THE WAY OF THE OLD ONES

"What sort of creatures live down here?" Duffy whispered in the dark tunnel. "Snakes? Trolls?"

"I suppose there may be snakes," the old enchanter replied impatiently. "No trolls. Not really trolls."

A hundred yards ahead, the Irishman noticed a hammocklike bundle slung from the ceiling. The bundle looked like a mummy bearing a sword. It struck him as a poor idea of a joke.

Then the thing opened its eyes. Duffy gulped and jumped backward.

The thing's mouth opened in a glittering yellow grin. "Halt," it said in an echoing whisper. "For the toll."

"What price for passage?" the old enchanter asked.

"Nothing exorbitant. There are two of you . . . I'll take the life of one."

THE DRAWING OF THE DARK

TIM POWERS

A Del Rey Book

BALLANTINE BOOKS • NEW YORK

To DOROTHEA KENNY
for measureless aid and advice,
and, once again,
to my parents,
NOEL and RICHARD POWERS

A Del Rey Book
Published by Ballantine Books

Library of Congress Catalog Card Number: 78-66095

ISBN 0-345-27604-3

Manufactured in the United States of America

First Edition: June 1979

Cover art by Doug Beekman

Contents

"If but we Christians have our beer,
Nothing's to fear."

—Sir William Ashbless

pROLOGUE

All Hallow's Eve, 1529

WITH ALMOST LUDICROUS CARE the old man carried the pitcher of beer across the sunlit room toward the still older man who reclined propped up in a bed by the window. A smear of dried mud was caked on the foot of the bed.

"Here you are, Sire," he said, pouring the black liquid into the earthenware cup which the old king had picked up from the table beside the bed.

The king raised the cup to his lips and sniffed it. "Ah," he breathed. "A potent batch this time. Even the vapors are strengthening."

The other man had now set the pitcher down on the table, pushing to one side a rusty lance head that had lain next to the cup. "It's a few ounces short," he confessed. "He sneaked down here Easter evening and stole a cupful."

The king took a sip, and closed his eyes rapturously. "Ah, that *is* good beer." He opened his eyes and glanced at the other old man. "Well, I don't think we can grudge him one cup of it, Aurelianus. I really don't think, all things considered, that we can honestly grudge him it."

BOOK ONE

"No familiar shapes
Remained, no pleasant images of trees,
Of sea or sky, no colors of green fields;
But huge and mighty forms, that do not live
Like living men, moved slowly through the mind
By day, and were a trouble to my dreams."

—William Wordsworth

Chapter One

ALL NIGHT the hot wind had swept up the Adriatic, and from the crowded docks down by the arsenale to the Isola di San Chiara at the western mouth of the Grand Canal, the old city creaked on its pilings like a vast, weary ship; and clouds as ragged as tatters of sailcloth scudded across the face of the full moon, tangling with the silhouettes of a hundred fantastic spires and domes.

In the narrow Rio de San Lorenzo, though, the smoky oil lamp at the bow of the gondola cast more reflections in the water than the moon did, and Brian Duffy reached over the gunwale to stir the black water was travelling at someone else's expense.
with his fingers and multiply the points of yellow light. He shifted uneasily on the seat, embarrassed, for he "I'll walk to my boat from here."

"Pull in to the *fondamenta*," he growled finally.

The gondolier obediently dug his long pole into the canal bottom, and the tiny craft heeled, paused, and then surged up to the embankment, its prow grating on a submerged step. "Thank you." Duffy ducked under the awning of the *felze* and took a long step to a dry stair while the boatman held the gondola steady.

Up on the sidewalk the Irishman turned. "Marozzo paid you to take me all the way to the Riva degli Schiavoni. Bring him back the change."

The gondolier shrugged. "Perhaps." He pushed away from the stair, turned his craft gracefully about, and began poling his way back up the glittering watercourse, softly calling, *"Stali!"* to draw any possible fares. Duffy stared after him for a moment, then turned on his heel and strode south along the embankment *calle* toward the Ponte dei Greci, the bridge of the Greeks.

He was reeling just a little because of the quantities of valpolicella he'd consumed that evening, and a sleepy footpad huddled under the bridge roused when he heard the Irishman's uneven tread. The thief eyed the approaching figure critically, noting the long, worn cloak, evidence of frequent outdoor sleeping; the knee-high boots, down at the heels, and twenty years out of fashion; and the rapier and dagger which looked to be the man's only valuable possessions. Edging silently back into the shadows, he let Duffy go by unaccosted.

The Irishman hadn't even been aware of the thief's scrutiny; he was staring moodily ahead at the tall bulk of the church of San Zaccaria, its gothic design undisguised by the Renaissance adornments that had recently been added to it, and he was wondering just how much he would miss this city when he left. "Only a matter of time," Marozzo had said over dinner. "Venice is more than half a Turkish possession right now, what with that grovelling treaty they signed eight years ago. Mark me now, Brian—before our hair is completely white, you and I will be teaching the uses of the scimitar instead of the honest straight sword, and our students will be wearing turbans." Duffy had replied that he'd shave his head and run naked with the jungle pygmies before he'd teach a Turk even how to blow his nose, and the conversation had moved on to other matters—but Marozzo had been right. The days of Venice's power were fifty years gone.

Duffy kicked a stray pebble away into the darkness and heard it plop into the canal after bouncing twice along the pavement. Time to move on, he told himself morosely. Venice has done its recuperative job, and these days I have to look closely to see the scars I got at Mohács two and a half years ago. And God knows I've already done my share of Turk-killing—let this city bow to the Crescent if it wants to, while I go somewhere else. I may even take ship back to Ireland.

I wonder, he thought, if anyone back in Dingle would remember Brian Duffy, the bright young lad who was sent off to Dublin to study for Holy Orders. They all hoped I'd eventually take the Archbishopric of Connaught, as so many of my forefathers did.

Duffy chuckled ruefully. There I disappointed them.

As he clumped past the San Zaccaria convent he heard muted giggles and whispering from a recessed doorway. Some pretty nun, he imagined, entertaining one of the young moneghini that are always loitering around the grounds. That's what comes of pushing your unwilling daughters into a nunnery to save the expense of a dowry—they wind up a good deal wilder than if you'd simply let them hang around the house.

I wonder, he thought with a grin, what sort of priest I would have made. Picture yourself pale and soft-voiced, Duffy my lad, rustling hither and yon in a cassock that smells of incense. Ho ho. I never even came *near* it. Why, he reflected, within a week of my arrival at the seminary I'd begun to be plagued by the odd occurrences that led, before long, to my dismissal —blasphemous footnotes, in a handwriting *I* certainly didn't recognize, were discovered on nearly every page of my breviary; oh yes, and once, during a twilight stroll with an elderly priest, seven young oak trees, one after another, twisted themselves to the ground as I passed; and of course worst of all, there was the time I threw a fit in church during the midnight Easter mass, shouting, they later told me, for the need-fires to be lit on the hilltops and the old king to be brought forth and killed.

Duffy shook his head, recalling that there had even been talk of fetching in an exorcist. He had scribbled a quick, vague letter to his family and fled to England. And you've fled quite a number of places in the years since, he told himself. Maybe it's time you fled back to where you started. It sounds nicely symmetrical, at any rate.

The narrow *calle* came to an end at the Riva degli Schiavoni, the street that ran along the edge of the wide San Marco Canal, and Duffy now stood on the crumbled brick lip, several feet above the lapping water, and looked uncertainly up and down the quiet shallows. What in the name of the devil, he thought irritably, scratching the gray stubble on his chin. Have I been robbed, or am I lost?

After a moment three well-dressed young men emerged from an arched doorway to his right. He turned on his heel when he heard their steps, and then relaxed when he saw that they weren't a gang of canal-side murderers. These are cultured lads, clearly, he reflected, with their oiled hair and their fancy-hilted swords, and one of them wrinkling his nose at the salty, stagnant smell of the nearby Greci canal.

"Good evening to you, gentlemen," Duffy said in his barbarously accented Italian. "Have you seen, by any chance, a boat I think I moored here earlier in the evening?"

The tallest of the young men stepped forward and bowed slightly. "Indeed, sir, we have seen this boat. We have taken the liberty, if you please, of sinking it."

Duffy raised his thick eyebrows, and then stepped to the canal edge and peered down into the dark water, where, sure enough, the moonlight dimly gleamed on the gunwales of a holed and rock-filled boat.

"You will want to know why we have done this."

"Yes," Duffy agreed, his gloved hand resting now on the pommel of his sword.

"We are the sons of Ludovico Gritti."

Duffy shook his head. "So? Who's he, the local ferrier?"

The young man pursed his lips impatiently. "Ludovico Gritti," he snapped. "The son of the Doge. The wealthiest merchant in Constantinople. To whom you did refer, this evening, as 'the bastard pimp of Suleiman.'"

"Ah!" said Duffy, nodding a little ruefully. "Now I see what quarter the wind's in. Well, look, boys, I was drinking, and kind of condemning anyone I could think of. I've got nothing against your father. You've sunk my boat now, so let's call it a night. There's no—"

The tallest Gritti drew his sword, followed a moment later by his brothers. "It's a question of honor," he explained.

Duffy breathed an impatient curse as he drew his rapier with his left hand and his shell-hilted dagger with his right, and crouched on guard with the weapons held crossed in front of him. I'll probably be arrested for this, he thought; engaging in a *duello alla mazza* with the grandsons of the Doge. Of all the damned nonsense.

The tallest Gritti made a run at the burly Irishman, his jewelled rapier drawn back for a cut and his dagger held at the hip for parrying. Duffy easily ducked the wide swing and, blocking the dagger-thrust with the quillons of his rapier, stepped aside and gave the young man a forceful boot in his satin-clothed backside that lifted him from the pavement and pitched him with an echoing splash into the canal.

Whirling around to face his other two assailants, Duffy knocked aside a sword-point that was rushing at his face, while another struck him in the belly and flexed against his shirt of chain mail.

Duffy punched one of the young men in the face with his rapier pommel and then hopped toward the other with a quick feint-and-slash of his dagger that slit the lad's cheek from nose to ear.

The Gritti in the canal was splashing about, cursing furiously and trying to find a ladder or a set of steps. Of the two on the pavement, one lay unconscious on the cobblestones, bleeding from a broken nose; the other stood pressing a bloody hand to his cut face.

"Northern barbarian," this one said, almost sadly, "you should weep with shame, to wear a concealed hauberk."

"Well for God's sake," returned Duffy in exasperation, "in a state where the nobility attack three-on-one, I think I'm a fool to step outside in less than a full suit of plate."

The young Gritti shook his head unhappily and stepped to the canal edge. "Giacomo," he said, "stop swearing and give me your hand." In a moment he had hoisted his brother out of the water.

"My sword and dagger are both at the bottom of the canal," snarled Giacomo, as water ran from his ruined clothes and puddled around his feet, "and there were more jewels set in their hilts than I can bear to think of."

Duffy nodded sympathetically. "Those pantaloons have about had it, too, I believe."

Giacomo didn't answer this, but helped his younger brother lift the unconscious one. "We will now leave," he told Duffy.

The Irishman watched as the two of them shuffled awkwardly away, bearing their brother like a piece of broken furniture between them. When they had disappeared among the farther shadows of the *calle,* Duffy sheathed his weapons, lurched away from the water's edge and leaned wearily against the nearest wall. It's good to see the last of them, he thought, but how am I to get back to my room? It's true that I have, on occasion, swum this quarter mile of chilly brine—once, to impress a girl, even holding a torch clear of the water all the way across!—but I'm tired tonight. I'm not feeling all that well, either. Heavy exertion on top of a full night of eating and drinking always disagrees with me. What a way to end the evening—"by the waters of the San Marco Canal I sat down and puked." He shut his eyes and breathed deeply.

"Pardon me, sir," came German words in a man's voice, "would you happen to speak the tongue of the Hapsburgs?"

Duffy looked up, startled, and saw a thin, white-haired old man leaning from a window two stories above; diaphanous curtains, dimly lit from behind, flapped around his shoulders like pale fire.

"Yes, old timer," Duffy replied. "More readily than this intricate Italian."

"Thank God. I can for the moment stop relying on charades. Here." A white hand flicked, and two seconds later a brass key clinked on the pavement. "Come up."

Duffy thoughtfully bent down and picked up the key. He flipped it spinning into the air, caught it, and grinned. "All right," he said.

The stairway was dark and cold, and smelled of mildewed cabbages, but the door at the top, when unlocked and swung open, revealed a scene of shadowy, candle-lit opulence. The gold-stamped spines of leather- and vellum-bound tomes lined a high bookcase along one wall, and ornate tables, shellacked boxes, glittering robes and dim, disturbing paintings filled the rest of the room. The old man who'd hailed Duffy stood by the window, smiling nervously. He was dressed in a heavy black gown with red and gold embroidery at the neck, and wore a slim stiletto at his belt, but no sword.

"Sit down, please," he said, waving at a chair.

"I don't mind standing," Duffy told him.

"Whatever you prefer." He opened a box and took from it a narrow black cylinder. "My name is Aurelianus." Duffy peered closely at the cylinder, and was surprised to see that it was a tiny snake, straightened and dried, with the little jaws open wide and the end of the tail clipped off. "And what is yours?"

Duffy blinked. "What?"

"I just told you my name—Aurelianus—and asked you for yours."

"Oh! I'm Brian Duffy."

Aurelianus nodded and put the tail end of the snake into his mouth, then leaned forward so that the head was in the long flame of one of the candles. It began popping and smoldering, and Aurelianus puffed smoke from the tail end.

"What in God's name are you doing?" Duffy gasped, half drawing his dagger.

"I beg your pardon. How rude of me. But it has been a day of . . . dire gambits, and I need the relaxation." He sat down and took a long puff at the ember-headed thing, letting aromatic smoke hiss out through his teeth a moment later. "Don't be alarmed. It's only a kind of water-snake which, when cured with the proper—*ahh*—herbs and spices, produces fumes of a most . . . beneficial sort."

"Huh!" The Irishman shook his head and slid his dagger back into its sheath. "Have you got any more *mundane* refreshments to offer a guest?"

"I am remiss. You must excuse me. Extraordinary circumstances . . . but yes, there is a fair selection of wines in the cabinet by your right hand. Cups behind you."

Duffy opened the cabinet and chose a bottle of sauternes, and deftly twisted the plug out of it.

"You know your wines," Aurelianus said, as Duffy poured the golden wine into a cup.

The Irishman shrugged. "You don't happen to own a boat, do you? I've got to get to San Giorgio, and three clowns sank the boat I had."

"Yes, so I heard. What's in San Giorgio?"

"My room. My things. It's where I'm currently living."

"Ah. No, I don't have a boat. I have, though, a proposal."

Duffy regarded Aurelianus skeptically. "Oh? Of what?"

"Of employment." He smiled. "You are not, I imagine, as wealthy as you have been at times in the past."

"Well, no," Duffy admitted, "but these things come in waves. I've been rich and poor, and will doubtless be both again. But what did you have in mind?"

Aurelianus took a long puff on the popping, sizzling snake, and held the smoke in his lungs for a good ten seconds before letting it out. "Well—*whoosh!*—by your accent I'd judge you've spent a good deal of time in Austria."

The Irishman looked annoyed, then shrugged and had another sip of the wine. "That's true. I was living in Vienna until three years ago."

"Why did you leave?"

"Why do you ask?"

"I beg your pardon; I don't mean to pry. I don't know why I have such difficulty in coming to the point." He ran the thin fingers of one hand through his hair, and Duffy noticed that he was trembling. "Let me explain: I have become the owner of the Zimmermann Inn."

Duffy raised his eyebrows politely. "Where's that?"

Aurelianus looked surprised. "In Vienna," he said. "Don't you—oh, of course. You've been away for three years. Before I took over it was called the St. Joseph Monastery."

"Oh yes. Where the Herzwesten beer comes from. You haven't shut down the brewery, I trust?"

Aurelianus laughed softly. "Oh no."

"Well, thank God for that." Duffy drained his glass. "How in hell did you get the Church to sell the place?"

"Actually, I inherited it. A prior claim on the land. Very complicated. But let me continue—I'm now running the place as an inn, and not doing a bad business. Vienna is a good location, and the Herzwesten brewery has as good a reputation as the Weihenstepan in Bavaria. My problem, though, you see, is that I haven't got—"

There was a hesitant rap-rap-rap at the door, and Aurelianus jumped. "Who is it?" he called in an agitated voice.

The answer came in a Greek dialect. "It's Bella. Let me in, little lover."

Aurelianus clenched his fists. "Come back later, Bella. I've a guest."

"I don't mind guests. I like guests." The latch rattled.

The old man pressed a hand to his reddening forehead. "Go away, Bella," he whispered, so quietly that Duffy barely heard it.

"Yoo hoo, guest!" came the raucous, liquor-blunted voice from beyond the door. "Tell the old juggler to let me in."

Good Lord, Duffy thought; *domestic embarrassments. Pretend not to notice.* He crossed to the bookcase and began squinting at the Latin titles.

"I've got news," Bella whined ingratiatingly. "Worth a ducat or two, I think you'll agree."

"News about what?" rasped Aurelianus.

"El Kanuni, as my dark-skinned friends say."

"You're a worthless trollop, Bella," the old man sighed unhappily, "but come in." He unlocked the door.

Preceded by an overpowering reek of stale perfume and grappa, a middle-aged woman in a somewhat sprung-at-the-seams skirt flounced into the room.

"Give me some wine, for the Virgin's sake!" she exclaimed, "lest I catch my death of the vapors."

"For *whose* sake?" Aurelianus inquired savagely. "Forget the wine. Vapors would be a blessing, considering what you've got already."

"Envy will rot your pale liver, little monk." The woman grinned. Duffy, having at least rudimentary manners, made a show of being absorbed by the books to the exclusion of all else.

Aurelianus turned to him apologetically. "Will you, sir, be so good as to excuse us for a moment?" He was all but wringing his hands with embarrassment.

"Of course," Duffy assured him with an airy wave. "I'll divert myself with your excellent library."

"Fine." The robed man took the woman roughly by the arm and led her to the far corner of the room, where they proceeded to converse in heated whispers.

Duffy buried his nose in a book, but, being a cautious man, strained his ears to catch as much as he could. He heard Bella's hoarse voice say, "The word is they've begun assembling the *akinji* in Constantinople . . . " Aurelianus asked a question about supplies and the Janissaries, but Duffy couldn't follow the woman's answer.

News of the Turks, the Irishman thought. It's all you hear these days. I wonder why this old bird's so interested.

"All right, all right," Aurelianus said finally, flapping his hands at the woman. "Your personal speculations don't interest me. Here . . . here's some money. Now get out. But first put that dagger back."

Bella sighed sadly and took a jewelled dagger out of the prodigious bosom of her dress. "I was only thinking a woman needs to be able to protect herself."

"Hah!" The old man chuckled mirthlessly. "It's the Turk sailors that need protection, you old vampire. Out!"

She left, slamming the door, and Aurelianus immediately lit several incense sticks in the candle flame and set them in little brass trays around the room. "I'd open a window," he said, "but in very old towns you never know what might be flying past in the darkness."

Duffy nodded uncertainly, and then held up the book he'd been leafing through. "I see you're a student of swordplay."

"What have you got there? Oh yes, Pietro Moncio's book. Have you read it?"

"Yes. As a matter of fact, it was Moncio and Achille Marozzo I was dining with this evening."

The old man blinked. "Oh. Well, I haven't used a sword myself for a number of years, but I do try to keep up with developments in the art. That copy of della Torre there, in the dark vellum, is very rare."

"It is?" remarked the Irishman, walking back to the table and refilling his glass. "I'll have to sell my copy, then. Might make some money. I wasn't real impressed with the text."

Long cobwebs of aromatic smoke were strung across the room, and Duffy fanned the air with a little portfolio of prints. "It's getting murky in here," he complained.

"You're right," the old man said. "I'm a damnable host. Perhaps if I open it a crack . . . " He walked to the window, stared out of it for a moment, and then turned back to Duffy with an apologetic smile. "No, I won't open it. Let me explain quickly why I called you in, and then you can be on your way before the fumes begin seriously to annoy you. I've mentioned the Zimmermann Inn, of which I am the owner; it's a popular establishment, but I travel constantly and, to be frank, there is often trouble with the customers that I can't control even when I'm there. You know—a wandering friar will get into an argument with some follower of this Luther, a *bundschuh* leftover from the Peasants' War will knife the Lutheran, and in no time at all the dining room's a shambles and the serving girls are in tears. And these things cut into the profits in a big way—damages, nice customers scared off, tapsters harder to hire. I need a man who can be there all the time, who can speak to most customers in their native languages, and who can break up a deadly fight without killing anybody—as you did just now, with the Gritti boys by the canal."

Duffy smiled. "You want me to be your bouncer."

"Exactly," agreed Aurelianus, rubbing his hands together.

"Hm." Duffy drummed his fingers on the table top. "You know, if you'd asked me two days ago, I'd have told you to forget it. But . . . just in the last couple of days Venice has grown a little tiresome. I admit I've even found myself missing old Vienna. Just last night I had a dream—"

Aurelianus raised his eyebrows innocently. "Oh?"

"Yes, about a girl I used to know there. I wouldn't really mind seeing her—seeing what she's doing now. And if I hang around here those three Gritti lads will be challenging me to a real combat in the official *champ clos,* and I'm too old for that kind of thing."

"They probably would," Aurelianus agreed. "They're hot-headed young men."

"You know them?"

"No. I know *about* them." Aurelianus picked up his half-consumed snake and re-lit it. "I know about quite a number of people," he added, almost to himself, "without actually knowing them. I prefer it that way. You'll take the job, then?"

Oh, what the hell, Duffy thought. I would never have fit in back in Dingle anyway, realistically speaking. He shrugged. "Yes. Why not?"

"Ah. I was hoping you would. You're more suited for it than anyone I've met."

He knotted his hands behind his back and paced about the cluttered room. "I've got business in the south, but I'd appreciate it if you could start for Vienna *tout de suite.* I'll give you some travelling money and a letter of introduction to the Zimmermann brewmaster, an old fellow named Gambrinus. I'll instruct him to give you another lump sum when you arrive there. How soon do you think that can be?"

Duffy scratched his gray head. "Oh, I don't know. What's today?"

"The twenty-fourth of February. Ash Wednesday."

"That's right. Monico had a gray cross on his forehead. Let's see—I'd take a boat to Trieste, buy a horse and cross the tail end of the Alps just east of there. Then maybe I'd hitch a ride north with some Hungarian lumber merchant; there's usually no lack of them in those parts. Cross the Sava and the Drava, and then follow the old Danube west to Vienna. Say roughly a month."

"Before Easter, without a doubt?" Aurelianus asked anxiously.

"Oh, certainly."

"Good. That's when we open the casks of bock, and I don't want a riot in the place."

"Yes, I'll have been there a good two weeks by then."

"I'm glad to hear it." Aurelianus poured himself a cup of the sauternes and refilled Duffy's. "You seem familiar with western Hungary," he observed cautiously.

The Irishman frowned into his wine for a moment, then relaxed and nodded. "I am," he said quietly. "I fought with King Louis and Archbishop Tomori at Mohács in August of 'twenty-six. I shouldn't have been there; as an Austrian at the time, Hungary was nothing to me. I guess I figured Vienna was next on the Turk's list." No sense telling him about Epiphany, Duffy thought.

The wine was unlocking Duffy's memories. The sky had been overcast, he recalled, and both sides had simply milled about on opposite sides of the Mohács plain until well after noon. Then the Hungarian cavalry had charged; the Turkish center gave way, and Duffy's troop of German infantry had followed the Hungarians into the trap. That was as hellish a maelstrom as I ever hope to find myself in, he thought now, sipping his wine—when those damned Turks suddenly *stopped* retreating, and turned on the pursuing troops.

His mouth curled down at the corners as he remembered the sharp thudding of the Turkish guns and the hiss of grapeshot whipping across the plain to rip into the Christian ranks, the whirling scimitars of the weirdly-wailing Janissaries blocking any advance, and the despairing cry that went up from the defenders of the

west when it became evident that the Turks had out-
flanked them.

"You obviously have luck," Aurelianus said, after
a pause. "Not many men got clear of that."

"That's true," Duffy said. "I hid among the river-
side thickets afterward, until John Zapolya and his
troops arrived, the day after the battle. I had to explain
to him that the idiot Tomori had attacked without
waiting for him and Frangipani and the other reinforcements; that nearly everyone on the Hungarian side—
Louis, Tomori, thousands more—was dead, and that
Suleiman and his Turks had won. Zapolya cleared
out then, ran west. I ran south."

The old man stubbed his smoking snake out in an
incense bowl and reluctantly exhaled the last of the
smoke. "You've heard, I suppose, that Zapolya has
gone over to the Turkish side now?"

Duffy frowned. "Yes. He just wants to be governor
of Hungary, I guess, and will kiss the hand of whoever seems to own it. I can still hardly believe it,
though; I've known him since 1515, and he was making
raids against the Turks even then. Of all the things
I would have sworn were impossible . . ."

Aurelianus nodded sympathetically. "If we could
rely on impossibilities we'd all be better off." He
crossed the room and sat down at a cluttered desk.
"But excuse me—I did not mean to stir up your past.
Here," he said, lifting a cloth bag from an opened
drawer, "is five hundred ducats." Duffy caught the
toss and slid the bag into a pocket. "And here," Aurelianus went on, flourishing a sheet of paper, "I will
write a letter of introduction." He dipped a pen in an
inkpot and began scribbling.

Duffy had long ago found it handy to be able to read
upside-down, and now casually glanced across the writing table at Aurelianus' precise script.

"My dear Gambrinus," Duffy read, *"the bearer of
this note, Brian Duffy,"* (here Aurelianus paused to
draw deftly a quick, accurate sketch of the Irishman),
*"is the man we've been looking for—the guardian of
the house of Herzwesten. See that he is paid five hundred ducats when he arrives, and subsequently what-*

*ever monthly salary you and he shall agree upon. I will
be joining you soon; mid-April, probably, certainly by
Easter. I trust the beer is behaving properly, and that
there is no acidity this season.—Kindest regards, AU-
RELIANUS."*

The black-robed old man folded the letter, poured
a glob of thick red wax onto it from a little candle-
heated pot, and pressed a seal into it. "There you go,"
he said, lifting away the seal and waving the letter in
the air to cool the wax. "Just hand this to the brewmaster."

Duffy took the letter. The seal, he noticed, was a
representation of two dragons locked in combat. "What
are my duties to be?" he asked. "Tell me again."

Aurelianus smiled. "Just as you said yourself: the
bouncer. Keep the riffraff out. Keep the peace."

The big Irishman nodded dubiously. "Seems odd
that you'd have to come to Venice to find somebody
to work in an Austrian tavern."

"Well I *didn't* come here to do that. I'm here for
entirely different reasons. Entirely. But when I saw
the way you dealt with those boys out front I knew you
were the man this job called for."

"Ah. Well, all right. It's your money." The wind
must be up, Duffy thought. Listen to that window rattle!

Aurelianus stood up. "Thank you for helping me
out in this matter," he said quickly, shaking Duffy's
hand and practically pulling him to the door. "I'll see
you in a month or so."

"Right," agreed Duffy, and found himself a moment
later standing on the dark landing while the door
clicked shut behind him. Now there's an odd fellow,
he thought as he groped his way down the stairs. I'll
be very curious to see if there actually are five hundred ducats in this bag.

A stale liquor scent lingered at the foot of the stairs,
and Bella sidled out of the shadows when he reached
the bottom. "The little eunuch gave you some money,
didn't he?"

"I beg your pardon, lady," Duffy said. "Nothing
of the sort."

"Why don't you and me go drink some wine somewhere?" she suggested. "There's lots I could tell you about him."

"I'm not interested in him. Excuse me." Duffy slid past her to the pavement outside.

"Maybe you'd be interested in a little feminine companionship."

"Why would that concern you?" he asked over his shoulder as he strode away. She shouted something after him in a rude tone of voice, though he missed the words. Poor old woman, he reflected. Gone mad from cheap Italian liquor. Shouting harsh words at strangers and harrying poor weird old men.

He glanced at the sky—an hour or so after midnight. No sense now, he thought, in going back to San Giorgio; the only thing worth mentioning that waits for me there is a landlord, justly angry about my failure to pay rent. I'd better find some kind of rooming house to spend the night in, and then get an early start tomorrow. A few hours' sleep in a moderately clean bed is what I need right now. It's been a tiring night.

"Stand aside, grandfather, we're trying to unload cargo here."

Duffy glared fiercely at the lean young dockworker, but moved obediently away. The morning sunlight was glittering like a handful of new-minted gold coins on the water, and Duffy was squinting and knuckling his eyes. He'd been told to look for a Cyprian galley called the *Morphou,* which was scheduled to make a stop at Trieste on its way home; "Look for a triangular sail with three sad eyes on it," a helpful little Egyptian had said. "That'll be the *Morphou.*"

Well, he thought irritably, I don't see any damned three eyes. Half these ships have their sails reefed anyway.

He sat down on a bale of cotton and watched disapprovingly the activity of all these loud, wide-awake people around him. Dark-skinned children, screaming to each other in a tangle of Mediterranean languages, ran past, flinging bits of cabbage at an indignant, bearded merchant; tanned sailors swaggered up from the docks, looking forward to impressing the Venetian girls with their foreign coins and fine silk doublets; and old, granite-faced women stood vigilantly over their racks of smoked fish, ready to smile at a customer or deliver a fist in the ear to a shoplifter.

Duffy had awakened at dawn in a malodorous hostel, feeling poisoned by the liquor he'd drunk the night before but cheered by his memory of opening the cloth bag beneath a flickering street lamp to discover that it did indeed contain five hundred ducats. And there are five hundred more waiting for me in Vienna, he thought, if I can just find this filthy Cyprian *Morphou*.

The gray-haired Irishman struggled to his feet—and a man on a porticoed balcony a hundred feet behind him crouched and squinted along the barrel of a wheel-lock harquebus; he pulled the trigger, the wheel spun and sprayed sparks into the pan and a moment later the gun kicked against the man's shoulder as its charge went off.

A ceramic jar beside Duffy's ear exploded, stinging his face with harsh wine and bits of pottery. He leaped back in astonishment and pitched over the bale of cotton, cursing sulphurously and wrenching at his entangled rapier.

The gunman leaned out over the balcony rail and shrugged. On the pavement below, two men frowned impatiently, loosened the daggers in their sheaths, and began elbowing their way through the crowd.

On his feet now, Duffy clutched his bared sword and glared about fiercely. It's probably one of those furioso Grittis, he thought. Or all three. And after I was so patient with them last night! Well I won't be this morning.

A tall, feather-hatted man, whose moustache appeared to be oiled, strode up to the Irishman and smiled. "The one who fired at you is escaping in that boat," he said, pointing. Duffy turned, and the man leaped on him, driving a dagger with vicious force at at the Irishman's chest. The hauberk under his much-abused doublet saved Duffy from the first stab; he caught the assassin's wrist with his right hand before another blow could be delivered, and then, stepping back to get the proper distance, ran his rapier through the man's thigh. Feather-hat sank to his knees, pale with shock.

I'm leaving Venice none too soon, Duffy reflected dazedly. He noticed with annoyance that his hands were trembling.

The frightened merchants and dockworkers were hurrying away, so he noticed immediately the two figures that were sprinting toward him—one was a stranger, one was young Giacomo Gritti, and both carried drawn knives.

"Fetch the guardia, for God's sake!" Duffy yelled shrilly at the crowd, but he knew it was too late for that. Sick with tension, he drew his own dagger and crouched behind his crossed weapons.

The stranger leaped ahead of Gritti, his arm drawn in for a solid stab—and then his eyes widened in pained astonishment, and he pitched heavily forward on his face, Gritti's dagger-hilt standing up between his shoulder blades.

Separated by ten feet, Gritti and Duffy stared at each other for a moment. "There are men waiting to kill you on the *Morphou*," Gritti panted, "but the old Greek merchantman anchored three docks south is also bound for Trieste. Hurry," he said, pointing, "they're casting off the lines right now."

Duffy paused only long enough to slap both weapons back into their sheaths, and nod a curt and puzzled thanks, before trotting energetically away south, toward the third dock.

Chapter Two

AFTER A BIT of token frowning and chin-scratching, the merchantman's paunchy captain agreed to let Duffy come aboard—though demanding a higher-than-usual fare "because of the lack of a reservation." The

Irishman had learned long ago when to keep quiet and pay the asking price, and he did it now.

The ship, he observed as he swung over the high stern, was notably dilapidated. God, dual steering oars and a square, brailed sail, he noted, shaking his head doubtfully. This one is old enough for Cleopatra to have made an insulting remark about it. Well, it's probably made the Venice to Trieste run more times than I've pulled my boots on, so I suppose it's not likely to founder on this trip. He sat down in the open hold between two huge amphorae of wine, and set one of the weather cloths, a frame of woven matting, upright in its notches in the gunwale. There, he thought, leaning back against it, I'm hidden from view at last, by God.

The sailors poled the vessel out past the clusters of docked galleys, and then the sail was unfurled on its dozen brailing lines, and bellied in the cold morning wind. The antique ship heeled about as the brawny steersman braced himself against the overlapping oar handles, and they were under way.

The captain sauntered about the deck criticizing the labors of his men until the Lido had slipped past on the starboard side; he relaxed then and strode to the stern, where Duffy was now perched on a crate, idly whittling a girl's head out of a block of wood with his dagger. The captain leaned on the rail next to him and wiped his forehead with a scarf.

He nodded at Duffy's sword. "You a fighting man?"

The Irishman smiled. "No."

"Why are you so anxious to get to Trieste?"

"I'm going to enter a monastery," Duffy said, paring the line of the girl's cheek.

The captain guffawed. "Oh, no doubt. What do you think you're going to find in a monastery?"

"Vows of silence."

The captain started to laugh, then frowned and stood up. He thought for a moment, then said, "You can't carve worth a damn," and stalked off to the narrow bow. Duffy held the block of wood at arm's length and regarded it critically. He's right, you know, he told himself.

The heavy-laden old vessel made poor time, despite the "new" lead sheathing which the captain announced, proudly, had been put on by his grandfather; and the quays of Trieste were lit with the astern sunset's orange and gold by the time the craft was docked. The captain was barking impatient orders at his tired crew as they kicked the wedges away from the step and lowered the mast backward across the decks, and Duffy unobtrusively climbed the ladder and walked up the dock toward the tangled towers and streets of the city. Many of the windows already glowed with lamplight, and he was beginning to think seriously about supper. He increased his pace and tried to estimate which section of town would be likely to serve good food cheaply.

The whitewashed walls of the narrow Via Dolores echoed to the clumping of Duffy's boot-heels as the salt-and-dried-fish smell of the docks receded behind him. An open door threw a streak of light across the pavement, and laughter and the clinking of wine cups could be heard from within.

Duffy strode into the place and was cheered by the hot draft from the kitchen, redolent of garlic and curry. He had taken off his hat and begun to untie his long, furred cloak when a man in an apron hurried over to him and began chattering in Italian.

"What?" the Irishman interrupted. "Talk slower."

"We," the man said with labored distinctness, "have —no—room. Already too many people are waiting."

"Oh. Very well." Duffy turned to go. Then he remembered his hat and turned around; a priest at a nearby table was nodding approvingly to the man in the apron, whom Duffy had surprised in the act of blessing himself. After a moment Duffy worldlessly took his hat and stalked outside.

Provincial idiots, he thought angrily as he shoved his hands in his pockets and trudged further up the street. Never seen a non-Mediterranean face in their lives, I guess. Thought I was some kind of bogey.

Patches of sapphire and rose still glowed in the late-winter sky, but night had fallen on the streets. Duffy had to rely on the light from windows to see his way, and he began to worry about footpads and alleybashers. Then, with a sound like branches being dragged along the cobbles, the swirling skirts of a heavy rain swept over him. Good God, he thought desperately as the cold drops drummed on the brim of his hat, I've got to get in out of this. I'm liable to catch an ague—and my chain mail shirt is already disgracefully rusted.

He saw an open door ahead, and loped heavily toward it, splashing through the suddenly deep-flowing gutter. Do I actually hear a mill-wheel pounding, he wondered, or is that just some overtone of the storm? No tavern sign was visible, but vine leaves were hung over the lintel, and he smiled with relief, when he'd stepped inside, to see the sparsely populated tables. They won't tell me they're too full here, he thought, beating the water off his hat against his thigh. He went to an empty table, flung his cloak on the bench and sat down next to it.

This is an odd place, he reflected, looking around; that drunken old graybeard by the kitchen door appears to be the host. Gave me a courtly nod when I came in, anyway.

A young man emerged from the kitchen and padded across the room to Duffy's table. "What can we do for you?" he asked.

"Give me whatever sort of dinner is in the pot, and a cup of your best red wine."

The lad bowed and withdrew. Duffy glanced curiously at the other diners scattered around the dim, low-ceilinged room. The rain had apparently got them down. They all seemed depressed—no, worried—and their smiles were wistful and fleeting. Duffy took the block of wood from his pocket and, unsheathing his dagger, recommenced his whittling.

When the food arrived it proved to be a bit spicier than he liked, and it all seemed to be wrapped in leaves, but the wine—of which they brought him a full flagon—was the finest he'd ever tasted. Dry but full-bodied and aromatic, its vapors filled his head like brandy. "Incredible," he breathed, and poured another cup.

*   *   *

After quite a while Duffy regretfully decided that the bas relief he'd been cutting into the surface of the table was no good. He shook his head and put his dagger away. Someone must have refilled the flagon, he thought, when I wasn't looking. Perhaps several times. I can't remember how many cups of this I've had, but it's been a respectable quantity. He glanced blurrily around, and noticed that the room was crowded now, and more brightly lit. I must be drunker than I thought, he told himself, not to have noticed these people arrive. Why, there are even a couple of people sitting with me now at this table. He nodded politely to the two bearded fellows.

Duffy knew he should try to snap out of this wine fog. I'm an idiot, he thought, to get drunk in an unknown tavern in a foreign city.

The young man who'd served him was standing on a table, playing a flute, and most of the people in the place were whirling in a mad dance, singing a refrain in a language Duffy couldn't place. The old bearded host, too drunk now even to stand unaided, was being led around the room by a gang of laughing boys. The poor old wino, Duffy thought dizzily—mocked by children. They're probably the ones that tied those ridiculous vine leaves in his hair, too.

Duffy could hear the mill-wheel rumble again, deeper and more resonant than before, like the pulse of the earth. The high, wild intricacies of the flute music, he now perceived, were woven around that slow, deep rhythm.

Suddenly he was afraid. A dim but incalculably powerful thought, or idea, or memory was rising through the murky depths of his mind, and he wanted above all to avoid facing it. He lurched to his feet, knocking his wine cup to the floor. "I'm . . ." he stammered. "My name is . . ." but at the moment he couldn't remember. A hundred names occurred to him.

The bearded man next to him had picked up the cup, refilled it with the glowing wine, and proffered it to the Irishman. Looking down, Duffy noticed for the first time that the man was naked, and that his legs were covered with short, bristly fur, and were jointed oddly, and terminated in little cloven hooves.

With a yell Duffy ran toward the door, but his own legs weren't working correctly, and he made slow progress. Then he must have fallen, for he blacked out and dropped away through hundreds of disturbing dreams . . . he was a child crying with fear in a dark stone room; he was an old, dishonored king, bleeding to death in the rain, watched over by one loyal retainer; he stood with two women beside a fire on a midnight moor, staring into the black sky with a desperate hope; in a narrow boat he drifted on a vast, still lake; he sat across a table from a shockingly ancient man, who stared at him with pity and said, "Much has been lost, and there is much yet to lose." The dreams became dim and incomprehensible after that, like a parade dwindling in the distance, leaving him finally alone in a land so dark and cold it could never have known the sun.

Several kicks in the ribs woke him. He rolled over in the chilly mud and brushed the wet gray hair out of his face.

"Damn my soul," he croaked. "Where in hell am I?"

"I want you to leave this city," came a man's voice.

Duffy sat up. He was in an empty, puddled lot between two houses. The rain had stopped, and the blue sky shone behind the crumbling storm clouds. He looked up into the angry and worried face of a priest. "You're . . ." Duffy muttered, "you're the priest who was in that first place I went last night. Where they turned me away."

"That's right. I see you found . . . another host, though. When are you leaving Trieste?"

"Damn soon, I can tell you." Pressing both hands into the mud, he struggled to his feet. "*Ohh.*" He rubbed his hip gingerly. "I haven't slept in the rain since I was eighteen years old. We middle-aged types would do well to avoid it," he told the priest.

"*I* didn't sleep in the rain," the priest said impatiently.

"Oh. That's right. I did. I knew one of us did."

"Uh . . ." The priest frowned deeply. "Do you need any money?"

"No, actually—wait a moment." His hand darted to his doublet, and he was a little surprised to find the hard bulge of the money bag still there. "Huh! No, I'm flush at the moment, thank you."

"All right. Be out of town today, then—or I'll tell eight of the biggest men in my parish to get sticks and beat the daylights out of you and throw you into the ocean."

Duffy blinked. "What? I—listen, I haven't done any—you little cur, I'll rip the livers out of your eight farmers." He took a step toward the priest, but lost his balance and had to right himself with two lateral hops. This jolted him so that he had to drop onto his hands and knees to be violently sick on the ground. When he got up again, pale and weak-kneed, the priest had left.

I wonder who he thinks I am, Duffy thought. I hate misunderstandings of this sort.

Cautiously he now asked himself, What *did* happen last night?

Very simple, spoke up the rational part of his mind hastily; you were stupid enough to get falling-down-drunk in a foreign bar, and they beat you up and dumped you in this lot, and you're lucky you look so seedy that no sane man would think of lifting your purse. Those dreams and hallucinations were of no significance. None at all.

His teeth were chattering and he shivered like a wet cat. I've got to get moving, he thought; got to find a friendly inn where I can pull myself together, clean up a bit. Buy some supplies. And then get the hell out of Trieste.

Taking a deep breath, he plodded unsteadily back down the Via Dolores.

Two hours later he was stepping out of a steaming tub and rubbing his head vigorously with a towel. "How's my breakfast coming?" he called. When there was no answer he padded to the door and opened it.

"How's my breakfast coming?" he bawled down the hall.

"It's on the table waiting for you, sir."

"Good. I'll be there in a minute." Duffy took his newly dried woolen trousers from a chair by the fireplace and pulled them on. He'd got them in Britain many years ago; and though they now consisted more of patches than of British wool, and the Italians laughed at the garment and called him an ourang outan, he'd become accustomed to wearing them. And in a late winter Alpine crossing I'll be glad I've got them, he nodded to himself. He flapped into his twice-holed leather doublet, jerked on his boots and tramped out to breakfast.

The innkeeper had laid out a bowl of some kind of mush with eggs beaten into it, black bread with cheese, and a mug of hot ale. "Looks great," Duffy said, dropping into a chair and setting to.

Four other guests sat nibbling toast at the other end of the table, and peered curiously at the burly, gray-haired Irishman. One of them, a thin man in a baggy velvet hat and silk tights, cleared his throat.

"We hear you are crossing the Julian Alps, sir," he said.

Duffy frowned, as he was wont to do when strangers expressed interest in his plans. "That's right," he growled.

"It's awfully early in the season," the man observed.

Duffy shrugged. "Too early for some, perhaps."

The innkeeper leaned in from the kitchen and nodded to Duffy. "The boy says he's got all the rust out of your mail shirt," he said.

"Tell him to shake it in the sand a hundred more times just for luck," said Duffy.

"Aren't you afraid of the Turks?" spoke up a woman, apparently Baggy-hat's wife.

"No, lady. The Turks couldn't be this far north this early in the year." And I wish I could say the same about bandits, he thought. Duffy busied himself with his food, and the other guests, though whispering among themselves, asked him no more questions.

They're right about one thing, he admitted to himself; it is early. But hell, I'll be prepared, the weather's good, and the Predil Pass is certain to be clear. It'll be an easy crossing—not like the last one, coming south in September and October of 1526, half-starved and with my head bandaged up like a turban. He grinned reminiscently into his ale. That's probably how I made it alive through the Turk-infested wastes of Hungary— Suleiman's boys, if they saw me, must have seen that bandage and figured I was one of their own.

The innkeeper leaned in again. "The boy says if he gives it a hundred more shakes it'll come apart."

Duffy nodded wearily. "He's probably right. Okay, have him beat the sand out of it, gently, and oil it." He stood up, nodded civilly to his fellow guests, and walked to his room.

His rapier lay on the bed and he picked it up, sliding his hand into the swept-hilt guard. The worn leather grip had become contoured to his fingers, and drawing the blade from the scabbard was like pulling his arm out of a coat sleeve. He had buffed the old sword and oiled it, and the blade gleamed shiny black as he sighted along it and then flexed it a bit to get rid of an annoying recurrent curve. He whished it through the air once or twice. Take that, Turkish infidel.

A knock sounded at the door. "Your hauberk, sir."

"Ah. Thank you." Duffy took the dissipirited-looking garment and stared at it judicially. Why, he thought, it doesn't look that bad. Some of the iron links had broken away here and there and been replaced with knotted wire, and the sleeves were uneven and ragged at the wrists, but on the whole it was still a valuable piece of armor.

A little wooden box lay on a chair, and Duffy opened it and looked at the collection of threads, dust, lint, feathers and shredded wood. He poked his finger in it—good and dry, he noted approvingly. Under it all was a small, round piece of glass, which he made sure was not broken. He closed the box and slipped it into the inside pocket of his doublet.

Time to go, he told himself. He took off the doublet, put on two rust-stained cotton undershirts and pulled the hauberk over them, ignoring the rattle of a couple of links falling to the floor. He shouldered on his doublet, belted on his rapier and dagger, and, picking up his fur cloak and hat, left the room.

"Landlord! Here." He dropped several coins into the innkeeper's palm. "By the way, where can I buy a horse?"

"A horse?"

"That's what I said. A horse. *Equus.* You know."

"I guess I could sell you one."

"A hardy beast? Able to carry me over the Alps?"

"Certainly, if you treat him right."

"He'd better make it. Or I'll come back here and do something awful."

Duffy concluded his examination of the horse with a long stare into its eyes. "How much for him?"

"Oh . . ." The innkeeper pursed his lips. "Sixty ducats?"

"Forty it is." Duffy gave the man some more coins. "I'm not kidding when I say I'll be back here, angry, if he drops dead."

"He's a good horse," the innkeeper protested. "I've cared for him since he was born. Assisted at his birth."

"Good heavens. I don't want to hear about it. Listen, I'll need some food, too. Uh . . . four, no, five long loaves of bread, five thick sticks of hard salami, a week's worth of whatever kind of grain the horse likes, two gallons of dry red wine, a bottle of really potent brandy . . . and a sack of onions, a handful of garlic cloves and two pounds of white cheese. Put all that in four sacks and tell me how much it adds to my bill."

"Yes, sir." the innkeeper turned and started back toward the building.

"And I mean potent brandy," Duffy called after him. "Dare to give me watered-down stuff and I'll be back here even if the damned horse can fly."

Chapter Three

THE SUN STILL LINGERED in the morning side of the sky when Duffy left Trieste, riding east, angling up through the foothills toward the white teeth of the Julian Alps. He'd stopped once more before leaving the city, to buy a pair of leather breeches and a knapsack, and he was wearing both items now. The bright sun sparkled at him from the new brooks that ran down through the hills, but he could still see the white steam of his breath, and he was glad he'd picked up a good pair of gloves during his stay in Venice.

Hunching around in the saddle, he nodded to the blue patch on the horizon that was the Gulf of Venice. So long, Mediterranean, he thought. It's been a pleasant interlude here, with your sunshine, Madeira wine and dark-eyed girls—but I guess I'm by nature more at home in the colder northern lands. God knows why.

The Irishman tilted back his hat and shook his head bewilderedly. Odd, he thought, how it got so weird there at the end. The Gritti boys try to kill me three-on-one Wednesday night, and then one of them saves my life and directs me to a safe ship next morning. And how did he know I needed a Trieste-bound ship, anyway? The Venetian citizens seem to know more about my business than I do myself.

And what *is* my business, anyway? I still can't see why that little old black-clad jack-in-the-box—God, I can't even remember his name—gave me all this money. Am I really the only man he's met capable of keeping the peace in his Austrian tavern? And since when do bouncers get this kind of money? It seems to me they're usually doing well if they get mere room and board. Oh, don't question it, old lad, he advised himself. The money's real, that's what counts.

32

The road wound now through tall evergreens, and the chilly air was spicy with the smell of pine. Duffy filled his lungs and smiled nostalgically. Ah, that's a smell from home, he thought. Austria, I've missed you.

And, he admitted uneasily, I've missed you, too, Epiphany. Good God—Duffy suddenly felt old—she's probably got a child by now. Maybe two of them. Or —he brightened—maybe that gargoyle Hallstadt fell off his horse one day while out hawking, leaving the old girl single and rich. Ho ho. Of course she might not speak to me. *Steward, dump chamber-pots on that derelict at the front door.* A quick vision of Duffy, befouled and berserk, kicking his way through a dining hall window, the ghastly spectre at the feast.

The thump of unhurried hoofbeats interrupted his reverie. He turned and saw, riding lazily fifty yards behind, a sturdy fellow wearing the laced-leather tunic and slung bow of a chamois hunter. Duffy waved politely but, not wanting conversation, didn't slow his pace.

Finally he focused his mind on the idea that was bothering him most. Could it be, he asked himself reluctantly, that I'm becoming a serious drunkard? I've been drinking since I was eleven, but it's never before given me hallucinations and blackouts. Well, you're getting older every day, you know. Can't expect to be able to toss it down the way you did when you were twenty. After this journey I'll stick to beer for a while, he promised himself, and not a lot of that. I certainly don't want to start seeing goat-footed people again.

The way was steeper now. A muddy slope, furred with brown clumps of pine needles, rose at his left hand, a similar one fell away at his right, and the tall pine trees stood up from every height like bushy green spectators seated in tiers. Bird-screeches echoed through the woods, and squirrels on high branches regarded the horse and man with great interest. Duffy flapped his arms and hooted at them and they fled in astonishment.

He was overtaking another rider, a fat friar on a plodding mule. The man appeared to be asleep, rocking loosely in the saddle and letting his mount navigate. Quite a busy road for this time of year, Duffy reflected.

Suddenly it was quieter. What sound just stopped? he asked himself. Oh, of course—the hoofbeats of the chamois hunter's horse. Duffy turned around again— and abruptly rolled out of the saddle as an iron-headed arrow split the air six inches over his saddle-bow. Somersaulting awkwardly across the path, boots flailing, he dived in a semi-controlled slide down the steep right-hand slope. For thirty feet he cut gouges in the mud and matted pine needles, then his clutching hand caught a tree root and he pulled himself hastily to his feet. He was behind a wide trunk and, he prayed, invisible to anyone on the road above.

He wiped cold mud off his face with a trembling gloved hand and tried to quiet his breathing. A bandit, by God, Duffy thought. I hope he leaves that poor friar alone. This makes three attempts on my life in three days—quite a coincidence. And it *is* simply a coincidence, he told himself firmly.

"Do you see his body?" asked someone up on the road.

"I tell you, idiot, you missed," came an answer. "Your arrow bounced away through the trees. He's hiding down there."

After a long pause the first speaker, more quietly now, said, "Well that's great."

Who's this other man, Duffy wondered. And where's the friar? Or is that the friar? I wish I could see up there.

"Hey," one of them shouted. "I know you can hear me. Come up right now and we won't hurt you."

Is that so, Duffy thought with a mirthless grin. Is that so, indeed?

"You know I've got a bow up here. I can just wait. You've got to come out some time, and I'll put an arrow through your eye when you do."

Well, if it comes to that, the Irishman reasoned, I can wait until dark and then creep unseen back up the hill and cut your vociferous throat, my friend. Where can my horse and supplies be getting to? Strange breed of bandits you two are, not to have gone after him instead of me.

There was silence from above for several minutes, then abruptly the rattle and slither of two men sliding down. "Careful! Do you see him?" one of them yelled.

"No," the other one shouted. "Where are you going? We've got to stay close."

When he judged that one of them was just about to slide past his tree, Duffy unsheathed his rapier and leaped out into the man's path. It was the fat friar, waving a long sword, and he screeched in terror and blocked Duffy's thrust more by luck than skill. He collided heavily with the Irishman and both of them skidded down the steep, wet incline—the fortes of their blades desperately crossed—unable to check their quickening slide. Duffy, keeping the friar's sword blocked with his own, tried to twist around and see what lay in their path. A blunt tree-branch in my back, he thought grimly, would pretty well conclude this.

The friar's trailing robe caught on a spur of rock, and he was jerked to a stop while the swords disengaged and Duffy slid on. Freed at last from the awkward *corps-à-corps,* the Irishman quickly dug in with the toes of his boots, his right hand and his sword pommel, and had soon dragged to a halt, sending a small avalanche of ripped-up dirt tumbling down the slope. Then he worked his boots into the hillside to get a firm footing.

The other bandit was climbing and hopping with panicky haste down the hillside, but he was still well above Duffy and the friar.

Then the fabric tore, and the friar was on his way again. He tried to block Duffy's sword as he'd done before, but this time the Irishman whirled his extended point in a quick *feint disengagé,* and the friar slid directly onto it, taking the sword through his belly. It was Duffy's hilt that stopped the man's downward course, and his face was less than a foot away from the Irishman's. The friar flailed his sword convulsively, but Duffy caught the wrist with his free hand and held it away. The two men stared at each other for a moment.

"You're no real friar," Duffy panted.

"You . . . go to hell," the man choked, and then sagged in death.

Propping the corpse up with his right hand, Duffy pulled his sword free, and let the body tumble away down the hill. He looked up. The chamois hunter was braced against a rock and a tree trunk about twenty feet up, unable to descend any further without being at the mercy of Duffy's rapier. The man carried a sword of his own, but didn't seem confident with it. The bow had been left up on the road.

"Come on, weasel," Duffy gritted. "Show us a little of that courage you had five minutes ago when you tried to shoot me in the back."

The man licked sweat off his upper lip and glanced nervously over his shoulder, up the slope. Clearly he was wondering if he could scramble back to the road before the Irishman could catch up with him and run him through.

"Don't think I'll hesitate," Duffy called, guessing the man's thoughts.

The chamois hunter reached out and scraped the ground with his sword blade, sending pebbles and clumps of leaves pattering down onto the Irishman.

Duffy laughed uproariously, sending echoes ringing through the trees. "Too late now, my friend, to begin tilling the soil! I don't know where you and your fat companion had your swords hidden when you were riding, but you should have left them there." A fist-sized rock bounced painfully off his head. "Ow! All right, you son of a dog . . ." Duffy began scrambling up the slope in a rage.

The man dropped his sword, turned, and scampered away upward like a startled squirrel. Duffy, being heavier and unwilling to relinquish his own sword, was left behind despite his ferocious efforts to catch up.

It may go badly, he realized, if he gets to the road and has time to draw his bow. Duffy stopped to catch his breath, and dug a stone out of the dirt. He tossed it up and caught it to judge its weight. Not bad. Drawing his left arm back and resting it against a tree limb, he relaxed and waited for a sight of the timorous bandit whose crashing, gasping progress must have been audible a mile away.

Finally he was visible, pausing at the lip of the road, silhouetted against a patch of sky. Duffy's arm lashed forward, flinging the stone upward with all the strength he could muster. A second later the bandit twitched violently and fell backward, out of sight.

Got you, you bastard, Duffy thought as he resumed his upward climb. It took him several minutes to work his way up the hillside, but when he stood at last on the road he'd still heard nothing from the stone-felled bandit. I suppose I hit him in the head and killed him, the Irishman thought glumly.

He brightened, though, when he saw his horse, the supplies still intact, nosing the muddy ground a hundred feet away. "Hello, horse," he called, walking up to the beast. The horse lifted its head and regarded its owner without enthusiasm. "And where were you, beast, when I was being done in down the hill? Hah?" The horse looked away, clearly bored. Duffy shook his head sadly and swung into the saddle. "Onward, you heartless creature."

By early afternoon the road had become a wide ledge angling steeply up the sloping face of a rock wall. Well-worn stones were pressed into the ground to serve as pavement, and the precipice side was bordered with a frail, outward-leaning fence of weathered sticks. When the sun hung only a few finger's-breadths above the western peaks Duffy came upon the St. James Hospice, a narrow-windowed, slate-roofed building nestled between two vast wings of Alpine granite.

Couldn't have timed it better, the Irishman thought as he led his horse up the path to the hospice. If those two assassins hadn't delayed me this morning, I'd have got here too early, and been tempted to press on for some other, probably not half so nice, shelter for the night. The heavy front door swung open as Duffy dismounted, and two monks strode across the snowy yard.

"Good evening, stranger," said the taller one. "Brother Eustace will take your horse around to the stable. Come with me." Duffy followed the monk inside and took off his hat and cloak as the door was drawn shut. The narrow vestibule was lit by a torch hung on the wall in an iron sconce, and a half dozen swords were stacked in one corner. "We insist," said the monk, "that all of our guests leave their weapons here."

Duffy grinned as he unsheathed his sword and handed it to the monk. "Sounds like a good idea, if you get everybody to go along with it."

"Not difficult," the monk said, setting Duffy's rapier with the others. "Any who won't comply spend the night outside."

After the evening meal, the half-dozen guests sat around the great fireplace and drank brandy. Several sat in wooden chairs, but Duffy lay stretched on the floor, his head pillowed on the flank of a big sleeping dog. The Irishman had allowed himself a cup of brandy, having chosen to regard it as a precaution against the cold.

Tacitly agreeing not to discuss the motives for their travelling, the guests passed the time by telling stories. An Italian told a morbid tale about a well-born girl keeping the severed head of her stable-boy lover in a flowerpot, and watering with her tears the plant that grew from it. The monk who'd let Duffy in related a riotous and obscene story of erotic confusions in a convent, and Duffy told the old Irish story of Saeve, the wife of the hero Finn Mac Cool, and how she was metamorphosed from a faun.

A tubby old gentleman had begun to recite a long poem about the Emperor Maximilian lost in the Alps, when the front door of the hospice banged open. A moment later a burly man in the heavy boots and coat of a guide strode into the room, impatiently brushing snow out of his moustache.

"A cold night, Olaus?" asked the monk, getting up to pour a cup for the newcomer.

"No," said Olaus, gratefully taking the liquor. "The winter is packing up and returning north." He took a long sip. "But there are monsters out tonight."

Duffy looked up, interested. "Monsters?"

The guide nodded as he sat down by the fire. "Aye. Griffins, snake men, demons of every sort."

"Did you see them, Olaus?" the monk asked, giving the other guests a broad wink.

Olaus shook his head gravely. "No. Damn few men see them and live. But today on Montasch I heard them singing choruses in the mountain, and coming here I crossed in the snow several tracks of unnatural feet. I wonder what it is that's got them roused."

"Oh, I don't know," the monk said airily. "It's probably some monster holiday today. They've opened their casks of Spring beer, I'll bet."

Olaus, aware that he was being ribbed, lapsed into sulky silence.

That reminds me, Duffy thought—I wonder how the Herzwesten Bock beer is coming. I trust this Gambrinus fellow knows his business, and hasn't let it go bad. Duffy yawned. The brandy, on top of the day's exertion, was making him sleepy. He stood up carefully, so as not to wake the dog.

"I believe I'll turn in, brother," he said. "Where would I find a bunk?"

The monk turned to the Irishman with a smile Duffy had seen before on the faces of old nuns attending to wounded soldiers—the easy grin of one who has pledged neutrality, and can afford to be courteous to all sides and factions. "Through that door," he said, pointing. "Breakfast is at dawn."

A little puzzled, Duffy nodded and walked to the indicated door, wondering briefly, and for no reason at all, whether the monk's incredulity at Olaus' statements might have been feigned. It was a pointless thought, and he threw it away.

There were twenty bunks in the next room, mounted in the walls like bookshelves. Duffy left his boots on the floor and climbed up into a high bunk. A blanket lay on the boards, and he stretched out on it, pulling his cloak over himself and using his knapsack for a pillow. In the next room he could hear the low mutter of the other guests saying a prayer. Got out just in time, he thought with a grin. He rolled over and went to sleep, dreaming of a Viennese girl named Epiphany.

It snowed during the night, and when Duffy went out to the stable next morning to saddle his horse, the air was so cold that his teeth hurt when he inhaled. The horse shook his head and snorted indignantly, unable to believe he was expected to work at this hour.

"Wake up, now," Duffy told him as he climbed into the saddle. "The sun's up, and it'll burn off this damned mist before ten o'clock. By noon we'll have forgot what this was like."

The fog hung on with tenacity, though, as if its wispy fingers were curled resolutely around every rock outcropping. Duffy was into the Predil Pass now, and to his right the precipice edge of the path dropped away as sharp and clean as a knife cut, giving the mist the illusion of a glowing wall to complement the dark stone wall at his left. Once, to test the depth of the invisible abyss, he pulled a stone out of the mountain face and tossed it out past the lip of the path. There was no sound of it striking anything.

At what he estimated was midmorning, the path widened as it curled over the broad shoulder of the Martignac ridge. Travellers' shrines, cairns and "stone men" marked the way clearly, even in the fog, and Duffy sat back comfortably and began to sing.

> *"Has aught been heard of the Fulgory Bird*
> *   in the isles to the west of Man?*
> *For hither the gilded galleys of men*
> *   have sailed since the world began.*
> *With painted sails and mariners' songs*
> *We come with trumpets and brazen gongs*
> *To procure that for which His Majesty longs,*
> *   The remarkable Fulgury Bird."*

Dimly through the vapors, Duffy had been seeing for some time a ridge paralleling his own, and now, glancing at it, he saw riding across it the silhouette of a vast horse and rider. "God preserve us," Duffy gasped, snatching instinctively at his hilt. That man is twenty feet tall, at least, he thought. Olaus was right.

The dim giant had reached for his own sword, so Duffy whirled his rapier out and brandished it—and the giant did exactly the same. The Irishman relaxed a little, skeptically. Then he resheathed his sword. So did the giant. Duffy now stretched out his arms and flapped them slowly, like a ponderous bird, and the shadowy rider simultaneously performed the same action.

Duffy laughed with relief. "No need to be scared, horse," he said. "It's simply our shadow on the mist." The horse flapped his lips disgustedly.

The milky brightness of the air was too dazzling and disorienting to stare into, and the Irishman kept his eyes on his hands, the path and the markers that jogged past. When he glanced at the shadow rider again, he was astonished to see a whole parade of silhouettes pacing along. He peered uneasily at the gray forms, and then stiffened with real fear.

One was a bird-headed animal with the body of a huge cat, and folded wings bobbed on its long back as it walked. Behind it trod a thing like a lizard, with the grotesque, wattled head of a rooster. A basilisk, or I'm a father confessor, Duffy thought as sweat began to trickle into the collar of his cloak. There were other figures in the murky, silent procession—dwarfs, monstrous crabs, and things that seemed to be nothing but knots of writhing tentacles. All of the shadows hopped, hobbled or strode along steadily, as if they'd walked for hours and were still leagues short of their destination. And in their midst rode stiffly the mounted figure that was Duffy's own shadow.

Like a child that fears it has seen a white, eyeless face moaning at the window, Duffy scarcely dared to breathe. He slowly turned away from the phantom ridge and stared straight ahead, where, to his horror, he could see a blurry outline in the fog. I suppose I'd see something behind me, too, he thought, but there's no way I'm going to turn around. One part of his mind, which he was trying hard to ignore, was fearfully shrilling over and over again, *What do they want?*

What do they want? His rational side advised him to avoid sudden moves and wait for the fantastic beasts to go away.

They didn't. When the glow in the sky began to dim with the approach of evening, Duffy was still being paced by his silent fellow travellers. The hollow chill of fright had, during the long day's ride, given way to a sort of unreal, fatalistic wonder. The horse, though, didn't even seem aware of the creatures.

With the numb calmness of a man in shock, Duffy halted his horse—the fabulous animals halted, too—and set about making camp under a low overhang of rock. I'm obviously either doomed or insane, he thought, but I may as well be warm. He set about collecting kindling, and even walked very near one of the monsters to pick up a particularly good stick; the creature, some sort of dog-faced bird, bowed and hopped back.

The Irishman crawled under the hood of rock and arranged the bits of wood in a pile. He took out his wooden tinder box and laid a few pinches of the carefully hoarded fluff at the base of the wood pile. The fog rendered the magnifying glass useless, so he dampened one corner of the tinder with a few drops of the brandy and then struck sparks from his sword hilt with the pommel of his knife. The *clink . . . clink . . . clink* was the only sound in the cold silence. Finally a frail brush-stroke of flame danced over the wood, and a minute later the fire had swelled enough to illuminate Duffy's meagre shelter. Acutely aware of being the only human within a dozen icy miles, he blessed the fluttering-flag sound of the fire because of the way it masked the ominous quiet of the blackness beyond.

He drank a good deal of the brandy, and then curled up in his fur cloak. It was now possible for him to suppose the monsters had been an illusion, an effect of the diffused sun, the mist and the snow. They'll be gone in the morning, he told himself.

They weren't. When he opened his eyes at dawn his heart sank to see a semicircle of tall gargoyle figures a dozen feet away from him; snow piled on their wings and horned heads showed that they had stood thus all through the night, and if it hadn't been for the bright alertness in every eye he would probably have tried to believe they were statues.

When he had roused and fed his unconcerned horse, nibbled a bit of salami and washed it down with cold wine, two of the things stepped back, opening the semicircle. Duffy obediently got into the saddle and rode forward, and the two that had stepped back strode ahead to lead the way as the rest got into motion behind the Irishman.

The sky on this Sunday morning was a clear cobalt blue, against which the mountain peaks might have seemed to be razored out of crumpled white paper if the sense of vast distance and space had not been so overwhelming. Duffy's steaming breath plumed away behind him in the thin, icy air of these cathedral heights, and he felt that he was treading the very rim of the world, closer to the kingdoms of the sky than to the warm heart of earth.

At one point there was a choice of ways around a towering granite shoulder: a new route, curling down to the left, whose well-maintained shrines and cairns indicated steady traffic, and a route that tacked steeply up, which, though a few old markers showed along it through drifts of snow, had clearly not been in use for at least several seasons; the odd parade wound its way without a pause up over the old path. Duffy frowned, having vaguely hoped to run into some large party of travellers that would chase these fantastic animals away. He turned and peeked at the dozen or so in his train. I suppose it doesn't matter, he reflected hopelessly. It would have had to be a damned large party anyway, and notably stout-hearted.

They shifted again, when the glittering sun was a few degrees past meridian. There were no markers to define this new, cliff-walled path, but a certain evenness and regularity implied that it had, at one time, been meant for traffic.

Duffy was near panic. Where are these things taking me? he almost whimpered aloud. We're still moving roughly east, thank God, but we're now several miles north of where I should be. Can I possibly ditch these beasts? And having done *that,* could I retrace the way back to the original path?

Their steep road changed direction several more times, and seemed with every league gained to become straighter and more consistent in width and surface. It was late in the afternoon, and Duffy was trying to work up the nerve to nudge his horse out of the procession, when, simultaneously, all of the hitherto-silent creatures joined voices in what might have been called song. It was a number of sustained single notes, like undiminishing reverberations of a dozen gigantic gongs, and the chord they combined in, echoing up and down the rock-walled pass and ringing away into the empty sky, actually filled the Irishman's eyes with tears, so great was the sense it conveyed of inhuman grandeur and loneliness. And as the song swelled, and rose by tremendous steps up some alien scale, the ascending pass levelled out onto an expansive plateau of snow-dusted stone.

Despite his profound surprise, Duffy simply closed his eyes for a moment before opening them again to stare. Tremendously old, weather-rounded pillars of uneven height stretched away across the top of the mountain, in two columns separated by nearly half a mile of crumbled pavement. Even the shortest of the pillars presented its eroded top to the sky a dozen feet over Duffy's head, and every one of them was wide enough to have housed a small temple.

The two guides ahead of him stepped aside, and Duffy's horse moved forward unprompted to take the lead. At a stately pace Duffy and his weird retinue proceeded down the center of the vast lane defined by the two ranks of pillars. The red sun hung directly behind, and the Irishman realized that if one were standing at the other end of the plateau, staring this way, the sun would be seen to sink precisely at the western end of the gargantuan, unroofed hall.

By God, said Duffy to himself, I wonder what this place looked like when it did have a roof, however many thousand years ago? Picture hundreds of torches carried by the congregation assembled on the ex-

quisitely worked mosaic pavement; the images painted
on the high, arched ceiling; and up front, the marble
altar, taller than a man but dwarfed by the towering
statue that stood behind it, the statue of a woman looking out over the heads of the faithful, directly into the
eye of the setting sun . . .

Duffy breathed deeply several times, fearing that the
rarefied mountain air might be inducing delirium. Take
it easy, lad, he pleaded with himself—you were on the
verge of losing the distinction between imagining and
remembering.

The walk across the plateau face took nearly an
hour, and when the Irishman reached the other side
his yards-long shadow had preceded him by several
minutes. A wide square mark lay before him, and looking closely he saw that it was a gap in the crumbled
paving, as if someone had carefully ripped up a square
section of it . . . or, it occurred to him, as if something had stood there before the floor was put down,
but had since been removed. Nervously he glanced left
and right, and his heart sank to see two weathered
columns of stone that, despite the blurring imparted
by the storms of thousands of Alpine winters, were
clearly the feet and ankles of a vanished colossus.

Duffy found that he was trembling, and reached
around into a saddlebag to fish out the brandy. He
unstoppered the bottle, but before he could raise it
to his lips the horse carried him across the dozen yards
that separated the two stone feet, and his chill abruptly
left him. Since it was in his hand, he took a swig of the
liquor—warm from having lain next to the horse's
flank—but now it was a sip to help savor the beauty
of the place, and not a gulp of oblivion to drive it
out of his mind.

An old stairway, wind-buffed to a sort of bumpy
ramp, led away down the mountain side from the end
of the plateau, and Duffy looked at the high peaks still
lit by the sun, seeming to see in their outlines the
shapes of primeval walls and battlements. He was in
the shadow now, and the Alpine cold was gathering
intensity along with the darkness, so he nudged the
horse into the shelter of a leeward alcove, dismounted,

and set about bedding down for the night. At last he lay wrapped in his cloak, wedged between the blanketed body of the horse and the wall of rock, watching the sky darken behind the stony silhouettes of his guides until all was a uniform black.

Chapter Four

FIVE DAYS LATER Johannes Freiburg sat in the taproom of the St. Mungo Inn and, putting down his mug of ale, nodded to the wide-eyed old man sitting across the table from him. "That's what I said. Escorted by every demon in the Alps. It was just at sunset, and I was crossing the Drava bridge with my goats, when I heard all this singing—hundreds of voices, all glass-rim high, whirling like birds around this one weird tune—and I figured for a second it was God and all the saints, come for me at last. So I turned around, back toward the moutnain, and here comes this tall, gray-haired man on a limping horse, riding down the path with the red sunlight on him like his own personal lantern; and behind him, perched on every ridge and crag, there were ranks and ranks of demons with bird heads, and wiverns, and every damned kind of monster you ever heard of, all singing like a church choir."

The old man crossed himself and gulped. "More ale here," he quavered to the innkeeper. "So who was he?" he asked his companion. "Beezlebub?"

"I don't know. I took off pretty quick—didn't want to let him get close enough to bewitch me—but he looked . . . *Oh my God, that's him just walked in the door.*"

Duffy didn't even notice the old man who clapped his hands over his face and, squeaking shrilly, bolted

out of the room as he entered it. The Irishman crossed
to the bar and calmly asked for a cup of beer. His
face was haggard and there were new wrinkles around
his eyes. When his beer had been drawn he took it to
a back table and sat down to drink it slowly, unaware
of Freiburg's intense, awed stare.

Well, thought Duffy, I can't pretend *that* was delirium tremens—not lasting six days like that. He
sighed and shook his head. I really was escorted
through the Predil Pass by a crew of fantastic beasts
only hinted at even in mythology. They guided me, led
me around areas I later saw to be unstable snow, kept
me on whatever track that was. They always main-
tained a respectful distance, too, and bowed when I
approached them! It was as if . . . as if I were a revered
and long-absent king passing through their district.

He remembered the odd fear he'd felt a week ago in
that mad tavern in Trieste—a fear of recognizing or
remembering something. That's another thing to worry
about, he thought; maybe the goat-footed man was
real, not a hallucination at all. Hell, he was an everyday sight compared to the company I've kept during
these past six days.

The tavern door swung open and a stout, bearded
man clumped in, wearing flared-top boots that came
up to his thighs. He glanced angrily around the room.
"Damn it, Freiburg," he growled, "have you seen Ludvig? He said he'd be drinking in here."

Freiburg bobbed his head. "Yes sir, Mr. Yount.
He . . . uh . . . just dashed out the back door."

"Saw me coming, did he? The lazy old monkey—
I'll break his jaw for him. He knows we—"

Freiburg was jiggling in his chair, winking, shaking
his head and waving his hands. Yount stared at him
in amazement, then caught on that the shepherd had
something confidential to whisper to him.

Yount leaned down. "What the hell is it?"

"Don't blame Ludvig," the shepherd whispered.
*"He's just scared of demons, which that gray-haired
man over there is on intimate terms with."*

Yount glanced across the room at Duffy, who was
still staring morosely into his beer. "Oh, hell," the

bearded man said to Freiburg, "you damned peasants can't take two steps without finding something to put the fear of the devil into you."

"Hey, it's true," protested the shepherd. "I'm not making it up—"

"Oh, no doubt. Like last year, when you crucified all the cats in town because they were witches' familiars."

"Now look, Mr. Yount, there were apparitions—"

Yount made a rude suggestion concerning what stance Freiburg should assume the next time he met an apparition. "Now where's my whimpering clerk? In here? Good Lord, hiding among the brooms and buckets. Out, Ludvig, you coward. We've got to be on the road, get those hides to Vienna before the rains can rot them."

Duffy looked up. "You're heading for Vienna?" he asked.

All three faces swivelled toward him, two of them pale and fearful and one thoughtful, appraising. "That's right, stranger," Yount said.

"I'd be glad to pay you to carry me," Duffy said. "My horse went lame on a . . . sort of forced march through the Alps, and I can't wait around for him to get straightened out. I wouldn't be much extra weight, and if you run across any bandits I imagine you'd be glad of another sword."

"For the love of God, master," Ludvig hisssed, "don't—"

"Shut up," Yount snapped. "Take holy water baths if you have to, or tattoo a cross on your forehead—I choose our personnel." He turned to Duffy, who was highly puzzled by these reactions. "Certainly, stranger. You can ride along. I'll charge you ten ducats, to be doubly refunded in the event that you help us repel any bandits."

Ludvig began weeping, and Yount clouted him in the side of the head. "Shut up, clerk."

Birds were calling to each other through the frees as Yount's modest caravan got under way. Four barrel-chested horses were harnessed to the lead wagon, on

the buckboard of which sat Yount and the clerk, while
Yount's two sons, having shed their shirts, were
stretched out on the bundled hides to get a tan. There
was another wagon being towed behind, and Duffy was
sprawled across its bench, half napping in the midmorning sun. Little boys lined the road as the wagons
rolled by, raising a cheer to see the departure of the
cargo that had for two days given their town the
pungent smell of a tannery. The Irishman tipped his
hat. So long, horse, he thought. I believe you're better
off without me.

In the morning sunshine, as he watched the birds
hopping about on the new-budding branches and listened to the creaking and rattling of the carts, it was
easy for him to regard the disturbing meetings in the
mountains and Trieste as flukes, chance glimpses of
survivals from the ancient world. Those things do still
exist, he told himself, in the darker corners and cub-
byholes of the world, and a traveller ought not to be
upset at seeing them once in a while.

They camped that night by the banks of the Raab.
Ludvig was careful to keep a distance between Duffy
and himself, and always to sit on the opposite side of
the fire; to make his feelings perfectly clear, every
half hour or so he fled behind one of the parked
wagons and could be heard praying loudly. Yount's
sons, though, got along well with the Irishman, and
he showed them how to play tunes on a piece of grass
held between the thumbs. They grinned delightedly
when he finished up his performance with a spirited
rendering of a bit from Blaylock's *Wilde Manne,* but
Ludvig, hiding behind a wagon again, howled to God
to silence the devil-pipes.

"That's enough," Yount said finally. "You're scar-
ing the daylights out of poor Ludvig. It's getting late
anyway—I think we'd all better turn in." He banked
the fire and checked the horses' tethers while his sons
crawled into sleeping bags and Duffy rolled himself
up in his old fur cloak.

Clouds were plastered in handfuls over the low sky
next morning, and Yount fretted for his hides. "To
hell with breakfast, boys," he shouted, slapping the

horses awake, "I want us five miles north of the river five minutes from now." Duffy climbed up onto the buckboard of the trailing wagon, turned up his frayed collar and resumed his interrupted sleep.

It was an oddly out-of-tune bird call that woke him again. I think that was a curlew, he told himself groggily as he sat up on the wagon bench, but I never heard one with such a flat voice. Then the call was answered, from the other side of the road, in the same not-quite-true tone—and Duffy came fully awake. Those aren't curlews, he thought grimly. They're not even birds.

Trying to make it look casual, he stood up, balanced a moment on the footrest and then leaped across the gap onto the leading wagon's back rail. He pulled himself over the bar, clambered across the rocking bales of hides—nodding cheerfully to the two young men as he passed—and tapped Yount on the shoulder. "Keep smiling like I am," he told him, ignoring the trembling Ludvig, "but give me a bow if you've got one. There are robbers in these woods."

"Hell," grated Yount. "No, I don't have a bow."

Duffy bit his lip, thinking. "You certainly can't outrun them with this rig. I'd say you've got no choice but to give up once they make their entrance."

"To hell with that. We'll fight them."

Duffy shrugged. "Very well. I'll go back to the rear wagon, then, and try to keep them from cutting it loose." He crawled back across the hides, told the boys to go talk to their father in a minute, and then half-climbed, half-leaped back to his own wagon.

Back up on the driver's bench, he pulled his hat-brim down over his eyes and pretended to go back to sleep. He kept his hands near his hilts, though.

A low tree branch sprang up into the air as the wagons passed under it, and four men leaped catlike to the caravan. Two of them tumbled sprawling onto the bundles in the second wagon, and Duffy was on his feet and facing them in an instant, his sword singing out of the scabbard.

One of them was now brandishing his own sword, and threw a powerful wood-chopping cut at Duffy's skull; the Irishman parried it over his head and riposted immediately with a head-cut of his own. The man hopped back out of distance, but Duffy managed to steer his descending blade so that it nicked the man's sword wrist.

"Hah!" the Irishman barked. "Robbers, Yount! Keep the horses moving."

Three men on horseback, he noticed now, were galloping alongside. Good God, Duffy thought, they really do have us. The two bandits in the wagon, swords out and points in line, made a stumbling but combined rush at him. Braced on the bench, though, Duffy had the steadier position—he knocked one blade away with his dagger and, catching it in the dagger's quillons, twisted the sword out of the man's hand and flipped it over the rail. The other man's blade he parried down, hard, so that it stuck in the wood of the bench-back for a second while the Irishman riposted with a poke in the trachea. Clutching his throat, the bandit rolled backward over the side rail. The other man, disarmed and facing Duffy's two blades, vaulted the rail and dropped to the ground voluntarily.

Perhaps ten seconds had passed since the two men had leaped from the tree onto the wagon. Duffy turned to see how the lead wagon was faring. One of Yount's sons was snapping the reins and shouting abuse at the laboring horses. Yount and his other son, both bleeding from minor cuts, were waving axes and holding at bay two of the robbers, who crouched at the rear of the first wagon.

Before the men on horseback could shout a warning, Duffy leaped again across the gap between the wagons, whirling his sword in a great horizontal arc, and a head bounced in the dust of the road a moment later. The other bandit, whom Duffy had only knocked sprawling, scrabbled frantically for his fallen sword, but the Irishman lunged at him with the dagger, burying it to the hilt under the man's jaw.

Two of the three riders were now leaning from their saddles and hacking at the hawser connecting the two wagons. "God," Duffy breathed wearily, getting up. He leaned out from the rail and brought the flat of his sword down hard on the skull of one of the galloping horses. The beast screeched, stumbled and fell in a thrashing somersault, pitching its rider headfirst onto the road. The horse behind tripped over the fallen one, and it too went tumbling.

The last rider, finding himself the only remaining representative of the robber gang, fell back, dismayed and uncertain.

"You'd be wise to go home while you still can," Duffy called to him.

Oh no, he thought, a moment later—he's got reinforcements. Two more riders were coming up fast from behind. Their swords were out and held low, and Duffy didn't relish the prospect of fighting them. They'll be passing that discouraged one in a second, he thought, and when he sees he's got support I'll have three of them to deal with.

Then Duffy blinked in astonishment, for one of the new riders had, in passing, casually leaned out and driven his blade through the back of the slower-riding robber. Why, they're reinforcements for *us*, the Irishman thought with relief. He grinned and sat back as one of them drew alongside, a blond, curly-haired young man.

"It's good to see you, lads," Duffy called. "Though a sooner appearance—" He leaped backward then like a startled cat, for the rider had made a terribly quick cut at his face. The sword point nicked the end of the Irishman's nose and then drove in at his chest; but Duffy had his own sword up by now, and parried the thrust.

"What's going on?" Yount called. "Who are *these* bastards?"

"I don't know," Duffy shouted, trying a feint and thrust at the young rider. The man effortlessly got a bind on Duffy's blade, and his parry and riposte were one movement. Not bad, considering he's fighting from the back of a horse, Duffy thought as he leaped back again and the stranger's sword lightly clipped his doublet.

The wagon rocked violently as the other of the pair leaped from his horse and swung aboard from the far side. Damnation, Duffy thought, whirling around just in time to block a flank cut from this new passenger, these boys are quick.

Yount and his son, hefting their axes, began clambering over the back rail of the first cart.

"Don't get yourselves hurt," the young man called to them. "It's him we want." He pointed at Duffy.

"I told you!" howled old Ludvig, peering above the foremost bench-back. "He's a devil!"

There was a quick whiz-and-thump then, and the young man cocked his head uncertainly, and a moment later toppled forward, a feathered arrow jutting from his back.

God help us, Duffy thought hysterically, what now? "Keep the horses moving," he yelled. "We've got to get clear of this madhouse."

There were men—little men—in the shrubbery beside the road. Duffy looked more closely, and saw to his astonishment that they were dwarfs, carrying bows and dressed in little suits of chain mail. The blond rider saw them too, paled, and spurred his horse to flee; before he'd got ten yards, though, a dozen hard-driven arrows had found the gaps between his ribs and he rolled out of the saddle as his horse galloped on.

The wagons rattled along down the road, the fletching-feathered corpse rolled limply to a stop, and the dwarfs slung their bows and knelt with lowered heads as Yount's hide shipment passed by.

The ranks of kneeling dwarfs stretched nearly a quarter of a mile, on both sides of the road. The Irishman slowly wiped his sword and sheathed it, but no one in the wagons spoke until the last dwarf had been five minutes passed.

"They . . . *rescued* you, didn't they? The dwarfs?" Yount's voice was thoughtful.

Duffy shrugged gloomily. "I don't know. I guess they did."

"I've carted hides through these woods for years," Yount said. "I've seen bandits before. This is the first time I've seen dwarfs."

"They bowed to him!" Ludvig called fearfully. "They knelt when he went by! He's the king of the dwarfs!"

"Oh, for God's sake, clerk," Yount said irritably, "he's taller than I am."

Duffy sat down on one of the bales, discouraged by these new developments. I hate times, he thought, when it seems like there's a . . . worldwide brotherhood whose one goal is to kill Brian Duffy. That's the kind of thing which, true or not, it's madness to believe. And even weirder is the brotherhood that seems to be dedicated to helping me. *Why,* for instance, did Giacomo Gritti save my life in Venice last week? Why did all the monsters in the Julian Alps get together to guide me through the pass? And now why did these dwarfs—famous for their sullen, secretive ways—turn out in droves and kill my attackers?

"I won't ride with him." Ludvig was in tears. "I'm a devout man, and I won't travel with a king of dwarfs and mountain devils."

Hmm, the Irishman thought uneasily—how did he hear of my Alpine guides?

"Shut up," barked Yount, his voice harsh with uncertainty. "We'll be in Vienna tomorrow afternoon, if we hurry. Whatever you are, stranger, I said you could ride with us, and I won't turn you out now, especially after you saved us from those highwaymen."

"Then turn me out," Ludvig said. "Stop the wagons and let me get my stuff."

Yount waved at him impatiently. "Shut up and keep still."

"I'm not joking," the clerk said. "Stop the wagons or I'll jump out while they're moving."

Duffy stood up. "Yes, Yount, you'd better put on the brakes. I'll walk from here. I don't want to deprive you of your clerk—he'd die for sure out here alone."

The old hides trader looked doubtful; clearly he'd be happy to be rid of the upsetting Irishman, but didn't want to violate travellers' countesy. "You're sure you want to leave us?" he asked. "I won't force you off, even to save poor idiot Ludvig."

"I'm sure. I'll do fine out here. If I get in any trouble I'll just whistle up some dwarfs."

The wagons squeaked and lurched to a halt as Duffy shouldered on his knapsack, bundled up his fur cloak

and swung to the ground. Yount's sons sadly waved
farewell—clearly they'd found him much more interesting a companion than the pious clerk. Duffy
waved, and the wagons strained and heaved into motion again.

The Irishman cursed wearily and sat down under
a tree to have a gulp or two of wine, for it had been
an exhausting morning. I suppose, he told himself,
savoring the lukewarm and now somewhat vinegary
chianti, I could somehow have avoided this maroon-
ment; turned on old Ludvig and hissed, *If you don't
shut up and let me ride along, I'll have my good pal
Satan chase you from here to Gibraltar.* Ho ho. Duffy
cut himself chunks of cheese, salami, onion and bread,
and washed it all down with some more of the wine.
Then he rubbed a split garlic clove around the cut in
his nose, to keep it from mortifying.

A minute or so later he stood up, set his hat firmly
on his gray head, and trotted away northward, following the wagon tracks in the dusty road. His relaxed,
jogging pace sent the miles pounding away behind
beneath his boots; toward midafternoon he permitted
himself a rest stop, but within five minutes he was
moving again. His breathing by this time was not as
easy and synchronized to his pace as it had been when
he started, but he forced himself, gasping and sweating, to cover as much ground as possible before nightfall.

The sky had already begun to glow in the west when
he rounded a curve in the road and saw before him
the narrow eastern arm of the Neusiedler Lake, gleaming like tarnished silver under the darkening heavens.
An abandoned-looking ferry dock and pulley were
tucked into a cove to his left. Time to rest at last, he
thought, sitting down right in the road and groping for
his wineskin. Nobody could expect me to try to cross
the lake at this hour.

A dot of orange light waxed and waned on the north
shore. That must be Yount, Duffy thought. I've nearly
kept up with him, in spite of being on foot.

The ground was damp, making him think of snakes
and ghouls, so he climbed an oak and settled him-

self in a natural hammock of branches that curled up around him like the fingers of a cupped hand. He had a supper of more bread, cheese, salami and wine, followed by a suck at the brandy bottle to keep off the chill. Then he hung his knapsack on a limb, wrapped up in the old cloak and heaved about on his perch until he found a comfortable posture.

Weariness and brandy made him sleep soundly in his treetop bed, but some time after midnight he was awakened by hoarse, deep-voiced calls. What the hell, he thought groggily; a gang of men on the road. Then he froze—for the voices sounded from above, and the speakers, unless Duffy was the victim of some kind of ventriloquism, were moving across the sky.

He couldn't recognize the language in which they called to each other, but it sounded eastern; Egyptian, he thought, or Turkish, or Arabic. *Can* this be real, he wondered, or is it some madness brought on by the brandy?

With a sound like banners flapping in a stiff wind, the voices whirled away to the north, and Duffy permitted himself a deep sigh of relief when he heard them echoing over the lake.

Never in my life, he thought, trying to relax again, have I been so mobbed by the supernatural as during this last week and a half, since leaving Venice. He could recall two or three odd sights during his childhood—an elderly gentleman he'd seen fishing on the banks of the Liffey, who'd disappeared when the young Duffy had looked away for a moment; two clouds that had uncannily resembled a dragon and a bear fighting above the Wicklow hills; a tiny man that had crouched on a tree branch, winked at him, and then hopped and scuttled away through the foliage—but it was easy, thirty years later, to believe they'd been games or dreams. These recent events, though, were hopelessly real. I wonder what's brought them all out of their holes, he thought. I wonder what's up.

He had begun to drift off to sleep again when a series of screams sounded faintly from the north; even from a distance Duffy could hear the stark fear in them. Good Lord, he thought, that must be Yount's

group. The flying things are over there. He sat up—
then shrugged helplessly and lay back down against
the branches. What can I do? he thought. It's the
middle of the night, the moon is down, and I'm on
the other side of the lake. Even if I was still with them
I don't think I could do anything against whatever
those things are.

In a few minutes the screaming had stopped. The
Irishman had another pull at the brandy—and another—and then closed his eyes and tried to sleep.

The next morning Duffy climbed down from his
bending, creaking tree while a furious wind from the
west flapped his cloak and blew his long hair into his
face. When he dropped to the ground, bits of twigs
and leaves were whipping through the air like debris
dashed before a flood, and the gray clouds twisted in
agonized tangles of muscular forms and ragged veils
across the sky. Good Jesus, Duffy thought, holding his
hat onto his head, I could believe this is the end of
the world.

He walked down the road to the lake, leaning into
the wind with every step and clutching the collar of
his cloak to keep it from whirling away like a furry
bat. I wonder, he thought, if I can possibly manipulate
the ferry in this weather. I can give it a try, he decided
—wondering, at the same time, why he was in such a
hurry to get to Vienna. Am I that anxious to see
Epiphany? He had for the moment nearly forgotten
Yount.

The lake looked like a vast pane of glass across
which an invisible army was marching in nailed boots;
the wind tossed it into hundreds of individual currents
and flecked it with whitecaps. He glanced down the
beach at the ferry platform, dreading the task of haul-
ing the barge back across the lake, and was surprised
to see the ferry moored on this side already. I know
it wasn't here last night, he thought. Who hauled it
back?

He plodded across the littered shore toward the
platform, and suddenly noticed the old man standing in
the ferry's bow. Although his fluttering hair and beard

were as white as bones, he was fully six feet tall, broad-shouldered and muscled like a wrestler. In spite of the chilly wind he wore only a loincloth and sandals.

"Two coins to cross," the old man said, his deep voice effortlessly undercutting the screech of the wind.

Duffy clumped along the platform and stepped carefully into the ferry. "What kind of coins?" he gasped, fumbling under his cloak. Thank God he's willing to risk a crossing, he thought; I damned well wouldn't, if it were my ferry.

"What do I care?" the ferryman growled. "Two coins."

Bless these unworldly backwoods men, Duffy thought, and dropped two sequins into the old man's leathery palm before sitting down on a section of bench somewhat sheltered from the wind by the high gunwale. The old ferrier untied the moorings, then braced his knotted legs below the bulwark and began laboriously pulling in the guide rope, and the flat craft, swinging and bucking in the agitated water like a fish on a leash, began moving away from the dock platform.

Duffy stared at the man in amazement, having expected to find, on one shore or the other, oxen turning a wheel. He's doing all the pulling himself, he marvelled. And in a sea like this? His heart will burst in two minutes. "Let me help you with that," the Irishman said, getting cautiously to his feet.

"No," said the ferrier. "Stay where you are." He does sound tired, Duffy thought as he shrugged and took his seat again, but with a more long-term weariness, in which this effort this morning is no more remarkable that the all-but-worthless coins I gave him.

Duffy glanced ahead across the choppy water, and suddenly remembered the calls and screams he'd heard the night before. I wonder, he thought with something of his boatman's weariness, if those screams across the lake really were Yount's party. I suppose they were. I'd like to think those flying things had nothing to do with me, but I think perhaps old Ludvig was right after all. I was a Jonah to Yount's people.

He looked nervously up at the shredding sky, half fearing to see bat-winged black figures wheeling above.

Then it occurred to him that, whatever they had been, they couldn't help being blown away east by this fierce wind. It's as if their presence here itched the earth, he thought, and it's sneezing.

The guide-rope was pulled tight across the water and thrummed like a bass lute string each time the old man clutched it. Duffy gripped the rail and held on, still half-expecting the old man to drop dead.

By imperceptible stages, though, the shoreline worked nearer, and eventually the ferry's ragged bow bumped the pilings of the north side dock. Duffy stood up. "Well, sir," he said, "thank you for the extraordinary—"

"Get out of the boat now," the old man told him.

The Irishman frowned and climbed out. Laconic, these rural types are, he thought.

There was a clearing littered with torn hides and splintered wood and the trampled remains of a camp-fire, but he could see no bodies. He wasn't sure whether to feel better about that or not.

Chapter Five

TOWARD MIDDAY the wind died down. It had blown away the cloud cover, and the sunlight began to make Duffy sleepy, so he laid his cloak under a tree and stretched out on it, dozing in the dappled evergreen shade.

He was snapped awake an hour later by a sound that was lately becoming uncomfortably familiar to him: the clang of swords. He got up, rolled his cloak, and padded a few yards deeper into the woods. This, at least, he resolved, is a fight I stay out of.

"Get the bastard!" someone was calling. "Don't you see him?"

"No," echoed a reply. "He was down in that thicket a second ago."

"Well—*Oh Jesus*—" Three quick clangs followed, and a gasping cry.

There was silence for a few moments, then the second voice spoke up again. 'Bob? Did you get the hunchback or did he get you?"

There was no answer. It's my guess the hunchback got Bob, Duffy thought with a hard grin.

Footfalls crackled somewhere near him, and he breathed a curse. Surrounded, he thought. I may have to climb a tree.

Exploding abruptly out of a bush in a spray of broken twigs and leaves, a little curly-haired man with an absurdly long sword leaped at the Irishman, whirling a quick cut at his head. Not having his own sword out, Duffy leaped up and parried the cut with the heel of his boot, and the impact flung him two yards away. The little man followed up the attack furiously, but Duffy had scrambled up and drawn his rapier now and was parrying the blows fairly easily, for the little man's two-handed sword was too heavy to be used deceptively.

I'm going to have to riposte soon, Duffy thought, exasperated, or he'll break my blade. "What is this?" Duffy asked, blocking a hard cut at his chest. "I've done nothing to you!"

The hunchback—for, the Irishman noticed, that's who it was—stared at him for a moment, choked with rage. "Is that right?" he yelled finally, redoubling his attacks. "You call all that *nothing,* do you? Watch, while I do *nothing* to your filthy entrails."

First demons, Duffy thought unhappily, and now madmen. I guess I've got to kill him.

He shifted his sword to his inside line, inviting a cut at the shoulder. When he goes for it, he calculated, I'll parry outside, feint a direct riposte to his inside line, then duck around his parry and put my point in his neck.

The hunchback cocked his arm for the expected blow, but at that moment four armed men strode up through the tangled brush. "Kill them both," growled one of the newcomers, and they advanced with their points extended.

"God help us," gasped Duffy, alarmed by this escalation. "We can finish our fight later," he barked to the hunchback. "Deal with these boys now."

The little man nodded, and they turned on their four attackers. Duffy engaged the swords of two of them, trying to draw one into an advance so he could put a stop-thrust in his face, but the hunchback leaped at his pair, whirling maniacal hammer-strokes at them. The forest resounded like a dozen smithies.

Duffy struck down one of his opponents with a lucky remise that sheared across the man's throat; the other man tried an attack while Duffy was thus occupied, but the Irishman bounded back out of distance immediately and let the blade swish through the air unobstructed. I'll cripple this one, he thought, and then grab my stuff there and run like a bastard. That crazed hunchback will just have to be satisfied with dismembering the *next* stranger he meets.

Beating aside a badly aimed thrust, Duffy threw himself forward in a *punta sopra mano*—but when his leading foot hit the ground the boot heel snapped off and he fell, twisting desperately in mid-air to keep his sword between himself and his attacker. Blows rained down on Duffy for a good ten seconds—while he lay in the leaves, parried desperately and tried to riposte at the man's legs—and then there was a meaty *chunk* and the man fell on him.

Duffy got his sword point up in time to spit the man under the breastbone, but when he threw the corpse aside and hopped to his feet, he saw a deep, spine-severing cleft dividing the dead man's back.

"I already got him," explained the hunchback, wiping sweat off his forehead. "What kind of move was that, anyway? Diving on the ground like that?"

Duffy grinned sourly. "It would have been a damned good move if you hadn't split my boot heel a few minutes ago." He looked past the hunchback, and saw the other two men sprawled gorily in the clearing. "I suppose you still want to kill me?"

The hunchback frowned. "Uh, no." He wiped the

blade of his two-handed sword and slid it into a scabbard slung over his shoulder. "I owe you an apology for that. These weasels have been following me for days, and I took you for one of them. I'm sorry about your boot."

"Don't worry about it. One of these lads doubtless has feet my size, and I see they were all high-class bravos, well-shod."

"I never could have stood the four of them off alone," the hunchback said. "I'm indebted to you." He stuck out his right hand. "I'm Bluto, a Swiss."

Duffy shook his hand. "Brian Duffy, an Irishman."

"You're far from home, Duffy. Where's your horse?"

"Well . . ." Inquisitive little bugger, he thought. Still, he did save my life—after jeopardizing it in the first place. "I'm afoot."

"Just out for a stroll, eh? Well, these gentlemen had horses. They left them tethered in a clearing about a half mile back. When you've chosen a pair of boots, perhaps you'd care to select a horse."

Duffy laughed and wiped his sword off on the dead man's shirt. "All right," he said, "let's go take a look at them."

Half an hour later the two men were riding north. Duffy allowed himself a gulp of the wine, which was running low, and offered the wineskin to Bluto.

"No, thank you," the hunchback said. "Not right now, or I'll get sick. You're bound for Vienna, I assume?"

Duffy nodded.

"So am I. I've been hired to organize the city's artillery."

"Oh? You know about that stuff, do you?"

"It's what I do. I'm a freelance bombardier. What is it that's bringing you to Vienna?"

"Nothing so dramatic. I've been hired to be the bouncer at an inn there."

"Hah! These Viennese range far afield for their employees. There was no local talent?"

The Irishman shrugged. "Apparently not. The guy who hired me—weird little man named Aurelianus—"

"Aurelianus?" Bluto exclaimed. "Black clothes? Trembly? Afraid to open windows?"

Duffy frowned, mystified. "That's him. How did you know?"

"I met him two months ago, in Bern. He's the one who hired me to take charge of the artillery." For a minute or two they rode along in silence. Finally Bluto spoke. "I don't suppose there have been murderers chasing *you* around, have there?"

"Well . . . there has been an incident or two."

"Ah. I might hazard a guess, then, that there are those, enemies of Aurelianus, perhaps, who don't want us to get to Vienna."

Duffy snorted skeptically. "Who'd care whether or not the Zimmermann Inn gets a new bouncer?"

"I couldn't say. I wonder, though, who else he's hired, and for what."

"Have you . . ." Duffy began. "Have you run into any odd types, besides common murderers? Stranger . . . things . . . that pay uncalled-for attention to you?"

The hunchback stared at him uncomprehendingly. "Aren't murderers enough? What kind of 'things' do you mean? Lions? Wolves?"

"Yes," said the Irishman quickly. "Wolves. I've been plagued by them."

Bluto shook his head. "No. But then we're coming from different directions. Wouldn't be likely to run across the same sorts of beasts."

"That's true," assented Duffy, letting the discussion drop. That's odd, though, he thought. Bluto has apparently seen no supernatural creatures at all. Why have I seen so many?

At midafternoon their horses' hooves clattered on the Leitha Bridge, and by sunset they had reached the high, stone, battlement-crowned walls of Vienna.

"God, she's big," Bluto remarked as they rode up to the Carinthian Gate. "Have you ever been here before?"

"I used to live here," Duffy said quietly.

"Oh. Can you tell me where I could spend the night?

I want a bit of rest before I present myself to the city council."

Duffy frowned. If there's one thing I don't want right now, he thought, it's company. But he's a decent sort, and if it weren't for him I wouldn't have this horse. "I imagine they'd give you a room at the Zimmermann. Aurelianus owns it. Did he give you some kind of letter of introduction?"

"Yes. Sealed with two fighting dragons."

"Well, show that seal to the innkeeper. I doubt if he'd even charge you any money."

"Good idea. I'm much obliged to you."

They rode under the old stone arch and clip-clopped at a leisurely pace up the Kartnerstrasse. Duffy breathed deeply, enjoying the smoky smell of the city. Damn my eyes, he thought, it's good to be back. I remember riding down this very street sixteen years ago with Franz von Sickingen's knights, to go push the French away from the Rhine. Yes, and I remember coming back, too, blind and half-paralyzed by a sword-cut in the base of the skull. The physicians told me I'd never again be able to get out of a chair unaided, much less fight. Hah. Brandy, my Irish blood and Epiphany made liars of them. I was reading, walking with a cane and giving fencing lessons a year later; and by the time I was thirty-three, and had let my hair grow over my collar in back, you wouldn't know I'd ever taken a wound.

"Where is this Zimmermann Inn?" asked Bluto, peering around.

"Up this street a bit farther, just off the Rotenturm-strasse."

"How are the accommodations?"

"I don't know. In my day it was a monastery. But they've always made great beer—even back in the days when it was a Roman fort, I understand."

People on the street paused to stare at the two barbarous-looking riders; Duffy tall, burly, and gray, and Bluto gnarled and hunchbacked, his long sword-hilt thrusting up from behind his shoulder like a cobra whispering in his ear. In the courtyard of St. Stephen's Cathedral children pointed at them and giggled.

And off to our port side, Duffy thought grimly, silhouetted by the sunset, is St. Peter's Church, where Epiphany married Max Hallstadt in June of 'twentysix. I haven't seen her since that afternoon, when she told me I'd behaved disgracefully at the wedding. She was right, of course.

And here I am home again, three years and a few scars later. Returning in dubious triumph to keep bums from throwing up on the Zimmermann's taproom floor.

The sky was darkening fast now, and clear for the first time in several nights. Duffy winked a greeting at the evening star. "We go left here," he said.

Three blocks later the Irishman pointed. "That's her, on the left. As I recall, the stables are around back." It was a long, two-storeyed, half-timbered building with an overhanging shingled roof and three tall chimneys. Yellow light gleamed cozily in nearly all the windows, and Duffy was looking forward almost carnally to a big mug of mulled Herzwesten ale and a real bed.

The stable boys reeled a little, and smelled of beer, but Duffy told the hunchback this was to be expected in the stables of any fine inn. They left the horses there and strode—rolling a bit from the hours in the saddle—back up the alley to the street and the front door.

They paused in the vestibule, under a ceiling fresco depicting an unusually jovial Last Supper. "You want to see the innkeeper," Duffy said, "and I've been told to report to the brewmaster. God knows why. So I may see you later tonight, or I may not."

Bluto grinned. "Got a little girl or two you want to get re-acquainted with, hey? Well, I won't tag along. In any case, I know now where to come for the best beer in Vienna, right?"

"That's right." They shook hands, and Bluto pushed open the public room door while Duffy stepped through the one marked *Servants*.

A thin-faced woman gasped when she saw him, and nearly dropped her tray of beer mugs. "It's all right, daughter," Duffy told her, reaching out to steady the tray. "I haven't come to rape the help. Can you tell me where I'd find—" he glanced at the envelope, "—Gambrinus? The brewmaster?"

"Certainly, sir," she quavered. "He's in the cellar —down those stairs at the end of the hall—testing the spring beer."

"Thank you." Duffy walked down the hall to the indicated archway, and descended the dark stairs slowly and noisily to avoid giving a similar fright to the brewmaster. There were many steps, and when he finally stood on the damp flags of the floor he figured he was about thirty feet below ground level. The air was steamy and rich with the smell of malt, but for the moment he could see nothing in the dimness.

"What can I do for you, stranger?" came a deep, relaxed voice.

"Are you Gambrinus?"

"Yes. Will you have a cup of new schenk beer?"

"Thank you, I will."

Duffy could see dimly now, and sat down on an up-turned bucket, dropping his knapsack beside him. A clean-shaven old man with thick white hair drew a cupful of draft beer from a keg nearby and passed it to him. "We won't make any more schenk this year," he said gravely. "When these kegs are empty we'll open the bock."

"Well, fine," Duffy said. "Look, I met a man named Aurelianus in Venice a few weeks ago, and he said I should give you this." Here he handed him the some-what travel-stained letter. Gambrinus broke the seal and scanned the writing. He must spend a lot of time down here, Duffy realized, to be able to read in this darkness.

The Irishman looked around, interested. I've poured down gallons of Herzwesten beer, he thought, but this is the first time I've seen, however dimly, the cellar where it's brewed. The ceiling was lost in shadow, but scaffolds were braced around copper tubs that stood an easy twenty feet above the floor, and long pipes slanted into and out of several of the old brick walls. Bell-shaped oak kegs lay everywhere; full ones were stacked narrow-side-down several layers deep along one wall. Gambrinus was sitting on an empty one, and other empties were scattered about as if someone had used them for bowling pins in a particularly wild game. The large tun-tubs in which the actual fermentation took place were not visible, and Duffy assumed they were behind one of the walls.

Gambrinus looked up at Duffy curiously. "He seems to think you're the man we're looking for," he said. "And I guess he'd know. Here." He scribbled in red chalk on the back of the letter. "Show this to the innkeeper and he'll give you your money."

"All right." Duffy drained the cup and got to his feet. "Thanks for the beer."

Gambrinus spread his hands. "Thank God for it."

Duffy nodded uncertainly, then picked up his old knapsack and climbed back up the stairs to the main floor.

The same serving woman he'd startled before was returning with an armload of empty pitchers. "Did you find him?" she asked, still a little uneasy.

"Yes." Duffy smiled. "Now can you tell me where the innkeeper is?"

"Werner? Certainly. He's the heavy-set gentleman drinking burgundy at the end of the bar in the taproom." She squinted at him. "Didn't you used to live around here?"

"I'm not certain yet," he told her. "Thanks."

I guess that dog-faced old fellow is the one, Duffy thought as he weaved his way through the crowded dining room to the raised, slightly offset area that was the taproom. The old, room-long monastic tables had been sawn into thirds and distributed about the hall in a less regimented way, and several obviously new chandeliers cast a bright radiance into every corner. I can almost see, Duffy thought with a grin, the outraged ghosts of old monks peering in through these windows.

He sat down beside the small-eyed man. "You, sir, are the innkeeper here?"

Werner stared at him mistrustfully. "Why?"

"I've got this letter—"

"Another freeloader! Aurelianus obviously wants to ruin us. Listen, if you intend to steal any lead or brass from the rooms, I swear to Christ——"

Duffy laid one hand softly but heavily on the bar, and Werner halted in his tirade. "I'm not a freeloader," the Irishman said quietly. "Aurelianus hired me to keep the peace here. So stop shouting."

"Oh. He did? Sorry. Let me see that." Duffy handed him the letter. "Well, I see our cellar-hermit has approved it. Uh . . . *five hundred ducats?* That's simply out of the question. Obviously a mistake. I'll let you sleep here, somewhere, and you can eat with the kitchen help——tonight you can even drink as much beer as you like!——but this money is out of the——"

"You won't meet the terms of the letter?" Duffy asked in a conversational tone.

"Certainly not. It's some kind of mistake."

Duffy stood up. "Then I'm leaving Vienna in the morning. Explain to Aurelianus when he gets here that I left because you wouldn't comply with his written instructions. Right now I'll take you up on that all-the-beer-you-can-drink offer."

"Wait a minute," Werner protested, getting flustered. "If you're not taking the job . . . but . . . are you really leaving in the morning?"

"Bright and early."

Werner gulped some of his wine unhappily. "Very well," he said finally. "I'll pay you. I guess he can't blame me for his mistakes and Gambrinus' carelessness. I'll get the money tomorrow sometime. We can fix a wage for you then, too." He glared at Duffy out of his pouchy red eyes. "But hear me——there will be no fights, not even a harsh word, in here. Understand? If I have to pay this kind of money for a bouncer, he's going to do one hell of a good job."

The Irishman grinned and clapped the innkeeper on the back. "That's the spirit, Werner lad! I'll earn my keep. You'll bless the day I arrived."

"Go drink your beer."

Duffy stepped down to the dining room level and walked across to a table by the wall so that he could keep an eye on the entire hall. Looks like a fairly quiet place, he thought as he sat down; though I can see I'll have to crack down on vandalism. Someone's been carving on this table.

The thin serving woman was back, handing out foaming mugs and pitchers of beer, and Duffy beckoned to her. "Bring me a big mug of mulled ale, miss, and draw one for yourself—it's on the house. I'm the new chucker-out here."

She smiled wearily. "I'll be happy to. You won't get insulted, though, if I check that with Werner." Then she cocked her head. "You're Brian Duffy, aren't you? The old landsknecht fencing master?"

He sighed. "Well, yes. I am. Who are you?"

"Anna Schomburg. Everybody figured you died years ago, fighting the Turks in Hungary."

"Must have been somebody else. Uh, tell me, Anna, do you remember a girl named Epiphany Vogel?"

"Girl? Hah. Yes, I remember Epiphany *Hallstadt*. She got married, you know."

"Where is she now?" Duffy kept his voice in a casual tone. "Where could I find her?"

"Right here, if you wait long enough. She works the morning shift."

"Damn it, Anna, where's my suffering beer?" came an impatient call from another table.

"Whoops." Anna picked up her tray again. "See you later," she said, and whisked away.

Duffy was stunned. Could this girl be telling the truth? If so, he thought, what an amazing coincidence! I never used to think much of coincidences, but these days I practically trip over them in the street. Well by God, I'll wait right here until morning; pull my hat down over my face and then whip it off when she walks up to take my order. *Guess who, Piff!* Ho ho.

But why is she working here? In a damned *inn?* Hallstadt was rich. I guess the money dissolved away somehow, as God knows I've seen it do myself. Maybe old Hallstadt works here too, brushing out the dirty pitchers in some back room. How very far all of us mighty have fallen.

Two men had begun shouting at each other at the table nearest his. Uh-oh, time to earn your keep, the

Irishman told himself as he quickly got to his feet. "Gentlemen!" he said. "What's the trouble?"

The men actually paled when they stared up at the craggy, gray-stubbled face of the new bouncer, and saw the well-worn hilts of his dagger and sword.

"Well," spoke up one of them after a moment, "Otto here says the Pope can't predict the weather."

Duffy looked shocked. "Whose mother?"

Otto blinked. "No," he said, "I told him the Pope—"

"I don't want to hear any filthy lies about the Pope and this gentleman's mother," Duffy said in a low but outraged tone of voice. "Are you drunk, to talk this way?"

"You misunderstand," protested the first man. "We were—"

"I understand perfectly. Your disgraceful talk has offended everyone in the room"—Actually no one was paying any attention.—"and I think you two had better buy a round of beer for the whole lot, including me, by way of apology."

"What? Good Lord, we don't have that kind of money on us. Can't—"

"Tell the innkeeper I said you could open an account. He'll be pleased. And then keep your voices down. If I hear you squabbling again I'll come over here and cut out your bowels."

Duffy sat down again just as Anna set his beer on the table. "What did you tell those men?" she asked.

"Told them I'd knife them if they didn't shut up. If Werner ever lets you take a break, draw yourself a beer and join me. Tell me what-all's been going on during these three years."

"All right. It'll be a few minutes yet."

Duffy watched her hurry away, and admired, as he always did, the sidling, half-on-tiptoes dance of an experienced barmaid carrying a tray across a crowded room.

Half an hour later Anna slumped down at his table. "Whew," she breathed. "Thanks for the beer. It's life and breath and mother's milk to me at times like this." She brushed a strand of damp hair back from her forehead and took a deep swig from her mug. "So where have you been for three years," she asked, setting the beer down, "if not in hell, like everybody thought?"

"In Venice," Duffy told her, "which is where I met Aurelianus, who gave me this job."

"Oh, yes," Anna nodded. "Our absentee landlord. I've only seen him once or twice—he gives me the creeps."

"I can see how he might, holding burning snakes in his mouth and all. When did he get this place? I don't remember seeing him around when I lived here."

"He got here about a year ago. From England, I think, though I might be wrong on that. He had a paper, signed by the bishop, saying that the St. Christopher Monastery belonged to him. His ancestors owned the land, apparently, and never sold it. The abbot sent a protest, of course, but the bishop came out here in person. Told them yes, this little old bird owns the place, all you monks will have to go somewhere else. The bishop didn't look happy about it, though."

"They just turned all the old monks out?"

"Well, no. Aurelianus bought them another place on the Wiplingerstrasse. They were still pretty upset about it, but since the Diet of Spires it's become popular to take property away from the Church, and everybody said Aurelianus had behaved generously." She chuckled. "If he hadn't promised to keep the brewery going, though, the citizens would have hanged him."

"He must be rich as Jakob Fugger."

"He's got the finances, beyond doubt. Spends it everywhere, on all kinds of senseless things."

In an offhand voice the Irishman now turned to the subject uppermost on his mind. "Speaking of money," he said, "wasn't Max Hallstadt rich? How come Epiphany's working?"

"Oh, he *looked* rich, with his big house and his land and his horses, but it was all owed to usurers. He kept borrowing on this to pay the mortgage on that, and one day he looked over the books and saw he didn't own anything, and that eight different money-lenders could validly claim to own the house. So,"

Anna said with a certain relish, "he laid a silver-plated wheellock harquebus on his carved mahogany table, knelt down in front of it and blew his lower jaw off. He meant to kill himself, you see, but when Epiphany came running in to see what the bang was, he was rolling around on the carpet, bleeding like a fountain and roaring. It took him four days to die."

"Good Jesus," Duffy exclaimed, horrified. "My poor Epiphany."

Anna nodded sympathetically. "It was rough on her, that's true. Even when everything was auctioned off, she still owed money to everybody. Aurelianus, to do him justice, did the generous thing again. He bought all her debts and now lets her work here at the same wage the rest of us get."

Duffy noticed Bluto sitting with a stout blonde girl a few tables away. The hunchback gave him a broad wink.

"Where is she?" Duffy asked. "Does she live here?"

"Yes, she lives here. But tonight she's off visiting her father, the artist. He's dying, I believe. Going blind for sure, anyway."

He nodded. "He was going blind three years ago."

Anna glanced at him. "I remember now," she said. "You were sweet on her, weren't you? That's right, and then she married Hallstadt and you took off to Hungary, after shouting a lot of rude things at the wedding. Everybody knew why you went."

"Everybody's an idiot," the Irishman said, annoyed.

"No doubt. Here, you finish my beer. I've got to get back to work."

The room had been swept before the lights were snuffed out, but mice darted across the old wood floors in the darkness, finding bits of cheese and bread in the corners and around the table legs. Every once in a long while a muffled cough or door-slam sounded from upstairs, and the mice would stop, suddenly tense; but ten seconds of silence would restore their confidence and they'd be scampering about again. A few paused to nibble the leather of two boots under one of the wall tables, but there was tastier fare elsewhere, and they didn't linger there.

When the sky began to pale behind the wavy window glass, the mice knew the night was nearly over. Occasional carts rumbled by on the cobbled street, crows shouted at each other from the rooftops, and a man tramped by the windows, whistling. Finally the rattle of a key in the front door lock sent them bolting for their holes.

The heavy door swung open and a middle-aged woman hobbled in. Her graying hair was tied back in a scarf, and her fingers were clumsy with the keys because of the woolen gloves she wore. "Well, how does the place look this morning, Brian?" she inquired absently.

Duffy stood up. "It's good to see you, Piff."

"Yaaah!" she shrieked, flinging her keys across the room. She stared at him in utter horror for a second, then sighed and dropped unconscious to the floor.

For God's sake, Duffy thought as he ran across the room to the crumpled figure, I've killed her. But why did she speak to me if she didn't know I was here?

Bare feet thumped down the stairs. "What have you done to her, you monster?" shouted Werner, who stood draped in a wrinkled white nightshirt on the first landing. He waved a long knife menacingly at the Irishman. "Who'll serve breakfast this morning?"

"She's only fainted," Duffy said angrily. "I know her. I said hello to her and she was startled, and fainted."

Other voices sounded now on the stairs. "What's happened?" "That gray-haired drunkard we saw last night just knifed the old lady who serves breakfast." "That's right. He tried to rape her." *"Her?"*

Oh God, Duffy thought, cradling Epiphany's head, this is the worst so far. Worse than the wedding. At least that had a little dignity, smacked of respectable tragedy. This is low farce.

Epiphany's eyes fluttered open. "Oh, Brian," she said. "It really is you, isn't it? And I'm not crazy or haunted?"

"It's me sure enough. Pull yourself together now

and explain to these citizens that I haven't murdered you."

"What citizens . . . ? Oh Lord. I'm all right, Mr. Werner. This gentleman is an old friend of mine. I came upon him suddenly and it gave me a fright. I'm terribly sorry to have waked you."

Werner looked a little disappointed. "Well, in the future conduct your horseplay on your own time. That goes for you, too, uh, Duffy." The innkeeper disappeared up the stairs, and the curious guests, muttering "horseplay?" in several tones of voice, went back to their rooms.

Duffy and Epiphany remained sitting on the floor. "Oh, Brian," she said, leaning her head on his shoulder. "I thought for sure you were dead. They said nobody but Turks survived the battle of Mohács."

"Well, damn few, let's say," the Irishman corrected. "But if you thought I was dead, why did you speak to me when you walked in? I didn't mean to scare you. I thought someone had told you I was in town."

"Oh—old women get into silly habits," she said sheepishly. "This last year, since Max died, I've . . . when I'm alone . . . well, I talk to your ghost. Only a sort of game, you know. I'm not going mad or anything. It's just that there's more variety in it than in talking to myself all the time. I certainly never thought you'd answer."

Half saddened and half amused, Duffy hugged her. Unbidden, the words of the old man in his Trieste dream came back to him: *Much has been lost, and there is much yet to lose.*

bOOK TWO

"...Age to age succeeds,
Blowing a noise of tongues and deeds,
A dust of systems and of creeds."

—Alfred, Lord Tennyson

Chapter Six

WHEN DUFFY AWOKE, his pillow was littered with debris from his dream. He had seen this before, this apparent survival into daylight of a few dream-images, and he patiently patted the sheet where the things seemed to lie until they dissolved away like patterns of smoke. He swung his legs out of bed and rumpled his hair tiredly, as a startled cat leaped from the bed to the windowsill. What kind of dream could that have been, he wondered, to leave such uninteresting rubbish —a few rusty links of chain mail and Epiphany's old coin purse?

He stood up unsteadily, groaning, wondering what time it was and what he had to do today. To his intense disgust he noticed that he smelled of stale beer. Christ, he thought; in these past three weeks as the Zimmermann bouncer I think I've consumed more beer than any three patrons—four, probably, if you count what I spill on myself. He dragged on his trousers and shirt and went to see about having a bath.

Downstairs, the back kitchen door squeaked open and the innkeeper strode into the servant's hall, his square-toed shoes thumping impressively on the stone floor. He was elegantly dressed, looking almost cubical in a broad burgundy-velvet tunic slashed and paned with blue silk.

Anna leaned in from the kitchen. "And where have you been all night, Werner?" she asked.

Werner cocked an eyebrow at her. "It happens," he replied, "I was the guest of Johann Kretchmer. I don't suppose you've ever heard of him."

Anna thought about it. "Not the cobbler over on the Griechengasse?"

The innkeeper cast his eyes to the ceiling. "A different Kretchmer, you idiot. The one I'm talking about is a famous poet."

"Ah. I'm not familiar with the famous poets, I'm afraid."

"Obviously. He's published books, and has been personally complimented by King Charles himself!" He sat down on a hamper. "Draw me a glass of the burgundy, will you?"

"Coming up." Anna disappeared for a moment, and came back with a glass of red wine which she handed to him. "So what are you to this poet?"

Werner pouted his lips and shrugged deprecatingly. "Well . . . a *colleague,* actually. It seems he somehow got hold of some bits I wrote when I was a younger man—adolescent stuff mainly, not a patch on what I've done more recently—and he said . . . I'm quoting him now, mind you . . . that it showed a lyric grace the world hasn't known the like of since Petrarch."

"Since when?"

"God damn it, Petrarch was a *poet.* What do I hire such ignorant girls for?"

Duffy, newly scrubbed and feeling much less like an illustration of the Wages of Sin, trotted down the stairs and stepped into the hall, where the smell of hot stew still hung in the air. "Anna!" he called. "What are the chances of getting some breakfast, hey?"

Werner got to his feet. "We've packed up breakfast," he snapped. "You'll have to wait until dinner."

"Oh, that's all right," Duffy said with an airy wave, "I'll just sneak into the kitchen and see if I can't dig something up." He peered more closely at the innkeeper. "My, my! Aren't we adorned! Going to sit for a portrait?"

"He's been visiting somebody who admires his poetry," Anna explained. "Some old bird named Petrarch, I believe."

"Yes, he would be getting old these days," Duffy assented. "Poetry, eh, Werner? Some time you'll have to put a funny hat on and strap a pair of cymbals to your knees and recite me some of it. You got any dirty ones?" The Irishman winked hugely.

The bells in the tower of St. Stephen's Cathedral rang while Duffy was speaking, and Werner pointed vaguely in their southward direction. "It's ten o'clock you sleep until, eh? Well, enjoy sleeping late while you still can."

Duffy knew Werner was expecting him to ask what he meant, so he turned back to Anna. "Seen Piff around? I'm supposed to—"

"It may interest you to know," the innkeeper interrupted coldly, "that I'm having three bunks set up in your room. Four, maybe! Every day more soldiers are arriving in town, you know, and it's our duty to see that they're lodged. You don't *object,* I trust?"

Duffy grinned. "Not a bit. I'm an old campaigner myself."

Werner gave the Irishman a hard stare, then turned and walked away toward the stairs, his ostrich-plumed hat bobbing behind his neck on a string like a bird on a difficult perch.

When he had disappeared Anna shook her head at Duffy. "Why can't you ever be civil to him? You're only going to lose a good job."

He sighed and reached for the dining room door-latch. "It's a terrible job, Anna. I felt more worth-while cleaning stables when I was twelve." He swung the door open and grinned back at her. "As for Werner, he strikes me as the sort of person who ought to be annoyed. Hah. *Poetry,* for God's sake." He shook his head. "Say, I think Piff left a package in the kitchen—food and stuff, could you look? I'm supposed to visit her father this morning and give it to him. And serve me a cup of the morning medicine in the dining room, hmm?"

She rolled her eyes and started for the kitchen. "If the Turks weren't sure to kill us all before Christmas, Brian, I'd worry about you."

In the sunlit dining room Duffy crossed to his habitual table and sat down. There were other patrons present, beering away the hours between breakfast and dinner, and Duffy looked around at them curiously. The half dozen at the largest table were mercenary soldiers from the troop of Swiss landsknechten that had arrived in town a week ago, hired, it had turned out, by Aurelianus; and in the corner behind them sat a tall black man in a conical red hat. Good God, a blackamoor, thought Duffy. What purpose can have brought him here?

Unprecedented numbers of people had been entering the city during the past weeks, and the Irishman had noticed that they tended to fall into three groups: most were either European soldiers of one sort and another, or the wagon-roving, small-time merchants that thrive on the economy of war; but there was a third type, odd, silent individuals, often evidently from the barbarous ends of the earth, who seemed content to look worried and stare intently at passersby. And the first and last groups, Duffy reflected, seemed to cluster thickest in the Zimmermann dining room.

"Ho there, steward!" bawled one of the landsknechten, a burly fellow with a gray-streaked beard. "Trot out another round for us, hey?"

Duffy was leaning back now, staring at the friezes painted on the ceiling, but desisted when a wooden mug ricocheted off his shin.

"Wake up," the mercenary shouted at him. "Didn't you hear me call for beer?"

The Irishman smiled and got to his feet. He reached out sideways and, taking a firm grip on an iron candle-cresset bolted to the wall, wrenched it right out of the wood with one powerful heave. Clumping heavily across to the mercenaries' table, he hefted the splinter-edged piece of metal. "Who was it asked for beer?" he inquired pleasantly.

The landsknecht stood up with a puzzled curse, dragging his dagger. "You're hard on the furniture, steward," he said.

"No problem," Duffy assured him. "I'll hang your skull up there instead, and no one will notice the difference. Have to use a smaller candle, of course."

The other man relaxed a little and cocked his head. "My God . . . is it Brian Duffy?"

"Well . . ." Duffy stepped back, "more or less. You know me?"

"Of course I do." The man slapped his dagger back

in the sheath and pulled his baggy sleeve up past the elbow, revealing a wide scar knotted across his hairy forearm. "You've got the other half of that scar on your shoulder."

After a moment Duffy grinned and tossed the cresset clattering away. "That's right. On the field of Villalar in 'twenty-one, when we kicked the stuffings out of the Communeros. And a four-pound ball shattered off a rock as we charged, and sprayed four or five of us with metal and stone."

"Damn right! But did that stop us?"

Duffy scratched his chin. "Seems to me it did."

"No! Slowed us down a trifle, perhaps."

The Irishman proffered his hand as the other mercenaries relaxed and turned back to their beer. "The name's Eilif, isn't it?"

"It is. Sit down, lad, tell me what troop you're with. Sorry I took you for a steward."

"You weren't far from the mark, really," Duffy admitted, dragging up a bench and straddling it. "Ah, bless your heart, Anna," he added as she arrived with mugs and a pitcher and the bundle for Epiphany's father. "Actually I'm not with any troop. I'm the bouncer at this inn."

Eilif snorted as he poured foaming beer into two mugs. "Christ, Duff, that's little better than being the man that sweeps off the doorstep in the morning. No, it won't do. Won't do! But fortunately you are in the right place at the right time."

"Oh?" Duffy had been having his doubts.

"Well, certainly. I ask you: is Suleiman planning to come up the Danube straight toward where we're sitting, and bring along every mad-dog Turk from Constantinople? He is indeed! And will there be battles, forced marches, panics, exodi, sackings of towns? Unless I'm much mistaken! And who best reaps from such grim sowings?"

The Irishman grinned reminiscently. "The mercenaries. The landsknechten."

"Correct! Not the knights, locked up in their hundred pounds of plate armor oven, as noisy and unwieldy as a tinker's cart, and not the bishops and kings, who have a stake in the land and can't scamper off to a better position; and God knows it isn't the citizens, with their homes getting burned, their daughters raped and their very ribs sticking out from starvation. No, lad, it's *us*—the professionals, who fight for the highest bidder and know the situation firsthand and can look out for ourselves with no one's help."

"Well, yes," Duffy acknowledged. "But I can remember times the landsknechten caught hell along with everyone else."

"Oh yes. It's to be expected any time, and you always take your chances. But give me a war over peace any day. Things are clear in a war, people fall in line and don't argue or talk back. Women do what's expected of them without you having to go through all the preliminary miming they usually expect. Money becomes less important than horseshoe nails, and everything is free. I say thank God for Luther, and King Francis, and Karlstadt, and Suleiman, and trouble-makers everywhere. Hell, when the big boys keep tossing the whole chessboard to the ground after every couple of moves, even a pawn can keep from being cornered if he's clever."

A slow smile deepened the lines of Duffy's cheeks as he savored the memories Eilif's words woke in him: visions of mad, sweaty charges under smoke-streaked skies, of looking out over shattered battlements at the patterns of soldiers' campfires that provided the only pinpoints of light in the night of raped cities, of wild, torchlit revels in overthrown halls, and of refilling his cup from a spouting, axed brandy cask.

"Yes, Duff," Eilif went on, "you'll have to get in on it all. Now the Imperial troops are expected any day, but you're too dire an old wolf to march rank-and-file with that lot of sanctimonious youngsters." The Irishman grinned at Eilif's typical mercenary's contempt for regular soldiers. "Fortunately there are a dozen independent companies of landsknechten in town that would take you on this very minute, with the credentials you've piled up over the years; even one or two you've served with, probably. After all, lad, it's what you know best, and it's a seller's market right now."

Before Duffy could reply, the street door swung open and a man in a long green robe swept into the room, the almond eyes in his high-cheekboned golden face darting about to scan the others present.

"What the hell is that?" demanded Eilif in an outraged tone of voice.

"Our mandarino," Duffy told him. "No morning here is complete without a visit from him."

The Oriental looked anxiously across the room at Anna. "Is there yet any word of Aurelianus?" he called.

The silent black man in the corner looked up, his eyes alight.

"No," replied Anna patiently. "But he is, as I've said, expected daily."

"I think I know what it is, captain," piped up one of Eilif's companions. "I believe it's a snake waiting for the old wizard to smoke him."

Amid the general hilarity that followed this, the robed man glanced scornfully at their table. "The livestock certainly are noisy in Vienna."

"What? Oh, livestock, is it?" roared the Swiss who'd spoken, suddenly enraged. He stood up so violently that the bench fell over behind him, spilling two of his companions onto the oak floorboards. "Get out of here right now, monkey, or I'll make cattle feed out of you."

The Oriental frowned, then his narrow lips curled up at the corners. "Why, I think I'll stay."

After a moment's pause Eilif threw two coins down on the table. "Two Venetian ducats on our boy Bobo."

"Covered," said Duffy, producing two coins. The rest of the landsknechten began shouting and making bets of their own, and the Irishman kept track of the money.

Bobo kicked a few benches aside and cautiously circled the slender Oriental, who just revolved on a heel and watched impassively. Finally the Swiss leaped forward, lashing out at the other man's head with a heavy fist—but the robed man simply crouched under the rush and then instantly bounced up again with a whirl of arms that sent Bobo somersaulting through five feet of air into, and finally through, one of the lead-paned front windows. The abrupt percussive crash died away into the clink and rattle of individual pieces of glass on the cobblestones outside, and after a few moments Duffy could hear Bobo's gasping groans wafting in with the cold breeze that now swept through the hole.

"If there is no one else interested in discussing the price of cattle feed," said the victor politely, "I think I'll leave you after all." There were no takers, so he bowed and walked out of the room. Duffy gathered in the coins on the table top and began doling them out among himself and the two others who'd bet against Bobo.

There was a quick thumping down the stairs, and then the innkeeper's voice screeched, "What the hell's going on? Duffy, why aren't you preventing this?"

"He's taking bets on it," growled one of the losers.

"Oh, of course!" said Werner with an exaggerated nod. "What else would a bouncer do? Listen to me, you old wreck: when Aurelianus gets back here—pray God it's soon!—you are going to be *unemployed.* Do you follow me?"

The Irishman pocketed his share and picked up Epiphany's bundle. "I do." After bowing to the company he crossed to the door and stepped outside. The air still had a bite of morning chill in it, but the sun was well up in the cloudless sky and steam was curling from the shingles of nearby roofs.

Bobo had got up on his hands and knees and was crawling toward the door. Duffy dropped several coins where he'd be sure to come across them, and then strode off, whistling.

Under the gaiety, the Irishman had been obscurely depressed all morning, as he always was when he intended to look in on Epiphany's invalid father. What is it, he asked himself now, that upsets me about the old artist? I guess it's mainly the smell of doom that clings to him. He's so clearly on the downward side of

Fortune's wheel—studied under Castagno in his youth, was praised by Dürer himself ten years ago, and now he's a drunkard going blind, drawing on the walls of his tawdry Schottengasse room.

As Duffy turned down the Wallnerstrasse a couple of mongrels smelled the food in the cloth-wrapped package he was carrying, and pranced around him as he walked. The street became wider as it neared the northwest face of the city wall, and the Irishman made his way right down the middle of it, following the gutter, weaving around vegetable carts and knots of yelling children. Where is it, he thought, craning his neck; I'm always afraid I've passed it. Ah, right here. He shook his free arm menacingly. "Off with you, dogs, this is where we part company."

Edging his way out of the traffic flow and pushing open the creaking boarding house door, the Irishman stepped reluctantly out of the morning sunlight and into the stale-smelling dimness of the entryway. Maybe, he thought, what bothers me is the possibility that I'll be like this myself soon, living in a crummy hole and mumbling jumbled memories to people who aren't listening anyway.

He crossed the dusty entry, stepped through the stairway door—and froze.

In front of him, beyond a narrow beach, stretched away to the horizon a vast, listless lake or sea, reflecting with nearly no distortion the full moon that hung in the deep night sky.

Duffy's stunned mind scrabbled for an explanation like an atheist at the Second Coming. I was slugged from behind, he thought, and brought here (Where's *here?* There's no body of water this size within a hundred miles of Vienna) and I've been unconscious for hours. I just now came to, and I'm trying to get away.

He took two paces toward the lake and tripped painfully over the bottom steps of an old wooden stairway. Leaping to his feet, he stared around him bewilderedly at the close walls and the stairs. He ran back through the entry hall to the street, stared hard at the front of the building, the crowded sunlit street and the blue sky, and then slowly walked back inside.

He winced when he stepped again into the stairwell, but the old, peeling walls remained solid, almost sneering at him in their mundanity. He clumped hurriedly up to the second floor and knocked on the door of Vogel's room. Then he knocked again.

A full minute after his third and loudest series of knocks, a chain rattled and the door swung inward, revealing the cluttered mess of blankets, books, bottles and paper-rolls that Duffy had always seen there.

"Who is it?" rasped the ancient, scruffy-bearded man who now poked his head around the edge of the door.

"It's Brian Duffy, Gustav. I've brought you food and ink."

"Ah, good, good! Come in, son. Did you bring any . . . ?" He did a pantomime of sucking at the neck of a bottle.

"I'm afraid not. Just ink." He held up the ink pot. "This is ink. Don't drink it this time, eh?"

"Of course, of course," Vogel said absently. "I'm glad you happened to drop by today. I want to show you how *The Death of Archangel Michael* is coming along." Duffy recalled visiting the old artist two weeks ago, for the first time in three years, and being greeted with the same casual "Glad you happened to drop by today."

"Come on," the old man wheezed. "Tell me what you think of it."

The Irishman allowed himself to be led to the far wall, which was fitfully illuminated by two candles. Filling the wall entirely, from floor to ceiling and corner to corner, drawn with painstaking care on the plaster in a near-infinity of fine, close-knit penstrokes, was a vast picture.

Duffy gave a polite glance to the maelstrom of churning figures. When he had first seen the picture, possibly seven years ago, he'd had to look close to see the faint outlines of the shapes on the white plaster; and when he left Vienna in 'twenty-six the wall was a finely shaded drawing, crowded and vague in subject but faultless in execution. Now it was much darker, for every day the artist added hundreds of strokes, deepening shadows and, very gradually, blacking out some peripheral figures altogether. Three years ago the scene pictured seemed to be occurring at noon; now the tortured figures writhed and gestured in the shade of deep twilight.

"It's coming along wonderfully, Gustav," Duffy said.

"You think so? Good! Naturally your opinion counts in this," the old man chittered eagerly. "I've invited Albrecht to come and see it, but lately he hasn't even been answering my letters. I'm nearly finished, you see. I've got to complete the thing before I lose my sight entirely."

"Couldn't you call it finished now?"

"Oh no! You don't know about these things, young man. No, it needs a good deal of work yet."

"If you say so. Here, I'll stash this food in your pantry. Don't forget it's there, either!" Still looking at the old man, Duffy pulled open the door of the narrow pantry; a gust of fresh, cold air, carrying a smell like the sea, ruffled his hair from behind, and he closed the door without turning around. "On second thought," he said, a little unsteadily, "I'll let you put it away."

Epiphany's father, intent on touching up the shading of a cloud, wasn't even listening. Duffy ran a hand nervously through his hair, then laid a small stack of coins on a box that seemed to be serving as a table, and left the room. Descending the stairs he was careful to stare straight ahead, and he won his way to the street without being subjected to any more visions.

He strode unhappily back toward the Zimmermann Inn. What, he asked himself, almost ready to cry, is going *on*? Until today I hadn't seen any outré things in nearly a month. I'd hoped I was through with all that. And at least those satyrs, griffins and unseen night-fliers last month were, I think, real, since other people saw or were affected by them. But what about this damnable lake? Would another person have seen that? Maybe I'm crazy *and* haunted. That's it. Epiphany, will you take an insane husband to match your father?

From the walls came echoing the boom of cannons as Bluto and his crew of assistants tested the city's artillery for range. I wonder, Duffy thought, not for

the first time, if the Turks really will try for Vienna
this year. I suppose they will. And what with the shape
the old Holy Roman Empire's in, they'll probably
sweep right through and be in Ireland in two years. I
should take Eilif's advice—just throw myself into the
tide of warfare and keep too busy to go mad.

The soldiers were rowdy downstairs, shouting for
the casks of bock to be opened just two days early,
and the clamor eventually helped rouse the Irishman
from his unusually deep and prolonged afternoon
nap. He stared at the ceiling for a few moments and
tried to remember what dream it was that had left
him with such an oppressive, though unfocused, sense
of dread.

There came a rapping at his door. "Mr. Duffy,"
called Shrub, the stable boy. "Werner says come down
or be evicted tonight."

"Coming, Shrub." He was glad of even this annoying interruption, for it was a summons to rejoin the
world, and for a moment the world had seemed on the
point of going to bits like a scene painted on shredding
canvas. "I'm coming." He put on his boots and sword
and left the room.

At the door to the dining hall he paused to run his
hands through his gray hair and shake his head a
couple of times. Odd, he thought—I feel as if I'm still
half asleep . . . as if that damned dream, the one I
can't remember, is still going on, and is in some way
more real than my perceptions of this old door, my
hands, and the smell of cooking beef in the warm air.

"Don't hang back," came Anna's cheerfully exasperated voice from behind him. "Push on."

He obediently stepped through into the wide hall
and moved aside for her to pass with her tray of
pitchers. All the candles were lit in the cressets and
wooden chandeliers, and the long room was packed
with customers of every sort, from foreign mercenaries
with odd accents to middle-aged merchants sweating
under the weight of many-pocketed display coats.
Probably a third of the company had upturned their
empty or nearly-empty mugs, and Anna and two other

women were kept busy refilling them. Several dogs who had got in somehow were growling and bickering for scraps under the tables.

It struck Duffy that a touch of hysteria had sharpened the good-fellowship tonight, as if the night wind whistling under the eaves carried some pollen of impermanence, making everyone nostalgic for things they hadn't lost yet.

A tableful of young students near the bar had struck up a song, a cheery sounding number with lyrics in Latin:

> *"Feror ego veluti*
> *Sine nauta navis,*
> *Ut per vias aeris*
> *Vaga fertur avis;*
> *Non me tenent vincula,*
> *Non me tenet clavis,*
> *Quero mihi similes*
> *Et adjungor pravis!"*

Calling on his rusty seminary skill, the Irishman was a little appalled when he translated it in his head:

> *I am carried violently off*
> *Like a captainless ship,*
> *Just as down the highways of the sky*
> *A vagrant bird is driven.*
> *I am not held by any fetters*
> *Or secured by any key.*
> *I look for others like me,*
> *And my companions are distorted outcasts.*

He frowned, and abandoned as hopeless the notion of finding an uncrowded bench. He decided to sit in the kitchen and just listen for sounds of major unrest.

Catching the eye of one of the serving women as she was sidling past, the Irishman called over the din, "Do you know if Epiphany's in the kitchen?"

A drink-ruddied face looked up from beside Duffy's elbow. "No, she's not," the man put in merrily. "She was under the table here a minute ago . . ." With a helpful air he peered around his feet. "Gone! Run off with Werner's mastiff, I expect, and there'll be another litter of pups about the place before long. Now a leash would—"

The Irishman's hand shot out and seized the knot of the man's wool scarf. With a rolling heave of his shoulders Duffy hauled the choking man right up out of his place, held him briefly overhead as he re-planted his feet, and then pitched the whimpering figure twisting through the air to violently sweep the beer mugs off a nearby table before crashing to the floor, which resounded like a great drum.

The roar of conversation halted abruptly, then resumed much louder. Casting his glance defiantly over the crowd, the Irishman happened to catch the narrowed eyes of the Oriental who'd dealt with Bobo that morning. Yes, Duffy thought, what with the mandarino and myself there have been a lot of people flying through the air around here lately. Then, catching a glint of speculation in the sardonic gaze, the Irishman suddenly realized something. Whatever it is, he thought, that's got me so keyed up—this frustration or anticipation or foreboding—that man shares it.

Werner was beginning to voice hysterical protestations on the far side of the hall, so Duffy turned and strode through the steamy kitchen and out the back door into the stable yard.

That was a damn fool thing to do, he reflected. Flying into a boyfriend-rage like some teenager. Where's my self control these days?

He breathed deeply the chilly air of evening, staring west over the high roof of the city hall toward the diming-to-black tiers of the sunset. In some land over there it's broad daylight, he told himself. Night rushing up behind me and day so distant in front.

Was that the scuff of a footstep? He turned and noticed a wooden bucket rocking where it hung on the brewery door. Ah, he thought, just a delivery. Probably the butter Anna's been expecting, hung on the wrong door by mistake. Well, Shrub can carry it in tomorrow morning, I don't want to be meeting any-one just at the moment.

Glancing up, he was reassured to see the thickening cloud cover. Best not to stand under the open sky in times like these, he thought. Pull all available covers right up over your head.

A breeze flitted through the yard, and the tang of gunpowder smoke stung his nostrils. Instinctively he spun and glanced about, then leaped to the bucket on the door. A fuse was poking out of it from under the hammered-down wooden lid, and quickly disappeared inside, sputtering like a grease-fire, even as the Irish-man let out a yell and lifted the bucket off the hook. Though it weighed a good thirty pounds, Duffy pitched the thing one-handed across the yard, letting the mo-mentum of the throw fling him face down onto the cobblestones.

A flash and deafening crack split the night, and splinters, spinning boards and bits of stone rebounded from the inn walls and clattered down into the yard as the explosion's roar echoed away through the dark streets. Duffy sat up, coughing in the dust-and-smoke-choked air, and blood spilled down his cheek from a gash a flying bit of wood had laid open in his forehead. He lurched to his feet and drew his sword, half ex-pecting a rush of hostile figures from out of the dark-ness. The only rush, though, was from the kitchen door behind him, as a knot of serving girls and customers elbowed their way outside to see what had happened.

One voice, Werner's cut through the babble. He pushed several people aside and stepped to the front. "God *damn* you, Duffy!" he shouted. "What have you done now? It wasn't enough to break my windows this morning, now you have to blow up half my stable? Get out of my house, you lazy, drunken son of a bitch!" By way of punctuation he punched the Irishman in his broad chest.

"Ho!" called someone in the crowd. "Werner's got a savage side!"

Duffy barely felt the blow, but something seemed to burst in his head. "City-bred dog!" he roared, all thoughts of explanation flown. "Will you lay hands on me? On *me*? Run, vermin, and rejoice I won't foul my sword with your whore's-spit blood!"

The spectators had automatically stepped back at the new, harsh authority in Duffy's voice, and he now gave the innkeeper a stinging slap with the flat of his blade. "Run," ordered the Irishman, "or by Manannan and Llyr, I'll cave in your head with the pommel!" Werner's nerve broke, and he bolted around the corner of the building. "And hear, this, servant!" Duffy shouted after him. "You haven't the competence to order me out of your master's house. Aurelianus governs here, not you."

Whirling to face the throng of uprooted diners, the Irishman stabbed a finger at two of the Swiss mercenaries he'd gambled with that morning. "You two," he pronounced, "will sleep out here in the yard tonight to make certain this doesn't recur. You may build a fire, and I'll see to it that blankets are sent out to you. Keep your swords ready to hand. Understood?"

The bewildered landsknechten gulped, looked helplessly at each other, and nodded.

"Fine." The crowd parted for him as he strode back inside through the kitchen door. After a few moments Shrub fetched a bucket of water and timidly set about extinguishing the several small fires the explosion had started, while two of the older stable boys began calming down the surviving horses. Cheated of an explanation, the chattering knot of people slowly filed back inside, concocting wild theories of their own to account for the blast, leaving behind the two mercenaries who began unhappily gathering up shattered pieces of wood for a fire.

An hour later Duffy hung his clothes on a chair and got into bed. He blew out the candle with, it seemed to him, his last bit of strength.

He was still a little awed by his spectacular rage earlier. I must be wound even tighter than I thought, he told himself. I've never before lost my temper so completely. It was as if I were someone else for a moment. He shook his head. I guess I'll put off until morning the question of who would want to blow up the brewery and bury poor old Gambrinus in his cellar.

His eyes snapped open then, for the thought of the cellar had recalled to him completely the hitherto-forgotten afternoon dream. He had been, he remembered now, pottering comfortably about in the old Irish cottage in which he'd spent his boyhood, but had after a while found one thing that didn't fit with his memories of the place: a trap door in the flags of the floor, still half-hidden by a rug someone had kicked aside. For some reason the sight of it filled him with fear, but he worked up the nerve to grasp its ring and lift it on its grating hinges. Climbing down into the cellar this revealed, he found himself in an archaically opulent chamber. His attention, though, was drawn to a stone bier on which lay the body of a man; a king, or a god even, to judge by the tragic dignity expressed in every line of the strong, sorrow-creased face. Duffy stood over the body—and then had recoiled all the way into wakefulness, glad of Shrub's knock at the door.

Duffy now shook his head, trying to shake from it the memory of the last few seconds of the dream; for, though the figure on the bier was not alive, it had opened its eyes and stared at him . . . and for a moment Duffy had been looking up at himself, through the dead king's eyes.

Chapter Seven

BLUTO PUSHED the wind-blown hair out of his face and squinted along the barrel of the iron cannon. "Give her a shove left," he said. Two sweating, shirtless men seized the gun's trunnions and, groaning with the effort, pulled the barrel an inch or two to the left. "Good," said the hunchback, hopping up, "I reckon she's in line. Give the ball a last tap with the rammer in case we've joggled it loose."

Duffy leaned back and watched as one of the burly men snatched up the rammer and shoved it into the muzzle. I'm damned glad it's not me wrestling these guns around in the dawn mist, the Irishman thought.

"What are you shooting at this time, Bluto?" he asked.

The hunchback leaned out over the parapet and pointed. "Notice that white square, about half a mile away? Can't see it too well in this light, but that's as it should be. It's a wood frame with cloth tacked over it. I had these boys build it and run out there and set it up. We're pretending it's Suleiman's tent." His assistants grinned enthusiastically.

These poor crazy bastards enjoy this, Duffy realized. It's play to them, not work.

Bluto hobbled to the breech and shook black powder into the vent hole. "Where's my linstock, damn it?" he yelled. One of the gunnery men stepped forward proudly and handed him the stick with the smoldering cord coiled around it. *"Deus vult,"* the hunchback grinned, and, standing well to the side, leaned over and touched the glowing cord-end to the cannon vent.

With a booming crack that numbed Duffy's abused eardrums and echoed from the distant trees, the gun lurched backward, gushing an afterburn of nearly transparent flame. Blinking through the great veil of acrid smoke that now churned over the parapet, Duffy saw a spurt of dust and bracken kicked into the air a dozen feet to the left of "Suleiman's tent."

"Ha *ha!*" crowed Bluto. "Very respectable, for a first try! You there—yes, you—give the barrel a kick from your side, will you? Then sponge her out and get ready to re-load." He turned to Duffy. "I'm finally getting this city's artillery in order. In the first two weeks we were in town, all I did was scrape rust out of the bores. These idiots left the guns uncovered during the rains; didn't even put the tompions in the muzzles. I believe the council looks on these things as some sort of . . . iron demons, able to fend for themselves."

"Bluto," the Irishman said quietly, "you more or less have charge of Vienna's arsenal until the Imperial troops arrive, don't you? Right. Well, listen—have you noticed any thefts of powder?"

The hunchback shrugged. "I haven't checked the quantities. Why?"

Duffy gave him a succinct version of the previous night's events. "It blew out two stalls in the stable," he concluded. "Killed two horses and scared the hell out of every man and beast within three blocks."

"Good Lord, a petard," Bluto said in surprise. "Hung on the brewery door?"

"That's right. I'm beginning to wonder whether, weird as it sounds, some rival brewery might be trying to put us out of business."

"But Herzwesten doesn't have any rivals," Bluto pointed out. "The nearest commercial brewery is in Bavaria."

"That's right," admitted Duffy. "Well, I don't know —a rival inn, a resentful monk . . . " He shrugged.

Bluto shook his head in puzzlement. "I'll run an inventory of the whole arsenal. Maybe powder isn't the only thing someone's been stealing."

"She's ready to load, sir," panted one of the gunnery men.

"Very well, out of the way." The hunchback picked up the long ladle-pole and dipped it like a shovel into the powder cask. He hefted it once or twice. "That's three pounds," he judged, and slid it into the bore; when it clicked against the breech he turned it over and pulled the empty ladle out. Then he rammed the wad in, followed by the six-pound ball. "Now then, gang," he said with a grin, "let's see if we can knock Zapolya's hat off. Give me the linstock."

"I thought you said it was Suleiman," Duffy said, a little sourly. A year had gone by since the Hungarian governor had defected to the Turks, but Duffy had known the man long ago, and it still galled him to hear Zapolya and Suleiman equated as enemies of the west.

"We figure they're both in there, playing chess," Bluto explained.

The hunchback touched off the charge, and again the

cannon roared and heaved and coughed forth a great gout of smoke to hang over the battlements. A couple of seconds later a tree to the left of the target abruptly collapsed, slapping up another cloud of dust.

"Closer still," Bluto said. "You—give her another kick."

Duffy got to his feet. "I can't linger here all morning," he said. "We broach the bock tomorrow, and I've got things to do in the meantime."

"See you later, then," Bluto said, preoccupied with the gun. "I'll drop by for a mug or two if it's on the house."

"Why should it be on the house?" the Irishman demanded testily.

"Hmm?" Bluto reluctantly turned away from watching his men sponge out the bore. "Well, for God's sake, I saved your life, didn't I?"

"When?"

"You forgetful bastard. A month ago, when you were attacked in the forest."

"You nearly *killed* me," Duffy said. "And it was you being attacked, not me."

"Here, what are you apes doing?" the hunchback shouted at his assistants. "Give me that." He pushed the gunnery men away from the cannon and seized the sponge-pole himself. "Three turns left and three right," he told them. "Or maybe you want a stray spark still in there when you put in the new powder, eh? Idiots." His assistants grinned apologetically and shuffled their feet.

Duffy shook his head and strode to the stairway that would take him down to the street. Truly a single-minded hunchback, he thought.

When he reached the pavement and looked up from his boots, he groaned inwardly. Oh hell, he thought, it's the Englishman, Lothario Mothertongue. Can I duck out? No, damn it, he's seen me. "Hello, Lothario," he said tiredly to the tall blond man who was walking toward the stairs.

"Hello, Duffy," boomed Mothertongue energetically. "I've come to inspect the artillery. Give yon hunchback a bit of advice on the placement of the guns."

Duffy nodded. "I'm sure he'll be grateful." Mother-tongue had been "inspecting the artillery" daily ever since his arrival in town a week ago, and Bluto had twice had to be restrained from shoving the man off the wall.

"I'll tell you something, Duffy, in strictest confidence," Mothertongue said more quietly, laying his hand on the Irishman's shoulder and glancing up and down the street. Duffy knew what he was going to say; he'd been saying it for days, in strictest confidence, to anyone who'd listen to him, and Duffy himself had heard it twice already. "Certain authorities . . . " He winked mysteriously. " . . . have called me back from quite a distance to defeat these Turks, and I intend to do it!"

"Good, Lothario, you do that. I'd like to stick around and talk, but I've got an appointment." He performed a smile and walked past.

"Quite all right. I'll be seeing you tomorrow."

Yes, Duffy thought glumly, I suppose you will. The damned bock is drawing everybody like a lighted window in a storm. Well, he told himself, see it through two more nights and you'll be square with old Aurelianus—you promised to be here Easter, and that's tomorrow. After that you can honorably decamp; take Epiphany and leave the city before they lock all the gates against the Turks.

Children were skipping past him, shouting, "Vikings! We're going to fight the Vikings!"

Give 'em a boot in the backside for me, kids, Duffy thought wearily.

When he stepped into the warmth of the dining hall a white-haired old man stood up from one of the tables. "Mr. Duffy!" he said cheerily. "You made it here alive, I observe."

The Irishman stared at him. "Why, it's Aurelianus!" he exclaimed. "I didn't recognize you behind the eye-patch. How did that happen?"

Aurelianus fluttered his pale hands. "It's nothing. I didn't lose the eye, just injured it during a scuffle in Athens, two days . . . I mean two *weeks* ago. Yes. I'll be able to throw away the patch before long." He waved at his table. "But join me! We've much to discuss."

Duffy sat down. A few moments later Anna had set two capacious mugs of beer on the table, and he sipped his gratefully.

"Oh, sir," Anna remarked to Aurelianus, "there have been some very weird gentlemen asking for you lately. A tall man who appears to be from Cathay or somewhere, several black Ethiopians, a copper-skinned man dressed all in feathers,—"

The old man frowned, then laughed softly. "Ah, the Dark Birds are here already, eh? I'm afraid I shall have to disappoint them this time around. Steer them away from me if you can, will you lass?"

"Aye aye." Before returning to the kitchen she rolled her eyes at Duffy behind Aurelianus' back.

"The girl tells me Werner isn't here," said the old man. "He's off somewhere, the guest of . . . did she say a poet?"

"Yes," assented the Irishman almost apologetically. "It seems our innkeeper can whip out the verses like nobody on earth since Petrarch. I haven't read any of it, thank God."

"Poetry-writing." Aurelianus sighed. "At his age." He took a long sip of the beer and thumped the mug down on the table. "In any case," he said, turning to the Irishman with a comfortable, if twitchy, grin, "I trust your trip here was easy and pleasant?"

Duffy thought about it. "Neither one, I'm afraid."

"Oh? Oh!" Aurelianus nodded understandingly. "You glimpsed, perhaps, some creatures of a sort one doesn't usually run into? Or heard odd sounds in the night that couldn't be attributed to wolves or owls? I thought of warning you about that possibility, but decided—"

The Irishman was annoyed. "I'm not talking about glimpses or night-sounds. In Trieste I met a man with goat's legs. I was escorted through the Alps by a whole damned parade of unnatural beasts. Dwarfs saved my life. Flying things that called to each other in Arabic, or something, destroyed a caravan I was travelling with." He shook his head and had another sip of beer. "And I won't bore you with an account of all the plain, everyday *men* that tried to put arrows and swords through me."

Aurelianus' good humor was whisked away like a veil, leaving him pale and agitated. "Good heavens," he muttered, half to himself, "things are moving faster than I thought. Tell me, first, about this goat-footed man."

Duffy described the nameless tavern in which he'd taken shelter on that rainy night, told him about the wine and finally, about his oddly built table-mate.

"Was there," Aurelianus asked, "the sound of a mill?"

"There was. You've been to the place?"

"Yes, but not in Trieste. Any street of any Mediterranean city could have brought you to that place. You were . . . attuned to it, so you saw it." He rubbed his forehead. "Tell me about these Arabian fliers."

"Well, I was sleeping in a tree and heard them circling in the sky, speaking some eastern lingo to each other. Then they swooped across a lake and kicked the stuffings out of the caravan of a poor hides-merchant who'd given me a ride earlier."

The old man shook his head, almost panicking. "They've been watching me for years, of course," he said, "and I guess I inadvertently put them on to you. Ibrahim is stepping up the pace, that's clear." He looked imploringly at Duffy. "Was there, I hope, some manifestation afterward? Those creatures don't belong here, and the very land knows it. Were there earthquakes, a flood . . . "

Duffy shook his head. "No, nothing like—wait! There was a tremendous wind next morning."

"Blowing which way?"

"From the west."

Aurelianus sighed. "Thank the stars for that, anyway. Things haven't gone *too* far."

"What things?" Duffy demanded. "Leave off this mystery talk. What's really going on? And what have you really hired me for?"

"In due time," Aurelianus quavered.

"In due time you can find yourself another down-at-heels vagrant to be your bouncer!" Duffy shouted. "I'm taking Epiphany and going back to Ireland."

"You can't, she owes me a lot of money." He quickly held up his hand to prevent another outburst from the Irishman. *"But!* Very well, I'll explain." He got to his feet. "Come with me to the brewery."

"Why can't you explain right here?"

"The brewery is the whole heart of the matter. Come on."

Duffy shrugged and followed the old man through the servants' hall to the cellar stairs.

"What do you know about Herzwesten?" Aurelianus asked abruptly, as they carefully felt their way down the steps.

"I know it's old," Duffy answered. "The monastery was built on the ruins of a Roman fort, and the beer was being made even back then."

The old man laughed softly, started to speak and then thought better of it. "Gambrinus!" he called. "It's me, Aurelianus!" Duffy thought the old man unduly emphasized the name; might Gambrinus otherwise have greeted him by another?

The white-maned brewmaster appeared below. "When did you get back?" he asked.

"This morning. Hah," he laughed, turning to the Irishman, "they didn't think I'd make it by Easter. Well, Gambrinus, I have to cut things close sometimes, I admit, but I haven't outright failed yet. Not significantly. Have you got three chairs? Our friend here feels he's entitled to some information."

Soon the three of them were seated on empty casks around a table on which stood a single flickering candle, and each of them held a cup of new-drawn bock beer. Aurelianus waved his brimming cup and grinned. "The bock isn't officially broached until tomorrow night, but I guess the three of us deserve a preview."

"Now then," Duffy said, more comfortably, "what's the real story here? Are you a sorcerer or something? And even if you are, I don't see how that would explain things like the lit petard I found on the brewery door last night. So fill me in."

Aurelianus had gone pale again. "You found a petard on the brewery door? Yesterday? That was the first day of Passover," he said, turning to the old brewmaster.

"I was the blood of the lamb, then," Duffy remarked. "I flung the thing away, so it just wrecked part of the stable."

"Things, you see, are much more accelerated than we'd supposed," Aurelianus said to Gambrinus. More softly, he added, "Mr. Duffy saw Bacchus's tavern—even drank the wine!—and reported afrits looking for him at night. Ibrahim isn't holding back; there can be no further doubt that what he's preparing is a shot to the very heart, and it's cracking open the secret places of the world. Things are awake, and stepping out into the daylight, that used to do no more than occasionally mutter in their sleep."

"Hold it, now," said Duffy irritably. "That's the kind of thing I mean. Who's this Ibrahim? Do you mean Suleiman's Grand Vizier?"

"Yes," said Aurelianus. "He is the chief of our enemies."

"*Whose* enemies? The brewery's?" The whole affair was making less and less sense to Duffy.

"The west's," Aurelianus said with a nod.

"Oh." Duffy shrugged. "You mean the Turks. Well, yes. I'd call Suleiman the actual chief, though."

"I wouldn't," Aurelianus said. "Neither would Suleiman, I think. How much do you know about Ibrahim?"

Duffy resolved to hold his temper until he got some coherent answers. "Well," he said, "I know Suleiman appointed him as his Grand Vizier six years ago, when old Piri Pasha was tossed out, even though everybody thought the post ought to go to Ahmed Pasha. Ahmed was pretty angry about it—raised a revolt in Egypt and got beheaded for his trouble, as I recall." He sipped his bock, wondering absently what its taste reminded him of. "Oh, and I've heard it said that Ibrahim's a eunuch."

Aurelianus looked shocked and Gambrinus laughed. "Talk of that sort is neither here nor there," Aurelianus said sternly. "But to move on: what have you heard about his . . . lineage, his nativity?"

The Irishman shook his head. "Nothing. Though I have the impression he's of low birth."

Aurelianus laughed this time, humorlessly. "Lower than you know. He was born in Parga, on the Ionian Sea, and they'll tell you his father was a sailor; that may in a sense be true, but he was not a sailor of earthly seas."

"What?" Damn this wizardly gibberish, Duffy thought impatiently.

"His real father was an air demon that visited his mother one night in the semblance of her husband."

The Irishman started to protest, then remembered some of the creatures he'd seen lately. Keep your mouth shut, Duffy, he told himself. Who are you to say there aren't air demons? "Go on," he said.

"Such conceptions do occur," Aurelianus said. "Uh, Merlin, to choose the . . . handiest example, was such a hybrid. They have great, albeit tainted, spiritual power, and usually drift into black magic and similar unfortunate areas of endeavor. A few resist or are prevented from this course. Merlin, you'll recall, was baptized. Ibrahim embraced the Islamic faith." Aurelianus frowned at Duffy. "The powers of such half-human, half-demon people, though, are seriously depleted by sexual intercourse, and so they learn to shun attractive members of the opposite sex. *That,* you see —to do our enemy justice—is doubtless the basis of that libellous rumor you referred to a moment ago."

"Oh," said Duffy uncertainly. "Sorry." Good Lord, he thought; I'm not even allowed to insult Turks? "And you say this halfbreed is telling Suleiman what to do?"

"That's right. Ibrahim is subject only to the will of the Eastern King."

"Damn it all," Duffy burst out, "make sense, will you? If he's subject to Suleiman—"

"Suleiman is not the Eastern King. There are always higher levels. Charles is not the Western King."

"He's not, huh?" Duffy was amused now. Aurelianus had gone too far. "Who is? You?"

"No. But the man is living just outside Vienna." Seeing the Irishman's skepticism, he went on, more harshly, "You think, perhaps, that the only orders and authorities—and wars—are the ones you can see from your front doorstep? I had hoped a man of your experience would have outgrown such country village ways of thinking."

After a moment Duffy nodded, genuinely abashed. "You're right," he admitted. "Certainly *I* can't claim to know what is or isn't possible."

"You of all people," Aurelianus agreed.

"I'll grant you, then," Duffy said, counting off the points on his fingers, "that this East versus West struggle may be a higher—or deeper—thing than simply a dispute between Charles V and Suleiman about the ownership of some land. Also, I can't rule out the possibility that the weapons of war include magic. Fine! But what have *I,* or this brewery, got to do with it? Why was I so fiercely hounded—and peculiarly aided —on my way here?"

Aurelianus leaned back, pressing his fingertips together. "I must phrase this carefully," he said. "Uh . . . just as in swordplay it is more efficient to thrust for the heart than to pick away forever at the man's arm and fingers—"

"That isn't always true, by any means," Duffy pointed out.

"It's just an analogy. Be quiet. So a general can save time and trouble by striking directly at the heart of his enemy's kingdom." He sipped the heavy bock. "Did it ever occur to you to reflect on this brewery's name?"

"Herzwesten," Duffy said thoughtfully. "West-heart." He frowned. "Are you trying to say—"

"Stop talking and find out. Yes; this brewery is one of the main—there aren't words—focuses, hearts, pillars, of the West. The East, of course, has similar centers, but at present the East is on the offensive."

Duffy was grinning in spite of himself. "But why a *brewery?* I'd have thought . . . oh, a cathedral, a library . . ."

"Oh, no doubt," said Aurelianus. "I know. Those things seem older, more dignified, more characteristic of our culture. But they're not. Listen, three thousand years before Christ was born, a people came out of Spain and spread across Europe. They were nomads, strangers wherever they went, but respected—nearly worshipped—because they brought with them the secret of beer-making. They spread the art of brewing with a missionary zeal—you can find their decorated beakers in graves from Sicily to the northern tip of Scotland. The fermented gift they brought to Europe is the basis of more beliefs than I dare tell you right now; but I will tell you that in the very oldest versions of the story, it was beer, not fire, that Prometheus stole from the gods and brought to man."

Duffy blinked, impressed by the old man's speech. "And that's why the Herzwesten is one of the most important centers, eh?"

"Possibly *the* most important." Aurelianus peered at the Irishman, as if gauging how much revelation he could take at one sitting. "Being Irish," he said slowly, "you've doubtless heard of Finn Mac Cool."

Duffy nodded.

"There actually was such a man," Aurelianus said. "He was the High King of these people I was speaking of, the nomadic beaker people—call them Celts if you like, it's not entirely inaccurate—and he died here." He pointed at the floor.

Duffy automatically peeked under the table. "Here?"

"He's actually buried under this building," Aurelianus told him. "You mentioned the old Roman fort that used to stand here; it was built around this brewing cellar, which had been producing beer for two thousand years when the first Roman saw the place. The brewery was built thirty-five centuries ago, to be a marker over Finn's grave." He paused. "You don't know the derivation of the name *Vienna,* do you?"

"No."

"It was originally called *Vindobona*—the city, you see, is even named after Finn."

This is all very interesting, Duffy thought, but a trifle beside the point. He spread his hands. "So?"

Aurelianus sagged like a dancer stepping offstage. "So . . . you've had a history lesson," he said tiredly.

"Anyway, all this is doubtless why you were attacked coming here: word must have reached Zapolya—Suleiman's man in Hungary—that you'd been hired to defend Herzwesten, and he sent assassins out to prevent you. Evidently you were aided by some of the old, secret folk; you're fortunate that they're loyal to the west, and recognized you."

The Irishman nodded, but frowned inwardly. There's a lot you're not telling me, little man, he thought. All this was just a glimpse at one or two of the many cards you're holding. Am I one of the cards? Or a coin in the pot? Your answers have only raised more questions.

"What is all this to you, anyway?" Duffy asked. "Why have you hired Bluto and me, and God knows how many others?"

"I'm not exactly a free agent. None of us is."

"Ah," Duffy said, "you're 'subject to the will' of this Western King."

Aurelianus' voice was barely audible. "All of us are."

"He's living near Vienna, you say? I'd like to meet him sometime."

The old man blinked out of his reverie. "Hm? Oh, you'll meet him, never fear. He's not well, though. He's injured, can't travel. But you'll be introduced to him."

A few moments of silence passed, then Duffy stood up. "Well, gentlemen, if that's that, I'll see you later. There'll be a big crowd tomorrow, and I've got to rearrange the tables and take down the more fragile wall hangings." He drained his cup of beer, and realized at last why it seemed so familiar to his tongue—it had something, a hint, of the deep, aromatic taste of the wine he'd drunk in the phantom tavern in Trieste.

Chapter Eight

THE LAST THING Duffy hoisted down from the dining room walls was a heavily framed painting of the wedding at Cana, and he peered dubiously at the smoke-darkened canvas as he carried it to the closet where he'd stashed the rest of the paintings, crucifixes and tapestries. Odd, he thought—this is the first time I ever saw the miraculous wine portrayed as a white. I'm not sure they *had* white wine in Palestine then. But in spite of the dimness of the scene, that's clearly a yellow stream they're pouring into Jesus' cup.

The Oriental had arrived, and was sitting at his usual table, sipping beer and occasionally turning on the Irishman a reptilian eye. Duffy had considered, and discarded, the idea of going down to the cellar to warn Aurelianus of the "Dark Bird's" presence. After all, he thought now, he didn't caution me at all about my journey here—why should I do him any favors?

Duffy was noisily dragging the tables around into a more regimented formation—much the way the monks used to have the room arranged, he reflected—when Aurelianus opened the hall door and strode into the room.

"Aurelianus!" spoke up the Oriental, springing to his feet and bowing. "It is a pleasure to see you again."

The old sorcerer started, then after giving the Irishman a reproachful glance bowed in turn. "It is likewise a pleasure to see you, Antoku Ten-no. It has been a long time since our last meeting."

Antoku smiled. "What are a few years between old

106

friends?" He waved at the other bench at his table. "Do me the honor of joining me."

"Very well." Aurelianus slowly crossed to the table and sat down.

And why, Duffy wondered idly as he slammed another table into place, the term "Dark Birds"? I could understand calling the blackamoor dark, or the feathered man a bird—but how, for example, does old Pitch-'em-out-the-window Antoku qualify?

Finally the last table—aside from the one at which the two men were talking in lowered but intense tones —was in place, and Duffy was turning to leave when a bench rutched sharply as Antoku stood up. "Are you trying to haggle with me?" he demanded of Aurelianus. "If so, simply name your price and dispense with the usurer's tricks."

"I'm being honest," Aurelianus replied sternly. "I can't help you this time . . . at any price."

"I'm not asking for *much*—"

"I can't help you at all."

"Do you know," there was fear in the Oriental's voice now, "do you know what you condemn me to? The flickering half-life of a phantom, a will-of-the-wisp *oni-bi* wandering forever on the shore at Dan-no-ura?"

"*I* don't condemn you to that," Aurelianus shot back strongly. "The Minamoto clan did, eight hundred years ago. I simply gave you a reprieve once . . . one which I can't now renew. I'm sorry."

The two men stared tensely at each other for several seconds. "I do not yet resign," said Antoku. He started for the door.

"Don't think of fighting me," Aurelianus said in a soft but carrying voice. "You may be as powerful as a shark, but I am a sun that can dry up your whole sea."

Antoku stopped in the vestibule. "A very old, red sun," he said, "in a darkening sky." A moment later he had gone.

Duffy's joking remark died on his lips when he glanced at Aurelianus and saw the lines of weariness that seemed chiselled into the stony face. The old sorcerer was staring down at his hands, and Duffy, after a moment's hesitation, left the room silently.

In the kitchen the Irishman drew a chair up to the open brick oven and began meditatively picking and nibbling at a half loaf of bread that lay on the bricks to one side.

There seem to be a few teeth left in the old wizard's head, he reflected. He wasn't mincing any words with Antoku in denying him whatever it was that he was after—filthy opium, it sounded like. I wonder why he's always so apologetic and hinting and equivocal with me. I wish he wouldn't be—knowledge is better than wonder, as my old mother always said.

Shrub leaned in the back door. "Uh . . . sir?"

"What is it, Shrub?"

"Aren't you going to come fight the Vikings?"

Duffy sighed. "Don't bother me with these kid games you've somehow failed to outgrow."

"Kid games? Have you been asleep? A dragon-prowed Viking ship sailed down the Donau Canal early this morning, and stopped under the Taborstrasse bridge." Shrub's voice rang with conviction.

Duffy stared at him. "It's some carnival gimmick," he said finally. "Or a travelling show. There haven't been real Vikings for four hundred years. What are they selling?"

"They look real to me," Shrub said, and scampered out into the yard.

The Irishman shook his head. I'm not, he told himself firmly, going to leave this warm room to go see a troupe of puppeteers or pickpockets or whatever they are. I'm at least old enough not to be tempted by cheap thrills. But good Lord, whispered another part of his mind . . . a *Viking ship*.

"Oh, very well," he snarled after a few minutes, eliciting a surprised stare from a passing cook. The Irishman got impatiently to his feet and strode outside.

The first thing that struck the roof-crowding, street-choking spectators—after the wonder of the painted sail and the high, rearing dragon figurehead had worn off—was the age and disspirited look of these Vikings. They were all big men, their chests sheathed most impressively in scale mail; but the hair and beards under the shiny steel caps were shot with gray, and the northmen eyed the thronged canal-banks with a mixture of apathy and disappointment.

Sitting in the ship's stern, by the steering oar, Rickard Bugge pulled his weary gaze from the Vienna crowd when his lieutenant edged his way aft between the rowing benches and knelt in front of him.

"Well," Bugge said impatiently, "what?"

"Gunnar says we're caught fast, captain, in the canal-weed. He thinks we'd better wade in with swords and cut our hull free."

Bugge spat disgustedly over the rail. "Does he know where we are? This isn't the Danube, I believe."

"He is of the opinion that this is Vienna, captain. We apparently turned into this canal last night without realizing we were leaving the river."

"Vienna? We overshot Tulln, then. It's those damned west winds this past month." He shook his head. "If only Gunnar could navigate. He's lucky a river is all he's got to contend with—what if we were at sea?"

"Listen," the lieutenant said, a little reproachfully, "Gunnar's got problems."

"So I should smile when he pilots us into a smelly ditch, to be laughed at by beggars and children?" He pointed expressively at the crowd. "Well, go on, then. Get them over the side and chopping the water lilies."

Bugge slumped back, trying to scratch his stomach under the sun-heated mail. But it's no good, he thought. We may as well go home. We'll never find Sigmund or the barrow now, even if they do, as Gardvord swore, exist.

The grizzled captain cast his mind back, nostalgically now, to the low-roofed, candle-lit room in which he and thirty other retired soldiers of the Hundested parish had sat at a table and cursed in astonishment and outrage at the tale told to them by old Gardvord, while the bitter wind whooped at them from the darkness outside and fumbled at the shutter-latches.

"I know many of you heard the untraceable voice

from the Ise fjord yesterday," Gardvord had hissed in that meeting five and a half weeks ago, "a voice that called, over and over for a full hour yesterday morning, *'The hour is come, but not the man.'*" The old wizard had spread his wrinkled hands. "It troubled me. I therefore spent most of last night laboriously questioning the senile and reclusive huldre-folk about that prodigy—and it's grim news I got for my trouble."

"What was it?" Bugge had asked, impatient with the old hedge-magician's narrative style.

With a have-it-then glare, Gardvord turned to him. "Surter, the king of Muspelheim in the distant south, is leading an army north to capture and destroy the funeral barrow of the god Balder."

Several of the assembled men had actually gasped at that, for the old legends agreed that when Surter of Muspelheim marched north, Ragnarok, the end of the world, was not far off; a couple of the men had spasmodically blessed themselves, scared by their old pagan heritage into taking cover under the newer Christianity; and one old fellow, gibbering the beginning of a *Pater Noster,* had even attempted to crawl under the table.

"Odin look away," Gardvord had sneered. "The men of the north aren't all they used to be."

Ashamed by the timorousness of his fellows, Bugge had pounded the table with his fist. "We will, of course, organize an army to repel Surter." This statement put a little heart back into the other old soldiers, and they had nodded with a tardy show of determination.

"Unless," one nervously grinning man had quavered, "this is all a fantasy, like the graveyard stories children invent to scare themselves, and wind up half-believing."

"Idiot!" Gardvord had shouted. "You heard the fjord voice yesterday! And the misty huldre-folk were more lucid last night than I've ever known them." The old man frowned around the table. "This is no mere guess-work, my stout warriors."

Bugge had leaned forward then. "Who's the man?" he asked. "The one who hasn't come, though the hour has?"

"It is the man who will lead you. Listen to me now, you complacent fathers and householders, and don't make up your twopenny minds that what I'm saying is necessarily a fable. Do you recall the stories of Sigmund, who drew out Odin's sword easily from the Branstock Oak when no other man in the Volsung's hall could budge it with his best efforts?"

"Certainly," Bugge had nodded. "And I also recall what became of that sword when the one-eyed god inexplicably turned on him. Odin shattered it in battle, and Sigmund, left unarmed, was killed by Lyngi's spearmen."

The magician had nodded. "That's true. Now listen. Odin has allowed—ordered, rather—Sigmund himself to return to the flesh, to lead you in pushing back Muspelheim's hordes."

The men around the table had been skeptical, but afraid to let Gardvord see it. "How will we meet him?" piped up one of them.

"You must sail up the Elbe, through various tributaries and overland crossings, and finally down the Danube. When you have reached the city that is built around Balder's barrow, you'll know it, because," he paused impressively, "Sigmund will actually rise from the water to greet you. I suspect the barrow is near the city of Tulln, but I can't be sure. You'll know the spot, in any case, by Sigmund's watery resurrection."

It proved impossible to raise an army, and so Bugge and twenty comrades, all unmarried or notably restless, had set off by themselves on the difficult land and sea journey. And here, he thought sadly now, our ill-considered quest ingloriously ends. Run aground on a clump of sewer weed in a Viennese canal, hailed by the citizens, who seem to think we're a company of jugglers or clowns. So much for our bid to thwart Surter and Muspelheim, and postpone doomsday.

Bugge shook his head disgustedly as he watched several of his men lower themselves into the canal, gasping and hooting at the chill of the water. We were mad to listen to the old fool, he told himself. It's obvious to me now that the whole tale was just a third-rate wizard's beery dream.

Duffy's scabbarded rapier knocked awkwardly against the back of his right thigh as he sprinted past St. Ruprecht's Church. He had to slow then, for the street below the north wall was packed with a collection of festive citizens. Housemaids called lewd speculations to each other, young men crouched and flexed their sword arms with a just-in-case air, and children and dogs scampered about in a frenzy of unspecific excitement. The wall-top was just as crowded, and Duffy wondered how many people would fall off it before the day was over. A little fearful of seeing the moonlit lake again, he was consciously making himself pay exclusive attention to this Viking spectacle.

And how am I to see what's going on? he asked himself, annoyed by the density of spectators.

He saw Bluto among the mob on the battlements, trying to keep children from uncovering the cannons. "Bluto!" the Irishman called in his most booming voice. "Damn it, *Bluto!*" The hunchback turned and frowned at the throng below, then saw Duffy and waved. "Throw me a rope!" Duffy shouted. Bluto looked exasperated, but nodded and disappeared behind the rim. The Irishman shoved, slipped and apologized his way to the base of the wall. I hope I can climb a rope these days, he thought. It would never do to reach the halfway point and come sliding clumsily back down, in front of what must be just about the entire population of Vienna.

After several minutes a rope came tumbling down the wall, and Duffy seized it before two other view-seekers could. Then, bracing his legs from time to time on the old stones of the wall, he began wrenching himself upward. Below him, in spite of the gasping breaths that roared in his head, he could hear people remarking on him. "Who's the old beggar climbing the rope?" "Watch him drop dead after ten feet."

Oh indeed? thought Duffy angrily, putting a little more vigor into each hoist of the arm. Soon he saw the hunchback's worried face peering down at him from the lip of the catwalk, and it grew closer with every desperate pull on the rope. Finally he hooked one hand over the coping and Bluto was helping to drag him up onto the warming flagstones, where he lay gasping for a while.

"You're too old to climb ropes," Bluto panted as he hauled the snaky length in.

"As I . . . just demonstrated," the Irishman agreed. He sat up. "I want to see . . . these famous Vikings."

"Well, step over here. Actually, they're kind of a disappointment. A few are in the canal now, chopping clumps of algae, but the rest just sit around looking wilted."

Duffy got to his feet and slumped in one of the north-facing crenels. Fifty feet below him was the Donau Canal, and a ship lay in the water under the Taborstrasse bridge, its red and white striped sail flapping listlessly.

"Are they real Vikings?" Duffy asked. "What are they doing here, anyway?"

Bluto just shrugged.

"I'm going to get a closer look," Duffy decided. "Tie that rope around the merlon here and throw it down the outside of the wall. Or no free beer tomorrow night," he added, seeing the hunchback's annoyed look. The Irishman pulled his gloves out from under his belt and put them on as Bluto dealt with the rope; then he stepped up on the crenellations—to the awe of several little boys—and slipped the rope behind his right thigh and over his left shoulder. "See you later," he said, and leaned away from the wall, sliding down the rope and braking with the grip of his right hand. Within a minute he was standing on the pavement next to the canal bank as Bluto pulled the rope up once again.

There were even people out here, elbowing each other and calling sarcastic questions to the dour mariners. Muttering impatient curses under his breath, Duffy walked west along the bank to a cluster of wooden duck-cages that formed a sort of pier jutting out into the green-scummed water. He cautiously got up on top of the first one—and it held his weight, though the ducks within set up a squawking, splashing clamor. "Shut up, ducks," he growled as he crawled out along the cage-pier, for their racket was drawing the amused attention of the canal bank crowd.

When he reached the outmost cage he sat down on it, and was rewarded for all his efforts with a clear view of the grounded but graceful ship. The oars, several of which were broken off short, had been drawn in and stuck upright in holes by the oarlocks, and nearly formed a fence around the deck. Duffy was trying hard to be impressed by the sight, and imagine himself as one of his own ancestors facing such northern barbarians in Dublin Bay or on the plain of Clontarf, but these weary old men languidly hacking at the canal weed put a damper on his imagination. These must be the very last of the breed, he decided, devoting their remaining years to a search for a fitting place to die.

A sharp crack sounded under him, and his perch sagged abruptly. Holy God, he thought, I'll be dumped in the canal if I don't move fast. He shifted back onto another board, which gave way entirely, leaving him hanging by his knees and one hand, nearly upside-down. There were roars of laughter from the bank. His rapier slid half out of its scabbard; he risked a grab for it, the last plank buckled, and he was plunged into the icy water in a tangle of boards and hysterical ducks. He rolled thrashingly over, trying to swim before his mail shirt could drag him down, and his sword caught against one of the floating planks and snapped in half. "God *damn* it!" he roared, snatching the hilt before it sank.

He swam clear of the wreckage, and found the meagre current carrying him downstream, toward the Viking ship and the rippling sheets of green canal scum. None of the northmen had noticed him yet, though the citizens on the wall and the bank were absolutely convulsed with merriment.

Still clutching his broken sword, Duffy dived and swam a distance under the surface—he'd discovered his mail-shirt to be a bearable encumbrance—hoping to avoid the worst of the scum and mockery. It's just possible no one recognized me, he thought as he frog-kicked his way through the cold water.

Bugge looked up when he heard splashing by the larboard gunwale, and at first he thought some Viennese had fallen into the canal and was trying to climb aboard. Then, the blood draining from his wide-eyed face, he saw two slimy green arms appear at the rail, followed a moment later by their owner, a tall, grim-looking man covered with canal scum and clutching a broken sword. In a moment this ominous newcomer had clambered aboard and was standing in a puddle of water between the rowers' benches.

Bugge dropped to his knees, and the rest of the Vikings on board followed his example. "Sigmund!" he gasped. "My men and I greet you and await your orders."

Duffy didn't understand Norse, but he understood that these Vikings had somehow mistaken him for someone—and who could *that* be? He simply stood there and looked stern, hoping some solution would present itself.

There was a commotion on the bridge above; several people shouted *quit shoving!* and then Aurelianus leaned out over the rail. "What is this?" he called anxiously. "I missed the beginning."

Duffy waved at the kneeling northmen. "They seem to think I'm somebody else."

Bugge glanced timidly up, saw Aurelianus' white-fringed, eye-patched face peering down at him, and simply pitched forward onto the deck. "Odin!" he howled. The other mariners also dropped flat, and the ones in the water, peeking now through the oarlocks, whimpered in the clutch of real awe.

"This is very odd," Aurelianus observed. "Did they say who they believe you are?"

"Uh . . . Sigmund," said the Irishman. "Unless that means 'who the hell are you.' "

"Ah!" said Aurelianus after a moment, nodding respectfully. "We're dealing with the real thing here, beyond a doubt!"

"What the devil do you mean? Get me out of here.

I'm a laughingstock—covered with filth and carrying a broken sword."

"Hang onto the sword. I'll explain later." With more agility than Duffy would have expected, the eternally black-clad old man vaulted the bridge rail and landed in a relaxed crouch on the ship's central catwalk. Then, to the Irishman's further surprise, Aurelianus strode confidently to the prostrate captain, touched him on the shoulder and began to speak to him in Norse.

Duffy simply stood by, feeling like a clown, as the Viking captain and his crew got reverently to their feet. Bugge answered several questions Aurelianus put to him, and then crossed to where the Irishman stood and knelt before him.

"Touch his shoulder with your sword," Aurelianus told him. "Do it!"

Duffy did it, with as much dignity as he could muster.

"Very good," Aurelianus said with a nod. "Ho!" he called to the interested gawkers on the shore. "Bring some sturdy planks here, quick! Captain Bugge and his men are ready to disembark."

It was a bizarre parade that Epiphany saw marching up the street, heralded by the wild barking of dogs. She stood in the Zimmermann's doorway and gaped at these twenty-one armed Vikings being led by what appeared to be a revivified drowned man. Then, paling, she recognized him.

"Oh, Brian!" she wailed. "They've killed you again!"

Immediately Aurelianus was behind her shoulder, having somehow got into the building unnoticed. "Shut up," he hissed. "He's in fine health, just fell in the canal. He can tell you all about it later. Right now get back to work."

Duffy led his gray warriors around back to the stables, and said hello to Werner, who was fastidiously picking up some lettuce leaves that had fallen out of a garbage bin.

"What's *this?*" the innkeeper demanded. "Who are these boys?"

Duffy answered as he'd been told to. "They're

twenty-one Danish mercenaries Aurelianus has hired to help defend the city against the Turks."

"What Turks? I don't see any Turks—just a crowd of old vagabonds who'll drink up my beer. And what did somebody dip *you* in? This is too foolish. Get them out of here."

The Irishman shook his head. "Aurelianus is in the dining room," he said. "You'd better go talk to him."

Werner wavered. "You won't do anything out here while I'm gone . . . ?"

"Well . . . he told me to turn the horses out of the stables so these gentlemen can sleep there. He said it's a mild Spring, and the horses ought to be able to survive the night air, and during any cold spells they could spend the night in the kitchen."

"Horses in my kitchen? Vikings in my stable? You're out of your mind, Duffy. I'll—"

"Go talk to Aurelianus," the Irishman told him again. The Vikings regarded the ranting innkeeper with great curiosity, and one of them asked him something in Norse.

"Silence from you, lout!" Werner barked. "Very well, I'll go ask him about this. I'll tell him to get rid of the whole gang of you—including you, Duffy! My opinion carries weight with him, or perhaps you didn't know!"

"Good!" Duffy grinned. "Go acquaint him with it." And he gave Werner a hearty slap on the back that propelled him half the distance to the kitchen door. Actually, though, the Irishman thought as he turned to the stable, Werner is the only one that makes sense anymore. Why in hell *should* we take in these decrepit Danes? They're sure to be always either rowdy-drunk or morose; and either way we'll get no work out of them.

"Now then, lads!" the Irishman called, clapping his hands to get their attention. "We movee horsies out of stable into yard, eh?"

The northmen all grinned and nodded, and even helped out once they saw what he was doing. "Hey, Shrub!" Duffy shouted when all the horses stood looking puzzled on the cobbles. "Bring us some beer!"

The boy peered around the kitchen door jamb. "Are those friendly Vikings?" he queried.

"The friendliest," Duffy assured him. "Get the beer."

"My men are not to be served alcoholic beverages," came a solemn voice from behind him. The Irishman turned, and sighed unhappily to see Lothario Mothertongue frowning regally at him.

"Oh, they're your men, are they, Lothario?"

"Indeed. It's been several lifetimes since we last met, but I recognize the souls behind their eyes. Bedivere!" he cried, attempting to embrace Bugge. "Ow, damn it," he added, for Bugge had elbowed him in the stomach. "Ah, I see. Your true memories are still veiled. That will doubtless be remedied when Ambrosius arrives." He turned to the Irishman now. "You may even be somebody yourself, Duffy."

"That'd be nice."

"It carries responsibilities, though. Heavy ones. When you're a martyr, as I am, you must count your life a trifle."

"I'm sure you're quite correct there," Duffy told him. "But surely there's a dragon or something that needs killing somewhere? I don't want to detain you."

Mothertongue frowned at Duffy's tone. "There are matters awaiting my decisions," he admitted. "But you're not to give these men alcohol; they're clean-living Christians . . . underneath it all."

"Of course they are."

A cask of beer was carried out a minute or so after Mothertongue's exit, and Duffy filled twenty-two mugs. "Drink up, now, you clean-living Christians," he told the northmen, unneccessarily.

Chapter Nine

BY LATE AFTERNOON the northmen were snoring in the hay, exhausted by their journey and made drowsy by the three kegs of beer they'd emptied. Duffy, nearly asleep himself, sat at his customary table in the dining room and watched the serving women ply brooms, mops and damp cloths about the walls and floor.

Presently listless footsteps dragged up to the front door and Bluto slouched in through the vestibule. He saw Duffy and started laughing. "Poseidon! You've taken a bath, I perceive, but you still smell like the canal."

The Irishman smiled sourly. "Go ahead and laugh," he said. "Those northmen think I'm God or somebody." He waved in grudging invitation toward the other chair at the table. "How was your day?"

"Oh, not good." Bluto sat down heavily. "Beer here, someone! A kid stuck his head in one of my best culverins and threw up."

"That'll surprise the Turks," Duffy observed.

"No doubt. Listen, Duff, do you really think it's likely Suleiman will be coming here? It's awful far north, in Turkish terms."

Duffy shrugged. "Unless Suleiman dies—and is replaced by a pacifist Sultan, which is nearly a contradiction in terms—I'd say certainly, the Turks will try to take Vienna. After all, why should they stop now? They've been moving steadily up the Danube: Belgrade in 'twenty-one, Mohács, Buda and Pest in 'twenty-six . . . and it's not as if Suleiman will be meeting a terribly organized front. Charles is too busy fighting the French king, Francis, to send us any troops, and Ferdinand alone won't be able to do much. Pope Clement has sent the customary good wishes, and little else. And then we've got good old Martin Luther wandering around saying idiot things like 'to fight against the Turks is to resist the Lord, who visits our sins with such rods'. Two years ago I'd have said Zapolya was our firmest hope against them, and now of course he's signed up as Suleiman's lackey. Actually, the Holy Roman Empire, the whole West, has never been so ripe for overthrow."

Bluto shook his head worriedly. "Right, then, so they come. Do you think we *can* turn them back?"

"I don't know. You're the gunnery man. But I think if we do rout them it'll be mainly because natural circumstances have weakened them—the weather, over-stretched supply lines, things like that. They'll be far from home, after all."

"Yes." The hunchback's beer was delivered, and he sipped it moodily. "Duff, as my closest friend, will you—"

"Hell," the Irishman interrupted, "you've only known me a month."

"I'm aware of that, of course," Bluto went on stiffly, making Duffy wish he hadn't spoken. "As my closest friend, I'm asking you to do a favor for me."

"Well, of course," said Duffy, embarrassed as he always was by any manifestation of sentiment.

"If I should happen to be killed . . . will you see to it that my body is cremated?"

"Cremated? Very well," Duffy said slowly. "The priests wouldn't like it, but I guess there'd be no reason for them to hear about it. You might outlive me, of course. Why do you want to be cremated?"

Bluto looked uncomfortable. "I guess if you accept the charge you deserve the explanation. Uh . . . my father was a hunchback, like myself. The whole line may have been, for all I know. He died when I was two years old. A cousin told me the following story, late one night; he was drunk, but swore it was true, that he'd been there."

"For God's sake," said Duffy. "Been where?"

"To my father's wake. Be quiet and listen. My father committed suicide, and the local priest said everybody's ancestors would be dishonored if my father was to be buried in consecrated soil. It was just as well— I don't think the old man would have wanted it anyway. So a bunch of his friends carted his body to an old pagan burial ground a few miles outside of town." He had another pull at his beer and continued. "There was a little house there, with a table, so they dug a grave right out front, broke out the liquor and laid the corpse out on the table. But he was a hunchback, as I've said, and he wouldn't lie flat. It wouldn't do to celebrate the wake with him face down, either—bad luck or something—so they found a rope somewhere, ran it over Dad's chest, and tied it under the table so tightly that he was actually pressed flat. So, now that the guest of honor was properly reclining, they hit the liquor. By nightfall a lot of other people had shown up; they were all crying and singing, and one of them was embracing the corpse . . . and he noticed the bowstring-taut rope."

"Uh-oh."

"Right. Nobody was watching him, so he sneaked out his knife and sawed through the rope. My father's corpse, with all that spring-tension suddenly released, catapulted right out the window. It scared the devil out of the mourners until the knife-wielder explained what he'd done. They went outside to bring the body back in, and saw that it had landed just a few feet to one side of the grave they'd dug. So they dragged him back inside, tied him down again, moved the table a little, made a few bets, and cut him loose again. *Boing.* Out he went. On the fourth shot he landed in the grave, and they filled it in and went home."

"Good holy Christ!" Duffy exclaimed. "I think your cousin was lying to you."

"Maybe. But I want to be burned."

"Look, just because something like that happened to your father—"

"Burned, Duff."

"Oh, very well. I'll see to it, if I survive you." They shook hands on it.

Looking over the Irishman's shoulder, Bluto remarked in a more casual tone, "Hm! The mandarino is giving one of us the fish-eye."

Duffy shifted around in his chair, and found himself once again meeting the cold stare of Antoku Ten-no. "You're right," he said, repressing a shudder as he turned back to Bluto. "An unpleasant customer, beyond doubt."

"Speaking of your customers," said the hunchback, "at what hour will you actually broach the bock tomorrow?"

"Can't get your mind off that, can you? Oh, tomorrow evening about five, I guess. I'll see you then, I assume."

"Me and everybody else in Vienna."

In the lamplit dimness of the kitchen hall several hours later Duffy strode up and down on the creaking boards, and hefted a sword with a dissatisfied air. "Well," he told Eilif, who sat on a barrel nearby, "I'll be grateful for the loan of it until I can get a sword made for me, but I wouldn't want to stay with this one."

The Swiss mercenary scratched his gray-shot beard. "Why not?"

"Look," said the Irishman, now rocking the rapier back and forth on his right palm, "the balance is wrong. All the weight's in the blade. I'd need a ten-pound pommel, and then it'd be too heavy to feint with."

"What do you want to feint for? Hit 'em hard straight off, and keep hitting 'em hard."

"I feel safer with the option. Also, look at that guard—it's just a loop of steel. Do you think a man couldn't get his point in under that, and clip off all my fingers with one poke?"

"God's hooks, Brian, why do you worry so much about the point? It's only effeminate Spaniards and Italians that use it—mainly because they don't have the strength or courage for a good chop." He swung an imaginary sword in a mighty arc. "Hah! Parry that, you Estebans and Julios!"

Duffy grinned. "For your sake, Eilif, I hope you never run into Esteban or Julio. He'll have you looking like St. Sebastian after they pulled out all the arrows."

"*Is* that so? I believe you spent too much time in Venice, Duff, that's all."

"No doubt. Well in any case, thank you. With this I can certainly deal with such swordsmen as are in Vienna. Uh, except, possibly, for a few of the landsknechten," he added, seeing Eilif's quick frown.

"Possibly a few," the Swiss agreed judiciously. "It sounds like the dining room's filling up," he observed, cocking a thumb at the double door. "Hadn't you better be getting in there?"

"No. I'm ditching it tonight," the Irishman told him. "Aurelianus suggested I give the innkeeper a respite from my abrasive personality for a bit—every time the man speaks to me he gets so angry he has to go unwind at that poet Kretchmer's house, where he's apparently something of a lapdog. Spent last night there after I allegedly tried to blow up the stables." Duffy sheathed the new sword and strapped it to his belt. "Drink up my share, though, will you?"

"Rely on me."

Duffy left the building through the kitchen, thrusting his hands deeply into the pockets of his cloak as the chilly wind found him. Patchy clouds hurried across the face of the just-past-full moon, and the gothic and medieval rooftops showed up dimly frosted against the sky's deep black. Feeling like a goblin of shadows, Duffy made his way silently past several oases of warm light and music, on a course that would lead him to the wide Rotenturmstrasse and, after a left turn, to the north gate of the city. Aurelianus had paid some of the local lads to keep a watchman's vigil on the Viking ship, and he had suggested that tonight Duffy earn his keep by checking up on them.

The west wind was sluicing down the street like water down a channel, and to stop his cloak from flapping around his ankles the Irishman turned left into an alley that would take him to the north gate by way of St. Ruprecht's Church.

He was aware of comforting domestic smells now, seeping out from under doors and around window-shutters: hot bread, and cabbage, and wood burning in fireplaces. It was on just such a night as this, he reflected, about fifteen years ago, that I first met Epiphany Vogel. She was about twenty-five, a slim—well, skinny, to be precise—dark-haired girl who somehow managed, as some people can think in a foreign language, actually to think in whimsy and endearing nonsense; forever depressed or elated over incomprehensible trifles, and supporting her statements with misquoted snatches of poetry and Scripture.

I was sitting, Duffy recalled, for a portrait by her father, who was then still a respected painter. It was supposed to be a picture of John the Baptist or somebody, and he had accosted me in a tavern, telling me I possessed exactly the visage he required. The painting, which come to think of it was called *St. Michael the Archangel,* had taken several weeks to finish, and by the end of that time I was hopelessly in love with his daughter.

And here the year 1529 finds us: Vogel is a mad, blind old drunkard, Epiphany is a gray drudge with nearly all the spice pounded out of her, and I'm a scarred old tomcat with a poor attitude and no prospects, and all of us sitting dumbly in the path of the vigorous Turkish onslaught. The Irishman laughed and did a few capering jig steps; for it seemed to him that, though that was unarguably how it would look to an outsider, and even to himself, it still wasn't quite the whole story.

He was crossing a small square that ringed a dormant fountain when a flapping from above made him glance up, and his quiet thoughts scattered like startled sparrows—for two black, man-shaped creatures were spiralling down toward him out of the sky. The moonlight gleamed on their billowing wings, curved scabbards and—a puzzling note—their high-soled clog shoes.

Horrified, Duffy reflexively snatched at his sword, but his darting left hand never reached the hilt.

He was abruptly seized, not externally but from

within, as if a hitherto-unsuspected fellow-driver had shoved him away and taken the reins. In a helpless panic he watched his own left hand draw his dagger instead, and then deeply plough its razor edge across his right palm, so that blood was spilling out even before the blade was clear.

Hold off, devils, he thought hysterically. Give me two minutes and I'll evidently chop myself to bits, and save you the trouble. With all the strength of his mind he struggled to regain control of his body, but it seemed that the more he tried to resist his present state, the more complete it became.

His slashed right hand drew the sword now, and held it down, so that the point scraped on the flagstones; blood trickled through his fingers and ran under the looped guard onto the blade. His left hand hefted the shell-hilted dagger—as the tall creatures folded their wings and touched down, their stilted shoes knocking on the flags—and extended it in a cautious en guarde.

Seen at this distance of only a dozen feet, the things did not really look very human. Their eyes were far too big, and their foreheads sloped back parallel with their long, many-fronded ears; their shoulders were broad but hunched, and a fixed, wolflike grin curled under their muzzles. Even as Duffy gathered these first impressions one of them raised to its lips a tiny pipe and began to play a shrill, wild melody.

Duffy growled a curse in a language he didn't understand and, painfully dragging his sword behind him on the pavement, made a long hop toward the piper and slashed at its head with the dagger.

The thing leaped back out of distance, blinking and confused. Its companion chittered in obvious disappointment and pointed at the Irishman's sword, down the channel of which his blood had already run all the way to the tip—then the creature drew a long scimitar and, poised tense as an insect, advanced on Duffy while the piper stepped back and resumed its eerie playing.

The scimitar lashed out in a lightning cut at the Irishman's neck, and Duffy knocked the blow away with the guard of his dagger . . . resisting the impulse to riposte, though, for his weapon didn't have nearly enough reach. Even so, he laughed with relief, for the move had been his own—he had regained control of his actions.

Another slash followed quickly, and as he parried it, low, he noticed out of the corner of his eye that, at the moment of dagger-and-scimitar contact, sparks flew from his pavement-scraping sword point; and suddenly he knew, with an unexplainable conviction, that to lift the sword from the ground would mean his own death.

The devil attacked fiercely now, and fending off the licking scimitar with only the dagger required every bit of skill and agility the Irishman could muster. The piping became louder and faster, and blue fire snapped and glowed around Duffy's trailing sword point as he hopped about in a desperately complicated dance of advance and retreat.

"Help!" he bellowed hoarsely. "Fetch the army, someone! Fetch a priest!" The pipe-music seemed to muffle his voice, though, and he couldn't even raise an echo.

The creature was inhumanly quick, darting now at Duffy's leg, an instant later at his face, then jabbing at his arm. Flailing the dagger in wild parries, Duffy managed to keep the long blade away from his vital parts, though he was soon bleeding from a dozen minor cuts. The Irishman was panting heavily, and already the rainbow glitter of exhaustion flickered at the edges of his vision.

Then he parried a thrust low and outside, and inhaled a grating sob as the scimitar edge rasped across the bones of his knuckles instead of the steel guard. In an instant the guard was full of blood, and his grip was perilously slippery.

His adversary launched a fast jab at Duffy's eye, and he heaved the dagger up to block it—but it was only a feint, and the sword edge flipped in mid-lunge toward his unprotected left side. Instinctively Duffy whirled his sword up and caught the blow on the forte . . . but the moment his point was lifted from the flagstones, the shrieking music extinguished all his strength, and he pitched limply forward onto the pavement.

Still clutched in his left hand, the dagger—now streaked with his own blood—stuck firmly in a crack as he collapsed on it; instantly warmth seemed to rush up the blade from the earth, lending the nearly unconscious Irishman just enough power to roll over and raise the heavy sword in a clumsy stop-thrust as the monster leaped forward to bestow the last stab. The thing lunged directly onto the extended blade, and its own impetus drove it forward so that the point sprang a foot out of its back.

The piping abruptly ceased, and the spitted creature, lurching backward off the Irishman's sword, let out a ululating death yell that echoed back unmuffled from every wall. With a convulsive shudder it threw its scimitar away, loudly shattering some window, and then slumped forward, curling as it fell to land with a crack on its head.

The piper ignored the prostrate, gasping form of the Irishman and rushed to its slain fellow, lifted the corpse, and flapped heavily away up into the night sky.

Duffy lay where he was, panting like a dog as his drying blood glued his hilts to his ravaged hands, and followed the flier with his eyes until the thing disappeared over the roofs.

"With all due modesty," Werner was saying, raising his voice to be heard over the usual dining-room din, "here I have been hiding my light under a bushel basket. Burying the talents I was entrusted with, instead of going out and investing them."

Aurelianus smiled. "You must let me see some of your verses before you go, Werner."

The innkeeper wrinkled his forehead. "Well, I'm not certain you'd get much out of them. They're pretty esoteric—full of obscure allusions to the classical philosophers; and I don't confine my muse to the pasture of any one language. I write, frankly, for the ultra-sophisticated . . . the *literati* . . . the initiates." He took a sip of his burgundy. "It's a lonely craft, fully appreciated only by others like myself. Why, Johann was telling me—that's Johann Kretchmer, you know—he was saying that when he read his *Observatii ab Supra Velare* to the Emperor Charles himself, Charles clearly missed half the references. As a matter of fact, he even missed a *very* derogatory reference to himself, so couched was the passage in oriental imagery!" Werner dissolved in giggles at the very idea, shaking his head pityingly.

"Think of that," sympathized Aurelianus. "Well, we'll miss you. About Christmas, you think?"

"Yes. Johann and I plan to tour Greece and Italy, bask in the auras left by the great minds of the past."

"A trifle cold for a long journey, won't it be? Midwinter?"

Werner looked around, then leaned forward. "Not necessarily. Johann has read the works of Radzivilius, Sacroboscus and Laurentius, and he has solved the mystery of radical heat and moisture."

"I'll be damned. In that case, then, I guess you— what is it, Anna?"

The serving girl's face was cross, scared and impatient. "It's Brian. He just came back and he's—"

"—Got into another drunken brawl, evidently," finished Werner, looking past Anna at Duffy's unsteadily approaching figure. "I don't like to be mundane, Aurelianus, but that man is one of the reasons for my planning to leave. In the grossest manner he has—"

Aurelianus was staring at Duffy, who now stood beside the table. "Leave us, Werner," he rasped. "No, not another word! Off!"

Duffy collapsed onto the bench Werner vacated. "A cup of beer, Anna," he whispered.

"Go to the cellar, Anna," Aurelianus said. "Tell Gambrinus I said to draw a tall tankard of the bock for Duffy." She nodded and hurried away. "What has happened?"

The Irishman laughed weakly. "Oh, nothing much. Two black devils came out of the sky and tried to make a shish-kebabby out of me." He reached across the table and tapped the old sorcerer's chest with a blood-browned finger. "And I want answers to some questions, clear and quick."

"Of course, of course. Black devils, you say? Flying ones? Great God. When Anna gets back we'll go . . . I don't know . . . into the kitchen, and you can tell me the whole story. Yes, yes, and I'll tell you what I know." He looked up. "Jock! Jock, lad! Get over here."

A tall, rangy young man loped across the room to the table. That's a familiar face, the Irishman thought. Where do I know you from, Jock?

Aurelianus' fingers clutched the baggy green satin of the man's sleeve. "Go to the King," the old sorcerer whispered hoarsely, "all four of you, and guard him—with much more than your lives! An expected danger has shown up at an unexpected hour. Stay with him through the night, and come back when it's full dawn. I'll have made some sort of arrangements by then, I trust. Go!"

Jock nodded and sprinted to the servants' hall without ever having looked at Duffy. The old man was snapping his fingers impatiently. "Where the hell— oh, here she is. Grab your beer and follow me."

"Somebody's got to bind up his cuts," Anna protested," or his hands will mortify."

"Hush, girl," said Aurelianus, flapping his hands at her. "I was patching up wounded men long before you were born. Come along, uh . . . Brian."

Duffy obediently took hold of the tankard, carrying it carefully in both mangled hands, and followed the old man through the ancient stone arch of the kitchen doorway. Aurelianus dragged two stools up beside the coping-stones of the open fire and shoved away several soot-and-grease-crusted iron poles; wrapping his hands first in an old towel, he carefully lifted down a pot of boiling water from a chain over the fire. He then fumbled about under his gown and at last produced a metal box and two small pouches. "Give me your hands," he snapped.

Duffy extended them, and Aurelianus dipped the towel in the scalding water, shook it out gingerly and then wiped the blood off the Irishman's hands. Duffy winced and was about to voice a complaint when the old man loosed the drawstring of one of the pouches and sprinkled green powder over the lacerations; a sharp coldness spread into Duffy's hands through the cuts, and the hot, throbbing pain went out like a snuffed candle flame.

"Well!" he said. "Thanks." He started to draw back.

"Not so fast, we're not through." Aurelianus was untangling a spool and needle from a lot of other litter in the metal box. "Look somewhere else, now, and tell me about these devils."

Staring a little nervously at the uneven stones of the ceiling, Duffy told him about the evening's bizarre, musically accompanied duel. "But I was certain I was a dead man, right at the start there," he said when he'd finished. "I just watched helplessly while my body performed actions I never willed. And, and somehow the harder I tried to shake off enchantments and let my real self take control, the stronger this . . . *other* control became."

"Yes, I can imagine. Look, I don't know how to tell you this gently, but there's an errand you and I have to run tonight before we can totter off to our beds. It shouldn't be too—"

"God damn it, *no!*" Duffy exploded. "You're insane! *Tonight?* I'm not even going to listen—"

"*Silence!*" Aurelianus thundered. "You *will* listen to me, and that respectfully, you ignorant, brawling fool. I wish I could give all this to you slowly, with lots of explanation, and time to assimilate it and ask questions, but if our situation was good enough to allow for all that, neither of us would have to be here in the first place." Aurelianus was angry, but in spite of his words Duffy suspected that the anger was not really aimed at him. "Do you want to know what happened to you tonight? Hah? Oh, you do? Then pay attention —those two creatures were . . . scouts, shall we say, advance riders of the Eastern Empire. God knows what they were doing here already—Suleiman hasn't even left Constantinople yet, and I didn't expect this kind

of thing to appear until he was well up the Danube."
He shook his head unhappily. "But one makes the best
preparations one can, and then deals with difficulties
as they arise." He was working busily over Duffy's
hands, but vague pressures and tugging were all the
Irishman felt. "The fact that these things focused on
you, rather than the city in general, or the brewery,
is particularly worrying. It indicates that they weren't
just blindly sent north by Ibrahim, but rather were
summoned and instructed by someone here. I'd give a
lot to know who that would be."

"So would I," Duffy growled. "But you haven't said
yet what this errand is."

"We're going to summon equivalent guards."

"And another thing—" Duffy paused. "Did you say
equivalent?"

"Yes. What other thing?"

"Oh. Uh . . . yes. What did exactly happen during
that fight? What *was* that when my body started acting
on its own, and cut my hand and went on guard with
only my dagger? If you say you don't know, I won't
believe you," he added.

"Very well. I think I can tell you that." He gathered
up his things. "Do you have a pair of gloves? Well,
here. Shake some of this powder into them before we
start tonight. It'll kill the pain and keep the cuts clean."
He sat back and smiled coldly. "This will of necessity
sound a trifle *mystical* to you. I hope you don't object."

"I can't object, if it's true."

"That's right. Doubtless you've heard of reincarna-
tion?"

"Yes. To have been an Egyptian princess in some
previous life." Duffy picked up his tankard and took a
long draught. "Why is it always Egyptian princesses
that they were?"

"Because most people weren't anything at all, and
they make up something that sounds glamorous to lend
a bit of color to the only life they'll ever have. But
I'm not talking about those fools. A few people really
have lived previous lives, and you are one of them.
When—"

"Who was I?"

Aurelianus blinked. "Hm? Oh, it's . . . hard to say. Anyway, when those two sky-creatures attacked you this evening, an earlier version of you obviously took over."

"And nearly got me killed," Duffy muttered.

"Oh, don't be an idiot. He had to take over. What would you have done if he hadn't? Just rushed at the things waving your sword and dagger, right?"

Duffy shrugged and nodded.

"Right. You have no experience in these matters, but your earlier self did. *He* knew that the monsters were on profoundly alien ground, and didn't dare touch the earth—hence those odd, stilted shoes. He knew, too, that the only way to resist the hypnotic, will-sapping magic of the pipe-music was to have an anchor, establish a connection in blood and steel with the earth of the west; very like Antaeus, you'll recall, who could out-fight anyone as long as he was in contact with the ground. When you lifted the sword from the pavement, and broke the contact, your strength left you—and thank Finn Mac Cool you happened to fall holding your dagger point-forward, so that the connection was immediately re-established."

The Irishman took another long sip, as two cooks came in and fussily hung the pot back up on the chain. "Well," he said finally, "that does seem to cover the facts."

The old sorcerer smiled. "Good! I'm glad your mind still has some stretch left in it. Finish that beer and come on. With any luck we'll be back by midnight." He stood up.

Duffy didn't. "I'm injured. Go summon your own guards."

"I can't do it alone," Aurelianus said quietly.

"That shouldn't be any problem. The city's—hell, this *inn* is full of husky swordsmen who'd do anything for five kronen and a mug of beer. Get one of them." The Irishman sipped his bock and watched the old man cautiously.

"It has to be you," Aurelianus said levelly, "and it

will be. I'd rather have you come along of your own free will, but I don't insist on it."

Duffy glared at him. "Meaning?"

"Meaning I *can*, if necessary, tell you certain things, show you things, *remind* you of things, that will bring back up to the surface the archaic personality that's dormant in you. Your body will come along in any case; it's up to you whether it's you at the tiller or . . ." He spread his hands. "Or him."

It required some effort for Duffy to conceal his sudden panic. He felt as if someone far away below in the darkness was chipping away at the pillars of his mind, and the steady *crack . . . crack . . . crack* of it was the only sound in the universe. Just like at Bacchus' place in Trieste, he thought nervously; I am tremendously afraid of remembering something . . . and I emphatically don't want to know why, thank you. He raised the still half-full tankard, but paused and then put it down. At that moment the beer seemed to be a part of what was threatening him.

Slowly he looked up and met the sorceror's eyes. "I . . . will go," he almost whispered. "As I guess you knew all along." He stood up wearily. "In my life I've sometimes had to make men do things they didn't want to—but I've never soiled my hands with such a lever as that."

"I'm sorry," Aurelianus said. "I wish the situation didn't necessitate it."

"I'll get my doublet." He sighed and rubbed his face gingerly. "Is this to be a full dress sword-and-hauberk affair?"

"Dagger and hauberk. There won't be room to swing a sword."

Duffy raised his eyebrows. "I see. Going to fight dust-mice under the beds, eh? Give me a few minutes." He walked out of the kitchen, consciously putting a bit of spring into his step.

The old man smiled sadly at the empty doorway. "You always did need some prodding," he muttered, "and I never have played fair. But you've always been the only piece solid enough to stand in the breach."

Chapter Ten

AURELIANUS LED THE WAY down several halls, of varying age and architecture, to the side of the rambling old building farthest from the brewing cellar. The low ceiling of the last corridor was black and greasy from centuries of candle smoke, and the oil-lamp in Aurelianus' bony hand sent up its own infinitesimal deposit.

"Where the hell are we going?" Duffy demanded, in a whisper so as not to awaken any tenants in the rooms on either side.

"The old chapel."

At the end of the hall stood two tall iron doors set in a Romanesque arch, and Aurelianus fished a ring of keys from under his gown and turned one of them in the lock. The doors swung open easily and the two men stepped through.

The moon lit the stained-glass windows in shades of luminous gray, and Duffy was able to see without the aid of Aurelianus' smoky lamp. The high, domed ceiling, the pulpit, and the pews and kneelers clearly identified the room as a chapel, in spite of the dust-covers pulled over the statues and crucifix, and the piles of boxes, buckets and ladders beside the doors.

Duffy waved at a stacked arsenal of mops and brooms. "All you use this room for is one huge maid's closet?"

The old man shrugged. "No one would hear of putting it to so low a use as an auxiliary dining room," he said, "and I can't use it as a chapel because the Archbishop forbade Mass ever to be said here again when I took over." He closed and re-locked the doors.

Chuckling softly, the Irishman followed him up the center aisle to the communion rail. Aurelianus unhooked a dusty velvet rope and let the free end's hook clank on the marble step. "Come on," he said, striding up to the altar.

Duffy did, and was amused to find himself uneasy at not genuflecting. His right hand even twitched in the reflex to bless himself. I know what previous self *that* is, he thought. It's ten-year-old Brian the altar boy.

Aurelianus stepped around to the right side of the high altar and then edged his way into the narrow gap between it and the wall. Though not pleased about it, Duffy followed. In that confined, shadowy space Aurelianus' lamp seemed bright again, and the Irishman was surprised to see painted shapes on the wall four inches away from his face. A fresco, by God, he thought, completely hidden by the altar. He was pressed too close to it to see what its subject was, but he did shuffle past one clearly visible detail: a procession of naked women carrying sheaves of grain to a mill. Ho ho, he thought. Those rapscallious old monks.

"There's a step here," said Aurelianus over his shoulder.

"Up?" inquired Duffy.

"Down." Aurelianus peered back at him with a cold smile. "Down and out."

Duffy carefully set both booted feet onto the stone step before trying for the next. When he'd taken a dozen of them he was below the level of the floor, and he found himself in a claustrophobically tight and low-roofed spiral stairwell, hunching and groping his way by the reflected light from Aurelianus' lamp. The old sorcerer was about half a spiral below him, and though the Irishman could clearly hear his scuffling steps and his breathing, he couldn't see him.

"Damn it, wizard!" exclaimed Duffy, lowering his voice in mid-word as he noticed how the tight-curled stone tube amplified sounds. "Slow up, will you? This stairway was obviously built for gnomes."

Aurelianus' head poked into view around the bricks

of the curved inward wall. "I must insist on complete silence from here onward," he hissed, and withdrew below.

The Irishman rolled his eyes and continued his awkward descent, bent-kneed and crouching to keep from bumping his head on the stone roof. The steps were rounded as if by millenia of use, but every time his boots slipped on one it was easy to catch himself by bracing his hands against the close walls. No sir, he thought, this isn't a stairway in which you'd have to worry about taking a tumble. Though, he reflected uneasily, if you *did* fall, and got jammed head-downward in here, somebody would have to come with hammers and break your bones to get you unwedged. He took a few deep breaths and forced the thought out of his mind.

The corkscrew shaft didn't go straight down; it seemed to Duffy that it slanted slightly north. By now we must be about thirty feet under the cobblestones of the Malkenstrasse, he thought. Maybe if we go deep enough we'll be outside the city altogether.

By the dim light he had noticed words scratched roughly in the bricks, and he paused to puzzle out a couple of the inscriptions. PROPTER NOS DILA-TAVIT INFERNUS OS SUUM, he read, and, a few steps later, DETESTOR OMNES, HORREO, FUGIO, EXECROR. Hm, he thought; the first graffiti was a comment on how eagerly the mouth of Hell awaits us, and the second is just somebody expressing a lot of hatred for "all of them." Evidently the foreman of this tunnel-digging job failed to keep the workmen happy. Well-educated workmen they were, too, to be scrawling in Latin instead of German.

"Hey," Duffy whispered. "Why are these inscriptions in Latin?"

The sorceror didn't even peer back. "This was a Roman fort once, remember?" came his whisper from below. "Romans spoke Latin. Now be quiet."

Yes, the Irishman thought, but Romans didn't have chapels, at least not Christian ones. What sort of chamber did this damned stair once lead down from?

His continually hunched posture was beginning to

give him knee-twitches and a throbbing headache, but when after a half-hour's steady descent they came to a wide landing and Aurelianus proposed a brief rest, the headache went away but the throbbing did not; a deep reverberation, like a slow drum-beat, was coming from below, vibrating through the stone, to be felt in the bones rather than heard. For one panicky moment Duffy thought something ponderous was walking slowly up the stairs, but after a few more seconds he decided the source was stationary.

As he sat panting and massaging his right leg he noticed more scratches on the walls, and lifted the sorceror's lamp to see what the sentiments were at this level. Instead of Latin words, though, he saw a number of horizontal lines hatched by short vertical and diagonal strokes. Well I'm damned, he thought—these inscriptions are in Ogham! I didn't think you could find this primordial script except in a few Celtic ruins in Ireland. I wish I could read them.

Then he had hastily clanked the lamp back down beside Aurelianus and said, "Let's push on, shall we?" —for it had seemed to him that he could have read them, if he'd really tried. And no one since the druids had ever been able to.

Aurelianus stared at him curiously, but shrugged and got to his feet. "Right." He padded to the end of the level stretch, where the stair resumed, and continued the downward course.

This deeper set of stairs was a long, steep ramp rather than a spiral, but Duffy had by now lost all sense of direction, and he had no idea of their position in relation to the city that lay somewhere above. The walls were still close, but the stone ceiling was a good deal higher in this section, and the Irishman was able to stand up straight.

Here too the stairs were worn down to low ridges, but the incline wasn't quite steep enough to make it dangerous. The arched mouths of side-tunnels yawned in the walls at intervals, and the deep drum-beat throbbed a little more noticeably each time the two wayfarers shuffled past one. It seemed to Duffy that the going was warmer on this stretch, as if the draft sighing out of the black tunnels was a long exhalation from the lungs of the earth, and the slow drum the beating of its molten heart.

Passing one of the openings he head a soft, slithering rustle, and he started convulsively, his hand leaping to his dagger hilt.

Aurelianus jumped too, then after glancing round-about turned to Duffy with his white eyebrows raised in annoyed inquiry.

"What sort of things live down here?" the Irishman asked, remembering to whisper. "Snakes? Trolls?"

"I suppose there may be snakes," the sorcerer answered impatiently. "No trolls. And no man has entered these tunnels since the Church took over the brewery, in the twelfth century. All right?"

"All right!" snapped Duffy, irritable now himself. After all, he thought, it wasn't *my* idea to go for a romp in a rat warren. They plodded on in silence.

After perhaps a hundred more yards the Irishman noticed something ahead—a hammocklike bundle slung from the ceiling, dimly visible in the flickering yellow light. Aurelianus nodded to show he saw it too, but didn't slacken his pace.

My God, Duffy thought as they drew closer, it's a mummy, wearing a sword, hung sitting in a sling. A poor idea of a joke, especially in a setting like this.

Then the thing opened its eyes, which brightly reflected the lamplight. Its pupils were vertical slits, like a cat's. Duffy yelped and jumped a full yard backward, fell, and regained the ground in a sitting slide. The sorcerer just eyed the sitter speculatively.

Its mouth spread open in a glittering yellow grin, making its face seem to be nothing but eyes and teeth. "Halt," it said in an echoing whisper, "for the toll."

Aurelianus stepped forward, holding the lantern low, as Duffy got back to his feet. "What price for passage?" the old man asked.

The thing spread long-fingered hands. "Nothing exorbitant." It hopped down from its sling, agile as a monkey, and caressed the hilt of its short sword. "There are two of you . . . I'll take the life of one."

Duffy had wearily dragged his dagger out now—

dreading the exertion of hacking this unwholesome creature to death—but Aurelianus just raised the lamp so that his seamed, craggy face was clearly visible. "Do you think you could digest my life, if you took it?" His voice was flat with contempt.

The thing shuddered with recognition and bowed, casting its ropy colorless hair over its face. "No, Ambrosius. Your pardon—I didn't know you at first." A glowing eye looked up from under the hair. "But I will have your companion."

Aurelianus smiled, and raised the lantern to show Duffy's face in sharp chiaroscuro. "Will you?" he asked softly.

The creature—which, a part of Duffy's mind had time to reflect, had probably once been a man—stared for a full minute, then whimpered and abased itself full length on the stones of the tunnel floor.

Aurelianus turned to the Irishman and, waving a hand forward, stepped around the would-be toll-taker. Duffy followed, and heard the degraded thing mutter, as he edged past, "Pardon, Lord."

For the next dozen yards they could hear it whimpering behind them, and Duffy shot the old man a venomously interrogative look. Aurelianus just shrugged helplessly.

When the stairs finally came to an end, widening out into a chamber whose walls and roof the lamp was powerless to illuminate, Duffy thought it must be dawn in Vienna, or even noon. And, he told himself grimly, there's about a mile of tangled tunnels between you and your bed.

Aurelianus was striding forward across the chamber floor, so Duffy wearily followed, and saw ahead of them the coping of a well wide enough to drop a small cottage into. The old sorcerer halted at the edge, fumbling under his gown. Duffy peered down over the stone lip, wrinkling his nose at a faint smell that was either spice or clay. He could see nothing, but the deep pounding seemed to emanate upward out of the well.

Aurelianus had produced a little knife, with which

he was carefully cutting a gash in his own left fore-
finger. Reaching forward, he shook the quick drops of
blood into the abyss for a few moments, then drew
his hand back and wrapped the finger in a bit of cloth.
He smiled reassuringly at Duffy and folded his arms,
waiting.

Minutes went past. The Irishman had again begun
to confuse his own pulse with the barely audible bass
vibration, and so his stomach went cold when it
abruptly ceased.

The lean hand of the sorcerer clamped on his shoulder. "Now listen," he breathed into Duffy's ear, "I am
going to recite some sentences to you, quietly, a phrase
at a time, and I want you to shout them into the well
after me. Do you understand?"

"No," returned the Irishman. "If you're the one
that knows the words, *you* shout them. I'll stand by."

The warm draft from out of the well was stronger
now, as if something that nearly filled the shaft was
silently ascending.

"Do as I say, you damned idiot," Aurelianus whispered quickly, his fingers digging into Duffy's shoulder.
"They'll recognize your voice—and obey it, too, if our
luck hasn't completely flown."

The well-draft slowed to what it had been before.
Duffy got the impression of something poised and at-
tentive. He kept his mouth resolutely shut as long as
he could bear it—perhaps thirty seconds. Then, "Very
well," he breathed weakly. "Go ahead."

The words Aurelianus whispered to him, Duffy realized as he called them out after him in a strong voice,
were in archaic Welsh, and after a few moments he
recognized them. They were lines from the hopelessly
enigmatic *Cad Goddeu,* the Battle of the Trees, which
his grandmother used to recite to him when he was a
child. He began to translate the lines in his head as he
pronounced them:

> "I know the light whose name is Splendor,
> And the number of the ruling lights
> That scatter rays of fire
> High above the deep.

Long and white are my fingers,
It is long since I was a herdsman.
I have travelled over the earth,
I know the star-knowledge
Of stars before the earth was made,
Whence I was born,
How many worlds there are.
I have travelled, I have made a circuit,
I have slept in a hundred islands;
I have dwelt in a hundred cities.
Prophesy ye of Arthur?
Or is it me they celebrate?"

At this point Aurelianus began giving him syllables
that carried no meaning for him, and weren't in Welsh.
Duffy guessed that the part he'd understood had been
a stylized greeeting. He stopped trying to follow it and
just called out the incomprehensible words as they were
muttered to him.

Aurelianus' relayed monologue went on for many
minutes, and the Irishman was getting sleepy. He
wondered if it would be all right if he sat down, and
decided regretfully that it probably wouldn't.

At one point his heavy-lidded eyes snapped fully
open in panic. Had he missed a phrase? But Aurelianus was calmly droning the next one, and a moment
later Duffy was instinctively repeating it in a loud voice.
I guess I haven't missed any, he thought. I must have
one of those household spirits crouched on my shoulder, the ones that breathe for you all night while you're
asleep, and it's maintaining my half of this bizarre
address while I doze.

With that reflection he really did stop paying attention to the words his mouth called out, and he even
let his eyes close completely. An old campaigner, he
was not incapable of falling asleep standing up.

Finally Aurelianus' promptings began to take on a
tone of conclusion, and there came at last a phrase
which, by its inflection, was obviously the last. A pause
followed, and then Duffy called one more sentence into
the abyss, in apparently the same language but a more
jocular tone. Only after the echoes had died away

down the well and up the stairs did the Irishman come fully awake and realize that the sorcerer hadn't fed him that one. Fearful of having ruined everything, he glanced at Aurelianus.

The old man, though, was smiling and nodding. "A nice touch, that last," he whispered to Duffy. "I'd forgotten their peculiar sense of humor."

And I recalled it, eh? the Irishman thought unhappily, too weary to let this new piece of evidence really upset him. I'll worry about all this in the morning. "Fine," he sighed. "Let's get the hell out of here."

"In a moment. Hush now."

For another minute or two they stood staring at the coping stones in the unsteady lamp light. There were age-blurred carvings on them, but Duffy was sick of deciphering things. He wanted only to get back up to the surface—he was beginning to fancy he could actually feel the weight of all the dirt and rock overhead.

Then a voice spoke out of the well—a deep voice that carried more than a lifetime's worth of strength and sadness—and it said, "Yes, Sire. We will be honored to stand one more time with you." The sound seemed to press outward against the walls and ceiling, uncomfortably constricted by the subterranean chamber.

Duffy was startled, but after a pause collected his wits and said "Thank you."

The old wizard stepped back now and waved the lamp toward the stairs. Duffy thought he looked cautiously pleased, like a chess player who manages to castle advantageously. Without a word they began the long ascent.

Before long they came to the sling, hung from two hooks wedged between stones in the ceiling, where the peculiarly devolved being had accosted them. There was no sign of it now. Duffy had paused to look around, but Aurelianus urged him on with a curt wave. The lamp still shone as brightly as ever, but the old man shook it worriedly and turned the wick lower, cursing softly as he burned his fingers.

When the steps levelled out at the short landing Duffy took a deep breath and ran his gloved fingers

through his hair. The last stretch now, he told himself. Or the last cramp, I should say.

"Come no further, topsiders," fluted a weirdly
whistling voice from the darkness ahead. The Irishman
leaped back and landed in a crouch, his dagger out,
and Aurelianus nearly dropped the lamp in his haste
to turn the wick up again. The glassed-in flame brightened, and glittered on the patchy white fur of three
man-tall creatures that Duffy took at first for spiders.

Then he decided that this species, too, might have
been human once, though much longer ago than that
of the grinner in the sling. Their ears had grown wider
than spread hands, at the evident expense of their
eyes, which were completely buried under thick fur.
Their limbs were grotesquely long and twisted, and
the Irishman suspected that when the things crawled
their knees and elbows would be above their heads.

"Put out the light," one of them said, and Duffy
saw why the voice was so odd—their cheeks had
retracted, leaving their mandibles projecting nakedly
under their wide-nostrilled noses.

"Get out of our way, vermin," Duffy growled, "or
we'll put out *your* lights."

The thing extended a hand tipped with five long
claws, and waved them in the air like the legs of an
overturned bug. "I don't think you can," it lisped.

"Dung beetles!" shouted Aurelianus angrily. "Listen
to my voice, Listen to *his*. Can it be you don't know
who you're confronting?"

The thing laughed softly, an odd sound like dice
shaken in a cup. "Of course we know, man."

The wizard stepped back. "Someone's bought away
their loyalty," he whispered. "I knew there were
dangers down here born of atrophy and neglect, but
I didn't expect outright treason."

Bought with what? Duffy wondered. Before he could
ask, all three of the things hopped forward at once
as if yanked by the same string. One landed on top
of Duffy and bore him to the floor, trying to claw in
under his upflung arm at his eyes while the Irishman
hacked at it with his dagger. Aurelianus dropped the

lamp, but it rolled, still burning and unbroken, into a corner.

Another of the things was at Duffy now, digging at his stomach but foiled for the moment by the chain-mail hauberk under the leather tunic. Though Duffy's flailing dagger seemed to be sinking into soft abdomen as often as it skidded off bone, the one on top of him kept dragging its claws across his forehead and cheeks. He could feel his own hot blood running into his ears, and other blood was sliming his dagger-gripping fingers and running down his wrist. All he could smell was goaty fur and all he could hear were his own involuntary screams.

Then something collided, hard, with the thing crouched on his chest. The Irishman rolled out from under and slammed his dagger to the hilt into the face of his other attacker, roughly where its eye would have been, and it rolled over backward so convulsively that the dagger was wrenched out of his hand.

Scrambling up into a crouch he turned to face the first one—and saw only two motionless bodies sprawled on the floor. He spun to see how Aurelianus was faring, and saw the old wizard pushing aside a limp form to go pick up the lantern.

Duffy straightened up and relaxed; then his knees buckled and he allowed himself to sit down heavily. "I thought . . . there were only . . . three of them," he panted. "Oh. I see." Aurelianus had approached with the light, and Duffy now noticed that the fourth creature, which had knocked the thing with claws off his chest, was different. He rolled it over with his foot, and saw again the slit-pupiled eyes and wide grin, now lifeless. Its throat had been sheared right across by the spider-thing's claws, but the hilt of its short sword stood up from the bristly white chest of its slayer. Which was nearly my slayer too, Duffy reflected.

"It seems he decided to pay the toll himself," Aurelianus remarked lightly. "Grab your dagger—and the little sword if you like, though I don't think we'll have any more trouble—and let's go. This lamp won't light us all the way to the top as it is."

Duffy resented Aurelianus' airy tone. "A brave thing died here," he said gruffly.

"Hm? Oh, the beastie with the big eyes. True. The wages of courage is death, lad, but it's the wages of everything else, too. The common penny, the coin of the realm. Stop to mourn for every good man that's died for us and you'd never get from bed to the chamber-pot. Come on."

The Irishman braced himself on his numb hands, got his legs under him and shakily stood up. His vision was flickering, and he had to lean against the wall and stare at the floor, breathing deeply, to keep from fainting.

"Your bed is waiting for you up there," said the old man. "Onward and upward."

The light did wink out while they were on the tightly twisting stairwell, but they groped their way to the top with no further incidents. Duffy was nearly unconscious, and no more aware of his situation than if he'd been dreaming. None of his injuries actually hurt, though he felt hot and swollen and throbbing all over. After a long period of stair-shuffling, a change in the air-temperature made him open his eyes and look around. They were in the dark, unused chapel again, faintly lit by the as-yet tenuous dawn.

"Why . . ." the Irishman croaked, "why *should* they have . . . recognized me or my voice? Any of them?"

"You need a drink," the sorcerer said, kindly.

"Yes," he agreed, after some thought, "but if I have one I'll be sick."

Aurelianus reached under his robe. "Here," he said, handing Duffy a straight, dried snake. "Smoke this."

The Irishman held it up and peered at its silhouette against the window, rolling it between his fingers. "Is it like that tobacco plant from the Evening Isles?"

"Not much. Can you get to your room all right?"

"Yes."

"Take this too," Aurelianus said, handing him a little leather bag sealed with a twist of wire. "It's an ointment to prevent flesh from becoming infected. Wash your face before you go to bed and then rub this into those cuts. With any luck they won't even leave scars."

"God. What do I care about scars." He plodded toward the door, opened it, and turned. "Why did they all speak contemporary Austrian, if no one's been down there for so long?"

He couldn't clearly see the old wizard's expression, but Duffy thought he was smiling a little sadly. "There was no Austrian spoken down there tonight, except for a couple of your whispers to me. All the conversations between us and those tunnel-rats was in an archaic Boiic dialect seasoned with corrupt Latin; and the thing in the well spoke a secret, nameless language that reputedly antedates mankind."

Duffy shook his head absently. "Then how did I understand . . . " He shrugged. "Why not? Very well. I'll be talking to badgers in finger-language next, I don't doubt. Yes. And what could I possibly have to say to them? Good night."

"Good night."

Duffy lurched away along the creaking boards of the corridor. Aurelianus stepped to the doorway and watched his unsteady progress; he saw the Irishman lean toward one of the still-burning wall cressets, puff the snake alight, and plod on, trailing clouds of white smoke.

Chapter Eleven

IT WAS EASTER MORNING, and the bells of St. Stephen's rang solemnly joyful carillons out across the sunlit roofs of the city; another winter had been survived, and the several churches were filled with citizens celebrating the Vernal Equinox, the resurrection of the young God. At midnight all candles had been put out —even the tabernacle lights—and a new flame had been struck from the flint and steel in the cathedral vestibule and carried by altar boys to the other churches, in order to begin the new liturgical year with a renewed light.

On the secular levels, too, it was a big day. Sausage vendors had set up little grill-carts at every corner, and sent spicy, luring smoke whirling away through every street; children, dressed up for Mass in their finest doublets and dresses, scampered about St. Stephen's square afterward, begging their parents for pennies to buy Easter cakes with; and the sellers of relics and sacred gifts had people waiting in line to buy holy cards, rosaries and bones of various saints—it was later estimated that six entire beatified skeletons changed hands that day. These branches of commerce enjoyed an ecclesiastical dispensation from the rule against working on Sunday, but other small businessmen had taken advantage of the obscuring crowds to peddle their own, unsanctified goods furtively. One of these, a self-styled troop outfitter, had parked his cart at a corner of the Tuchlauben and folded down its wooden sides, revealing racked assortments of swords, hauberks, halberds, helmets and boots, some of them in fact old enough to be plausibly offered as relics.

He had done a fair amount of business this morning, and brightened still more when he saw a battered-looking old warrior come weaving through the crowd, his gray head standing a full foot above the tide of passersby.

"Ah, you there, sir," piped the merchant, hopping nimbly down from the cart's seat to land on the pavement in front of Brian Duffy. "Do you call those *boots?*" He pointed at the Irishman's feet, and several people paused to look. "I won't say what I'd call 'em, since I suspect you'd swipe my head off, heh heh. But do you think you can defend Vienna in those, charging —God forbid!—over the jagged rubble of our city's walls, as like as not? Say no more, sir, I can see you hadn't given it any thought, and now that you have, you agree with me. I happen to have a pair here that were made for Archbishop Tomori, but never worn because he was killed by the Turks before delivery. I

see you and that courageous soldier of God have the
same size feet, so why don't you just—"

"Save Tomori's boots for somebody with as little
sense as he had," Duffy advised gruffly. "I might,
though," he added, remembering the sword he'd broken
in his canal-fall the day before, "be able to use a new
sword."

"It's the right man you've come to! This two-handed
thing, now—"

"Might conceivably make some Jannisaries laugh
themselves to death. Be quiet. I want a rapier, with a
left-handed grip, a full bell-guard and quillons, heavy
but with the balance point about two inches forward
of the guard. Made of Spanish steel. A narrow blade
with—"

He stopped, for someone had grabbed his arm and
pulled him back. Turning irritably, he saw Aurelianus'
crumpled-parchment face framed by a black hood.
"Damn it, wizard," Duffy snapped, "what's the matter
now?"

"You don't need to buy a sword," Aurelianus said.
"I've got a good one you can have."

There were a few hoots from the crowd, and Duffy
stalkingly dragged the sorcerer several paces down the
street. When it no longer seemed that everyone was
paying attention to them, he stopped and turned to the
old man. "Now, what are you saying?"

"Why do you walk so fast? I've been following you
for blocks. I said I have a sword you can use. You
don't have to buy one."

"Oh. Well thanks, I'll take a look at it," the Irishman said, trying to be reasonable, "but I'm damned
particular about my weapons—I wasn't really expecting to get one from that fellow. Hell, I usually have to
have my swords made to my own specifications. And
I am left-handed, you know."

"I think you'll like this one," Aurelianus insisted.
"You've, uh, liked it before."

"What do you mean? Is it an old one of mine you've
magicked from the bottom of some ravine or bay?"

"Never mind. Come back to the inn and take it."
Aurelianus took a step back the way they'd come.

Duffy didn't move. "You mean right now? No. I'm off to the barracks to visit some friends. I'll look at it later."

"These are dangerous times. I really wish you'd come get it now," Aurelianus pressed.

"Well, what's wrong with this?" Duffy asked, slapping the scabbard of the sword he'd borrowed from Eilif. "I'm beginning to feel moderately at home with it."

"Why do you—" A child dashed past, yelling and waving a whirling firework on a stick. "Damn it, why do you have to be so difficult? Certainly, that sword will do against a pickpocket or a drunken bravo, but you're just as likely to run into other things, and the blade I'm offering you has special properties that make it deadly to them. Listen, guess who didn't show up at the inn for his morning beer today, for the first time in months?"

Duffy rolled his eyes impatiently. "Methuselah."

"Almost right. Antoku Ten-no, the bad-tempered Oriental. And I'm now fairly sure it was he who called those two devils last night and set them onto you."

Duffy sighed. That morning he had, to his own delighted surprise, awakened from four hours of sleep clear-eyed and energetic; he remembered opening his casement to let the cold, diamond-crisp air flap at his night shirt, and remembered filling his lungs and expelling the breath in a shout of laughter that had echoed away up the street as an escort for the melody of the bells, and drawn the startled glances of several boys on the pavement below. Aurelianus now seemed bent on deflating that exhilaration.

"Why *me?*" he almost yelled. *"You're* the one that wouldn't give him his opium or whatever the hell it was he wanted. Why didn't he send his winged musicians to you? I don't believe you know nearly as much about all this as you pretend to. Why don't you just *leave me alone,* understand?—and all your sorcerous cronies, too!"

The Irishman strode angrily away through the crowd, followed by wondering stares. An elderly, well-dressed man sidled up to the wizard and inquired as to the price of opium. "Shut up, you fool," Aurelianus told him, elbowing him aside and returning the way he'd come.

Six hours later the low sun was casting a rust-colored light in through the three west-facing windows of the Zimmermann dining room. There was the usual pre-dinner clatter and laughter from the kitchen, but aside from the weary Aurelianus there was no one in the dining room. The table candles and wall cressets would not be lit for another hour or so, and shadows were proliferating in the corners and under the chairs.

The old sorcerer looked furtively around, then laid his fingers on the glass cup in which sat his table's candle. He lowered his head and frowned. After a minute he raised his eyes to the wick, which was still a curl of lifeless black; his eyebrows went up in uneasy surprise, and he bent his head again, frowning more deeply. Several minutes went by while wizard and candle were as unmoving as a painting—then a solid yellow flame shot with a rushing roar out the top of the cup, which cracked into several pieces, spilling steaming wax out onto the table top.

The front door had just opened, and Brian Duffy stood in the vestibule doorway, staring skeptically at Aurelianus. "Was there some purpose in that, or are you just clowning around?"

The sorcerer fanned at the cloud of smoke. "A little of both. How was your day?"

Duffy crossed to Aurelianus' table and sat down. "Not bad. Drank up a lot of French wine and traded reminiscences with the landsknechten. No devils of any note approached me. Did I miss anything around here?"

"Not much. I broke the news to Werner that you're still an employee here, and he shouted for ten minutes and then stormed out. Tells me he's going to celebrate the vanquishing of winter in more edifying company—which I take to mean he's going to spend the night reciting poetry at Johann Kretchmer's place again. Oh, and the Brothers of St. Christopher set up their usual puppet show in the yard, as they do every Easter, but your crew of Vikings thought the puppets were homunculi—they smashed up the box and chased the monks away. The kids were all crying, so I had to go out there and do juggling tricks to restore order."

Duffy nodded with a satisfied air. "All emergencies kept well in hand, eh? Good work."

Aurelianus smiled. "And I did have a long talk with old Werner, before he made his exit."

"Oh? That seems a waste of time."

The old man reached behind him and picked up a candle from another table. "Not completely. He tells me you are a perfectly *disastrous* bouncer—says you encourage fights when they start and start 'em when they don't."

Duffy rocked his head judiciously. "Well . . . a case could be made for that point of view."

"No doubt. At any rate, as your employer, I have a proposal to present to you. I'd like to double your salary and promote you out of the bouncer position."

"To what position?"

Aurelianus shrugged and spread his hands. "Bodyguard, shall we say?"

"Whose body? Yours?" He watched as the sorcerer produced a tinder box from under his robe, opened it, and took out flint, steel and a handful of tinder.

"No, mine can take of itself. I mean the King."

Duffy laughed. "Oh, certainly. Hell, I can't imagine how Charles has got along until now without—no; I see. You mean this other king of yours." Aurelianus nodded, watching the Irishman closely. "The one living outside Vienna," Duffy went on, "who outranks Charles, though nobody's ever heard of him."

"A lot of people have heard of him," corrected Aurelianus, striking sparks into the tinder; "damn few know he actually exists."

"Very well, what's his name?"

"He doesn't really have a name. He's known as the Fisher King." The tinder was alight, and he held a sputtering straw to the wick of the new candle. It caught, and in a moment was burning brightly.

Duffy abruptly had the feeling that this conversation had occurred before, perhaps in a dream. The sensation puzzled and obscurely frightened him. "And he's in danger, is he?" The Irishman's voice was gruff.

"Potentially. Some time during the next couple of days we'll have to go fetch him, bring him inside the city walls. He hates the confinement, you see, of streets and gates and masonry—especially in his sick, wounded condition—and he'd prefer to stay out in the woods until the last possible day. He is safe *now,* what with a dozen of our pit-summoned defenders circling over his cabin, and Suleiman an easy three months away, but Antoku's tricks have me worried—I'd sooner not take any chances. We'll bring him inside within the week."

A sick hermit living in the woods, Duffy thought. I've never heard of him, but he's a greater king than the Emperor, Charles V, eh? No doubt, no doubt! Hah. Just another sad old phony, like those British shopkeepers who claim to be druids, and dance, rather self-consciously, at Stonehenge every midsummer's eve.

Duffy sighed. "Yes, for double my salary I'll watch over this old king of yours—just so these . . . what? 'Pit-summoned defenders'? . . . keep their distance."

"They're on your side."

"Still, I don't want to meet any. And what do you mean, Suleiman three months away? He's further off than that."

"Not much further. His advance scouts left Constantinople today. He won't be more than a month behind."

"Today? How can you know already?"

Aurelianus smiled tiredly. "You know me better than *that,* Brian."

The street door rattled and creaked open, and the hunchbacked figure of Bluto bulked against the late afternoon glow. "Damn," exclaimed the Swiss bombardier, "I thought I'd be the first in line. I might have known you two would be here before anyone else."

Aurelianus pushed back his bench and got to his feet. "I was just chatting with Brian. I'm not much of a beer drinker, actually—my share of the bock is all yours." He bowed and walked quietly out of the room.

Bluto crossed to Duffy's table and pulled up the

bench at which Aurelianus had been sitting. "Speaking of beer . . . "

Duffy grinned. "Yes. Anna or Piff is in the kitchen. Why don't you have them pour us a last pitcher of the schenk beer, eh?"

"Good idea. My God, what happened to your face?"

"I was attacked in my sleep by mice. Go get the beer."

Bluto did, and for twenty minutes the two of them sipped cool beer and discussed the possible Turkish lines of attack, the weak points in the city wall, and various defense arrangements.

"Charles has *got* to send reinforcements," Bluto said worriedly. "Pope Clement, too. Can it be they don't see the danger? Hell, Belgrade and Mohács were costly defeats, yes. They were the stepping-stones to the Holy Roman Empire. But Vienna is the damned *front door*. If the Turks take this place, the next spot to hold the line will be the English Channel."

Duffy shrugged. "What can I say? You're right." He poured the last of the beer into Bluto's cup.

Shrub and a couple of the other yard boys had come in with ladders and were hanging cagelike grilles over the wall cressets. The hunchback watched them. "Really expecting a wild crowd tonight, aren't you?"

"Evidently," Duffy agreed. "Back when this place was a monastery they used to drag kegs out and have the bock festival in the street. It got pretty berserk sometimes. Easter, the bock beer, and Spring are all the same thing in everybody's mind, and they really dive into it head first after a hard winter."

Bluto drained his glass and stood. "Say, Duff, it must be half past four now. When should I make sure to be here, to be at least among the first in line?"

"I don't know. Supper time, I guess." He too stood up and stretched, yawning like a cat. "Maybe I'll trot downstairs and ask Gambrinus. See you later." He ambled off toward the cellar stairs, secretly hoping to get another advance taste of the Spring beer.

Duffy could hear someone moving about in the darkness below as he descended the stairs. "Gambrinus!" he called, but there was no answer. Remembering the

petard he'd found on the brewery door, he closed his
fingers around his dagger hilt and took the remaining
steps as quietly as possible.

When he stood at last on the damp paving stones,
he peered cautiously around the dim cellar, but didn't
see anyone. Maybe I'm now having auditory hallucinations to complement my moonlit-lake visual ones, he
thought unhappily. Wait a moment! Who's that?

A tall figure had stepped out of the shadows behind
the brick chimney, and now crossed to a door set in the
wall next to the high-set copper tubs; in a moment he
had opened the door and stepped through into the
blackness beyond. The Irishman had caught only a
quick glimpse of the stranger, but had noticed that he
was blond or red-haired, and wore a loose cloak
fastened at the throat by one metal button.

Duffy had his dagger out and strode to the door.
"Come out of there," he barked.

There was only silence from the dark room beyond,
and an intensification of the steamy malt smell.

Duffy retreated to the fireplace, picked up a coal with
the tongs and held it to the wick of Gambrinus' lantern.
Armed now with the light, he returned to the doorway
and peered warily into the stone-walled room revealed
within. He couldn't see anyone, and, assuming the
intruder was hiding to one side of the door, leaped
through with a whirl of the lantern and an intimidating
yell.

The room was empty. "Enough now, what *is* this?"
the Irishman snarled. Setting down the lantern, he
examined the walls for evidence of a secret door, but
found none. The floor was simply moist earth, and the
high-ceilinged room contained nothing but a monstrous wooden vat, taller by half than Duffy, the broad
slats of its sides green with the moss of decades, perhaps centuries.

Duffy was about to go back to the dining room and
worry about this new symptom of madness when he
noticed three big, discolored wooden spigots set in
the side of the vat, one at chest level, one at knee level,
and one only a dozen inches above the dirt floor.
Tarnished brass plates were nailed above the spigots,

and he looked closely at them. The top one read LIGHT; the middle one BOCK; and the bottom one was so scaled with verdigris that it was indecipherable, and he had to scrape at it with the edge of his dagger. After a minute he had got it fairly clean, and could read its single word: DARK.

Now what the hell, he thought, forgetting the elusive intruder in his immediate puzzlement. He glanced up and saw a number of pipes emerging from the cellar wall and entering the vat at the top. Can this thing, he wondered queasily, be substituting for the tun tubs of a normal brewery? Does the fermentation of all Herzwesten beer take place, as it appears to do, in this great moldy vat? I wonder if they ever clean it.

After extinguishing the lantern he made his way thoughtfully back up the stairs. Maybe, he speculated, that fair-haired man, whoever he was, led me into that room intentionally; wanted me to see that enigmatic vat.

He paused at the top of the stairs. I've frequently tasted Herzwesten Light, he thought, and every Spring I can have the Bock. What, though, is Herzwesten Dark, and why have I never heard of it?

Bluto had wandered off, and the only person in the dining room besides Shrub and his helpers was Epiphany. She had wiped down the tables and washed and stacked the serving-boards for dinner, and was now slumped at the traditional employees' table, wearily slurping small beer.

"Piff, my love," the Irishman exclaimed. "Where have you been hiding?"

Epiphany started when he spoke, then smiled worriedly. "You're the one that's been hiding, Brian," she said. "I've been looking for you all day. Anna tells me you were in a sword-fight last night. Good God!" she gasped as he approached her table, "How did your face get all scratched?"

"Oh, the usual monsters have been giving me a rough time. But I give them a rough time, too. Are you working dinner?"

"No, thank God." She brushed a damp strand of

gray hair back from her forehead. "I guess it'll be a real madhouse."

"It's a madhouse anyway. I believe our employer is insane." He reached across the table, picked up her beer and drank it off. "Let's go up to your room. I've got a few things to tell you."

She eyed him cautiously. "Brian, you look like an old tomcat: this season's cuts crossing last year's scars." After a moment she grinned and stood up. "My room? This way." Duffy followed her up the stairs, reflecting that it might still be possible to talk some of the old woman out of the girl.

Epiphany's room, a narrow one overlooking the stables, was neat, but not intimidatingly so. Framed paintings leaned out from every wall, mostly religious canvasses of her father's; though Duffy thought he recognized one as the work of Domenico Veneziano. A bird twittered manically in a cage that hung over a chessboard, the pieces of which stood unmoved in their four basic ranks. Duffy absently moved the white king's knight to the third row, over the ridge of the pawns.

"Sit down, Brian," Epiphany said. Duffy dragged a chair up from beside the dresser and sat down on it while she perched on the bed.

"Let's see," the Irishman said. "I don't know where to start, Piff. Well. Do you know why Aurelianus lured me here from Venice?"

"To keep peace in the dining room . . . which you really—"

"Never mind. No. That was the story, yes, but he's dropped hints that that's not what he wanted me for at all. He thinks the Turks are coming to Vienna just to wreck this brewery, and he thinks—equally insane— that *I* can prevent them. Me, a stranger he just encountered at random hundreds of miles from here. And listen, that isn't all, he's got a madman's explanation for everything. You think Suleiman is the head man of the Ottoman Empire? Not according to Aurelianus! No, it's Ibrahim, the Grand Vizir, who also happens to be the son of an air-demon or something. And maybe you imagined Emperor Charles counted for something here in the West? Hell, no! There's an old fisherman in the forests outside town that's the *real* king." Duffy kicked the bed post, secretly irritated to find some of his scornful incredulity feigned.

"It *is* all a lot of senile fantasies on Aurelianus' part," he went on, trying to convince himself almost as much as Epiphany. "Certainly, the old fellow can work magic tricks and conjure spirits out of holes in the ground . . . but, Christ, we're dealing with modern warfare here: cannons, troops, swords and mines. How can *I* save the damned *brewery* if the Hapsburg and Vatican armies fail to save *Vienna?* And if they do save the city, what point will there be in me standing vigilantly in front of the brewery flexing my sword-hand? Hell—Aurelianus might have been something once, but he surely doesn't know what's going on now. The fact is that Suleiman wants the empire of Charles V, and is coming to break the eastern wall of it—and Aurelianus thinks the whole affair revolves around me, Herzwesten beer, and some old hermit in the woods who imagines he's a king!"

He had stood up in order to gesture more effectively during this speech, and now he sat down beside Epiphany on the bed. Her face was lit by the reflected, curtain-scrimmed orange light from the west, and for the first time since his return to Vienna she really looked familiar to him. This was Epiphany Vogel at last, beginning to shed the gray, acquired personality of Epiphany Hallstadt.

"Listen, Piff. I've done my share of killing Turks, and I don't see how my presence in Vienna could affect the coming battle one way or the other. Now I happen to have saved some money, and on top of that for some reason they're paying me a princely salary. I figure in a few weeks, early May, let's say, we'll have enough . . . that is, if it sounds as good to you as it does to me . . . what I mean is, what would you think of hoofing it to Ireland with me, before they lock Vienna's gates? We could get married—finally!—and live in a real slate-roofed cottage and, I don't know, raise goats or something. Don't tell anybody, though."

"Oh, Brian, it sounds wonderful!" She blotted a tear

with a beer-damp sleeve. "I'd given up ideas like that till you came back from the dead. But can't I tell Anna?"

"Nobody. Aurelianus could legally prevent you from leaving, because you owe him money."

She scratched her head. "Do I?"

"Yes. Don't you remember? He bought up all the debts and bad accounts that were your legacy from that worm-gut son of a bitch Hallstadt, may he be turning on a spit this minute in hell."

Epiphany was shocked. "Brian! Max was your best friend once. You shouldn't hate him."

"It's because he was my best friend that I do—did—hate him. I wouldn't have minded so much if a stranger had taken you from me."

She put a hand on his arm. "Don't dwell on all the stuff that's behind us. We can still spend our twilight years together."

"*Twilight* years? I don't know about you, lady, but I'm as nimble and sharp as I was at twenty-five, which wasn't all *that* long ago."

"Very well," she said with an indulgent smile. "Our . . . early afternoon years. Oh, God . . . do you really think it's a possibility, after all this time?"

"After all this time," Duffy asserted, "it's an inevitability."

He leaned forward and gave her a kiss, and it lingered past the point of being perfunctory. Gently transported by the dimness, and the brain-fumes of an afternoon's wine-drinking, he was at last in the arms of Gustav Vogel's impossibly attractive daughter; and he had, unnoticed, become again the Brian Duffy of 1512, whose glossy black hair did not yet have to be grown long in the back to cover a knotted white scar.

They fell back across the bed with the ponderousness, and something of the sound, of an old stone wall collapsing, and Epiphany pulled her mouth free and gasped, "You're on duty tonight, aren't you? And dinner is probably being served this minute."

"Damn duty and dinner," the Irishman muttered thickly; then, "Oh, hell, you're right," he said. "Easter evening, the drawing of the bock, is what Aurelianus specifically hired me to watch over. For the money he's been paying me I guess I owe this much to him."

He stood up reluctantly and looked down at Epiphany, who in the diminishing light was an indistinct figure stretched across the bed. "I'll be back sometime," he said.

"I hope so," she answered in a small voice.

Chapter Twelve

CROWDED INTO A SHADOWY CORNER, Duffy and Aurelianus watched three beer-crazed shepherds jigging on one of the tables while nearly everyone in that quarter of the dining room sang and clapped in accompaniment.

"Don't you think you should get those men down from there?" Aurelianus asked anxiously.

Duffy shook his head. "No. The celebration spirit would only break out in some other activity, like maybe pitching beer mugs through the window. They're just enjoying themselves, and they're paying you for the beer. Why interfere?"

"Well . . . all right. You're the chucker-out, after all." The old man leaned against the wall, apparently a little bewildered by the rowdiness of the bock celebration. "Are you quite up to all this?" he asked. "Have you rested up at all since our underground enterprise last night?"

"What? I can't hear you in this pandemonium." Aurelianus repeated his last sentence, louder. "Oh! Don't worry about me, I'm fine. These days it takes more than a few hobgoblins to disorder me."

"Good. It's a wise tolerance to cultivate."

"It's what? I didn't—God help us." Duffy shoved several people aside, spilling their beer in all directions, and, taking a flying hop over a table, bowled off their feet two mercenaries who had begun trading knife-thrusts. Before they could roll to their feet the Irishman had unsheathed his own dagger and cut, with two quick flicks of the blade, their belts, so that their hands now had to be occupied with holding their clothing together. They left the room, red-faced, accompanied by howls of laughter.

"Mr. Duffy!" Shrub cried, waving from atop the bar.

"In a minute, Shrub," Duffy called, for on the other side of the room a suddenly irate merchant was slapping his wife and calling her vile names. Muttering a quick apology, the Irishman snatched up a brimming mug from a table he passed, and then dashed its foaming contents forcefully into the face of the misogynist shopkeeper; the man had just been filling his lungs for another burst of abuse, and was choking now on a couple of ounces of beer he'd inadvertently inhaled. Duffy lifted him from his chair by a handful of hair and gave him a resounding slap on the back, then slammed him back down into his seat. "There y'are, sir," said the Irishman cheerfully. "We don't want any of our patrons choking to death, eh?" He leaned down and said more sharply but in a whisper, "Or getting their ribs kicked in, which will happen to you if you touch that lady again or say any more insulting things to her. Do I make myself clear? Hah? Good."

"Mr. Duffy!" Shrub called again. "There's a man to see you—"

The table on which the shepherds were dancing collapsed then, spilling the three fuddled jiggers against the bar, which fell over against the wall with a multiple crash. Shrub leaped clear, but landed in a dish of roast pork on another table, and had to flee from the wrathful diners.

A little while later Duffy saw Bluto edge through the front door, and waved. The Irishman opened his mouth to shout that he'd squared it with the serving girls about Bluto's free beer, then decided that such a statement, shouted across the dangerously crowded room, could only cause a riot. I'll tell him when I can whisper it to him, Duffy decided. I wonder who this man is that Shrub tried to tell me about.

A youth with black curly hair was slouched against the wall, and pulled his hat down over his eyes as Duffy sidled past. That's what's-his-name, the Irishman thought, Jock, the lad Aurelianus sent out last night to keep an eye on that precious king of his. I'd swear I've seen him somewhere outside Vienna. Where?

Duffy tried to pursue the memory but was distracted by the necessity of rescuing one of the serving women from an old priest turned amorous by the evening's heady brew. After encouraging the clergyman to recall the dignity he owed the cloth, Duffy lifted a mug from a passing tray and drained it in two long swallows.

"Here, here! Pay for that, sir!" came a voice from behind him. He turned and Bluto grinned at him.

"Hello, Bluto," Duffy said. "I've told the girls you're to get free bock till ten."

"Till ten? What happens at ten?"

"You start paying for it."

"I'd better get busy then. Oh," Bluto spoke more quietly, "I finished checking the stores this afternoon. There's about a hundred pounds of black powder missing."

The Irishman nodded. "Nothing else?"

"No. Oh, maybe. One of the old forty-pounder siege bombards seems to be missing, but the armorer probably miscounted them when he made the list back in 'twenty-four. I mean, how could anyone carry away a gun like that?"

Duffy frowned. "I don't know. But I'll keep my eyes open. You haven't seen Shrub around, have you?"

"Yes. He's in the kitchen. I saw him peeking in here a minute ago, looking scared. Where are your Vikings?"

"In the stable, drinking and singing. I'm hoping that if I keep sending beer out to them they'll stay there, and not try to join the party in here. Oh no, what are those shepherds doing to that guy over there?"

"Baptizing him with beer, it looks like."

"Excuse me."

Twenty minutes later Duffy sank exhausted onto a bench in the corner and signalled to Anna for a pitcher. He had put down so many uprisings in the still noisy room that people within earshot of him—not a great distance, to be sure—kept a wary eye on him; the rowdier drunkards were shaken and, in some cases, pulled down from chandeliers or out from under tables and told to stop it by their more sober friends.

Shrub edged his way nervously through the crowd, leading a tall, dark-faced man who wore a heavy cloak and a wide-brimmed hat. "Mr. Duffy," the boy said before darting out of the room, "this gentleman wanted to see you. He's a Spaniard."

He looks more like a pirate than a gentleman, the Irishman thought, but I may as well be civil. "Yes, sir?"

"Can I sit with you?"

Duffy's pitcher arrived then, giving him a more tolerant outlook. "Very well," he said, "pull up a bench. Have you got a mug to drink from?"

The Spaniard swiped an empty one from the nearest table. "Yes."

"Then have some beer." Duffy filled both their mugs. "How can I be of service to you? Uh, the boy was mistaken, I assume, in describing you as a Spaniard."

"Eh? Why do you say that?"

"Well, you're stretching your vowels, but your accent's Hungarian. Or so it seems to my possibly beer-dulled ears."

"No, damn you, you're correct. I'm Hungarian. But I think it's your eyes that are beer-dulled if you don't recognize me."

The Irishman sighed, and with some effort focused his attention on the man's shadowed face, expecting to recognize some old comrade-in-arms who would probably want to borrow money.

Then his stomach went cold, and he suddenly felt much more sober; it was a face he had last seen on that awful morning in the late summer of 1526 when

Duffy, wounded and exhausted, had breasted the broad tide of the Danube and dragged himself onto the north bank. The Turkish banners had been flying over the conquered town of Mohács behind him, and sixty thousand slain Hungarian soldiers were being buried on the battle-furrowed plain. That morning, on the river's north side, he had met the army of John Zapolya, for whom Archbishop Tomori and King Louis, both at that moment being laid unmourned in unmarked graves, had not waited. The battered Irishman had described to Zapolya the disastrous battle and rout of the previous afternoon, and Zapolya, shocked and angry, had within the hour led his army away westward. Duffy had rested in the woods for another day and then beaten a furtive, solitary retreat to the south, over the Alps to Venice. Years later he heard of Zapolya's subsequent defection to the Turkish side.

"By God," he breathed now, "how do you dare come here? After you sold your homeland to Suleiman I never thought I'd see you again . . . except perhaps over a gun-barrel or sword-point."

John Zapolya's eyes narrowed, but his sardonic smile didn't falter. "My loyalty is and has always been to Hungary, and it has been for her welfare that I have done everything . . . even this tonight."

Duffy was still appalled at the man's very presence. "What *are* you doing here tonight?" he asked. "And why do you evidently suppose that I won't shout to this roomful of people the fact that this 'Spaniard' is the man they've practically come to equate with Satan?"

"Well, lad, first because I've got a short-barrel monk's gun levelled at your stomach under the table. Yes, I'm afraid it's true. And second, there are four of my men in the alley out back, in what appears to be a haywagon."

Duffy sighed wearily. "And what is it really, John?"

Zapolya sipped his beer, keeping his eyes on Duffy and his right hand under the table. "Oh, it's a haywagon, but it holds more than hay."

"Damn it, John, can't you—"

"Very well, take it easy. There's a siege bombard

in it, loaded with a forty-pound ball of iron. Its barrel is laid horizontal, pointing at this building, and my men are carrying slowmatches."

"If you'll pardon my saying so, John, *none* of this makes any sense. Why should you risk your life sneaking into Vienna, and then settle for just killing me and blowing up this inn?" Keep him talking, Duffy told himself; play for time and maybe some drunk will lurch into him, spoil his aim for one precious second.

"Don't play ignorant with me, old Duff," said Zapolya with an easy smile. "You wouldn't be here if you didn't know what this place is, and who you are."

"Why must everyone speak to me in riddles?" Duffy complained. "What is it you want? Why are you sitting in here if you've got a damned siege-gun levelled at the back door?"

"Keep your voice down. I'm sitting here because I'm a dispensible piece in this game, a rook they're willing to sacrifice for a solid checkmate. I've been sent here—at great personal risk, as you've noted—by my master, Ibrahim, to offer you a very high, very powerful position in the Eastern Empire."

The amorous priest reeled by behind Zapolya's chair in pursuit of one of the serving women, but earned a mental curse from the Irishman for failing to collide with the traitorous Hungarian's chair. "Position?" Duffy sighed. "What sort of position?"

Zapolya stared at him with something like envy. "A higher one than mine. If you play this game right, you could replace Suleiman himself."

Duffy laughed derisively and gulped some beer, using the motion to let his hand fall nearer his dagger. "I hate to be the first to tell you you're crazy, John. If I am." He strove to keep his tone light while trying to guess the position of the other man's gun. "Why should Ibrahim want *me* to replace the *Sultan?* The greatest Sultan the Ottomans have ever had! This really is madness. And I can just imagine the delight the Turks would exhibit at being led by an Irishman. Ho ho."

"Much the same, I imagine, as their delight at having an orphan from Parga appointed Grand Vizir over Ahmed Pasha, who'd deserved the post for years.

These things do happen, and the next step is always unimaginable until it's occurred."

Can I flip this table over before he can pull the spark rasp of his gun? Duffy wondered. Probably not. "Why me, John?" he stalled. "Why Brian Duffy from Dingle? You haven't explained that yet."

Zapolya, for the first time during the conversation, looked disconcerted. "Brian . . . honestly, don't you know who . . . what . . . you are?"

A wrenching thunderclap sounded from the rear of the building, and the windows rattled furiously. Ladies screamed, serving women dropped laden trays, and Zapolya instinctively half-turned in his chair. Duffy leaped to his feet, overturning the table on the Hungarian, whose pinned gun sent a lead ball splintering into the floor between Duffy's boots.

There were screams and sword clangs from the back alley, and a fog of gunpowder smoke blew through the kitchen into the dining room, where the beer-fuddled crowd had united in a desperate, shouting rush for the front door. Duffy was knocked sprawling by a fat lady who was bulling her way through the press, and he lost sight of Zapolya.

"Bluto!" Duffy yelled. "Aurelianus, anyone! Grab that Spaniard! He's Zapolya!"

No one heard him, and by the time he'd kicked and cursed his way clear of the shouting crowd, the Hungarian was nowhere to be seen. The Irishman gritted an oath and ran through the smoke-fogged kitchen.

The stableyard beyond was all aglare, lit by a furiously burning haywagon that sat on its collapsed axles in the middle of the yard. A great gap had been torn in the back fence, and through it he could see flames licking about among a scattered rubble-heap that had been a leather shop that afternoon. Bugge's Vikings fingered the grips of their bared swords and kept wary eyes on the shadows; and after a moment the Irishman noticed three bodies sprawled on the paving stones.

"Aurelianus!" he called. "Bluto! Damn it, we can still catch him!"

"Who?" asked Aurelianus, who had followed him

through the kitchen and now stood wringing his hands behind Duffy.

"Zapolya! He was here. Take a horse and race to the north gate. I'll take the Carinthian gate. Have them close it and let no one out." Duffy had seized a wild-eyed horse as he spoke, and now scrambled up onto its bare back. "Go!" Not pausing to see if the trembling old man obeyed him, Duffy put his heels to his mount's ribs and galloped out of the red-lit yard.

Bluto cut another notch in the candle's rim and watched the hot wax spill down the side. "Anna," he said. "Another cup of bock."

"It's after ten, you know."

"I know." The hunchback looked around the dining room. Most of the revellers had trickled back, but the room's warmth had been let out, and the chilly air reeked of gunpowder—it was a more subdued crowd gulping the beer now.

At the same moment, Duffy strode in from the kitchen and Aurelianus pushed open the street door. Both men looked tired and less than pleased. Without looking at each other they pulled up a chair and a bench at Bluto's table.

"Uh, make that a pitcher, and two more cups, Anna," the hunchback called. Duffy and Aurelianus nodded agreement.

"Did he leave through the Carinthian gate?" the old man asked after a minute of breath-catching. "I've got the north one closed and triply guarded."

Duffy nodded. "He did. Three minutes before I got there. I followed him south for a half mile, but even in this moonlight I lost his tracks."

Aurelianus sighed. "Are you sure it was him?"

"Yes. I used to know him, remember? He came to entice me over to the Turkish side, and to blow this place up. By the way, Bluto, I believe the missing siege mortar is in the middle of that bonfire out back."

"It is," Bluto confirmed. "You can see it through the flames."

"I wonder," Duffy sighed, filling a cup with the newly arrived beer, "why they aimed the thing the wrong way. Was it all a bluff? But why bring the gun at all if that was the case?"

"It wasn't a bluff," Bluto told him. "When your northmen saw those four men roll the wagon into the yard, they told them, in Norse and sign-language, to get it the hell out of there. Zapolya's men told them to shut up, so the Vikings turned the wagon around themselves, intending to shove it back out into the street. That started a fistfight, and apparently these haywagon boys were carrying firepots or slowmatches. One of them was knocked unconscious and fell into the hay. A minute later the wagon was in flames, and a minute after that the mortar let go, taking out the fence and two buildings on the next street. Your Vikings figured this was an unfair weapon, so they unsheathed their swords and killed the remaining three intruders immediately."

Duffy laughed grimly. "And I thought they'd never earn their keep."

"He tried to entice you, you say?" Aurelianus asked, leaning forward. "By what persuasions?"

"Crazy things. He talked like you frequently do, as a matter of fact. That stranger-things-are-possible-than-you-know sort of nonsense." Duffy refilled his mug. "He said if I went along and signed up, that Ibrahim would make me Sultan—and just depose old Suleiman, I guess." He shook his head and sighed with genuine regret. "Poor old John. I remember him before he lost his mind."

Aurelianus was deep in thought. "Yes," he said finally, "I can see what Ibrahim must have had in mind. A wild gambit indeed! Zapolya's mission was to buy you over or, failing that, to kill you. And to blow up this inn in any case."

"Ibrahim could have sent a better messenger," Duffy observed. "John never got around to mentioning money."

Aurelianus stared at him. *"Money?* He offered you the third highest position in the Eastern Empire!" He shook his head. "Oh hell. I don't know; maybe it's a good thing you persist in regarding these matters in such a mundane light. Maybe that's your strength."

"Ibrahim wants Duffy here for a sultan?" Bluto snickered. "I thought sultans were supposed to be tee-totallers."

The Irishman wasn't listening. "He did seem a little . . . at a loss, right at the end, like a man offering gold coins to a savage whose tribe barters only hides and fish. He said, 'Do you honestly not know who you are?' and then that gun went off." He turned hesitantly to Aurelianus. "Do you think . . . you don't think . . . Ibrahim *really* sent him? To offer me . . . *that?*"

Aurelianus looked away. "I can't be sure," he said, but Duffy got the impression that the old man's uncertainty was feigned.

"Who am I, then? What did he mean by all that?"

"You'll know soon enough," Aurelianus said pleadingly. "This is the sort of thing it's no use telling you about until you've more than half figured it out already. If I explained everything now, you'd laugh and say I was crazy. Have patience."

Duffy was tired, or he might have pursued the point. As it was, he just shrugged. "Let it lie, then. I'm fast losing interest in all this anyway." His decision to flee with Epiphany had given him a pleasant sense of dissociation with all of Aurelianus' schemes and theories. "More beer here, Anna! This pitcher's suddenly empty. Oh, by the way, Aurelianus, when do they draw the Herzwesten Dark?"

Aurelianus blinked. "Who in hell have you been talking to? Bluto, would you leave us for a moment? This is a private business."

"Certainly, certainly!" Bluto stood up and went to another table, intercepting, to the Irishman's chagrin, the new pitcher.

"Who," Aurelianus asked earnestly, "told you about the Dark?"

"Nobody told me. I heard a noise in the cellar and found some red-haired fellow wandering around down there. I followed him through the door in the wall, and saw that huge vat. Is all Herzwesten beer drawn from that?"

"Yes. Do you . . . have any idea who he was?" The old man's voice quivered with supressed excitement.

"Me? No. He disappeared in the vat room. I looked all over for a secret door, but couldn't find one." Duffy laughed. "I figured he must have been a ghost."

"He was. Did he speak?"

"No. You've seen him yourself?" Duffy didn't relish the ghost idea, and wanted to establish the intruder's identity.

"I'm afraid I haven't. I've only heard him described by those who have."

"Who," Duffy asked, "is he?"

Aurelianus sat back. "I'll tell you that. But first let me mention that the vat you saw has been in operation ever since this brewery was started three and a half thousand years ago. Parts of it have been replaced, and it's been enlarged twice, but we . . . they . . . always kept the beer that was in there. It's a lot like the solera method of blending sherry. We pour the new wort in at the top and draw the beer out further down, so there's always a blending and aging process going on. In fact, there are probably still traces of the first season's barley in there, thirty-five hundred years old."

Duffy nodded civilly, reflecting, though, that the surest way to get Aurelianus to talk about chickens was to ask him about cheese.

"Ordinarily," Aurelianus went on, "such a vat would have to be cleaned annually. We've avoided that necessity by leaving out the bottom boards entirely, so that the staves, and the beer, rest directly on the naked earth."

Duffy gagged and set down his cup. "You mean the beer is mixed right in with the *mud?* God help us, I never thought—"

"Relax, will you? The beer seeps down into the dirt, yes, but the dirt doesn't rise. We don't stir it. We just gently drain off the beer at various levels, and the mud isn't riled. Have you ever tasted better beer?"

"Well, no."

"Then stop acting like a kid who just learned what tripes are." The old man squinted critically at Duffy.

"I hope you're ready for all this. You ask questions and then get all upset at the beginnings of an answer."

"I'll be quiet," Duffy promised.

"Good enough. The man you saw was a ghost. Sorry. When you saw him he was returning to his grave." He leaned forward again. "By Llyr, I'm going to give it to you direct—it was the ghost of Finn Mac Cool, returning to whatever remains today of his earthly dust. Finn is buried, you see, six feet directly below that fermenting vat."

Duffy blinked. "And there's no bottom to it? He must be absolutely dissolved in beer."

"Right. And the beer upward is saturated with his . . . essence and strength, the lower levels most strongly."

"Then this Dark, being the lowest, must be nearly Finn-broth."

"Spiritually speaking, that's right," Aurelianus agreed. "Though physically it's just unusually heavy, superaged beer. Don't get the idea that it clots, or that we get bones and teeth clogging the spigot."

"Oh no!" Duffy said airily, though privately resolving never to drink any of it. "So when is it drawn? I've never heard even a hint of it."

"That's because the last time the Dark was drawn was in the year 829; when the sons of poor Emperor Louis were turning against him, as I recall. We'll draw it again on the thirty-first of October of this year. That's right, we let every drop of Dark age seven hundred years."

"But good Lord," Duffy exclaimed, "beer can't age that long. Brandy or *claret* couldn't age that long."

"Well," Aurelianus admitted, "you can't really call the stuff beer after all that time, that's true. It becomes something else. Something similar in many ways to the wine you drank in Bacchus' tavern, in Trieste. And you noticed, I assume, that the Dark spigot was only a few inches above the dirt floor? Only the next three or four inches above that are drawn at a time, so the Dark is always a terribly limited quantity."

"Is there much demand for it?" Duffy asked, certain that there couldn't possibly be.

"Yes . . . but not from beer drinkers. Because of its, ah, source, the Dark is very potent stuff, psychically, spiritually . . . magically. Physically too, as a matter of fact—it often shows levels of alcohol content theoretically impossible from a natural fermentation process. Anyway, yes, much more demand than the meagre supply can accommodate. It, in fact, is what Antoku wanted from me—a cupful of it to maintain the life he should have given up a thousand years ago. He was killed as an infant in a Japanese sea-battle, you see. I did let him have a cupful last time—" He halted and glared defensively at Duffy; then smiled awkwardly, coughed and went on. "In any case, he thinks it is now his right. He is, I'm afraid, incorrect. And all the other Dark Birds, the Ethiopian, the several Hindus, the New World aborigine and the rest of them, they too hope for a sip of it, and some of their cases are nearly as desperate as Antoku's. But they won't get any, either."

"Who will you give it to?" Duffy asked, beginning in spite of himself to get curious about the brew. After all, he thought, that wine in Trieste was very nice.

"Antoku evidently thinks I intend to give it to you," said Aurelianus, "since he set those afrits onto you. Or maybe that was supposed to be a warning to me that he *could* kill someone even more vital."

"Uh huh. So who *does* get it?" Evasion is this man's second nature, the Irishman reflected.

"This time? Our King—the Fisher King. I told you, didn't I, that he's ill? And so is the West. Which way the connection works I'm still not certain, but the connection unarguably exists; when the King is well, the West is well."

"And this beer will cure him?" asked Duffy, trying to keep the skepticism out of his voice.

"Yes. Our King is weakened, injured, his strength dissipated—and there's the strength and character of Finn, the first King, in the Dark. He'll be able to put his lands in order again."

"And you'll draw the stuff in October? Can't you do it a bit early? After all, when you're talking about seven centuries, a few months one way or the other . . ."

"No," said Aurelianus. "It can't be hurried. The cycle has to come round completely, and there are stars and tides and births to be taken into account as much as fermentation and beercraft. On October thirty-first we'll draw the Dark, and not a day before." He raised worried eyes to Duffy. "Perhaps you can see now why Ibrahim is so anxious to destroy the brewery before then."

At two in the morning the remainder of the crowd was sent home, and the lights were put out as the employees, having decided the clean-up could wait until the next morning, stumbled off to bed. Duffy took a walk out back, but all fires had been put out, his northmen snored peacefully in the stable and there was no evidence of smoldering bombs, so he went back inside.

Somehow he wasn't sleepy, in spite of having slept only four hours the night before, and all the drinking and running around of this evening. He sat down at his table in the dark dining room. As usual, he thought, Aurelianus managed to duck the question I most wanted an answer to, which is: *Who or what am I in this vast scheme? Why has everyone from Ibrahim to Bacchus taken an interest in me?*

He silently lifted his chair further back into the shadows then, for he heard two low voices in the kitchen conversing in Italian.

"Is there any word from Clement?" asked one.

"As a matter of fact," replied the other, "it looks like he will send troops this time. He's even trying for some kind of temporary truce with Luther so that the West can unreservedly unite against the Ottoman Empire."

The two speakers emerged from the kitchen and started up the stairs without noticing Duffy. One was Aurelianus and the other was the swarthy, curly-haired young man, Jock, who'd pulled his hat down over his face when Duffy had passed him earlier in the evening.

Huh! the Irishman thought; didn't Aurelianus tell me in Venice that he didn't speak Italian? And speaking of Venice, it was *there* I first saw this Jock fellow, who introduced himself, that Ash Wednesday evening, as Giacomo Gritti. What connections are these?

The sorcerer and the young man ascended the stairs, and their whispering voices died away above. Those two are working together, then? Duffy mused. That would explain why young Gritti saved my life and directed me to a safe ship, that morning on the Venice docks, though it certainly doesn't shed any light on the ambush he and his brothers sprang on me the night before. Unless that fight was somehow staged . . . ?

One thing is sure—I've been lied to a number of times, and can't even guess why. I don't like it when strangers pry into my affairs, but I absolutely can't bear it when they know more about my affairs than I do myself.

He stood up and walked to the servants' hall, picking up an empty beer mug on the way.

He placed his feet carefully on the cellar stairs as he descended them so as not to awaken the sleeping Gambrinus, and then padded cautiously across the stone floor to the door the ghost had gone through that afternoon. The hinges must have been recently oiled, for they didn't squeak when the Irishman slowly drew the door open. He groped his way to the huge vat in the pitchy blackness, and then felt for the lowest of the three spigots. It turned grittily when he exerted some strength; then when he judged he'd drawn half a cup he shut the valve and, closing the vat-room behind him, hurried up the stairs to the dining room.

He lit the candle at his table and peered suspiciously at the few ounces of thick black liquid that swirled in the bottom of the mug. Looks pretty vile, he thought. Then he sat down, and even without bringing the cup to his nose he smelled the heady, heavily aromatic bouquet. God bless us, he thought rapturously, this is the nectar of which even the finest, rarest bock in the world is only the vaguest hint. In one long, slow, savoring swallow he emptied the cup.

His first thought was: Sneak downstairs, Duffy lad, and *fill* the cup this time. He got to his feet—or tried to, rather, and was only able to shift slightly in his chair. What's this? he thought apprehensively; I recover from a lifetime's worth of dire wounds only to be paralyzed by a mouthful of beer? He attempted again to heave himself out of the chair, and this time didn't move at all.

Then he was moving—no, being carried. He was exhausted, and a frigid wind hacked savagely through the joints in his plate armor. He rolled over, moaning with the pain in his head.

"Lie still, my King," came a tense, worried voice. "You'll only open your wound again if you thrash about so."

He groped chilly fingers to his head, and felt the great gash in his temple, rough with dried, clotted blood. "Who . . . who has done this?" he gasped.

"Your son, King. But rest easy—you slew him even as he dealt you the blow."

I'm glad of that, anyway, he thought. "It's frightful cold," he said. "My feet are as numb as if they belonged to someone else."

"We'll rest soon," came the voice of the attendant. "When we reach the bank of yonder lake."

He painfully raised his head from the pallet on which he was being carried, and saw ahead a vast, still lake reflecting the full moon. After a while he was set down by his two panting companions, and he could hear water splashing gently among rocks and weeds, and could smell the cold, briny breath of the lake.

"My sword!" he whispered. "Where is it? Did I—"

"Here it is." A heavy hilt was laid in his hand.

"Ah. I'm too weak—one of you must throw it into the lake. It's my last order," he added when they began to protest. Grudgingly, one of them took the sword and strode away through the shadowy underbrush.

He lay on the ground, breathing carefully, wishing his heart wouldn't pound so. My rushing blood is sure to force the wound open again, he thought, and I'll die soon enough even without that.

The attendant came back. "I've done as you said, Sire."

Like hell, he thought. "Oh? And what did you see when you threw it in?"

"See? A splash. And then just ripples."

"Go back, and this time do as I said."

The man shambled away again, confused and embarrassed. It's the jewels in the hilt, the dying man thought. He can't bear to think of them at the bottom of the lake.

The attendant looked subdued and scared when he returned this time. "I did it, Sire."

"What did you see?"

"A hand and arm rose out of the water and caught the sword by the grip, before it could splash, whirled the sword three times in the air, and then withdrew below the surface."

"Ah." He relaxed at last. "Thank you. I want to leave no debts."

A boat rocked at the edge of the water now, and a woman in muddy shoes leaned worriedly over him.

"Our son has killed me," he told her, controlling his chattering teeth long enough to speak the sentence.

"Put him aboard my boat," she said. "He's not long for this world."

He awoke frightened, on a hardwood floor, not daring to move for fear of attracting the notice of something he couldn't name. It was dark, and he didn't want to rouse his memory. Whatever has happened, he thought, whatever this place is, whatever is the name of my enemy—and myself—I'm better off ignorant of them. If I know nothing, admit nothing, acknowledge nothing, perhaps they'll leave me alone at last, and let me sleep. He drifted again into treasured oblivion.

Chapter Thirteen

"INSENSIBLY DRUNK! I expected it, of course. And on my beer, which I daresay you neglected to pay for, eh?"

Duffy opened his eyes and blinked up at Werner. He tried to speak, but produced only a grating moan; which was just as well, since he'd intended to voice only reflexive abuse. The Irishman loathed waking up on the floor, for one couldn't, in that situation, pull the covers up and postpone arising. One had immediately to get up and begin dealing with things.

Getting to his feet proved a little easier than he'd expected. "Shut up, Werner," he said quietly. "Don't mess about in things that don't concern you. And tell one of the girls to bring me a big breakfast." Werner just stared at him, anger growing in his face like a spark on a fur cloak. "Did you even *hear*," Duffy went on, "about the siege gun somebody tried to blow this place up with last night? If it hadn't been for those Vikings in the stable, you and the rest of the city's dogs would right now be scavenging through a rubble pile on this spot." Werner looked only bewildered now. "*Your* beer," Duffy added contemptuously, shambling to his table and collapsing into a chair.

Like a man beaten by bandits who sits up in the ditch later and feels for broken teeth or ribs, the Irishman gingerly prodded his memories. I'm Brian Duffy, he thought with cautious satisfaction, and I'm in love with Epiphany Vogel and employed by Aurelianus. It's the day after Easter, 1529. I'm Brian Duffy, and no one else.

His breakfast and Lothario Mothertongue arrived simultaneously. Duffy concentrated on the former.

"Brian," Mothertongue said, tossing his cloak across

a bench and rubbing his chilly hands together, "the time draws nigh. I am gathering my knights about me once more. And," he smiled graciously, "there is a place for you at my new round table. I heard of your courageous behavior last night." He turned a speculative eye on the Irishman. "Tell me, do you feel anything, any long-lost echoes, when I say the name . . . *Tristan?*"

Duffy, his mouth full, shook his head.

"Are you sure?" Mothertongue went on, his voice tight with an intensity of emotion. "Tristan! *Tristan!*" He leaned forward and shouted in the Irishman's face, "Can your hear me, Tristan?"

Duffy seized a bowl of milk from the table and flung it into Mothertongue's face. "Snap out of it, Lothario," he said.

Mothertongue got to his feet, outraged and dripping. "I was wrong," he hissed. "There's no place in Camelot for you. I don't know who you may once have been, but your soul is now polluted and corrupt, a swamp wherein crawl mind-adders."

Duffy wanted to be angry, but was laughing too hard. "By God," he gasped finally, "it was looking like a gloomy day till you showed up, Lothario! Mind-adders, hey? Ho ho." Mothertongue turned and stalked out of the room.

Shrub came dashing in as Duffy was polishing off the last of his black bread. "Mr. Duffy," he said. "Was there really a swordfight in here last night?"

"No. Not while I was sober enough to notice, anyway."

"There was a Turkish bomb out back, though, wasn't there?"

"I guess you could say so. How does the yard look this morning?"

"Like a battlefield. That burned-up wagon is sitting right in the middle like a black whale-skeleton, and there's dried blood on the cobblestones, and Mr. Wendell's leather shop and warehouse are kicked to bits. He's real mad. Says Aurelianus is going to pay through the nose." The image obviously impressed Shrub.

"Ah. No other damages, I trust?"

"No. Well, some kids were up on the roof, I think. Messing around."

"Kids? Did you see them?"

"No, but there's little faces carved all over the roof, and stars and crosses and Latin words written in chalk on the walls."

"Well, get a couple of the other boys, fill some buckets and climb up there and wash as much of it off as you can, will you? I suppose——"

"No, don't, Shrub," interrupted Aurelianus, who had padded up behind Duffy's chair. "Leave those markings alone, and don't let anyone try to clean them off."

"Yes, sir," Shrub nodded, and darted through the kitchen door, eager to leave with the easier order.

Duffy looked up as Aurelianus pulled out the bench Mothertongue had vacated; the old man was paler than usual, but his eyes glittered with extraordinary vitality, and his black clothes seemed to fit his narrow frame better today. "May I sit down?" he asked.

"Of course. Why leave those drawings on the walls?"

"Why leave your armor on in a fight?" He let out a bark of laughter. "After all the trouble you and I went to, down below, to summon guards, do you want to erase their warding marks? Be satisfied with human adversaries—you wouldn't want to take on the . . . creatures that are repelled by those runes and cantrips and faces."

"Oh." The Irishman scowled. "Well, for matter of that, I don't feel like taking anybody on, these days."

Aurelianus laughed again, as if Duffy had made a joke. "Eat up, there," he said. "I figure you and I can ride out this morning and bring the King inside."

"An interesting idea," said the Irishman, "but no, I'm afraid not this morning. I don't feel well, and I'm supposed to visit Epiphany's crazy old father." Actually he had no plans for the morning, and would have preferred nearly any activity to calling on the old painter—especially after having suffered those lake-hallucinations at his boarding house three days ago—but he wanted to test Aurelianus, see how much latitude and freedom his new position was to allow him.

"Well, I guess it doesn't matter too much," said the old sorcerer with a shrug.

Duffy was pleased. I'm my own man at last, he thought.

"That's Gustav Vogel, isn't it?" Aurelianus asked suddenly. "I remember him. He did me quite a service at one time—it's one reason I'm helping his poor daughter. Is he doing any paintings these days?"

Duffy thought about it. He couldn't remember the old artist working on anything but that pen-and-ink wall drawing. "No . . ." he began.

"I didn't think so," interrupted Aurelianus, who seemed to have no patience with slow speech this morning. "But this is beside the point. I told you I've got a sword to replace the one you broke two days ago; come up to my room now and take a look at it."

"You can't bring it down here?"

Aurelianus was already on his feet. "No," he said cheerfully.

Duffy stood and began unsteadily to follow the old man up the stairs. The action reminded him of having seen Aurelianus with Giacomo Gritti the night before, and he halted. "Didn't you tell me in Venice that you can't speak Italian?" he asked suspiciously.

"Why are you stopping? I don't know; I may have. Why?"

"What's your connection with Giacomo Gritti? Or Jock, as you call him now? I saw you chatting with him last night. You had better tell me the truth this time, too."

"Oh, you saw us? He's been in my employ for years. His name's not really Gritti, by the way. It's Tobbia. I have to have a lot of agents in that area—Venice, the Vatican. And I do speak Italian. If I told you I didn't, though, I'm sure I had some good reason." He took another step up.

"Not so fast. If he works for you, why did he and his 'brothers' try to kill me the night I met you?"

"Honestly, Brian, can't you trust me? I told them to provoke a fight with you so that I'd have an excuse to speak to you and offer you the job you now have. And they weren't really trying to kill you. I'd instructed them to make the skirmish look convincing, but to deliver no real, damaging blows. Besides, I knew you could take care of yourself. Now come on."

He got three steps higher before the Irishman's hand on his shoulder stopped him again. "What if I'd delivered a real, damaging blow to one of them? And what do you—"

"If you'd killed one of them," Aurelianus interrupted impatiently, "I'd simply have phrased my proposal to you differently. Instead of praising your tolerant restraint in a fight, I'd have complimented you on your decisive, no-nonsense reactions. It doesn't matter. There are much more important—"

"It matters to me. And what do you mean, you knew I could take care of myself? I thought that evening was the first time you'd seen or heard of me. Why did you go to so much trouble to get *me* here, when there must have been a dozen guys in Vienna alone that could do the job better than I can? Damn it, I want some explanations that don't raise a hundred more questions. I—"

Aurelianus sighed. "I will," he said, "explain all when we get to my room."

Duffy squinted suspiciously at him. "All?"

The old man looked vaguely offended as they resumed their ascent of the stairs. "I'm a man of my word, Brian."

Aurelianus' room at the Zimmermann Inn looked very like his room in Venice. It was a clutter of tapestries, books, scrolls, jewelled daggers, colored liquids in glass jars, odd sextant-like devices, and a cabinet of good wines. The curtains were drawn against the morning brightness, and the chamber was inefficiently lit by a half-dozen candles. The air was close and musty.

"Sit down," he said, waving Duffy to the only chair free of piled clothing. Aurelianus lifted from a small box another of his dried snakes, bit the end of the tail off and lit the thing in a candle flame. Soon he was seated on the floor, leaning against a bookcase and puffing smoke contentedly.

"I'll try to start from some sort of beginning," he said. "I've mentioned that this brewery is, in a sense, the heart of the West, and the tomb of an ancient king whom your Vikings are not entirely incorrect in calling Balder. Suleiman is the spearhead of the eastern half of the world, which is trying to strike at us now, while we're in a state of discord and weakness."

"Which is because the Western King isn't well . . . ?" Duffy hazarded.

"Right. Or else he's not well because his kingdom is unsteady. It's the same thing, really. Cure one and you've cured the other. And he'll be strengthened and renewed in six months, come the drawing of the Dark. Suleiman, knowing that, is going to try to destroy this brewery, and take Vienna into the bargain, before then. Before long Ibrahim will make some efforts, I expect, to send supernatural combatants down on us, but the elf-signs and faces on the walls should guard us from that. See that Shrub keeps those markings from being cleaned off.

"Anyway, this is a . . . dire pass we've come to. The East has flexed her sword-arm against a number of our eastern outposts, and is now limbering up for a lunge directly toward the heart, while the west languishes in defenseless chaos. Observing the seeds of this situation many years ago, our Fisher King made a tremendous request of the gods. God, if you prefer the singular." He took a long, popping draw on the snake, and puffed out a startling succession of smoke-rings.

Duffy pressed his lips together and shifted in his seat. "What request?"

"To return, for a while, the greatest leader the West ever had. To loan us one hero from the domains of death long enough to parry this eastern threat. The request was granted . . . and the man was born again, dressed in flesh once more."

"Uh," Duffy said hesitantly, "who is he?"

"He's remembered by a number of names. The one you'd know best is Arthur. King Arthur."

"Oh no!" Duffy burst out. "Wait a moment—are you trying to tell me there's truth in Lothario Mothertongue's babblings? All this round-table-and-Camelot stuff he's always spouting? Listen, if he's King Arthur, the one these fool gods have sent to save us, the Turks will have taken Vienna by the end of next week."

"There *is* some truth in his babbling," Aurelianus said. "But no, relax, he's not Arthur. He must be a powerfully sensitive clairvoyant, though, to have grasped the situation unaided and come directly to Vienna. It's very sad, really." He shrugged. "Many are called, but few are chosen."

Suddenly Duffy suspected where all this was leading. Well, he thought, let the old bastard say it. "So who is Arthur?" he asked carelessly. "You?"

"Good heavens, no." The old man laughed and took another long pull on the snake, making the head glow nearly white. "I'm coming to it; let me unravel the story in order. It was my job to find this reincarnated Arthur, for I knew—by certain signs and meteorological phenomena—*when* he was born, but not where. I began searching the western lands for him about twenty years ago, when he'd have been in his mid-twenties. I found traces, psychic footprints, of him in a number of countries, but the long years passed—"

"Did you find him?" Duffy asked.

"Well, yes, to omit a lengthy but fascinating tale."

"And," said Duffy tiredly, feeling like a participant in some ritual dialogue, "where is he?"

Aurelianus puffed on the snake and stared curiously at the Irishman. "Sitting in the chair across from me."

"You mean me?"

"Yes. Sorry."

The Irishman started snickering, and it built up to a laughing fit that lasted half a minute, at the end of which time his eyes were wet with tears and he'd begun to twist the straw plug out of a bottle of Spanish red wine. "This is certainly my week," he observed, a little hysterically. "First those northmen decide I'm Sigmund, and now you tell me I'm Arthur."

"They're two names for the same person. Didn't you ever even wonder about the parallel between Arthur demonstrating his right to the throne by being the only man able to pull the sword from the stone, and Sig-

mund proving his by being the only one who could
pull Odin's sword out of the Branstock Oak?" He
nodded. "Obviously there's another true clairvoyant
in Denmark somewhere, who sent Bugge and his men
here so unerringly."

"God help us," Duffy said, adding with some sar-
casm, "Were they correct also, then, in assuming
you're Odin?"

Aurelianus narrowed his eyes mysteriously, then relaxed and grinned. "Well, no. That was an excess of
religious enthusiasm on their part. Helpful, though."

Duffy felt vaguely nauseated, and blamed it on the
snake fumes. He'd got the plug out of the bottle, but
now couldn't imagine drinking any of the wine. I don't
care if I *was* Arthur in that lake-dream last night, he
thought, I'm Brian Duffy now and I'll not have my
identity usurped by some old dead king. He looked at
the litter surrounding him in the artificially dimmed
room. I'm *not* a part of this morbid, dusty, sorcerous
world, he told himself insistently.

"That, of course," Aurelianus was saying, "is why
the dwarfs and mountain creatures protected you—
they knew who you were, even though you didn't yourself. And that's why Ibrahim tried to prevent your
arrival here by sending winged afrits, and having his
lackey Zapolya send conventional assassins, to inter-
cept you. When he failed to kill you he tried to bribe
you over to the eastern side. The offer of the sultanate,
I believe, was genuine."

The little black-clad man hopped to his feet, opened
a cabinet and groped in its dark interior. "Here," he
said softly, lifting out a long, straight sword and handing it to the Irishman. Duffy stared at it; it was longer
and heavier than the swords he was used to, and the
hilt, above a grip long enough for two hands, was a
simple crosspiece.

Memories now rushed vehemently through his mind,
uncontrollable. Calad Bolg, he thought, the sword remembered in the legends as Excalibur. He recognized
it also from his dream—it was the sword he'd ordered
his attendant to throw into the lake—and from other
dreams he'd had during his life, all of which he'd for-

gotten upon awakening, but which came back to him now. I've killed quite a few men with this, he thought, many long years ago. I killed Mordred, my son, with it.

"You recognize it." There was only a hint of a question-mark at the end of Aurelianus' sentence.

"Of course," Duffy nodded sadly. "But what about Brian Duffy?"

"You're still Brian Duffy. As much as you ever were. But you're Arthur, too, and that kind of outshines everything else. Brandy and water tastes more like brandy than water, after all."

"I suppose so." He hefted the sword and tried a ponderous cut-and-thrust, chopping a notch in the cabinet. "It's awful heavy," he said, "and I like a fuller guard. Swordplay has changed since the days when this was forged. They . . . we . . . wore heavy armor then, and swords weren't used for defense."

"It's a good sword," Aurelianus protested.

"Certainly, to hang on a wall or chop trees down with. But if I were going to use this in combat, I'd want the blade narrowed and shortened by at least a foot, the grip shortened by five inches, and a solid bell-guard welded around this crosspiece."

"Are you out of your mind? That's the finest sword ever made. I don't think you *could* shorten the blade— that isn't everyday steel, you know."

"I remember how well it hews armor. But we never parried in those days, just traded axe-type blows until one guy's armor gave way. I'd take a swing at someone now with this, and he'd disengage and put his point in my nose before I'd even begun to swing mine back in line. I think I'd be more comfortable with a regular rapier, thanks. Save this for scything wheat."

Aurelianus was outraged. "This is the most foolish thing I've ever heard. It's Calad Bolg, damn it! Show some respect."

Duffy nodded, acknowledging the reproach. "Sorry. I'll take it out back and try a few passes at a fence post."

"Fine. In about an hour we'll ride out for the King."

Duffy nodded and turned to leave, then halted and

spun to face Aurelianus again. "You . . . wore your·
hair longer then. And you had a beard."

The old man laughed softly and nodded. "Your
memory is clearing, Arthur."

"Yes." At the door Duffy paused, and said over his
shoulder, "You used to be a much calmer man,
Merlin."

"Times were simpler then," Aurelianus nodded
sadly.

The Irishman slowly picked his way back down the
stairs. He felt as if the walls and roofs of his mind
were being shaken, and falling away here and there to
reveal an older landscape. But those walls and hall-
ways are what's Brian Duffy, he thought mournfully.
And now that I can remember both lives, I can see
I've had much more enjoyment and relaxation as Duffy
than I did as Arthur.

At the bottom of the stairs he stopped. I may be . . .
this primordial king, he thought, but by God I'll live
in the crumbling personality that is Brian Duffy. And I
won't carry this sword; the very sight and feel of it are
impacts against those poor mind-walls.

He bounded back up the stairs and rapped on
Aurelianus' door with the sword's pommel. The sorcerer pulled the door open, surprised to see him back
so soon. "What is it?" he asked.

"I . . . I don't want this sword. I'll get another somewhere. Here." Aurelianus just stared at him. "Look,"
Duffy insisted, almost tearfully, "You'd better take
it, or I'll pitch it into the canal—or that moonlit lake
next time I come across it," he added, half to himself.

At that Aurelianus paled and reeled back. "What?
What moonlit lake? Llyr help us, it's only April! Tell
me."

The Irishman was surprised by this response. "Don't
get excited," he said. "To tell you the truth, I think
it's probably just an alcohol-hallucination. I'm sure
it's nothing to—"

"Tell me."

"—get upset about . . . Oh, very well. Twice on, uh,
Friday, in the middle of the day, I saw very clearly—

even felt the cold wind of it—a wide lake under a full moon. And then—"

"Who were you with?" Aurelianus snapped. "You must have been with some doomed or dying person, for whom death's door was already ajar."

Duffy was impressed and uneasy. "Yes, I was. Epiphany's father, as a matter of fact."

The sorcerer looked a little relieved. "I hoped it was something like that. What you were seeing in these . . . visions? . . . was—"

"It was where King Arthur died," Duffy said.

"How did you know that?" exclaimed the sorcerer, upset again.

"Because last night I saw it again, much clearer and for a longer time. I was a wounded, dying king being carried to the marge of this lake. I had one of my few remaining retainers throw my sword—this sword —into the water, and he said a hand rose from the water to catch it. Then there was a boat I was being lifted into, and my sister was in it, and I told her our son—*our* son?—had killed me."

The wizard was gaping at him in dismay. "Even having remembered Arthur's life, you shouldn't yet be able to see the end of it. Where were you when you saw this one, and who were you with?"

Duffy didn't want to admit having stolen a cupful of the Dark, so he just shrugged and said, "I was alone. In the dining room after everyone went to bed."

Aurelianus fell into the one uncluttered chair. "This is terrible," he muttered. "Something is fast approaching, something your mind can recognize only in terms of that lakeside memory. The last time this thing came, you see, that's the form it took." He looked up. "In other words, the spirit that is Arthur will shortly be returning to . . . death, Avalon, the afterlife."

Duffy raised his eyebrows. "Where does that leave me?"

"I don't know, damn it. Probably dead, since of course when you die his spirit would automatically be forced to go."

"Great. Couldn't Arthur make his exit and leave me alive?"

"Choose to leave, you mean, without being evicted from your body by your death? I suppose so. Though you'd probably die anyway, of psychic shock from the mental amputation."

The Irishman was not as frightened as he would have been if he didn't know that last night's vision had been prompted more by the cup of Dark than the imminency of death, Arthur's or his own or both; but this was still far from reassuring news. "Well, why the hell don't you know any of this?" he demanded angrily. "You're a sorcerer, aren't you, a wizard, a witch-doctor, a scrutinizer of chicken entrails? Fine! Haul out your crystal ball and take a look! *See* if I survive all this."

"You have no idea how much I wish I could," Aurelianus said, in quiet contrast to Duffy's shouting. "The fact, though, is that all auguries and portents are blind to our current situation and the coming battle. I don't like it at all—it appalls me to think that Zapolya could have been so near and so well-informed without my having any indication of it; and to realize that he could be *anywhere* right now with, not impossibly, a force of armed men at his disposal. You can see why we've got to get the King safely inside immediately."

The wizard shook his head, staring at the old sword. "For fifteen hundred years all the precognitive arts have been gradually dimming out, like vision as twilight falls; they're all based, you see, on the old Chaldean principles of astrology, which relied on the existence of predictable courses, a predetermined world history. And they did work well for thousands of years. But in the last fifteen centuries the equations of predestination have been increasingly fouled by an element of . . . randomness, or something I can only perceive as randomness . . . " His voice trailed off. His eyes were on the sword, but his gaze had turned inward.

The Irishman thought about it, then shrugged. "I'm afraid I'm on the side of the randomness. The idea of predestination, lack of free will, disgusts me. Astrology, in fact, has always disgusted me. And I think you picked the wrong picture to illustrate your point—it doesn't sound to me like a man's vision dimming as night approaches, so much as an owl's when the sun rises."

Aurelianus' face slowly wrinkled itself into a wry smile. "I'm afraid," he admitted, "your analogy *is* better. Ibrahim and I, and Bacchus, and your mountain guides, and your winged adversaries of the other night, are creatures of the long, brutal night of the world. You and the Fisher King are creatures of the coming day, and you can't really feel at home in this pre-dawn dimness. In any case, to return to my point, though the prescient arts are deteriorating, they've still got a clear century or two of effectiveness left. I, in common with a lot of other beings, am accustomed to relying on them as you do on your eyes and ears. But in *this* conflict, this problem of Vienna and the beer and Arthur and Suleiman, they're completely in the dark, blinded."

Duffy raised his eyebrows. "And what is so bright about any light here that it should so dazzle all you cellar-denizens?"

Aurelianus was getting annoyed. "Don't run it into the ground," he snapped. "It's because you are or will be centrally involved in it all. You're an anomaly, a phenomenon not allowed for by the natural laws, and therefore you and your actions are unreadable ciphers to the old natural magics."

At this the Irishman brightened. "Really? Then you don't have any idea of what I'm going to do?"

"Well, I do have clues," Aurelianus allowed. "Indications. But in the main, no—I can't see you or the things you affect."

Duffy reached across a table and with two fingers snagged the bottle he'd opened earlier. He took a liberal sip from the neck and put it back. "Good enough. I'll be downstairs whenever you want to leave." He picked his way around the ornate obstacles and again left the room.

Chapter Fourteen

"EPIPHANY!" he yelled when he reached the dining room. "Damn it, *Epiphany!*" There's no reason for me to obey that old monkey, he thought. Why should I trust him? He's never had my genuine interests at heart; he's always just used me like a chess-piece in his filthy wizardly schemes. Trusting Merlin is like giving a migrant scorpion a lift inside your hat.

Epiphany stood in the kitchen doorway, wiping her hands with a towel and staring at him worriedly. "What is it, Brian?" she asked.

"Get some travelling clothes and any cash you've saved—we're leaving this minute. I'll go saddle a couple of horses."

Dawning hope put a youthful brightness in her smile. "You mean it? Really?"

"I do. Hurry up, the little sorcerer may try to stop us."

He snatched his cloak from a hook and strode through the kitchen to the stableyard. "Shrub!" he yelled, blinking in the sudden daylight. "Saddle up my horse, and one for Epiphany. We're going for a ride."

He took a hurried step toward the stable, and tripped over a charred board; snarling a curse, he put out his hands to catch himself.

His hands and aching head plunged into the dark, icy water, but a moment later soft arms had pulled him back from the gunwale and gently lowered him onto a seat, and the boat soon stopped rocking. Terribly weak, he slumped back onto some kind of cushion, and lay there gasping, staring up at the stars and the moon in the deep black sky.

"Are you all right, Mr. Duffy?" Shrub sounded worried.

The Irishman rolled over on the sun-warmed cobbles and brushed dry ashes out of his face and hair. "Hm?

Yes, Shrub, I'm all right." Looking past the boy, he could see several of the northmen grinning at him. He got to his feet and rubbed bits of grit out of his abraded palms.

"I'll go saddle your horses, then," the boy said.

"Uh, no . . . thank you, Shrub, I've . . . changed my mind." A weighty depression had emptied his heart of everything else: enthusiasm, hope, and even fear. I was out on the lake, he thought, and without a sip of the Dark this time to prompt it. Hell, I can't run off with what's-her-name if I'm going to be dead in a few months, and probably insane long before that. Besides, I can't disobey Merlin, my old teacher. I've known him much longer than I've known this woman. Women are unreliable anyway—didn't Gwenhwyfar run off with my best friend? No, that was Epiphany . . . well, both of them . . .

Epiphany's voice interrupted his confused thoughts. "I'm ready, Brian! How's that for hurrying?"

With some effort he turned and stared at the gray-haired woman standing in the back doorway. "What?"

"I'm ready to go! Are the horses saddled?"

"No. I'm sorry, Piff, I don't seem to be able . . . we can't go. I can't leave. It's impossible to explain."

She let drop the bundle she'd been holding, and glass broke inside. "Do you mean we're not going?"

"Yes. That's what I mean." Enunciating words seemed dreadfully tiresome. "I'm sorry," he managed to add.

Her face was stiff. "Then when will we? You said in a few weeks . . . " The new tears on her cheeks glistened in the morning sun.

"I can't leave. I'll die in Vienna. Try to understand, Piff, my will doesn't have enough strength in this, it's like trying to swim clear of a whirlpool."

He stopped talking then, for she had turned away from him and trudged with heavy footsteps back into the dimness of the kitchen.

When Aurelianus came outside several minutes later, uncharacteristically dressed in a long woolen tunic, black tights and a tall sugar-loaf hat, he found Duffy sitting in the shade of the kitchen wall with his head in his hands. The sorcerer pursed his lips and hefted the half-dozen rattling swords that were cradled awkwardly in the crook of his left arm.

"What, lad?" he said chidingly. "Moping here, in the early morning when there's work for all of us to be doing? Up! Melancholy is best indulged at night, over wine."

Duffy exhaled sharply, and was surprised to find he'd been holding his breath. He stood up smoothly, without using his hands. "Not the way the nights have been around here lately," he said, and smiled bleakly. "Horror and fear and rage get a lot of indulgence, but melancholy needs more quiet surroundings." He peered at the old man. "Why all the swords? Are you going to conjure up an octopus to come with us?"

"I figured we might as well bring your northmen along," Aurelianus explained, crossing the yard to dump the swords with an echoing clatter into the bed of a large wagon. "How many of them have their own weapons?"

"I don't know. Most of them."

"These will be enough to make sure everyone is armed, then. I even brought Calad Bolg for you."

"If it comes to it, I'll use a plain rapier, thanks," Duffy said. "No guns?"

"I'm afraid not, what with the King being involved."

"He doesn't approve of them?"

"No."

"Huh." Duffy, though leery of the innovative firearms himself, shook his head wonderingly. "Well, I hope we don't run up against someone who *does* approve of them."

"Why don't you see if you can coax those beery Aesir into the wagon," the sorcerer suggested, "while I get the lads to harness up a couple of horses."

Twenty minutes later the crowded wagon creaked and bounced out of the city through the west gate; once outside, they were soon deserted by the gang of prancing, cheering boys that had accumulated around the vehicle during the ride from the Zimmermann Inn. Guided by Aurelianus, the horses picked their way through the unpaved lanes between the livestock pens and were soon trotting briskly through open meadows of new spring grass, along the only wide track that led over the near hills and up into the dense Wienerwald, the Vienna woods.

When they had traversed perhaps a mile, the wizard slowed the horses and yanked the reins so that they'd step over the shallow ditch on the right side of the path. Then the wagon lurched and rocked up a patchily shadowed slope, between occasional twisted trees. Twice they got stuck, and both times Duffy and the northmen climbed out, wrestled a wheel free of some entanglement, and laboriously gave the vehicle a gasping, back-wrenching shove to give the horses a little slack in which to get moving. Finally they had crested the first hill and were precariously teetering down the far side; Aurelianus was leaning ineffectually on the back brake, and the wagon would have rolled over the horses and tumbled into the narrow ravine if Duffy hadn't flipped the old wizard over backward into the packed northmen and borne down on the brake himself.

"You just call directions, huh?" the Irishman shouted, angry at having been scared.

Aurelianus stood up in the wagon bed and leaned his elbows on the back of the driver's bench. "Sorry," he said. "I never brought a wagon here before. That's right, kind of slant it across the slope. And then take it between those two big oaks."

"Right." The northmen bunched up on the uphill side of the wagon and leaned parallel to the slope, while Duffy did some tricky work with brake and reins.

The wagon's shadow, which had been stretched out in front of it across the damp, grassy earth, abruptly swung around like the boom of a jibing sailboat; in a moment it lay almost directly behind them, and the morning sun was in Duffy's eyes. He gasped and locked the brake. "What the hell happened?" he exclaimed. "Did we hit slippery mud? I didn't feel anything."

"Keep going," Aurelianus said. "You're still on course. Pay no attention to any whirling effects—they're just a few local direction-confusion and disorientation spells I laid down a number of years ago."

"Oh." It occurred to Duffy that this would not only make it difficult to get into the area, but difficult also to get out, especially in a panicky haste. He glanced furtively to both sides, looking for skeletons of any wayfarers who might have blundered into this wall-less labyrinth. He didn't see any bones, but, glancing up, he did see figures circling high in the air—figures he thought were hawks until he looked more steadily and saw the manlike forms between the vast wings. He quickly snapped his gaze back to the landscape ahead, uneasy to think that it was he who had called those things out of their deep retreat.

He sneaked a glance over his shoulder to see how Bugge and his men were taking these outré phenomena, and was surprised to see no dismay or fear in their faces. Several were watching the fliers, but all seemed tensely cheerful. Bugge grinned at the Irishman and muttered something in Norse, so Duffy grinned back and raised a clenched fist before returning his attention to the horses. Well, why should I be worried, he thought; nobody else is.

They proceeded for another hour into the wooded hills, and three more times the sun did its trick of shifting about in the sky. The whole adventure had by this time taken on a dreamlike unreality to the Irishman, and if the wagon had rolled up across the side of the sky, swerving between clouds, he would not have thought it incongruous.

Finally the wagon bumped down through a narrow, greenery-roofed tunnel, in which gravity for one awful moment seemed to be pulling upward, and emerged into a small glade.

For a moment Duffy just sat, clutching the edges of the seat and trying to get his bearings—that last bit of sorcery had convinced him that the wagon was going into a forward tumble—then he opened his eyes and saw the cabin.

It was a low, thatch-roofed, stone-walled, one-storey affair, and could credibly have been five years old or five hundred. He glanced questioningly at Aurelianus, who nodded. "This is the place," the wizard said.

Duffy bounded over the side onto the grass. "Let's

get him and get the hell out of these woods, then. Bugge! Come on, drag your lads out of there! There's work to be done, old kings to be carried about!"

"This is entirely the wrong spirit," Aurelianus protested, climbing down beside the Irishman. "Now listen, there's a question you must ask and one you mustn't, so—"

"Damn it, I'll ask any questions that occur to me, and none that don't. Come on, now, lead the way. You're the one that knows him, after all." He strode toward the cabin with the sorcerer scurrying alongside and the stolid northmen bringing up the rear.

"All this is difficult enough," Aurelianus complained, "without you acting like a damned—"

"What did you think you were going to get, when you . . . placed your order for me? A tame, all-powerful giant who'd cheerfully jump at your every order? If so, you made a mistake—you didn't want King Arthur, you wanted a village idiot."

The sorcerer threw up his hands. "Maybe you've got a point and maybe you haven't," he said. "Quiet now, here we are." He rapped respectfully on the thick oaken door, and a faint voice answered within. Frowning a warning at Duffy, Aurelianus opened the door and led the way inside.

Duffy followed, and was surprised; he had expected to see the same depressing gloom that cloaked Aurelianus' chamber at the inn, and the same sort of ominous and ill-smelling objects scattered carelessly about. Instead he saw a pleasant, sunlit room, aired by two open windows; the only jarring note was several handfuls of mud caked on the foot of the bed. The Irishman didn't look at the man in the bed, but turned to his northmen and, with expressive grunts, began pantomiming the act of lifting the occupant and carrying him outside. It looked as if he were imitating a careless furniture mover.

"Brian," came a weak but humorous voice from behind him. "Surely it's Brian Duffy?"

Duffy turned and looked at the King, who was sitting up in the bed. He was clean-shaven, though his white hair hung down around his shoulders, and his face was seamed with what the Irishman thought must have been centuries of experience. Aside from the bandage around his hips, he didn't appear to be in bad shape.

Then Duffy met his gaze, and to his own surprise remembered having met and talked to the old man, decades ago, while out on a boyhood ramble along the banks of the Liffey. "Hello, sir," Duffy said now. "I thought you lived in Ireland."

"I live in the west."

Aurelianus was surprised and annoyed. "What's this? Why didn't you tell me you'd met him?" he demanded of the King. "I had to search twenty years for him."

"Don't get upset, Merlin." The old monarch smiled. "You've found him now. In any case, I didn't know then who he was—just that he was something considerably more than the average eight-year-old."

Duffy relaxed, and glanced around. On a table beside the bed lay an earthenware cup and a rusty lance head, both of archaic and evidently Mediterranean workmanship. He looked up with a grin, and was a little disconcerted to see expressions of anxious suspense on the faces of the King and Aurelianus. "Uh," Duffy said uncertainly, gesturing at the cup, "I was just going to say that that cup will come in handy when it comes time to . . . have your swig of the beer." He had the feeling he'd unwittingly touched an awkward subject, but he decided he must have dealt with it correctly, for the two old men broke into reassured smiles; and he guessed, without knowing why, that this was the crucial matter Aurelianus had tried to warn him about as they'd been walking to the cabin. Somehow it was fortunate that he'd referred to the cup rather than the lance.

Bugge and his men grasped what was expected of them, and six of them proceeded gently to lift the Fisher King from the bed and hobble toward the door. Aurelianus halted them long enough to put a hat on the aged King, then waved them to go on.

"I don't suppose he can ride?" Duffy asked. "It's going to be cramped in that wagon."

"No, he can't," the sorcerer said. "Even when he's

well, he's not permitted to. There are all sorts of restrictions that apply to him—he can't wear a garment with knots in it, or a ring that's an unbroken circle, he can't touch a dead body or be where one is buried . . . he could never, for example, actually go down into the Zimmermann brewing cellar . . . hell, even that mud on the bed there is a requirement."

Duffy's gray eyebrows were halfway to his hairline. "Huh! That's as bad as all the Old Testament do's and don't's."

"Same kind of thing," said Aurelianus, moving toward the door.

The Irishman followed him outside. "How *did* you find me?" he asked. "I gather Venice wasn't the first place you looked."

The wizard sighed. "It certainly wasn't. Anyone else I could have located in two hours by thaumaturgical means, but, as I told you, you're a walking blind-spot where those arts are concerned. So I simply had to travel about and look for you. You did leave indications of your passage here and there, which helped, but my real clue was a painting I found two years ago here in Vienna—*Michael the Archangel* by Gustav Vogel, which you were the model for."

"That's right," Duffy said. "That was in 1512 or 13; he liked my face or something, and I liked his daughter. And I was recuperating from a wound and had nothing much else to do."

The northmen had got the King to the wagon and were carefully raising him toward the back of it. Aurelianus seemed satisfied, for he didn't rush over to criticize their efforts. "Yes," he said reflectively, "Vogel, in spite of being deeply religious—or because of it, conceivably—apparently recognized what sort of . . . thing . . . you are, and put it so clearly onto the canvas that I recognized you from it. He is allied with the new power in the world, the dawning day, if you prefer, which is blinding all the old magics, and—"

"Do you mean the Church?"

"More or less. And so he could recognize you more easily than I could. He has a real clairvoyant spark—it's too bad he's given up painting."

"It certainly is," agreed Duffy, without conviction. "Look, they've got him in the wagon. Hadn't we better be going?"

"I guess we should," said the wizard, starting across the grass. "It's so pleasant out here, though."

Duffy, who felt more comfortable in crowded, tangled city streets, where, for one thing, gravity was consistent and the sun moved slowly along a predictable course, didn't concur, but said nothing and followed Aurelianus to the wagon.

The first ten minutes of the return trip passed quietly enough. Duffy again drove, and was almost beginning to get used to the tricks of the enchanted environment. A half-dozen of the northmen got out of the vehicle and paced alongside, kicking stones and branches out of the way of the wheels and giving the Irishman directions by pounding on the wagon's sides. The only disconcerting note was one he should have expected: the high-flying sentinels no longer circled over the cabin, but swung in wide arcs several hundred feet directly overhead. "Those things are pacing us," he remarked quietly to Aurelianus.

"You're damned right they are," the wizard said with a pleased nod.

For several minutes then neither of them spoke, and the creak and rattle of the wagon, and the chatter of birds, were the only sounds.

Duffy had just wiped his forehead with his sleeve when he saw three of the winged guards stoop like striking falcons out of the sky, plummeting toward a point in the woods not far ahead. "Look out," he snapped, sitting up straight, "I think someone followed us through your web of direction-confusion spells."

For a while those were the last words he was to speak in German. He turned, and seemed to see Bugge and his men for the first time. "Viking, rush ten of your men into the trees ahead," he barked, using an archaic Norse dialect, "and have them conceal themselves on both sides of the path. Now!"

Bugge had heard that style of speech used by the very old folk in the Roskilde hills, and understood it well enough to follow the order. He snapped a quick phrase of clarification to his men, took in ten of them with a wave, and leaped over the side of the cart, followed a second later by the men he'd designated. Screams and sword-clangs had begun to sound from the woods ahead.

"You three take the King out of the chariot," Duffy went on, and three northmen leaped up to obey him. "Lay him down by the side of the path, out of sight; then race back here." He turned to Aurelianus and spoke in Dumnoiic Celtic, "Go, Merlin. Stay with the King."

"Of course, Sire," the sorcerer answered in the same tongue. He climbed down and followed the burdened northmen, who sprinted back to the wagon a few moments later.

The Irishman rummaged among the swords piled in the wagon bed as the three men clambered aboard, and sat back up with the heavy hilt of Calad Bolg in his fist. He whirled the long blade once in the air and stung the horses' flanks with a snap of the reins. As the wagon surged forward he snarled up into the sky, "Ride with us, Morrigan, and rend these dogs limb from socket!"

A tight knot of yelling men burst out of the forest just in time for Duffy's hard-driven wagon to plow into them; at least two went down under the horses' hooves, and then the Irishman and the ten northmen in the cart vaulted into the mêlée, swords swinging, while Bugge and his men charged in from behind the trees on both sides.

Landing on his feet, Duffy swept several extended swords out of line with a momentous flail of Calad Bolg, and his shoulder-straining return stroke cut one man nearly in half; the others fell back, frightened, for the real use of the longsword had been a lost art for at least a century. The Irishman, though, waded in with the thing, whirling it in deft parries and devastating ripostes as if he'd used one all his life.

A furious crashing and snapping sounded in the tree branches above, and Duffy's force was joined by five of the winged sentinels. Appalling when seen at close range with their long, tusked muzzles and fish-like eyes, they flapped heavily to and fro in the clearing, tearing at the heads of the opposite force, and twice lifted a man a dozen yards in the air to tear at him with tooth and claw before releasing the mangled body to fall back into the press.

John Zapolya, loitering toward the rear, deflected with his dagger the sword of one of the northmen, and put his own rapier-point into the man's neck. As the body fell away he stepped back and looked quickly around him. This was a disaster. He'd have to flee if reinforcements didn't arrive within seconds—

Then, as he looked over the warriors' heads toward the northeast, a hard smile narrowed his eyes. "Hang on, men!" he shouted to his panicky band of renegade Hungarians. "Here come some of our own!"

Duffy turned around just in time to parry a scimitar wielded by a swooping creature of the same species, though of obviously different allegiance, as the things that were decimating the Hungarians. It blocked his riposte, but the force of the blow flung the creature flat on the ground, and it thrashed once and then went limp in death; and before the next one came at him he had a second to notice the stilt-soled sandals on the thing's misshapen feet.

The battle was joined in deadly earnest now, and retreat was no one's option any longer. An unholy racket compounded of shouts, sword-clangs, inhuman screeches and the flapping of heavy wings crashed away through the trees, as the two forces surged in tangled eddies back and forth, and the airborne warriors tore at each other overhead; sorcerous blue fire snapped and leaped from the spot where Aurelianus defended the King against three of the afrits. Noticing this last development, Duffy chopped and hewed his way back through the chaos of struggling bodies toward the King. With the longsword he was wreaking tremendous damage on the Hungarians, who, on the uneven and crowded ground, could not bring into play the natural advantages of their newer, lighter rapiers.

Another figure was angling through the press toward Aurelianus' position, and Antoku Ten-no was cutting nearly as wide a swath as Duffy. The Oriental wielded a long, two-handed sword of alien design and was, like the Irishman, managing to keep out of any close, *corps-à-corps* confrontations that would put him at the mercy of a short dagger. And when Duffy caught the blade of one of the Hungarians low and split his skull with the answering stroke, it was Antoku alone who stood between him and the embattled Aurelianus.

The eyes of the Oriental lit with recognition, though Duffy's registered no more than one competent warrior's quick appraisal of another. "Ah, now, darling of the west," hissed Antoku, "what—*ahh!*" He hopped backward and managed to catch a jarring cut on his hilt, and a moment later to deflect over his head a backhanded remise.

Evidently angry at not being listened to, he swung in with a roundhouse chop at Duffy's ribs. Duffy yanked his hilt down to belt level and let the Oriental's sword rebound ringingly from the upright blade, and then he lunged forward.

Antoku's face had one instant to gape in horror before the fiercely driven edge sheared half of it away. As the body crumpled, the Irishman paused only long enough to strike off the maimed head before running forward toward Aurelianus and the King.

The crouching sorcerer was desperately flinging his arms about, directing the bolts of blue light that were jumping, ever more weakly, from the ground up toward the three hovering, flapping devils, whose claws and scimitars licked hungrily down at him. The magical lightning appeared to be doing no more now than jolting the creatures, and they were beginning to close in.

"Merlin!" the Irishman shouted hoarsely. "Use it all up in one flash!" He stopped and turned, staring back at the fight.

Falling to his knees, the exhausted sorcerer threw both arms toward the closest afrit, and with a thundering crack a man-thick blast of sunfire arced up from the soil and punched the thing out of the sky.

Duffy turned and leaped even as the first echoes were booming in the trees and Aurelianus was toppling forward onto the ground. Calad Bolg, swung overhead at the apex of the leap, clanked through the spinal column of one of the blinded devils. The thing screeched and thrashed heavily to earth as the Irishman landed bent-kneed and spun away toward the remaining one, which was flapping sightlessly upward, chittering in panic and becoming entangled in the branches. It was out of Duffy's reach, but two of the King's winged guards noticed its plight and, arrowing across the clearing, made short work of the creature.

Leaning on his sword and panting like a bellows, Duffy surveyed the scene: the Hungarian force was routed, and being pursued south toward the Wienerwald track by several of the remaining northmen; the wagon stood where he'd left it, though surrounded now by sprawled corpses, and one of the horses slumped dead in the harness; and Rikard Bugge sat on the grass, humming a tune and knotting a length of blood-spotted cloth around his thigh. Duffy glanced toward the prostrate Fisher King, who smiled wanly and held up two crossed fingers.

Aurelianus got shakily to his feet and leaned against a tree trunk. "That was . . . close to the bone," he gasped, speaking contemporary Austrian again. "You're all right, Brian?"

All right? Duffy thought irritably. Why shouldn't I be all right? Then the sword slipped from his numb fingers and he looked quickly around, suddenly conscious of great fatigue.

"What the hell just happened?" he asked, trying to keep the shrillness of sudden fright out of his voice.

Aurelianus, staring at the battle-debris down the slope, nodded almost absently. "You don't remember."

"No, damn it—the last thing I remember is . . . seeing the flying sentries stoop from the sky."

The sorcerer nodded. "I thought so. It was Arthur who fought here."

Duffy turned, punching a finger toward the magician. "It was *not*," he shouted. "I'll remember in a moment —I've often seen people temporarily lose the memory of something rough, some violent action." Savagely he kicked the hideous foot of the dead afrit, and added, in a whisper, "Which this evidently was." He paced back and forth, pursing his lips as he stepped around the wide burned spot in the grass. "Very well," he snapped finally, pointing down the slope, "who *are* those men?"

"Hungarian, mostly," answered Aurelianus calmly. "I have hopes, though not much confidence, of finding Zapolya's corpse among them. The one halfway up here is Antoku. You apparently killed him."

"Who? Oh, the mandarino? Oh." Duffy shrugged. "I guess that's good."

"Yes."

"What the hell went wrong, anyway, with all your turn-'em-around and get-'em-lost spells?"

The wizard frowned defensively, with a furtive glance down at the King. "Nothing. These lads didn't have the sorcerous talents to penetrate my magical camouflage . . . but I guess they had enough skill in forest-craft to follow someone who did." He had got his breath back now, and stepped briskly away from the trunk. "Round up those of our lads who can stand," he told Duffy, "and get them to carry the King to the wagon. I'd counsel you to jettison the dead horse, too. I'll see to the wounded." To the King he added, "Excuse me, Sire," then he started down the slope.

Duffy stooped to pick up his dropped sword, and noticed which one it was. "Hey," he called after the wizard. "Why was I using this? I thought . . . he and I . . . agreed it was outmoded."

Aurelianus half-turned. "That was when you and he were kind of talking in unison," he called. "I guess when it's him alone, he still prefers it. Good thing I thought to bring it along." He strode onward a few paces, then stooped to examine one of the wounded northmen.

"Take it easy, lad," said the Fisher King to Brian, softly. "I know it's hard. But if it were easy, they'd have got somebody else to do it."

Duffy stared after Aurelianus and shrugged helplessly. "Then it must be easy," he said, "because it certainly looks like they've got somebody else to do it."

BOOK THREE

"And there was a tumult as of great battles out upon the plain that night, and shifting fires no man could explain, and wonders in the sky . . ."

—from the journal of
Kemal Pasha Zadeh,
official scribe to the Sultan
Suleiman el Kanuni

Chapter Fifteen

THE SQUARE OF early afternoon sunlight had shifted a few inches up the plaster wall, and Brian Duffy straightened up a bit more to keep his face clear of it; if he didn't get up and move soon, he knew, he'd have to give up staying above it and slide down almost prostrate on the bench in an attempt to get his face under the dazzling beam instead.

"Do you want one or not?" the young man who stood in the doorway repeated, a little impatiently. He jiggled a tiny gray manlike figure on the end of a string.

Duffy blinked owlishly at him and had a long sip of lukewarm red wine to postpone the effort of answering. The boy is far too elegantly dressed, the Irishman decided. Those baggy blue sleeves, ornamentally slashed to admit puffs of red satin, are good enough for swaggering in front of the ladies, but when it's fighting to be done give me old leather and thick-backed gloves. "Are you going to go out dressed that way?" he asked. "If so, I hope that's your second-best suit." Then, remembering the lad's question, he answered, "No, thank you. I don't need any mandrake roots. I'll just duck and weave and take my chances."

The young landsknecht shook his head dubiously and replaced the ugly little root in his pouch. "It's your life," he conceded. "Say, when were you born?"

Several joking answers occurred to the Irishman, but he was too sleepy to voice them. "Huh?" he contented himself with saying.

"What month were you born in?"

"Uh . . . March."

"Hm." The young man pulled a chart out of his pouch and scrutinized it. "Well, you'd be better off if you were a Libra or a Cancer, but being a Pisces you needn't fear being shot in the feet." He grinned, bowed and walked outside.

"Do you mean it won't happen, or I just shouldn't fear it?" Duffy called after him, but got no reply.

Though he was sitting up as straight as he could, the sun was now lancing at his eyes from the top of the window. Not wanting to be found slouched on his back messily finishing a cup of wine just before combat, he swung his legs down off the bench and stood up and stretched, thus accidentally spilling the rest of the wine onto the dirt floor. Well, he thought, taking it philosophically, it was about time to get ready anyway. He sat down on one of the bunks and pulled on his boots, then stood and picked up his sword, hauberk, doublet and helmet, and walked outside into the shifty and heatless mid-October sunlight.

A series of warehouses in the southeast corner of the city had been hurriedly converted to barracks, and several companies of landsknechten, including Eilif's, were quartered in them. Duffy emerged from the southernmost of them and pushed his way into the mob of mercenary soldiers assembled in a square of the Schwarzenbergstrasse. He found the table at which Eilif's armsmaster was dispensing harquebuses, and took a long-barrelled matchlock and pouches of powder and balls.

"Duff," the old soldier said, "I've got a wheellock back here I was saving. You want to take it?"

"You take it," Duffy told him with a grin. "Last time I tried to fire one of them I got my hair caught in the wheel. Had to retreat waving a sword and dagger, with the damned gun attached to my head."

"*I* won't call you a liar," the man said amiably, handing Duffy several lengths of matchcord.

The Irishman carried all his stuff away to one side of the square and laid it on a curb while he put on his hauberk and leather doublet. Sporadic gunfire popped and spattered from the top of the wall, and he looked up for a moment. That'll be the sharpshooters, he thought, warming up with some long-distance covering fire from rifled guns. He listened, but could hear no answering gunfire from outside the walls. He sat

down and began the task of loading his matchlock.
Vienna had been totally invested by the Turks now for
twelve days.

The young man he'd seen in the barracks, whose
mandrake root dangled now from his belt, ambled up
and watched Duffy's efforts critically. "Your matchcord
is supposed to go through that little metal tube on top
of the barrel," he pointed out helpfully. "So the sparks
from your first shot don't light it in the middle somewhere."

Duffy sat back and grinned up at him, squinting
against the sun. "Well now, that's the first time I ever
heard that," he said gently. "Here I thought that tube
was for grating cheese with, after the battle."

A white-bearded landsknecht who was crouched
several feet away looked up from whetting his sword
and barked a laugh. "If you young calves could grasp
the idea of aiming," he said, "you'd see how that match-
guide can be used as a sight. Hell, Duffy's an old
soldier; he wouldn't let his cord get near the flashpan."

"I've been known to do some beastly things, but
never that," the Irishman agreed.

Guns cracked again along the wall and the young
mercenary jumped, immediately hopping through a
few practice sword-thrusts to disguise the involuntary
motion. An eddy in the breeze brought down to the
street the curried smell of gunpowder. Straightening
and stretching after his extempore exercises, he asked
Duffy offhandedly, "Do you think this is it?"

"Hm? What's what?"

"This sortie this afternoon. You think this'll be the
one that breaks the siege one way or the other?"

The older man laughed scornfully, but Duffy just
smiled and shook his head. "No," he said. "They
know they can't hold that little rise. It's mainly a gesture. So we make another gesture: we run out there
and push them back. Men will be killed, but this won't
be a decisive encounter."

"Well, when *will* there be a decisive encounter?" In
his efforts to keep his expression unconcerned, the lad
had let some hysteria enshrill his voice. "If they back

off, why don't we just keep pushing?" he went on, in a deeper voice. "Or for matter of that, if we fall back, why don't they?"

Duffy carefully laid his loaded gun on the pavement. "Why, because we're old veterans, on both sides. The landsknechten know the wages of hot-headed charges—and those Turks out there are Janissaries, the best fighting men in the East. They're not just fierce, like the akinji or the iayalars; they're smart as well."

"Ah." The young man looked then across the street at the shot-scarred faces of the nearer buildings. "They're . . . *Christians,* aren't they?" he asked. "The Janissaries?"

"Well, they *were,*" Duffy said. "The Turks conscript them from Christian families inside the Ottoman Empire, but they take them before the age of seven. Then they bring them up as the most fanatical Moslems and highest-favored soldiers of the Sultan. They've been baptized, yes, but you couldn't call them Christians any longer."

The lad shuddered. "It's like the old stories of draugs or changelings. To take our own people away, and change them, and then send them back to destroy the place they can no longer even recognize as their fatherland."

"True," agreed Duffy. "The men we'll be shooting at this afternoon could well be the sons of men who fought beside the knights at Belgrade."

"As men further west will be shooting at *our* turbanned sons if we don't turn them back," the young man said. "But we shouldn't have any trouble holding out, should we? I mean even if the Imperial reinforcements don't come?"

"It's a race," Duffy said, "to see which gives out first: our walls or their supplies. At night you can already hear their miners digging away at the foundations underground."

"Defeatist talk!" snapped the white-bearded mercenary, hopping nimbly to his feet and whirling his newly sharpened sword in a whistling circle over his head. "It takes a besieging force a hell of a lot longer to undermine a city's walls than to shatter them down with big guns. You'll notice they've got nothing but light cannon out there—good for arcing over the walls to break windows and knock in a few roofs, but useless for battering a way inside. Fix your mind on what a lucky thing it's been that the heavy rains these past months forced the Turks to leave all their heavy artillery bemired on the muddy road behind them!"

He strode away, still brandishing the blade, and the somewhat cheered young man wandered off a few moments later.

Duffy remained sitting where he was, frowning and suddenly wishing he'd had more wine that morning; for the old landsknecht's words had reminded him of the last time he'd spoken to Aurelianus, just a day or so before the Irishman had left the Zimmermann Inn to live in the barracks.

It had been a bright morning in mid-May five months earlier, and the old sorcerer had approached him in the Zimmermann dining room, smiling as he set down beside Duffy's beer a small wooden chest that rattled as if it were full of pebbles.

"Suleiman and his entire army left Constantinople yesterday," he said. "Let's you and me go for a walk out by the east end of the Donau Canal."

Duffy sipped his beer. "Very well," he said, for it was a pleasant day and he hadn't been out of the city in weeks, "but I don't think we'll be able to see them—much less hit them with your collection of sling-stones."

"Not hit them with them, no," Aurelianus agreed cheerily. "Come on, now, finish your beer while I go tell Marko to saddle us a couple of horses."

Duffy was happy to comply, for Epiphany was due back before long; and she'd shown a tendency, lately, to burst into tears every time he spoke to her. The most recent example had occurred in the dining room during dinner.

Shuddering at the uncomfortable recollection, he drained the beer and followed Aurelianus outside. He helped Marko saddle the second horse, and mounted quickly. "After you," he said to the sorcerer with as sweeping a bow as is possible on horseback.

They rode out of the north gate, and then let the horses choose their own lazy pace southeast across fields of new grass starred with peonies. After about two miles Aurelianus bore left, toward the willow-banked southern arm of the canal, and soon they were drawing to a halt in the waving green shade.

"What *do* you intend to do with that box of rocks?" asked Duffy finally; he hadn't inquired during the ride, not wanting to let Aurelianus know how curious he was.

"Make rain magic. They're meteoric stones—bits of falling stars," replied the sorceror, dismounting and scrambling down to the water's edge.

"Rain magic, hey?" Duffy peered up into the cloud-less blue vault of the sky. "A likely day for it," he observed. "Wait up."

"Hurry. It's just about noon right now."

When he reached the water Aurelianus crouched down, and waved Duffy to be silent. He dipped a cupped hand into the water and sipped some of it, then rubbed the rest into the dirt. He opened the wooden chest—Duffy, peering over the old man's shoulder, was distinctly disappointed to see the little raisin-wrinkled lumps it contained—and sprinkled a second handful of water over the stones. He closed the lid, stood up with the chest, and began to shake it rhythmically, whispering in a language Duffy was careful not to listen to.

The willow branches began swaying in the still air as the percussive rattle took on a faster and more complicated pace. Soon the leaves were rustling to-gether, and though Duffy tried not to notice it, he had to admit the new sound was in the same rhythm.

Then the tempo of the shaken stones quickened again—it was almost twice as fast—and then again. Aurelianus' hands were moving so fast that they were actually just a blur to the sight, and no intervals could be heard in the rattling: it was just a loud, textured hiss. The thrashing willow branches were being all but ripped from the trees.

Duffy took an involuntary step back, for the sustained pitch of it all seemed suddenly to be a line of entry for something, something that existed always at such a pitch. The air was tense and close, and Duffy felt the pregnant tingle of the moment between a gasp and a sneeze.

Then with a shout the wizard flung the box at the water. It opened in mid-air and the stones ripped up the water like grape-shot, and a gust of wind from behind them accompanied the shout with such abrupt force that Duffy nearly followed the stones into the canal.

The burst of wind whipped past the two crouching men for a dozen seconds; then Duffy's hair fell back into place and the willows went limp, though the Irishman could see the trees flailing further south. After a few seconds they too were still.

Aurelianus sat down heavily, letting his hands rest on the ground. "Ah," he sighed after a minute of open-mouthed panting. "There are . . . many more *powerful* spirits, but these rain spirits certainly are among the most . . . *energetic*." He started to stand, then thought better of it. "And they demand a good deal of energy on the part of their conjurors, too." He lifted his trembling hands and peered at them. "It must have been almost precisely noon when I started," he said, "for them to have come through so quickly and easily. The last time I did this trick, several years ago, I had to shake the damned box for nearly half an hour."

Duffy watched the wooden chest bobbing slowly away downstream. "Noon?" he repeated absently. "What's so special about noon?"

Aurelianus tried standing up again, and made it this time. "All these magics involve a breaking or violation of the natural laws," he told Duffy, "and those laws relax just a little, are weakest, at noon and midnight."

Duffy was about to frame some statement about himself being weakest at those hours, when Aurelianus started energetically toward the horses. "I'm glad I got that done," the old wizard said. "With the kind of pace Ibrahim has been keeping up, I'm afraid this magic will be impossible before long. But those rains should considerably hamper Suleiman's northward progress." He swung into the saddle.

The Irishman followed suit. "Why impossible? Will there soon be no more noons or midnights?"

"No, but when two adepts, such as Ibrahim and myself, come into close, proximate conflict with one another, a deadlock of magic results—like two knife fighters gripping each other's wrists. Whole categories of higher magic are damped out by the disharmony of our overlapping auras. When that happens, the issue has to be settled by swords and cannon; sorcery is stifled." He turned his horse about and nudged it up the bank to the level expanse of the grassy plain.

"Ah," said Duffy, following him and squinting in the suddenly unobstructed sunlight. "So when the Turks get here you won't be able to . . . say . . . send a flock of giant wasps out at them, or turn the ground to quicksand under their feet?"

"I'm afraid not. In fact this, today, may be the last bit of major sorcery I'll be able to do until it's over; I've already noticed a trace of resistance in certain everyday spells and tricks."

"Like that candle you tried to light a few weeks ago, that blew up?"

"Yes. In such a deadlock of contending adepts, minor hearth-and-kitchen magic *can* still operate, but even it is much more difficult. And the big stuff, as I say, is out."

"I don't know why you old lads even bother to show up, then," remarked Duffy. "What's the use of you, if this deadlock is completely unbreakable?"

"Well . . . *virtually* unbreakable," corrected Aurelianus. "Why, to advise the rest of you, I suppose. I think before too long you'll be Arthur completely, all the time, and you'll . . . he'll . . . need coaching and re-educating."

Duffy had said nothing, though his eyes narrowed; and by the time they'd returned to the Zimmermann he had made a decision. Gathering together his few belongings and Eilif's sword, he quietly vacated the premises. Eilif was happy to sign the Irishman on as a member of his company, and Duffy took up residence with the landsknecht mercenaries, who were at that time quartered in the north barracks, near the Wollzelle.

A month or so later word had officially reached western Europe that Suleiman was advancing toward Austria with seventy-five thousand men. Charles had been too busy pursuing his conflicts with the French king to send troops to Vienna, so his brother Ferdinand had gone before the Diet of Spires to beg aid from the princes of the Holy Roman Empire, and to point out to them that if Austria were to fall to the Turks, they would be moving on into Bavaria with little delay. And, despite the pressing Lutheran controversy, Protestants and Catholics had agreed on providing a *Reichshilfe,* a collection of troops for the defense of the empire. A month was spent assembling this force, but finally on the twenty-fourth of September, 1529, Count Nicholas von Salm had arrived in Vienna with eight thousand professional fighting men and took command of the defense. He'd beaten Suleiman to the city by only three days—and if it hadn't been for the inexplicably heavy rains that had dogged the Sultan's entire progress northwest along the Danube, von Salm would have arrived much too late to be anything more than a harrassing spectator at the siege of Vienna.

Duffy now shook his head and stood up, pleased to feel the buoyancy of the wine still filling his head. He had, several months ago, hit upon drunkenness—with wine, *not* Herzwesten beer—as a cure and preventative for lake-visions and Arthur-visitations; and to judge by their total absence since, the remedy was an effective one.

A horn's sharp blare cut through the babble and clatter that filled the crowded square, and the mercenaries began forming into lines. The Irishman flipped his Venetian salade to the back of his head and then pulled it down in front by the nose-piece so that his cheeks, jaw and nose were protected. Then he drew on his heavy gloves, hefted his matchlock and sprinted over to where Eilif's company was assembling.

The seething crowd of soldiers had separated into four columns of about forty men apiece, some dressed more grandly than the young man with the mandrake root, some more shabbily than Duffy. There wasn't much talking now. The firemasters of each company, carrying their long torches, worked their way up and down the lines, stopping beside each man to set his matchcord-end aglow. Duffy had Eilif's man light his at both ends, for the Irishman could recall times when an unexpected tumble had extinguished the one lit end.

Eilif and Bobo left a group of company captains and lieutenants and crossed the square to their assembled men. "We're going to escort fifty of von Salm's knights out toward the Turk position," Eilif barked, "which, as you've probably seen from the walls, is a hill topped with a low stone wall. The idea is for us to drive them back to a point where our cannons can get at them and blow them back to their own lines—then we stand around behind the wall long enough to show we could keep it if we wanted to, then we come back inside, knights first. We'll be on the left front flank, and I want you to stay there, don't go running around. And make this look good—all the landsknecht captains and lieutenants are meeting with von Salm and the city council at the Zimmermann Inn tomorrow morning to ask for more money, so I want you lads to look like indispensible professionals. Right?"

"Right!" roared the whole company in unison.

"Right. So keep your heads, give the men behind you time to re-load, and let the Turks put themselves where you can kill them. No heroics—this isn't the last card to be dealt."

The horn was blown again, and the landsknechten filed out of the square to the Kartnerstrasse, where they turned left. The knights were already mounted and assembled in the yard inside the gate, and the fitful sunlight gleamed on a polished helmet or gauntlet here and illuminated a bobbing plume there. The tall, armored figure of von Salm himself was visible, bestowing last-minute afterthoughts on the warriors.

The landsknechten marched up in two columns that enclosed the knights. These knights too were battle-tempered professionals, veterans of the Peasant Wars and Tokay and a dozen other campaigns. They had outgrown the dilettante horseman's contempt for the footsoldier, having too often seen the inverted-turtle fate of knights unhorsed when there was no friendly infantry to keep the enemy away.

A wide cloud had glided like some gray sea-bottom creature across the face of the sun; and when a priest stepped up beside von Salm to pronounce a blessing, several men swore and cupped their hands over their match-ends, thinking the drops of holy water sprinkled in the dust to be the beginnings of rain.

A groom hurried up with a portable framework of steps and set them beside a richly caparisoned white horse; von Salm stepped up them and lowered himself into a saddle as high in front and back as a Spanish galleon. Even from this distance, Duffy could see the black spheres of two deeply incised fragmentation bombs lashed forward of the stirrups. The count raised a hand—cannons abruptly boomed along the top of the wall and the great bolt of the Carinthian gate was noisily ratcheted back—and then pointed forward. Added to the din then was the rattle of hooves and boot-heels on the cobblestones as the troops got into motion and began filing, four footsoldiers and two knights abreast, through the gate.

The covering cannon fire, shooting mostly grapeshot and the rubble of newly shattered house walls, was only intended to disorganize the Turks and kill any who might be poking their heads up for a look. The light barrage ceased as soon as the defenders were all outside the gate. Duffy, standing in the indistinct shadow of the wall, could see the plumes of cannon smoke drift away to eastward, white against the gray of the clouds.

"Landsknechten advance two hundred yards," barked von Salm, "then split to make room for us, dig in and give covering fire. When we charge through and hit them, you follow us into the mêlée."

There were curt nods from the four captains, and the hundred and fifty mercenary soldiers broke into a matched jogging trot forward. Duffy craned his neck as they rounded the southeast corner of the wall, but the only motion at the Turk position was a cloud of dust raised by the scattered shot. He could hear the bells of St. Stephen's beginning to peal behind him—they were the church bells announcing one o'clock mass, not the strident, clanging alarum bells that would have warned of an attack. He sneaked a look over his shoulder a moment before the southernmost of the immobile knights receded out of sight around the high shoulder of the wall. We're alone out here now, he thought, still breathing easily as he trotted across the ripped-up plain. I hope they follow quickly when we start shooting.

They ran for many long minutes due east on a course that would bring them around the southern end of the low wall that was sheltering the venturesome band of Turks. Duffy was keeping a cautious eye on the established Turkish lines, but no evident activity there hinted at a counter-charge. The Irishman was panting now, and dreading the possibly frantic run back.

As the jogging body of soldiers crested a shot-scarred rise, he took the opportunity to get a comprehensive look around. The Mohammedan host bulked in solid ranks ahead and further away to his right. Barely visible in the southern haze was the red spot that was the tent of Suleiman himself. Greetings, exalted sultan, thought the Irishman dizzily. Greetings from one who was once offered your job.

When the two first shots were fired, the wind blew most of the sound away, so that all Duffy heard was a dry knocking like stones being struck together; an instant later, though, two of the landsknechten reeled backward and fell, tripping several of their fellows.

By God, thought Duffy, experiencing his first real chill that day, they've got harquebuses now. They didn't three years ago, at Mohács.

Eilif had sprinted to the front; still running, he turned to the mercenaries. "Split now!" he shouted. "Advance another fifty yards, then halt and fire!"

There was more firing from the Turkish position, and several mercenaries fell during that fifty-yard run. Eilif had planned it well, though, for when they halted they were a little to the east of the wall, which they now viewed end-on, and could plainly see the white robes of the several dozen Janissaries.

Duffy, being in the front line, knelt to prepare his gun for firing. He was panting, welcoming the cool western breeze on his sweaty face and neck. Another popping burst of harquebus-fire sounded from the Turkish emplacement, and a ball struck just in front of the Irishman, spraying dirt in his face as it rebounded away over his shoulder. The morning's wine fumes had worn off, and he had to force himself to be calm as he screwed one end of his matchcord into the top of the S-shaped serpentine bolted to the side of his gun. His powder-flask hung from his belt, and he fetched it up with his left hand and tapped a pinch of the gray powder into the flashpan.

The Janissaries still stood in the lee of the wall, apparently re-loading for another volley. Duffy braced his right arm on his knee and aimed at a tall one, lining him up through the match-guide tube. He squeezed the trigger, which threw the top of the serpentine with its glowing match-end into the flashpan. The charge went off with a bang, burning the Irishman's cheek with the flare of the priming. He was deafened, too, for most of the landsknechten fired at about that same second. When he'd blinked the tears out of his eye and looked up again, he couldn't tell whether he'd hit his man or not, for the remaining Janissaries had flung down their guns and were charging with drawn scimitars.

Where are the knights? Duffy thought desperately as he commenced re-loading his matchlock. The wild, wailing cry of the Janissaries was all around him like the racket of insects or tropical birds, and very soon he could hear also the rapid, heavy scuff of the Turks' sandals. It quickly grew louder.

He risked a hurried glance up. God, they were close! He could see the white teeth snarling in the brown, straining faces, and actually met one man's eyes. Powder in the pan, now, he snapped at himself; there! As much of it in the pan as on the ground, anyway.

One of the white-robed Turks was only three strides

from being on top of him, so Duffy thrust the gun at him like a spear and yanked the trigger. The match was slammed into the pan so hard that it was extinguished.

Sparks actually flew as the Irishman parried the hard-driven scimitar with the barrel of the useless gun; then the man had collided with him, and they were both tumbling in the dust. Duffy rolled to his knees and drew sword and dagger. He sank the dagger into the slower recovering Turk's neck and blocked another whistling scimitar with the sword, riposting with a short, hard chop to the leg. The Turk's wobbly remise clanged off Duffy's salade, and the Irishman hopped to his feet and punched his dagger into the man's face.

Without pausing, he kicked away a crescent blade that was coming at him in a low line, and clubbed the wielder in the jaw with the heavy sword-pommel. Another of the battle-maddened Turks was rushing at him, and he knocked the scimitar away with a high parry and let the man run onto the extended dagger.

Then a physical shock whiplashed through the press as the galloping knights ploughed into the Janissary-choked gap between the two groups of landsknechten. The huge broadswords in the hands of the steel-cased riders rose and fell, and the Turks gave way like a tangle of driftwood before a crashing wave.

Duffy took advantage of the distraction to strike the head off one Turk with a whirling chop, axe-style. A moment later there were two landsknechten beside him and one hard-pressed Turk in front; then that one turned and was running, along with perhaps a dozen other remaining Janissaries.

"Let them go!" boomed the deep voice of von Salm. "Advance at a walk to the place they held!"

A walk was all Duffy could have done anyway. He managed to lift and sheathe his weapons, and plodded forward, panting, lacking the strength to reach up and wipe the froth from his lips.

In a few minutes they stood on the wall-topped rise. Ignoring an admonitory bark from von Salm, Duffy sat down on the masonry and stared back at the high walls of Vienna. The city looked impossibly safe and far away. If Suleiman orders a vigorous counter-charge now, he thought dully, the knights would make it back, but damned few of the landsknechten. *I* wouldn't make it, for damned sure.

He heard a heavy, multiple-clank thud and looked behind him. One of the knights had fallen from his horse, though whether from a wound or heat-prostration Duffy couldn't tell. "Strip off his armor," von Salm ordered. The count had raised his visor, and with his red, sweat-gleaming face looked on the verge of heat-prostration himself.

"Do we have time?" one of the mercenaries asked anxiously. The silence was beginning to weigh heavily on the small, isolated group. "We could just carry him—"

"Damn it, will you . . . obey me?"

With a shrug the mercenary squatted and began tugging at the straps and buckles. He was quickly joined by two of his fellows, and in a few moments they had unfastened all the armor—revealing the knight to be dead, of a thrust in the side between the breast and back plates.

"Very well," said von Salm wearily. "Now untie these two bombs, join their fuses and splice a length of matchcord to them. I want a long fuse."

The dozen retreating Janissaries had reached the Turkish lines, and there seemed to be activity there. *What is he clowning with?* Duffy wondered impatiently. *This is a time for retreating, not cleverness.*

"Good," said the count. "Now reassemble that armor with the bombs inside." He looked at the knight beside him. "I had planned only to demolish this wall, but possibly we can lure in an eager Moslem or two as well."

When the sweating footsoldiers had done as he ordered, and leaned the suit of armor in a standing position against the wall, von Salm had them light the cord that dangled from the empty helmet. "Back home now!" he called. "At a leisurely pace, landsknechten flanking."

Duffy had almost completely got his breath back,

and walked around the assembling horses to where Eilif's company was regathering. Eilif stood apparently unscathed at the front, but Duffy didn't see Bobo. The Irishman got in line and just stared at the ground, channeling all his attention into the tasks of breathing and relaxing his cramped hands.

"I see you've made it so far," came a voice from beside him.

He raised his head. It was the young man of the mandrake root, his clothes dusty and torn and his face already showing bruises, but evidently unhurt. "Oh, aye." He looked the young man up and down. "I warned you about those clothes, if you recall. And I see you lost your magicus."

"My what?"

"Your root, your mandrake charm." He pointed at the lad's undecorated belt.

The young man looked down, startled, saw it was true and pressed his lips together. He stretched on tiptoe to see von Salm, off to his right, and muttered, "When are they going to get us *moving?*"

Before Duffy could answer, von Salm had flicked the reins of his horse and the several columns got under way, marching at a slow, easy walk west, toward the high city walls.

Though he had always been as at home in forests or at sea as in cities, the twelve-day confinement of the siege had given the Irishman something of the habitual city-dweller's point of view; it now felt unnatural to be seeing the walls of the city from the outside—an unnatural perspective, like looking up at the hull of a ship from under water, or seeing the back of one's own head.

They tramped on and the walls slowly drew nearer and still they heard no wailing battle cries or thunder of hooves from behind. Duffy could recognize men on the battlements now, and saw Bluto peering along a cannon barrel.

Then there was the drumming of hoof-beats from the east, and von Salm raised his hand to check the instinctive increase in speed. "We will not run!" he shouted. "They cannot reach us before we are inside.

Anyway, I believe they want to deal with the guard we left by the wall."

So the columns of knights and landsknechten marched on at the same agonizingly restrained pace, while the pursuit grew audibly nearer. The men on the walls were now calling to them to hurry.

Duffy turned to stare behind—a mercenary's luxury; the knights were etiquette-bound to look straight ahead and take their leader's word for what was happening— and saw perhaps two dozen mounted Janissaries riding after them, their long white robes whipping about like wings in the head-on breeze. He's right, the Irishman admitted to himself. They can't possibly get here before we get through the gate, and they'd be mad to ride within cannon-range in the attempt. I guess they must really think we've left men to guard that damned little wall.

Then the Janissaries had reached the wall, and were wheeling around it; and a moment later the wall's mid-section silently turned into a skyward-rushing dust-cloud, and Duffy saw several horses and riders on the periphery flung to the ground. After a second or two the boom of the explosion rolled across him.

They could hear the Carinthian gate being opened as they rounded the southeast corner, and von Salm, swaying in his saddle, did not object when they all quickened their pace.

Chapter Sixteen

As HAD RECENTLY BECOME his involuntary habit, Duffy awoke as suddenly as if someone had punched him. He rolled out of his bunk and stood up, glaring round-about in an unspecific panic, wondering where he should have been at this moment and whether the dim light beyond the window was that of early dawn or late evening.

At Duffy's abrupt movement another man gasped and scrambled out of a bunk. "What the hell?" he shouted, blinking rapidly and grabbing for his boots. "What the hell?"

Several groans arose out of the room's shadowy expanse, and one voice at the other end called, "What's the trouble, Suleiman goosing you in your sleep? Get drunk before you go to bed—then you won't dream."

Well, I'm not sure that's true, Duffy thought. He relaxed and sat down on the bunk, having remembered, in less than the usual ten seconds, who he was, and where, and when. That's evening out there, he told himself proudly; this afternoon we sallied forth to drive the Turks back from that little rise, and my gun misfired, and poor old Bobo ate one scimitar while parrying two others. I remember it all.

He pulled on his boots and stood up again, wishing, not for the first time during the last twelve days, that there was water to be spared for bathing.

"That you, Duff?" came another voice, nearby.

"Yes."

"Where you headed?"

"Out. Go drink somewhere."

"Eilif's at the Peerless Ploughman, on the other side of the Kartnerstrasse by the Capuchin church. Know the place?"

"Oh, aye." Duffy had, during the last five months, been making up for his three-year absence from the legendary mercenaries' tavern, which had been founded in 1518 by an expatriate Englishman who'd lost a leg in a minor skirmish on the Hungarian border. "Perhaps I'll trot round that way myself."

"A wise plan," the other man agreed. "He said he had something he wanted to tell you anyway."

"That's where I'm likely to be, then. Come yourself whenever you think you've had enough sleep."

Duffy stepped outside, breathing deeply in the cool west breeze that hadn't slacked in the last two weeks. The day's cloud cover was breaking up, and he could see Orion lying almost prone across the rooftops. Bonfires and braziers already flickered here and there on the rubble-strewn pavement; groups of soldiers hurried by with an air of purpose, and the little boys who sold firewood were scrabbling about in the wreckage of several shattered buildings, cautiously pleased by the quantity of windfall kindling they were able to fill their baskets with. Someone was strumming a lute in the next barracks, and Duffy hummed the tune as he strode away up the Schwarzenbergstrasse.

There was nothing much about the exterior of the Peerless Ploughman to distinguish it from any other building in the area; it was a low, shingle-roofed house whose small, leaded-glass windows spilled only a slight gleam of light out onto the cobblestones, and its sign, a rusty plough, was bolted flat against the bricks of the wall and practically invisible at night. Duffy clumped up to the heavy oaken door and pounded with his fist on the worn spot below the empty knocker-hinge.

After a few seconds the door swung inward, letting more light and a mixture of smells—beef, beer, spices and sweat—out into the street. A big, sandy-haired young man with pop eyes peered at him over the top of a foaming beer mug.

"Can I come in?" Duffy asked with a smile. "I'm with—"

"I know," said the beer drinker, lowering the mug and wiping his mouth with the back of his hand. "Eilif's company. I saw you from the wall today. Come on in." He stepped back and waved Duffy inside.

There were five steps down to the main floor, which made the heavy-beamed ceiling seem high. Lamps and candles cast a diffused yellow light from a dozen tables, and the surf-roar of conversation and laughter and rattling cups surged back and forth in the place, so completely contained by the massive walls and thick door that a passerby in the street outside would scarcely have known the house was occupied. There was music, too, for old Fenn, the host, had got out his antique harp—booty from God-knew-what long-forgotten campaign—and was strumming on it old country airs to which he'd improvised filthy and blasphemous lyrics. Duffy picked his way down the steps and began weaving through the crowd toward where he knew the wine was.

"Duffy!" sounded a shout through the babble. "Damn it, Brian! Over here!"

The Irishman looked around and spotted Eilif, sitting with a couple of other landsknecht captains at a table by the wall. Several men stepped out of his way and he crossed to the table and sat down. Bits of bread and sausage-ends on the table top told Duffy that the captains had been there since dinner.

"Brian," said Eilif, "meet Jean Vertot and Karl Stein, captains of two of the Free Companies."

Duffy nodded at the two men. Stein was tall and rangy, with an old scar curling vertically through the network of wrinkles around his left eye and down his cheek; Duffy had met him fifteen years ago, during the fighting on the Rhine. Vertot was a burly giant whose full beard was still pure black, despite at least two decades of being captain of one of the most savage bands of landsknechten—or lasquenets, as they were known in his native Normandy—in all of Europe.

"What are you drinking, Duffy?" asked Stein in a gravelly voice. Then before Duffy could answer Stein had reached behind him and snared one of the men from his own company. "Ebers," he said, "bring us over the cask of that bock beer."

"The *cask*, sir?" repeated Ebers doubtfully. "Isn't it bolted down? How about—"

"Damn you, if you were this slow to obey me in battle we'd all have been wiped out years ago. You've got your orders—go!"

Duffy had opened his mouth to voice his preference for wine, but now shut it. I guess I can't turn down the beer, he thought helplessly, now that poor Ebers is off risking his life to bring it to us. He shrugged inwardly and turned to Stein with a smile. "Bock beer? In *October*? Where does Fenn get that?"

"It's Herzwesten," Stein said. "The owner of the Zimmermann Inn—what's his name, Eilif? He hired your company."

"Aurelianus," Eilif answered.

"That's right. Aurelianus evidently saved a lot of the

spring production for just such an emergency as this—"
The broad wave accompanying the statement took in,
Duffy gathered, the Turkish ranks massed outside the
city, "—and now he's distributing all of it among the
troops. It's been twelve days now, and there must be
ten thousand soldiers of one sort or other in the city;
I'm amazed there's still any left."

"Maybe its like the loaves and the fishes," Duffy
suggested.

"I like this fellow Aurelianus' miracle better," commented Vertot.

"Anyway, Duff," said Eilif, who hadn't followed that
last exchange, "I called you over here because poor old
Bobo was killed out there today. Tomorrow morning
all the landsknecht captains and their lieutenants are
meeting at the Zimmermann Inn with von Salm and
some highly placed boys to ask for more money—our
feeling is that we've got them over a barrel, you see—
and we want to be well-represented. You, therefore,
are hereby promoted to the post of lieutenant."

"Me?" Duffy felt vaguely frightened by the sudden
conjunction of drinking the Herzwesten bock and visiting the Zimmermann Inn. For the first time in five
months he felt his sense of independence begin to
waver. Maybe none of this, he thought, from Bobo's
death to Ebers' beer-fetching mission, was accidental.
"But good God, Eilif, I'm your most recently acquired
man! A dozen of your old wolves deserve the post
more than I do, and they'll probably mutiny if I'm put
over them." There was shouting from the other end
of the room, and the sound of splintering wood.

"To hell with that," said Eilif carelessly. "They've
tried to mutiny before, and with a lot more cause than
that. I have a talent for putting down mutinies. Besides,
you are the man for the job—few of my lads have had
the years of experience you have, and you're lots
smarter than they are."

"And for you to refuse," Vertot pointed out with a
smile, "would almost constitute a mutiny right there."

"Duffy knows that," snapped Eilif.

"Of course," acknowledged the Irishman. "And I'm
not going to refuse." He looked away and saw Ebers,

a cask under one arm, elbowing angry drinkers out of his way as he struggled back toward the table.

"The beer arrives," Stein pronounced, getting to his feet. He drew his sword with a ringing rasp of steel and confronted Ebers' pursuers. "What he has done was by my order!" he shouted. "Back, you dogs, unless you want to leave here carrying your livers in your hands."

The gang of irate landsknechten fell back, grumbling about the privileges of rank. Ebers set the cask on the table and saluted. "Mission accomplished, sir."

"Well done. Draw yourself a cup and then go away."

"That's settled, then," said Eilif, who had opened the tap and was filling several cups from the steady brown stream. "You'll accompany me to the Zimmermann in the morning." He turned the tap off and set one of the filled mugs in front of the Irishman, then commenced wiping up the puddle of spilled beer with a crust of bread.

"Right." Duffy took a deep breath and drained half the mug at one draught. Damn, he thought. The stuff is good. Eilif, chewing with relish on the soggy bread, seemed to be of the same opinion.

Fenn stumped up to the table, pivoting expertly on his wooden leg. "What's the riot here?" he inquired, grinning wolfishly. "I run a quiet, family-type place."

"We know you do, Fenn, and that's why we brought your excellent beer over here for safekeeping," Duffy told him, "away from those damn drunkards." By way of punctuation he drank off what remained in his cup and refilled it.

"Am I to understand you are buying the whole cask?"

"That's right," confirmed Stein. "In celebration of Duffy's promotion to lieutenant."

"Hah!" barked Fenn, pounding his peg leg on the floor in what was evidently a substitute for slapping his knee. "Duffy? The human wineskin? A wise move! That way you're sure to have Dionysus and Silenus and Bacchus watching over you." The Irishman looked up suspiciously at the last name, but Fenn was just laughing good-naturedly. "This calls for a song!" the host shouted.

There was scattered applause at that, and a slight quieting of the steady din of voices, for Fenn's songs were popular. "Give us *The Signifying Monkey*," bawled one soldier. "No, *Saint Ursula Going Down for the Third Time*," yelled another.

"Shut up, you rats," said Fenn. "This is a serious occasion. Brian Duffy has been promoted to the office of lieutenant in the company of Eilif the Swiss." There were cheers, for despite Duffy's predictions of mutiny, he was liked and respected among the troops. The one-legged man moved quickly, with a gait like a barrel being rolled on one corner, to the counter on which sat the wine kegs and his harp. Picking up the latter, he caressed a long, soft chord out of the instrument; then he smote the strings with the first notes of the old goliard song, *Fortuna, Imperatrix Mundi*.

Fenn sang, and nearly the entire crowd raised their voices in approximate harmony in the chorus, shouting the ancient lyrics that celebrated the vagaries of Fortune's wheel. Duffy sang as loudly as the rest, after pausing only long enough to drain his refilled cup so that he might beat time with it on the table top.

When Fenn finished the song, the company showed no intention of ceasing to sing the choruses, so the host shrugged and began it a second time. Duffy sat back and filled his cup once again with the brown beer. He sipped it thoughtfully.

Just as certain tunes will bring clearly back decades-old memories, and occasional untraceable aromas call up long-forgotten emotions of childhood, so the taste of the beer, combined with the antique goliard melody, was prodding some sleeping memory of his, something pleasant he'd forgotten long ago. Usually reluctant to rouse his faculties of recollection, he pursued this one elusive scrap with all the recklessness and single-mindedness of a drunkard.

Then Eilif was blinking up at him with an expression of puzzlement, for the Irishman had risen to his feet with a shout that broke the back of the song, which had been limping a bit by this time anyway. He glanced around at the merry and curious faces, and, raising his foaming cup, called something in a language no one in the room understood.

"That's Gaelic or something," Fenn said. "Ho, Duffy! None of your barbaric tongues here! You're lucky I don't make everyone speak God-fearing Latin in my house."

The Irishman seemed to see that no one had understood him, so he laughed and strode up to where Fenn stood, and held out his hands for the harp.

The host laughed uncertainly, as if not entirely sure he knew who this was; but after only a moment's hesitation he let him have the harp. Duffy took it, and his fingers played softly over the strings, wringing out soft flickering snatches of melody, like music faintly heard from far away. He looked up, started to speak, and paused. Then, "Aperte fenestras!" he called.

"Hah!" Fenn was delighted. "Latin I asked for and Latin I get. Didn't you hear him, you clods? Open the windows!"

Puzzled but drunkenly willing to go along, a number of the mercenaries leaped to the several narrow windows, unlatched them and pushed them open. Duffy turned to a heavy door behind him, slid back its bolt with one hand and drove it open with a forceful shove of his boot. It couldn't have been a door Fenn intended for use, for there was the sound of boxes falling on the other side, but the host just laughed as the western breeze swept through the room.

Then the Irishman began to play, and it was a quick, darting tune in which tension and menace were tempered by a strong note of exhilaration. There was in it the wary excitement of crouching in the chill of dawn, fingering the worn grip of a trusted weapon and eyeing the near gap from which the enemy would appear; the cold-bellied, dry-mouthed thrill of charging a horse down a dangerously steep slope; and the wonder of standing at the bow of an outward-bound ship, watching the sun sink ahead over uncharted seas. The room became almost quiet as the soldiers harkened to the music, and much of the haze of drunkenness was sluiced out of their eyes as if by the fresh breeze.

A certain tune had been building up in the background of his playing, and now he brought it to front and center, giving full rein to the alternately regal and elfin melody. His audience stirred with recognition, so the Irishman began to sing, in the language Fenn had described as "Gaelic or something."

Several German voices joined him, and a moment later several more. But it was an ancient song that had passed through many languages, and soon Fenn was roaring English lyrics, and Vertot's Frenchmen were singing along in a minor key that reflected the main theme and was almost a mirror image of it, convex to concave.

Before long the room thundered with the song, and many of the men had got to their feet to give their lungs fuller play, and the interweaving polyglot chorus set the fancy glass beer pitchers rattling musically on their high shelf.

The Irishman wrung stronger chords from the instrument as the song neared its crest, and then, just as it did, the bells heralding eight o'clock mass began ringing in the tower of St. Stephen's. The song reached crescendo gracefully, effortlessly taking in the pealing of the bells as accompaniment; and a moment later a deep, window-rattling bass was provided by rumbling cannon-fire from the city walls.

After whipping the tail end of the melody through a couple of unnecessary flourishes Duffy handed the harp back to Fenn. All the men were on their feet now, clapping and cheering, and Duffy bowed and made his way back to his table.

His eyes looked a bit haunted and scared, but nobody noticed it. "That was good," pronounced Stein. "After twelve days of being cooped up within these walls, the men tend to lose heart. Music like that gives it back to them."

"And you can fight too, from what I hear," Vertot commented. "Yes, you have picked a good man to be your lieutenant, Eilif."

The cannon-fire was not followed by the alarum

bells, so they knew Bluto was just sending a few balls arcing through the night to remind the Turks he was there. More beer was poured, and the evening proceeded noisily but uneventfully. After a while someone complained of the draft, and the windows were closed again.

A couple of hours later Eilif and Duffy were staggering back toward the barracks. "Grab as much sleep as you can," Eilif advised. "We've got this meeting to go to tomorrow morning."

"Meeting! What meeting?"

"Never mind. I'll have one of the lads dump a bucket of water over you when the time comes."

"Make it beer."

"Right. A malty baptism. Say, when did you learn to play the harp?"

Duffy stared at the street, which seemed to be rocking in front of him. "I never did," he said. "*I* never did."

The second hour after dawn found Eilif and Duffy, both dressed fairly respectably, striding up the Rotenturmstrasse. The sky was overcast and the air was chilly, and the Irishman pulled the gauntlets of his gloves up over his tunic sleeves.

"How are we doing for time?" he asked, his breath steaming.

"We're a bit early—I don't think Stein had left yet when we did. Von Salm will probably be late anyway, to show us that he isn't impressed by our position. I think we can make a good case, though—and you just nod and look determined at whatever I say, got it?"

"Certainly," Duffy agreed airily, though privately resolving to speak up if he should want to. They turned left, and soon he could see their destination, several blocks ahead.

The Zimmermann Inn stood at the wall end of the Tuchlauben in the north section of the city, a good half mile from the actual focus of the Turkish offensive, and something very like Vienna's normal daily life still went on here. No soldiers trooped by, the streets were free of rubble and charred lumber and masonry-scarred cannon balls, and the west wind kept the smoke away; it was possible to imagine, seeing the usual milkmaids and beggars, that there were not seventy-five thousand Turks only three miles to the south.

The place looked, in fact, just as it had five months ago when he'd last seen it, and he couldn't suppress a reflexive *home-at-last* feeling. He had to remind himself that this was also the home of a sorcerer whose goal it was to drive him literally out of his head.

And it's also Epiphany's home, he thought, my old girl-friend who, until I finally left here, had got to the point of bursting into tears every time she saw me. The Irishman had a tendency to let long-standing guilt dry out into annoyance, and it had happened in his dealings with Mrs. Hallstadt. Why do women have to *be* that way, he wondered impatiently. Very well, I *did* let her down, broke a promise—I admit it! But do you suppose a man would let something like that sour the rest of his life? Hah! Why, you could show me the Nine Virgins of Luxor this minute, all of them naked and beckoning, and spirit them away from me a minute later, and a cup of wine would clear me of the tragedy. And it's been five months, after all. Hell, maybe she *has* got over me by now.

He strode on more cheerfully then, ignoring a faint, uneasy suspicion that he had not quite honestly assessed Epiphany's feelings, nor his own.

Eilif led the way up to the step and pulled open the front door. They stepped through the vestibule and entered the dining room, where a couple of captains already sat at a long table by the windows. From a corner of his eye Duffy noticed Lothario Mothertongue sitting by himself at a table in the far corner. I see nothing's changed, he thought—except that Lothario is looking a bit more haggard. But so are we all.

"Good morning, lads," Eilif greeted. "This is my second-in-command, Brian Duffy. Brian, this is Fernando Villanueva of Aragon, and Franz Lainzer of the Tyrol."

Duffy nodded as he sat down, and the Spaniard smiled. "I enjoyed your harping last night," he said. "You must play for us all once again before the walls come down."

"I'm not sure that gives me enough time," replied Duffy with a grin. "I have to have drunk a huge quantity of beer to do it, and Suleiman's likely to have the wall down by mid-day."

"Then you'd certainly better start now," Villanueva decided. "Ho, someone in the kitchen there! Beer for our musical friend! And for the rest of us, too!"

Eilif was looking out the window, which had been repaired with clear glass after Bobo's passage through it. "Several people coming," he said.

Behind him the kitchen door swung open, and Epiphany came walking across to the table, carrying a tray with a pitcher of beer and a half dozen mugs on it. Duffy averted his eyes uncomfortably, reflecting that she looked both older and dearer. Then she saw him— he heard a gasp, and a moment later a clatter and splash as the tray hit the floor. He looked up in time to see her run, weeping, back into the kitchen. Mother-tongue got up from his seat and hurried after her.

The Spaniard blinked in astonishment. "She obviously disapproves of drinking in the morning," he said. "Ho, miss! Landlord! Anyone! We don't intend to lap it up off the floor like cats!"

After several moments Werner appeared at the kitchen door, his eyebrows raised in impatient inquiry. Then he saw the foamy puddle on the floor. "Epiphany did that?" he asked of no one in particular. "This is positively the last! Anna," he called over his shoulder, "don't you go look for her. She just ran off because she spilled all this beer, and knows what I'll do this time —which is sack the lushy bitch!" He disappeared back into the kitchen.

"It's Vertot," said Eilif, who'd been ignoring the noise and was still watching the street. "Aha! And von Salm right behind. He's punctual—a good sign! Sit tight, lads, this is where we straighten everything out."

Well, Duffy thought bitterly, perhaps not quite everything.

Epiphany did not reappear during the meeting, in which Duffy found he could take no great interest. Anna served beer and sausage, giving the Irishman occasional glances of angry reproach.

Damn it, he thought during a long statement by the elegantly dressed and bearded von Salm, it wasn't my fault. Was that any way for the old girl to go on, after all this time? It *must* have been affectation, a pose—surely Anna can see that! Hell, no romantic reverse ever gave *me* more than a week's upset . . .

Oh? spoke up sarcastically another part of his mind. Then I guess it must have been some other Irishman that went off to fight the Turks at Mohács in 'twenty-six, just because his girl married another man; it took him three *years* to face her again.

". . . isn't that right, Brian? Or would you say I've overstated the case?" Eilif was eyeing him expectantly.

Duffy raised his head, letting his frown of worry look, he hoped, like one of grim determination. "There was no exaggeration in what you said," he told Eilif.

The Swiss turned again to von Salm. "Hear? And that from a man who fought with Tomori! You can't deny . . ." And the discussion swam away again out of the Irishman's focus of attention. Despite a vow he'd made at dawn, he was doing more than his share of putting away the beer.

At last the captains were pushing the benches back and standing up.

"As a limited representative of Emperor Charles V, that is all I can offer to add," von Salm said. "You can be sure, though, that when the Turks are driven off —assuming you landsknechten maintain your present level of performance—I will vehemently recommend a fuller payment for you all."

The captains nodded and broke up into conversing groups, having evidently got as much as they'd hoped for.

Eilif turned to the Irishman. "Heading back, Duff?"

"Uh . . . no." Duffy grimaced at the kitchen door. "No, I've got to settle a thing or two."

"Well, I'll see you back there." The grizzled Swiss captain grinned at him. "Don't give it all more worry than it's worth, lad."

Duffy shrugged. "I forget what it's worth."

Chapter Seventeen

HE FOUND HER in the flour-dusty storeroom, sitting on a keg of salt and sobbing so convulsively that it looked as if a pack of invisible dogs was mauling her.

"Epiphany?"

She turned a tear-streaked face up toward him, then looked away, crying harder than before. "Why did you come back?" she asked finally. "Just to make me lose this job?"

"Hey, Piff," Duffy said. "Don't cry. Werner can't fire you; it's Aurelianus who owns the place, and I've still got influence with him. Hell, I'll tell him to give you a raise."

"Don't," the old woman choked, *"mention* the name . . . of that little snake."

"What little snake?" Duffy asked, bewildered. "Aurelianus?"

"Yes. He's the one that put . . . some kind of filthy spell on you, to make you indifferent and cold toward me. *Ohhh."* She went off into howls of grief again.

Duffy considered it unfair of her to switch the subject around like that. "It's Werner we're talking about," he said. "And I'll see to it that he behaves himself in the future."

"What do I care about the future?" Epiphany moaned. "I have no future. I'm counting the hours until the Turks cut down the walls and knock my head off." Duffy guessed she'd said that last sentence so often lately that she didn't even bother to get the verbs in the right order anymore. "I haven't even seen my father in two weeks," she said brokenly. "I simply intended to abandon him when you and I left . . . and now, remembering that, I just can't face him anymore!"

"Good Lord," Duffy said. "Who's bringing him food, then?"

"What? (*sniff.*) Oh, I've got Shrub doing it." She looked up at him blearily. "Brian, if you do talk to that horrible Aurelianus, could you have him speak to Werner about my brandy? I've always been in the habit of having just a sip before I go to bed and when I get up in the morning, to help me work, you know, but now Werner insults me and says I can't have any, so I have to sneak it when no one's looking, which is so degrading. As if Werner ever does any work himself—he's always hidden away talking to that damned poet friend of his. Talk to him about it, Brian. You'll do at least that for me, won't you?"

The Irishman stared at her thoughtfully. Is this a gambit, he wondered, a story to make me feel properly guilty? *Oh, Brian, look, you've driven me to drink, you heartless wretch.* Is that what I'm supposed to understand?

My God, he thought suddenly, listen to yourself, Duffy. You *are* a heartless wretch. This old girl was quietly happy here until you showed up and made crazy promises to her that you couldn't keep. You *have* driven her to drink.

He reached out a hesitant hand and lightly squeezed her shoulder. "I'll talk to him," he said softly, and left the room.

Anna was in the kitchen, and looked up when, simultaneously, Duffy appeared from the storeroom and Mothertongue stepped in from the yard.

"Where is—" both men began at once.

"After you, sir," said Mothertongue.

"Thank you. Anna, where is Werner?"

"The same place he was before all the racket and weeping brought him out here a few minutes ago: his private wine cellar." As the Irishman turned in the direction she'd pointed, she added, "I wouldn't just barge in; that poet Kretchmer's in there with him—they're writing an epic or something, and won't have interruptions."

"They'll have one," Duffy predicted, walking on.

Behind him he heard Mothertongue ask, "Where did Mrs. Hallstadt go? She isn't out in the yard."

"She's in the storeroom," replied Anna tiredly.

Duffy paused and looked over his shoulder at Mothertongue, who, facing the storeroom door, had paused to look back at *him*. The two men stared at each other for a second or two, then thoughtfully resumed moving in their separate directions.

The Irishman had never been in Werner's wine cellar, but he knew it was tucked under the main stairs, a step or two below floor level, and in a moment he stood before the low door, his hand raised to knock. Before he did, though, it occurred to him that there was no reason to be polite—so he just grabbed the latch and yanked the door open.

The low-ceilinged room beyond was perhaps twelve feet long by eight wide, and bottles, casks and amphorae cluttered the shelves from floor to ceiling, softly lit by a lamp on the small table in the middle of the floor. Two men who had been sitting at the table had now sprung halfway up from their chairs, startled by Duffy's entrance, and he stared at both of them.

Werner was a bit heavier than Duffy remembered him, and his unusually fine clothes only served to set off the powdered pallor of his face and the gray in his oiled hair. Kretchmer was a tougher-looking man, his face tanned behind a startling red beard, but he was the one who seemed most upset.

"Ach!" the poet exclaimed in a high, hoarse voice, staring nervously at the Irishman's feet. "Common ruffians interrupt the sacred labors! A man of bloody hands intrudes into Aphrodite's very grove! I must avaunt!" He edged past Duffy, eyes still downcast, and hurried away down the hall.

Werner resumed his seat and threw up his hands. "Can art not be wrought without all these mundane *distractions?*"

Duffy stared at him. "What?"

Werner took a deep breath, then let it out. "Never mind, Duffy. What do you want?"

The Irishman looked at the littered table and picked up a little wooden whistle that had only one finger-hole. "Don't tell me: you're composing a musical High Mass." He blew through it, but failed to get any audible note. "I'd recommend a new pitch-pipe."

Werner got up from the table and, with much suppressed wincing, limped around the table and snatched the whistle from Duffy's hand, then just as awkwardly returned to his chair. "*Was* there something you wanted to say, or are you just bored?"

Duffy started to ask about the innkeeper's injuries, then remembered why he'd come.

"I want to tell you that you can't fire Epiphany Vogel. You—"

"I can do as I please in my place."

The Irishman smiled and sat down in Kretchmer's chair. "That's the crux of it, all right. How is it that you keep forgetting this *isn't* your place? Aurelianus owns it, and he's an old friend of mine. He won't—"

"You've been gone half a year. I don't think he's a friend of yours anymore. And in any case," he added with sudden heat, "I *run* this place, damn you! I have my finger on the pulse at all times. He listens to *me* when it comes to operating the inn. Do you think he could do it himself, without me? No sir! The little old—"

Duffy laughed. "Finger on the pulse? I like that! This place must be able to run itself, for as I recall you're hardly ever on the premises. You're always over at the house of that caricature of a poet. Hell, I remember Easter night, when Zapolya nearly blew this inn to bits—and you hadn't even heard of it the next morning! You were over at his place . . . quoting Petrarch and kissing Kretchmer's boots, I expect . . . "

Oddly, a sly look had sprung up in the innkeeper's eyes. "Well . . . it wasn't exactly his *boots*."

The Irishman squinted at him. "What the hell do you mean?"

"Well, if you must know, Kretchmer wasn't home

that night—but his wife was." Werner smirked. "His marvellously young and attractive wife, I might add."

Duffy was genuinely puzzled. "Do you mean to tell me his wife . . . and you . . . ?"

"I say nothing!" exclaimed Werner, still smirking. "I merely observe that sensitive, pretty young ladies tend to be swayed by the sort of verse I write. Swayed to an astonishing degree." He actually winked.

Duffy stood up, somewhat surprised and disgusted. "Swayed right over to horizontal, I gather. Where was Kretchmer when all this wonderful stuff was going on? Over here swigging the new bock, I suppose."

"Possibly. I only know she gave me to understand he'd not be back until morning, at the soonest."

"If you'll excuse me," Duffy said, waving at the papers on the table, "I'll leave you to your epic now, and—vacate poor Aphrodite's grove. But Epiphany still works here, do you understand? And she's permitted to keep a bottle of brandy in her room. I'll have Aurelianus trot down presently and confirm it for you." He walked to the door and turned around. "You know, you'd better be careful. Have you taken a good look at the shoulders on that Kretchmer fellow? Damned wide, for a poet. He could rip you to hash."

The powdered innkeeper chuckled confidently. "I am not physically unfit. In fact, I have consistently beaten him at arm-wrestling."

Duffy paused another moment, then shrugged. "You'd know best," he said, and left, closing the door behind him.

There's no way, he thought as he headed back to the kitchen, that Werner could honestly beat Kretchmer at arm-wrestling; either Werner lied or Kretchmer voluntarily allowed himself to lose. And why would he do that? And why—weirder still—would the wife of a big, healthy-looking fellow like that be attracted to the likes of Werner? And why do you bother your head about it? he asked himself impatiently.

He found Anna scraping a pile of chopped, dried meat off a board into a pot. "Genuine beef," she announced when she looked up and saw him. "Most of the inns have been serving dog and cat since before the weekend, though not calling it that, of course. We were better stocked—we'll have real pork and beef till about Thursday." She laughed wearily. "And even then we'll probably keep our integrity, because there won't be any dogs or cats left."

"I've been in long-besieged towns where even the rats were all eaten," Duffy said softly, "and we ate ants, termites and cockroaches. Some ate worse things."

Anna put on a fair imitation of a bright smile. "Really? I must say this does open up whole vistas for a revised menu."

He hooked a thumb at the storeroom. "Piff still in there?"

"Well," she answered cautiously, "yes . . . "

He pushed the door open quietly so as not to startle her, and saw her and Lothario Mothertongue sitting together on one of the few remaining hundred-pound sacks of flour. They were talking in low mutters and Mothertongue was stroking her hair. The Irishman closed the door as silently as he'd opened it.

He stood beside Anna and watched her chop an onion and then dice it. "How long has that been going on?"

She scooped up the white bits and flicked them off her hand into the pot. "A few days. It seems like everybody's behavior has changed during these last two weeks."

"Do tell. Well, I'll still speak for her to Aurelianus."

"Now *there's* generosity!"

He nodded. "Biting, Anna, very biting. Rest assured I'm cut to the quick. Where will I find him?"

"Hell, I'm sorry. In the old chapel, probably. He spends a lot of time in there, doing all kinds of peculiar things with weights and pendulums and little tops like the ones Jewish children play with. And any time there's a bit of sun he'll be waving a little mirror out one of the windows. Like he was signalling, you know, but it's a windowless, high-walled court out there—the only ones who could see the flashes would be birds overhead."

"That's the sort of thing these magicians like to do," Duffy told her. "See you later."

The long hall to the western side of the inn was just as dark at mid-day as at night, and it took Duffy several minutes to grope his way through its length of varying height, width and flooring all the way to the two tall doors of the chapel. He had been hearing voices for the last hundred feet, and now saw that one of the iron doors was ajar.

Though he couldn't hear distinct words, there was something in the tone of the voices that made him cover the last few yards silently, his hand dropping to loosen his dagger in its scabbard. The same piles of boxes and stacked mops obstructed the doorway, and he carefully sneaked around the side so that he could peer into the chapel from between two inverted metal mop buckets set atop a stack of ancient carpet rolls.

Though the light through the stained glass windows was gray and dim, Duffy's long grope through the dark hall had made his eyes sensitive to the slightest illumination. The tableau he saw at the altar looked, he thought, like the frontispiece of a treatise on some League of Outlandish Nations; of the six—no, seven—men confronting Aurelianus, two were blacks (one in feathers, the other in a long robe and a burnoose), one was the copper-skinned, leather-clad savage Duffy remembered seeing about the place five months ago, another seemed to come from the same far isles as had Antoku Ten-no, and the other three were apparently Europeans, though one was a midget.

"You've asked this before," Aurelianus was saying with perhaps exaggerated patience, "and I've answered before."

The midget spoke up. "You misunderstand, sir. We aren't *asking* any longer."

Duffy softly drew his dagger.

"You'd take it by force?" Aurelianus was grinning. "Ho! You're children with sticks coming to rescue a favorite lamb from a hungry lion."

The black man in desert garb stepped forward. "Two things, Ambrosius, are unarguably true. First, your power is severely circumscribed by the proximity of your inimical peer, Ibrahim, while our powers, though initially less, have remained undiminished—

you are on nearly an equal footing with us now, and I don't think you could overcome all seven of us if we were to work together."

"Were those both true things," Aurelianus asked politely, "or was it just one?"

"That was one. The second is this: Ibrahim will *have* this city, and he'll have it long before the thirty-first. The walls are tottering already, and there are fifty thousand fanatic Janissaries out on the plain waiting for a gap to run in through. There's no way on earth this brewery will last these two weeks until All Hallow's Eve. Ibrahim will be in here in half that time, and he'll poison the Mac Cool vat, or more likely just blow it to splinters and vapor with a bomb. Do you understand? What *you* hoped to accomplish with the Dark is simply impossible."

"I'm being a dog in the manger, you're saying."

"Precisely. You would preserve the Dark beer untouched—which only means that Ibrahim will be able to destroy every last drop of it, thus insuring that it will never do *anyone* any good. On the other hand, if you sell some of it to us—at a fabulously high price, never fear!—it will have served a purpose, two purposes, actually: it will have saved our lives; and out of gratitude we will help you and your King to escape from this doomed city. For though the Dark, if drawn now, would not have quite attained its full empire-redeeming strength, you know it would certainly be powerful enough to restore and rejuvenate a few old men."

"What makes you think escape is possible for anyone?" Aurelianus asked. "The Turks surround the city completely, you know."

The midget spoke up again. "You're not dealing exclusively with foreigners, Ambrosius. You and I both know half-a-dozen subterranean routes out of Vienna—one of them," he added, nodding at the altar, "accessible from this very room."

Aurelianus stepped up onto the dais around the marble altar, giving the seven men the look of supplicants. "The battle being fought here," he said, "is not the concern of any of you, for you have all dispensed with whatever allegiances you may once have had to East or West. My counsel to you is that you flee, by any of the routes your colleague here knows of—and bring water or wine to quench your thirst, for you won't have a drop of the Dark."

"Very well," said the black man in the burnoose, "you force us to—"

"Don't talk, old man," Aurelianus interrupted. "Show me. Come up here." He stepped back and spread his arms wide, and Duffy, peering from his hiding place, thought he could see the old sorcerer's hands flickering almost imperceptibly, like a mirage. The seven Dark Birds hesitated. Contempt put a sneer in the wizard's voice as he went on: "Come up here, you children-playing-at-magic! Try your little spells and cantrips against the Western Magic that was growing in the roots of Britain's dark forests ten thousand years before Christ, the magic at the heart of storms and tides and seasons! Come up to me! Who is it I shall face?" He threw back his black hood. "You know who I am."

Duffy was actually brushed with tingling awe, for the gray light seemed to make ancient, weather-chiselled granite out of the face that looked down on them all. This is *Merlin,* the Irishman reminded himself, the last prince of the Old Power, the figure that runs obscurely like an incongruous thread through the age-dimmed tapestry of British pre-history.

The sorcerer reached out a hand—it wavered, as if seen under agitated water—and seemed to grab an invisible loop or handle, and pulled. The black man stumbled forward involuntarily. Aurelianus stretched forth the other hand toward the midget, whose hair Duffy saw twitch and stiffen at a straight-out angle; the wizard closed the fingers of that hand and the little man yelped in pain. "I'm going to show you another way to leave Vienna," Aurelianus said softly.

Then all seven of the Dark Birds were running for the doors, the two held ones having wrenched themselves out of Aurelianus' magical grip. Duffy scarcely had time to scuttle around to the other side of the carpet stack before they rushed past him and were sandal-slapping away down the hall.

He looked back at the altar, and saw Aurelianus staring at him. "You appear out of a carpet, like Cleopatra," the old wizard observed.

Duffy stood up and walked to the communion rail. "I see Antoku wasn't the only one to get demanding," he said. "I'm glad I didn't ask for permission before snitching my sip of it."

Aurelianus cocked an eyebrow at him. "The Dark? You tasted it? When?"

"Easter night."

The wizard frowned, then shook his head. "Well, you wouldn't have been able to turn the tap if they didn't want you to have any." He looked intently at Duffy. "Tell me—how was it?"

The Irishman spread his hands. "It was . . . incredibly good. I'd have gone down for more, but it seemed to paralyze me."

The old man laughed quietly. "Yes, I've heard of it having that effect." He crossed to a couple of narrow chairs by the windows, sat down in one and waved at the other. "Drop anchor. Drink? Snake?"

Duffy thought about it as he walked over. "Snake," he said, and kicking his rapier out of the way, perched on the edge of the chair.

Aurelianus opened a little box and handed Duffy one of the sticklike things. "You've been fighting these days. How does it look? Was our thirsty friend correct about the walls?"

The Irishman leaned forward to get the snake's head into the flame of the candle Aurelianus held toward him. "They've got miners and sappers under them, yes," he said when he'd got it well lit, "but your blackamoor is wrong in thinking that it's decisive. You've got to keep in mind that October is insanely late in the year for the Turks to be here—as far as supplies go, I suspect they're in worse shape than we are, and they still have to turn around and face a damned long trip home." He puffed a smoke ring, grinned, and tried without success to do it again. "The walls could probably be tumbled in a day or two; the question is, do they dare wait another day or two? To say nothing of the—I'd estimate—additional day or two of street-to-street fighting that would be necessary for them actually to take the city."

Aurelianus waited a moment, then raised his white eyebrows. "Well? Will they dare it?"

Duffy laughed. "God, I don't know."

"Would you, if you were in charge?"

"Let's see—no, I don't think I would. Already the Janissaries are probably on the brink of mutiny. They'll be wanting to get back home to Constantinople.—They'll it will take months for them to get home, and even now they've waited too long to hope to elude winter. If Suleiman stays for the—let's say—additional week it would require to break and seize Vienna, he'd almost have to winter right here, and leave in the spring; and that's long enough for even Charles the Tardy to do something about it." He shrugged. "Of course guessing is just guessing. He may think he could keep his Janissaries in line and hold the city till spring, crumbled walls and all. It's hard to say. I think he's shown inexcusably bad judgment in hanging on here as long as he has."

Aurelianus nodded. "I suppose you're right, militarily speaking."

The Irishman grinned sarcastically. "Ah. But I'm all wrong spiritually speaking, eh?"

"Well, you've got to remember that Ibrahim is the one who finally decides, and his first concern is ruining the beer—when it comes to betting on the last card, he doesn't really care if Suleiman actually *takes* Vienna, or if the Janissaries all die on the way home, or if Charles bloodily evicts them all from here during the winter. If he can wreck the beer before the thirty-first of this month, when we hope to draw the Dark and give it to the Fisher King, he'll have done what he set out to do—and no cost will have been too dear."

The Irishman stood up, trailing smoke. "Then we'll have to rely on the homesickness of the Janissaries."

"Tell me, are Bugge's Vikings proving to be of any use in the defense?"

"Well, no. Von Salm says they're unsuited for disciplined warfare. I suppose they'll be useful if it does come to hand-to-hand fighting in the streets, but right now they're just sitting idle and frustrated in a lean-to by the north barracks. You might as well have kept them living here."

"I couldn't. It seems one of them mauled Werner and pitched him down the stairs, and he insisted they be thrown out. Bugge denied it, but Werner was adamant. Poor fellow still limps." He tapped the ashen head off his snake. "You know, I still have hope that they'll figure in this in some significant way. They were sent here so . . . purposefully . . ."

"They're a bunch of old men."

"Yes. This is a war of old men. Oh, I know Suleiman is only thirty-four, and Charles isn't yet thirty, but the conflict is old, the true kings are old—and I am perhaps the oldest of all."

Unable to think of a reply, Duffy turned to leave.

"Will you have a drink with me tonight in my room?" Aurelianus asked.

"No," said the Irishman, recalling what had prompted him to leave five months ago. Then he remembered the harp-playing episode of the previous night, and he shrugged fatalistically. "Oh, why not," he sighed. "I'm not really due back at the barracks till noon tomorrow. What time?"

"Nine?"

"Very well."

Duffy left the chapel and made his way back to the dining room. The Zimmermann was too far north and west to attract many soldiers these days, and it was haggard citizens that filled the tables around him. A new girl was working, and he signalled her.

"I'll have a bowl of whatever Anna's got in the pot," he told her, "and a flagon of Werner's burgundy—oh hell; forget the wine, make it a flagon of beer." Speaking of Werner had reminded him that he'd intended to talk to Aurelianus about Epiphany's job. I'll tell him tonight, he thought. "Say, does Bluto come in here anymore?"

"Who, sir?"

"The man in charge of the cannons. He's a hunch-back."

"I don't think so." She smiled politely and went on to the next table.

Duffy sat quietly waiting for his beer, savoring the weirdly wheaty aftertaste of the snake—which he'd ditched before entering the dining room—and ignoring the curious stares of the citizens around him. When the beer came, he poured himself a mug and sipped it slowly. After a while he noticed Shrub helping to carry steaming plates out to the tables.

"Hey, Shrub!" he called. "Come here a minute."

"Yes, Mr. Duffy?" said the stable boy when he'd delivered a plate and made his way to the table.

"You've been bringing food to old Vogel? Epiph-any's father?"

"I did for a few days, but he scares me. He kept calling me by the wrong name and telling me to get liquor for him."

"You don't mean you just *stopped?* Holy—"

"No no!" the boy said hastily. "I got Marko to do it. He's not scared of crazy old men."

"Marko? Is he the kid with the red boots?"

"Yes *sir*," assented Shrub, obviously impressed by the idea of red boots.

"Very well. Uh, carry on."

Perhaps as an apology for her shortness with him earlier, Anna had the new girl carry out to Duffy a capacious bowl of the stew, and he laid into it man-fully, washing it down with liberal draughts of cool Herzwesten Light. At last he laid down his spoon and struggled to his feet; he looked around the room, but there was no one in the scared-eyed crowd he knew to say good-bye to, so he just lurched to the front door and out into the street.

To the plodding Irishman the whole outdoors seemed far too bright—though gray clouds hid the sky and made a diffused glow of the sun—and the breeze was too cold, and the yells of the ragged children were unbearably loud. How many hours of sleep did you get last night, Duff? he asked himself. Well, I don't know, but it was something less than adequate for a tired, middle-aged soldier with a primordial king riding on his shoulders like the Old Man of the Sea.

He sighed heavily, and turned right at the corner of the inn instead of pressing on toward the Rotenturmstrasse. Soon he had come round into the inn's stableyard, and he leaned on a clothesline pole for a few moments and looked reminiscently about.

I see Werner hasn't re-roofed the stalls that were blown up by that petard, he noted. I wonder if he still thinks I was responsible for that. Probably he does. At least somebody patched the fence where Zapolya's damned forty-pound iron ball passed through it. And over there's where the northmen were quartered.

He crossed the yard to the stables and saw that there were still several straw-filled bunks against the back wall. Almost without conscious thought he rolled into the lowest, closed his eyes and was soon asleep.

With the lucidity typical of afternoon dreams, he was sitting across a table from Epiphany. Her hair was still more dark than gray, and her expressions and gestures hadn't yet lost the careless spontaneity of youth.

Though he couldn't hear his own words—in fact could apparently only speak as long as he didn't try to listen to himself—he knew he was talking earnestly to her, trying to make her understand something. What was it he had been trying to make her understand, that long-ago morning? Oh, of course! That she'd be mad to go through with her planned marriage to Max Hallstadt—that she ought instead to marry Duffy. He paused in his speech for a sip of beer, and had a moment of difficulty in regaining the thread of his faultlessly logical argument.

"Oh, Brian," she said, rolling her eyes in half-feigned exasperation, "why do you only bring these things up when you're sick, drunk or tired?"

"Epiphany!" he protested. "I'm *always* sick, drunk or tired!"

The scene flickered away, and he found himself shoving his way into the vestibule of St. Peter's Church. Several of Hallstadt's friends were there, evidently posted for the specific purpose of keeping the Irishman out if he should attempt to get in and disrupt the wedding.

"Come on, now, Brian," spoke one—what had his name been? Klaus somebody. "You're not a part of this picture anymore."

"Out of my way, you poxy toad," Duffy said, in a voice loud enough to turn heads in the nearer pews. "Hallstadt! Damn your eyes, you won't—" A fist in his stomach doubled him up and silenced him for a moment, but then he had lashed out with a punch of his own, and Klaus was jigging backward at an impossible-to-maintain angle, and colliding with the baptismal font . . .

The yard-tall pillar with its marble bowl tottered, leaned—as Klaus rolled off to one side—and then went to the floor-tiles with a terrible echoing crash. Holy water splashed up into the faces of appalled ushers, and shards of marble were spinning across the floor. Another of Hallstadt's friends seized Duffy by the arm, but the Irishman shook him off.

He took a step up the aisle. "Hallstadt, you son-of-a-whore, draw your sword and face me if you're not the eunuch everyone takes you for!"

People were leaping to their feet, and he caught one glimpse of Epiphany's veiled, horrified face before a hardy altar boy felled him unconscious with a tall iron crucifix.

Then he was simply falling through a vortex of old scenes and faces, over the muted babble of which he could hear an older man's voice raised in strong, delighted laughter.

Chapter Eighteen

WHEN HE OPENED HIS EYES he was in deep shadow, and the wall of the inn, which he could just see from where he lay, showed dark gray around the yellow of the windows. God, he thought blurrily. Just a dream this time, was it? It was bad enough to go through those unhappy days in early 'twenty-six, without having to re-live them in my dreams. Ah, but at least they're *my* memories; better a dozen such than one of those damned dreams of that moonlit lake—which you were risking, drinking all that cursed beer. Stick to wine, lad. He rolled to his feet, slapped straw from his doublet and combed his hair with his fingers, then took a deep breath, let it out, and started toward the building.

From habit he walked in through the kitchen's back door, and caught the red-booted Marko snitching a sweet-roll from a cupboard. "Marko," Duffy said, stopping. There was something he'd meant to ask this boy about. What had it been?

"Werner said I could have it," the boy said quickly.

"I don't care about your damned pastry. Uh . . . oh yes, you've been bringing food to Gustav Vogel, I understand?"

"I was for a while. Werner said I didn't have to anymore."

"Well who is?"

Marko blinked. "Is what?"

"Bringing the old man food, you idiot."

"I don't know. Why can't he go out and scavenge it, like everybody else?" The boy dashed out the back door, leaving the Irishman wearing a scowl of annoyance and worry.

The new girl who'd served him earlier was staring

at him from the other side of the fireplace, where she was ladling out bowls of apparently the same stew. "Where's Epiphany?" Duffy asked her.

"She went to bed early," the girl answered. "She didn't feel well. What are you doing in the kitchen? Guests are supposed to—"

"Where's Anna, then?"

"Around at the taproom end of the dining room, I believe. If you want supper you'll have to—"

"You can have mine," Duffy told her with a smile as he strode past her into the hall. The dining room was full, and alive with the gaiety that comes to people who know they might well be dead in twenty-four hours. Beer was being drunk at a prodigious rate, and Duffy found Anna crouched beside one of the decorated casks, holding a pitcher under the golden stream from the tap.

She looked up and saw him. "I thought you left."

"No, just fell asleep out back. Epiphany's gone to bed?"

"That's—Shrub! This is for Alexis and Casey's table, hurry up—that's right. Why?" She glanced at him suspiciously.

"Oh, give it a rest, Anna, I'm not planning to go up and force any attentions on her. Listen, she had Shrub bringing food to her father, and—"

Shrub scampered up again. "Hello, Mr. Duffy! Anna, two more pitchers for Franz Albertzart and that old lady."

"Coming up. What were you saying, Brian?"

"Well, Shrub here got Marko to do it, but I ran into Marko just now and he says he stopped."

"There you go, Shrub." The boy took the pitchers and hurried guiltily away. "Stopped what?"

"Damn it, listen to me. Nobody's been bringing food to old Vogel. Now *I'm* not going to be too upset if he turns up dead, but I think his daughter might be."

"Oh, hell," Anna said quietly. "You're right. I'll tell her first thing in the morning." She stood up and brushed a lock of hair out of her face, then looked at him with a little sympathy. "Brian, what *did* go wrong, anyway, between you and her?"

As Duffy paused to frame a credible and more or less accurate answer, the door banged open and five young men stamped in. "Anna!" one of them bawled across the room. "Five pitchers, pronto!"

The Irishman grinned with one side of his mouth and punched her very softly on the shoulder. "I'll tell you sometime," he said, and walked away toward the stairs. He turned and saw that she was watching him. He mouthed the name, *Aurelianus,* pointing upward.

There was a man asleep on the stairs, and Duffy stepped carefully around him, reflecting that besieged towns probably tended to surrender sooner if there was no wine or beer inside to divert the defenders, now and then, from the bleakness of their position. He got to the top landing and found Aurelianus' door, but just as he was about to knock he remembered that the old sorcerer had told him nine o'clock.

Damn, he thought. It's probably not even eight yet. I should have slept a bit longer, maybe carried the dream on to when I left town to go fight at Mohács. He started to tip-toe away, then snorted impatiently, strode back and rapped sharply on the door.

There was a squeal from inside, and overlapping it came Aurelianus' flustered but authoritative, "Who is it?"

"Finn Mac Cool."

After a moment the door opened and one of the maids, with face averted, ducked around the Irishman and hurried away. "Come in, Brian," said Aurelianus with weary patience.

The room might have been completely rearranged since Duffy's last visit, but it hadn't changed; it was still a heaped, candlelit collection of tapestries, jewelled weapons, beakers a-bubble with no source of heat, books big enough to serve as walls for a small man's house, and obscure animals stuffed in unlikely postures. The old wizard sat cross-legged on an upholstered stool.

Duffy jerked a thumb after the retreating maid when he'd shut the door. "I thought that kind of thing wasn't good for you half-breeds."

After closing his eyes for ten seconds, Aurelianus

stared at him and shook his head. "Your years as a mercenary soldier have coarsened you, Brian, to the point where you're unfit for gracious company. I was merely asking her if any of the maids had tried to come into my room recently; a new girl might not have been told that this room isn't to be entered. And didn't I say nine o'clock?"

"I decided I might have to be heading back to the barracks at around nine. Why don't you just lock your door?"

"Oh, I do, most of the time, but I forget occasionally, and I often misplace my keys."

"Isn't that kind of careless?" Duffy found a chair, tipped a cat out of it and sat down. "After all, I suppose some of this junk must be valuable to somebody . . ."

"Yes," the old man snapped. "Very valuable, quite a lot of it. The thing is, I tend to rely—perhaps too heavily!—on other protections." He nodded toward the door, above and around the top of which Duffy noticed a structure that combined the features of a parrot-perch and a dollhouse. "Would you like some brandy?"

"What? Oh, certainly." He waited until the wizard had poured two glasses of a golden Spanish brandy and handed him one. "Thank you. What was it you wanted to see me about?" He took a sip, swallowed it, then took a bigger one.

"Nothing special, Brian, I just wanted to chat. After all, I haven't seen you in months."

"Ah. Well, there's one thing I wanted to talk to you about. Werner intends to fire Epiphany, and this job is just about all she's got in the world. I'd be grateful if you'd tell him she's a permanent employee, and that he'd better not torment her."

Aurelianus blinked at him quizzically. "Very well. I gather you and she are not . . . seeing each other any-more?"

"That's right. She blames you for it, and I'm not sure I don't agree with her."

To the Irishman's surprise, Aurelianus did not raise his eyebrows and protest. Instead, the old man took a long sip of his wine and said, "Maybe that's fair and maybe it's not. If it is, try to imagine what things would have broken it up, if I hadn't. Or do you really think you would have run off and lived happily ever after in Ireland?"

"I don't know. It's not—it wasn't—impossible." Duffy picked up the bottle and refilled his glass.

"How old are you, Brian? You ought to know by now that something always breaks up love affairs unless both parties are willing to compromise themselves. And that compromising is harder to do the older and less flexible and more independent you are. It just isn't in you, Brian. You could no more get married now than you could become a priest, or a sculptor, or a greengrocer."

Duffy opened his mouth to voice angry denials, then one corner turned up and he closed it. "Damn you," he said wryly. "Then why do I want to, half the time?"

Aurelianus shrugged. "It's the nature of the species. There's a part of a man's mind that can only relax and go to sleep when he's with a woman, and that part gets tired of always being tensely awake. It gives orders in so loud a voice that it often drowns out the other components. But when the loud one is asleep at last, the others regain control and chart a new course." He grinned. "No equilibrium is possible. If you don't want to put up with the constant seesawing, you must either starve the logical components or bind, gag and lock away in a cellar that one insistent one."

Duffy grimaced and drank some more brandy. "I'm used to the rocking, and I was never one to get motion-sick," he said. "I'll stay on the seesaw."

Aurelianus bowed. "You have that option, sir."

The Irishman smiled at the sorcerer with something akin to affection. "Do I gather you've been through one or two of these affairs yourself?"

"Oh, aye." The old man leaned back against a bureau, reached up over his head and found one of his dried snakes. He rolled it unlit between his fingers, staring at it thoughtfully. "Not in the last three centuries, thank the heavens, but in my comparative youth —yes, a number of entanglements, artfully baited, but each one eventually ending with its own version of the one standard ending."

Duffy drained his glass again and set it on the table. "This is a side of you I never glimpsed," he said. "Tell me about these girls—tell me about the last one, three centuries ago, for God's sake."

The wizard's glass was empty, too, and for a moment he goggled at the snake in his left hand and the glass in his right. Then, coming to a decision, he held the glass out for Duffy to refill. "She was a Sussex witch named Becky Banham," he said as the liquor splashed messily into his glass. "She was a small-time country witch, but definitely the real thing—not one of these horoscoping crystal-gazers."

"And this . . . liaison broke up because you were too old to compromise and didn't care to starve your logical—"

"Well, no. Not this one."

"Oh? It was her decision, then?"

"No. She—" He glared defensively at the Irishman. "She was burned at the stake."

"Oh! Sorry to hear it." Duffy didn't know what more to say about a woman who, whatever else might be said of her, had still been dead longer than his great-great-grandfather.

Aurelianus nodded. "Sorry, you say? So was I, so was I. When I heard of it, a week or two later, I . . . visited that village." He sipped his brandy thoughtfully. "You can still see a chimney or two of the place these days, sticking up from the grassed-over mounds."

Getting up abruptly, the old man lurched over to a chest in the corner. "Somewhere in here," he said, lifting back the heavy lid and flinging small objects carelessly to the side, "is a book of her country-spells she gave me. Ah? Aha!" He straightened up, holding a battered, leather-bound little book. He flipped open the front cover and read something on the flyleaf, then slammed it shut and stared at the ceiling, blinking rapidly.

Duffy found himself regretting his momentary flash of sympathy. For God's sake, man, he thought, show a little restraint, a little control. To steer the sorcerer onto less maudlin ground, he asked, "And how does the siege look to *you* lately? Any sorcerous hints or glimpses of the outcome?"

Aurelianus put the book down on a cluttered table and resumed his seat, a little self-consciously. "No, nothing. Sorcerously I'm blind and deaf, as I'm sure I explained to you. When I want to know how Vienna stands I ask someone like yourself, who has been out there and seen it happening." He put the snake in his mouth at last, and stared hard, cross-eyed, at the thing's head. After perhaps a minute a red glow showed on the end, and then with a brief gout of flame the thing was lit, and he was cheerfully puffing smoke.

Duffy cocked an eyebrow. "How much of that sort of thing can you still do?"

"Oh, I can do small things only, tricks, like making beetles stand up and jig or making girls' skirts blow up over their heads. You know the sort of thing? But I can do *nothing* that is directly aggressive to the Turks, not even send them scalp-itch or foot-stink. Of course we're protected to the same degree from Ibrahim . . . it's simply a deadlock of all the powerful areas of magic, which I think I predicted to you five months ago."

Duffy was refilling his glass again. "Yes. You wanted to get your rain-magic done while you still had no restrictions on your power—and it may well have worked."

The old wizard was mildly annoyed. *"May* have worked? It did work, you clod. Have you seen any big cannons among the Turk formations, like the ones they overthrew Rhodes with? No, you haven't. My heavy rains forced Suleiman to leave them behind."

"The rain was damned fortunate, certainly," Duffy agreed. "But can you be sure it was *summoned* rain, and not a natural phenomenon that was going to happen anyway?"

"You were there. You know. You just want to argue with me."

"Very well, I admit it worked that time in May. But what's the use of having a wizard on our side if he can't do any wizardry?"

Aurelianus let a long stream of smoke out in a sigh. "Picture yourself in a *corps-à-corps* with a swordsman who is your equal in skill; your dagger is blocking his dagger, and your sword his sword. Now your dagger isn't free to stab with—but would you say it's useless?"

"No . . . but I wouldn't just stand there straining. I'd knee the bastard and spit in his eyes. Listen, when you were describing this deadlock in advance, you said it would be virtually unbreakable."

Aurelianus frowned. "Yes. It is."

"*Virtually* doesn't mean the same thing as *absolutely*."

"Hell, man, the sun is virtually certain to rise tomorrow morning, the sea is—"

"It could be broken, though? It'd be tremendously difficult or unlikely, but it could?"

"Could a man amputate, butcher and cook his own legs to avoid starvation? Yes."

"How? Not this starving man, I mean—"

"I know. Very well, there are two courses I could take that would free all the potency of military magic. One is horribly uncertain, and the other is horribly certain. Which one would you like to hear about?"

"Both. What's the uncertain one?"

"Well, the present balance is between Ibrahim and me; it would tilt in our favor if the Fisher King himself were actually to ride out and join his will with mine in a battle. Do you understand? He'd have to *be* there physically and *take part* in it. That's unthinkably dangerous, like recklessly advancing your king out from behind the pawn wall in a chess game when your life and the lives of everyone you know are somehow at stake." He spread his hands. "After all, Vienna isn't the absolutely final place in which to make a last stand against the East. There are other strength-spots where we could regroup and not be too much worse off than we are now.

"But there is no other Fisher King to be had. If he were to be struck by a stray harquebus ball, or cut down by a particularly energetic Janissary, or simply suffer heart failure from exertion or tension . . . well, that would be the end of the story. If the West seems chaotic and disorganized now, when he's only injured, try to imagine how it will be if he dies."

"Pretty bad, no doubt. Uh . . . there'd be no way for the Turks to counter this escalation?"

"Not as things stand, no. The only way would be for the Eastern King to join in the conflict too, which would simply maintain the deadlock; it would just be tenser, with more force being exerted on both sides. But of course their King is safely hidden in Turkey or somewhere."

Duffy scratched his chin. "Would it really be so mad to bring the Fisher King into a battle? It seems to me—"

"You have no conception of the stakes," Aurelianus snapped. "If anything went wrong we'd lose *everything*. There would be no kingdoms of the West, just a waste-land of hastily organized tribes, living in the burned-out ruins of cities, waiting, probably eagerly, for Suleiman to ride through and take formal possession."

"Oh, come *on*," Duffy protested, "let's be realistic. I'll take your word that it would be bad, but it couldn't be *that* bad."

"Said the expert on metaphysical history! Brian, you've never seen a culture that has lost its center, its soul. I was not exaggerating."

The Irishman took a deep sip of the brandy. "Very well. Tell me about the other way, the . . . 'horribly certain' way."

Aurelianus frowned deeply. "I will, though it will mean breaking a fairly important vow of silence. There is a . . . process, a certain unholy gambit, which would shatter the deadlock and blow away all obstacles for any number of devastating magical attacks on our enemies. It would be equivalent to—"

"What *is* it?" Duffy interrupted.

"It's a physical action which, with certain entreaties, becomes an invocation, a summoning of a vast spirit that is old and evil beyond human understanding. His —its—participation would break this present balance of power like a keg of bricks dropped on one tray of a jeweller's scale."

"What is it?" Duffy repeated.

"To the handful who know of it it's known as Didius' Dire Gambit Overwhelming; it was discovered by a Roman sorcerer roughly a thousand years ago, and it has been hesitantly preserved and recopied through the centuries by a few notably educated and unprincipled men. It has never actually been used. At the present time I believe there are only two copies of the procedure in the world—one is said to exist in the most restricted vault of the Vatican Library, and one—" he pointed at his bookcase, "is in a very old manuscript there." The Irishman started to speak, but Aurelianus raised a hand for silence. "The action that opens the gates for this dreadful aid is, baldly stated, the blood sacrifice of one thousand baptized souls."

Duffy blinked. "Oh. I see."

"I could be done, of course. I imagine I could exert all my influence and trickery and engineer a suicide charge of a thousand men, and then watch from the battlements as they died, and pronounce the secret words. And it would certainly save Vienna . . . from the Turks. I think, though, that it would be better to die clean, without such assistance. A black gambit like that would ruin the soul of the sorcerer who performed it—among other effects, I'd likely be nothing but a drooling idiot afterward—but more importantly, it would taint the entire West. A connoisseur would be able to taste the difference in the very beer."

Duffy drained his glass again. "I notice," he said finally, "that you . . . haven't destroyed your copy of the thing."

Aurelianus didn't answer, just gave him a cold stare. "Do I tell you how to grip a sword?"

"Not lately. Sorry."

In the awkward silence that followed, Duffy refilled his glass yet again, and took a healthy swig. Good stuff, he told himself, this Spanish brandy. He sat back in his chair and had another sip. Yes sir, truly excellent . . .

For several minutes Aurelianus puffed on the short stub of the burning snake and stared at the snoring Irishman with a dissatisfied air. Finally it was too short to hold comfortably and he ground it out in the open mouth of a stone gargoyle's head on the table. He was about to awaken Duffy and send him back toward the barracks when the Irishman's eyes opened and looked at him, alertly and with no sign of drunkenness. He looked carefully around the room, then just as carefully at his own hands.

When he spoke to Aurelianus it was in a Dumnoiic Celtic dialect. "I was wondering when I'd meet you," he said. "I've been drifting back into wakefulness for some time now." He smacked his lips. "What the hell have I been drinking?"

"Distillate of wine," Aurelianus said. "Are you Brian Duffy at all?"

"Not at the moment. Did . . . did I dream a conversation with you, Merlin, in which you offered me the sword Calad Bolg and I refused it?"

"No. That occurred—right in this room a little more than five months ago."

"Oh? It seems more recent. I wasn't quite awake, I think. I could remember and recognize things, but not control my speech."

"Yes. It was still mostly Brian Duffy, but there was enough of you present to give him inexplicable memories . . . and thoroughly upset him, incidentally."

"I know. Before that I had been dreaming, over and over, of the end of things before—that last cold night beside the lake. Then afterward there was that fight in the forest—I was fully awake then, but very briefly. I saw you, but was snatched away before we could speak."

"He's been out of my sight for the last several months. Have you been completely awake at any time since that day?"

"I seem to recall waking up in the night three or four times, seeing torches and sentries and then going back to sleep. I don't know when—they could even be memories from my . . . life. And then last night I found myself in a soldiers' tavern, and wound up playing a harp and leading them in one of the old, heartening songs. They all knew lyrics for it, in one language or another—things like that never really change." He smiled. "And here I am now with, evidently, time to talk. What are the stakes and how do they stand?"

"Let's see, what terms shall I use?" For a full minute he sat silent, his fingertips pressed together; then he leaned forward, and in the rolling syllables of a tremendously old precursor of the Nørse language, asked, *"Do you remember, Sigmund, the sword you pulled from the Branstock Oak?"*

Duffy's face had turned pale, and when he spoke it was still in the Celtic. "That . . . that was a *long* time ago," he stammered.

"Longer than I like to think about," Aurelianus agreed, also in the Celtic. "But what's happening now is something we saw coming then."

Duffy was sweating. "Do you want me to . . . withdraw, and let *him* surface? I fear it has been too long —I don't think there is much of him left—but I'll try if you say to."

"No, Arthur, relax. You have most of his important memories, I think, and that will do. You see, it may be want maps of the local terrain, and an accounting of last. The entire West—which means more than you know—is menaced and tottering, and for what it's worth I think this is the battle we heard prophecies of so long ago."

The Irishman had got his color back, though he still looked shaky. "Do you mean . . . actually . . . that Surter from the far fiery south . . . ?"

"His name is Suleiman."

". . . and a horde of Muspelheimers . . ."

"They call themselves mussulmen."

"And they are menacing . . . who? The Aesir? The Celts?"

"Aye, and the Gauls and the Saxons and the Romans and everyone else west of Austria, which is where we are."

Duffy frowned. "We fight in Austria? Defending Saxons? Why don't we fall back and fortify our own lands, so as to be ready for them when they get there?"

"Because if they crash through here there may not be enough stones in all of England to build a wall they couldn't shatter. We can't let them work up the momentum. And they induct and train as soldiers the children of conquered nations, so the families we'd pass in our retreat would be the source of men we'd have to fight someday." The old man sighed. "It may indeed prove necessary to abandon Vienna and fall back—but it would be like falling back from the sundered walls of a castle to defend the keep itself. It's not a move you'd make if there was any choice."

"I see. Very well, then, we fight them here. I'll want maps of the local terrain, and an accouting of our army and a history of how the siege has gone so far. We do have cavalry, don't we? I could lead them in a—"

"It's trickier than that, Arthur," Aurelianus interrupted gently. "Listen—can you hover, awake, just below the surface of Duffy's mind, so that you could take over if I called you?"

"I think so. He might sense me, of course. You have a plan, do you?"

"Oh, no, no. I do have one option, but it's a thing," and suddenly he looked old and frightened, "it's a thing I'd . . . almost . . . rather die than do."

Duffy's knees popped as his body stood up. "It sounds like sorcery, and it sounds like something better left alone." He walked to the door. "It's late—I'll let you get some sleep. I think I'll walk around the city for a while."

"You don't speak the language. Wait until morning and I'll give you a tour."

"I think I'll manage well enough." He smiled, opened the door and was gone.

Chapter Nineteen

RAIN SWEPT IN WIDE SHEETS along the cobbled avenues, and the splashed-up mist on the stones as each gust went by looked like waves. The air in the Zimmermann dining room was a marbling of cold drafts carrying the dry-wine scent of wet streets and hot stale air smelling of candle grease and wet clothing.

At a small, otherwise unoccupied table in the kitchen-side corner, Lothario Mothertongue dipped black bread into a bowl of hot chicken broth, and chewed it slowly. His eyes were anxious as they followed the frequently interrupted course of the new serving girl. Finally as she was moving past him he caught her elbow. "Excuse me, miss. Doesn't Epiphany Hallstadt usually work this shift?"

"Yes, and I wish she was here this morning. I can't handle all this alone. Let go."

Mothertongue ignored the order. "Where is she?"

"I don't know. Let go."

"Please, miss." He stared up at her earnestly. "I have to know."

"Ask Anna, then. Anna told Mrs. Hallstadt something that made her upset, early this morning. And Mrs. Hallstadt ran out without even taking off her apron. *He may be dead,* she yelled, and just ran out."

"Who may be dead?"

"I don't *know.*" With the last word she yanked her arm free of his grip and flounced off.

Mothertongue got up and went looking for Anna. He was ordered out of the kitchen by the cooks, and earned a few impatient curses by staying long enough to make sure she wasn't in there; he opened the side door and peered up and down the rain-veiled alley;

he even barged in on a no doubt glittering conversation between Kretchmer and Werner in the wine cellar, and was rudely told to leave. When he returned to his table he saw her helping the new girl carry trays.

He waited until she was nearby, then called to her. "Anna! Where is Epiphany?"

"Excuse me, gentlemen. She's off visiting her father, Lothario, and I don't know where he lives, so leave me alone, hm? Now then, sirs, what was it you wanted?"

For several minutes Mothertongue sat dejected, reflexively looking up every time he heard the front door creak open. After a while a tall man came in, his hair plastered down by the rain, and Mothertongue recognized Brian Duffy and waved, a little reluctantly. He pursed his lips then, for Duffy had returned the wave and was crossing the room toward him.

"Hello, Brian," he said when the Irishman stood over him. "I don't suppose you'd know where Epiphany's father lives, would you? Or that you'd tell me, if you did?"

The Irishman sat down, eyed him narrowly and said something in a language Mothertongue didn't understand. Mothertongue cocked his head and raised his eyebrows, and Duffy frowned with concentration, then spoke again in Latin. In spite of an unusual accent, the Englishman was able to understand it. "You seem unhappy, friend," Duffy had said. "What troubles you?"

"I'm worried about Mrs. Hallstadt. She's been—"

"In Latinae."

Mothertongue stared in surprise at Duffy, trying to decide whether or not he was being made fun of. The intentness of Duffy's gaze reassured him, and though still puzzled he began to speak haltingly in Latin. "Uh . . . I am concerned about Epiphany. She has been feeling bad lately, and then—I am sure unintentionally —you upset her yesterday morning by abruptly reappearing after an absence of many months. Now she has evidently received some bad news about her father, whom she has gone to see, and I would like to be with her in this crisis."

"Ah. You care for this woman, do you?"

Mothertongue looked at him cautiously. "Well . . . yes. Why, do you—still have affection for her?"

The Irishman smiled. "Still? I see. Uh, no, not the sort you mean, though I naturally have a high regard for . . . the woman. I am glad she has found as worthy a man as yourself to be concerned for her."

"Why, thank you, Brian, it is good of you to be that way about it, rather than . . . be some other way. Damn this language. It has all looked completely hopeless to me of late, but perhaps something can still be salvaged of the old order."

"The old order?" Two citizens shambled past, gawking at these men speaking church language.

"Yes. Perhaps . . . perhaps you remember certain hints I was making, when I first got here, this last spring."

"Remind me."

"Well, certain powerful authorities have summoned me—" His face had begun to brighten, but now it fell. "But they might better have saved the effort. It has all failed."

"Why don't you just tell it to me."

"I will. It's an outmoded secret now. I—" he looked up, with a certain battered dignity. "I am the legendary King Arthur, re-born."

Duffy's gray eyebrows were as high as they could get. "Would you please repeat that, giving special care to your use of the verb?"

Mothertongue repeated it as before. "I know how fantastic that sounds, and I doubted it myself for years; but a number of visions, supplemented with a lot of logical reasoning, finally convinced me. As a matter of fact, I was aware that Arthur had come back long before I deduced that it was I. I believe several of my men have been re-born as well, and that some high power intended us to meet and lead the way to a final dispersal of the Turks." He shook his head. "But it has failed. I found the men, but was unable to awaken the older souls in them. I told my secret to Count von Salm, and offered to assume command of a part of the army, and I was actually *mocked*—actually laughed at and ordered to leave." Mothertongue waved in the direction of the door. "And then, idle here in my defeat, I noticed Epiphany. I happened to look in her eyes one day, and got a conviction as clear as my first convictions that Arthur had been re-born—I suddenly *knew* that this woman had known Arthur very well." He shrugged. "Need I say more?"

"Just a bit, if you would."

"She is Guinevere. The gods are kind! I was unable to awaken the dormant souls of my men with a call to duty, but I think I can awaken her soul with love."

The Irishman stared at him with the wondering respect one feels for a child who has done some tremendously difficult, absolutely pointless thing. "I wish you well," he said.

"Thank you, Brian! I would like to say I am sorry for the way I—"

He was interrupted by a sudden jolt and rumble that seemed to come up through the floor. Duffy's face changed in an instant, and he leaped up and sprinted to the front door, wrenched it open and stood there listening. Several patrons cringed at the gust of cold air and the louder hiss of the rain, but nobody dared voice any objections. After several seconds another sound cut through the rain: the strident clangor of the alarum bells in the tower of St. Stephen's.

"My God," Duffy breathed, speaking contemporary Austrian for the first time that day. "That was the *wall.*"

He ran back through the dining room, flinging several people out of his way, through the steamy kitchen and out the back door into the yard; splashing across to the stables, he dragged a reluctant mare out of the shelter, leaped and scrabbled up onto the creature's bare back, and rode her out to the street, goading her to a gallop when they reached the southward-stretching, rain-swept expanse of the Rotenturmstrasse.

The echoing pandemonium of the bells was deafening as he drummed past the cathedral square. Though the rain was thrashing down out of the gray sky as hard as ever, quite a number of people were kneeling on the pavement. Make it count, you silly bastards, he

thought grimly. If ever there was a morning for a
high-density volley of prayers, this is the one.

Soon he could hear the thousand-throated roar of
battle, and he had taken a left turn and ridden halfway down a narrower, slanting street when he saw
ahead of him, dimly through the curtains of rain, half
of a great, ragged-edged gap in the high wall, and a
maelstrom of men surging back and forth over the hills
of rubble. Even from this distance he could see the
white robes of the Janissaries. "Holy God," he murmured, then whirled out his sword and put his heels
to the mare's flanks.

The Viennese forces had been assembled within
minutes of the mine-detonations, and were now
grouped in two tightly packed divisions, trying by
sheer weight and advancing force to drive back the
waves of wailing Janissaries. This was desperate, hacking savagery, in which there was no thought except to
press forward and kill. Long gone was the almost
formal restraint of yesterday afternoon's sortie. A
culverin hastily loaded with scrap metal and gravel
had been unbolted from its moorings and was being
awkwardly manhandled by a dozen men along the top
of the wall toward the jagged edge, where it could
be re-positioned to blast its charge down into the
massed Turks; but the rain made the use of match-
locks impossible—point and edge were the order of
the day, with all the bloody intimacy of hand-to-hand
combat.

Duffy charged headlong into one of the peripheral
skirmishes that were clogging the wall street to the
north of the main fighting. He parried a scimitar and
then chopped down into a Janissary's shoulder, and the
force of the swing sent him tumbling off the back
of the wet horse so that he rode the Turk's body to
the ground. Rolling to his feet with the sword he
somehow hadn't dropped, he waded into the mêlée
with wide-eyed abandon.

For ten minutes the battle raged at a maniacal pitch,
like a bonfire into which both sides were throwing
every bit of fuel they could find. The culverin was
wedged into an adequate position on the crumbled

lip of the wall, and two men were hunched over the breech, trying to ignite the charge.

A blade rang off the slightly too large casque Duffy had earlier snatched from the head of a slain soldier, and the helmet skewed around so that one eye was covered and the other blocked by the chin-guard. With a yell of mingled rage and fright, the Irishman ducked his head and dove at his assailant, both his weapons extended. The scimitar edge, being whipped back into line, grated against Duffy's jawbone, but his own sword and dagger took the man in the belly, and Duffy fell to his knees, losing the helmet entirely, as the Turk's body folded. An eddy in the tide of battle left him momentarily in a corpse-strewn clearing, and he knelt there for a moment, panting, before unsheathing his weapons from the Janissary's vitals, struggling to his feet and lurching back into the fight.

At that moment the culverin went off, lashing thirty pounds of scrap into the heaving concentration of Turkish soldiers and killing three of the gunnery men as it tore free of its new mooring and went tumbling away outside the wall.

As if it were one huge organism the Turkish force recoiled, and the Viennese soldiers crowded up to re-take every slack inch of ground. Men were still being skewered and chopped and split by the dozens with every passing minute, but the Eastern tide had slowed to a pause and was now ebbing. The European force pressed the advantage, crowding the enemy back into the gap. At last the Janissaries retreated, leaving almost half of their number scattered broken and motionless across the wide-flung heaps of rubble. The rain made their white robes gray.

During the battle Duffy had eventually found himself among Eilif's company of mercenaries and stayed with them; when the Turk retreat left the defenders clumped like driftwood on the new stone slope, the Irishman and Eilif were only a dozen feet apart. Eilif was bowed forward, hands clenched on his knees, gasping through a slack mouth, while Duffy sat down on the bright, unweathered face of a split block of masonry. The cold air was sharp with the acid smell of new-broken granite.

Finally Eilif straightened and took off his helmet, letting the rain rinse his sweat-drenched hair. "That . . . could have tilted either way," he panted. "I don't . . . like it that fast and hard. There's no control. You can't survive . . . many of those."

"Spoken like a professional," commented Duffy, wincing in mid-word at the flash of pain in his jaw. Hesitantly he fingered the gash—the cold rain seemed to have stopped most of the bleeding, but the edges of the wound were far apart, and he could feel fresh air in unaccustomed places.

"Damn it, lad!" exclaimed Eilif, noticing the cut. "They landed one on you, didn't they? I can see one of your back teeth peeping through. As soon as we get reassembled and take roll, I'll sew that up for you, eh?"

Duffy managed to unclench his sword hand, and the released blade clattered on rock. *"You'll* sew it up? No chance—" Then he looked around and noticed for the first time the appalling casualties the Vienna force had suffered. There were arm-stumps to be cauterized and tarred, jetting wounds to be staunched, crushed limbs to be set and splinted or amputated—the surgeons would be far too busy during the next several hours to attend to so relatively minor a task as sewing up Duffy's jaw.

"Half my boys need plucking from the fire," Eilif said softly.

"Of course," Duffy said, trying to speak out of the right side of his mouth. "I just don't trust your seamstress skills. Look, I think Aurelianus is versed in the surgical arts. What would you think if I trotted back to the Zimmermann and had him stitch me up?"

Eilif regarded him narrowly, then grinned. "Why not? I'd probably sew your tongue to your cheek. And God knows we can't leave you like this—you'd lose as much beer as you swallowed. In fact, you might be wise to catch a nap there, where there's still a roof." He pointed. "Their damned mine collapsed our barracks. Lucky most of us were outside. But I want you back here by midnight, understand? There will be a heavy watch kept here, and I'll oversee our part of it until then."

"I'll be here," Duffy promised. He stood up on fatigue-trembling legs, sheathed his sword and began picking his way over the wet, tumbled stones.

By the time he had walked all the way back to the Zimmermann Inn—God knew where the mare had wound up—the rain had stopped and his wound had started to bleed again, so it was a gruesome figure that finally pushed open the front door and lurched into the dining room. There was a large but silent crowd, and they all looked up fearfully at him.

The black man in the burnoose stood. "What news?"

Duffy didn't relish the idea of a long speech. "The wall is down at one point," he said hoarsely. "It was a near thing, but they were beaten back. Heavy losses on both sides."

The man who'd asked looked around significantly and left the room, followed by several others. The Irishman paid no attention, but let his blurring gaze waver around the room until he saw Anna.

"Anna!" he croaked. "Where is Aurelianus?"

"The chapel," she said, hurrying to him. "Here, lean on me and—"

"I can walk."

The Irishman clumped heavily down the long, dark hall, and when he reached the tall doors he pushed through without stopping, stumbling over a half dozen brooms on the other side. In the chapel Aurelianus stood facing the same seven men that had been there the day before, but today each of them carried a drawn sword.

The midget looked around at the interruption. "Why it's Miles Gloriosus. Out of here, clown." He turned back to Aurelianus, extending a short blade. "Did you understand what Orkhan just said?" he asked, indicating the black man. "The wall is *down*. They'll be in by dusk. Lead us to the cask now, or be killed."

Aurelianus looked indignant, and raised a hand as if he were about to throw an invisible dart at the man.

"Be grateful, toad, that I am at present too occupied to punish this trespass. Now get out of here—while you can."

The midget grinned. "Go ahead. Blast me to ashes. We all know you can't." He jabbed the old sorcerer lightly in the abdomen.

The quiet, incense-scented air of the chapel was suddenly shattered by a savage yell as the Irishman bounded forward into the room, doing a quick hop-and-lunge that drove his sword-point through the midget's neck. Whirling with the impetus, he slashed black Orkhan's forearm to the bone. The copper-skinned man raised his sword and chopped at Duffy, but the Irishman ducked under the clumsy stroke and came up with a thrust into the man's belly. Duffy turned to face the remaining four, but one of them cried, "Why kill Merlin? It's the Dark we want!" The five survivors ran from the chapel, angling wide around Duffy.

As soon as they were running away down the hall he collapsed as if dead. Aurelianus hurried to him, rolled him over onto his back and waved a little silver filigreed ball of the Irishman's nostrils; within seconds Duffy's eyes sprang open and a hand came up to brush the malodorous thing away. He lay there and stared at the ceiling, doing nothing but breathing.

Finally, "What . . . just happened?" he gasped.

"You saved my life," the sorcerer said. "Or, more accurately, Arthur did; I recognized the old battle-cry. I'm flattered that the sight of me in peril brings him out."

"He . . . does the heroics . . . and leaves the exhaustion to me."

"I suppose that isn't quite fair," said Aurelianus brightly. "And what have you done to your jaw?"

"Sew it up, will you? Surgeons too busy." He flicked his eyes around without moving his head, and saw nothing but dusty pews to one side and shifting rain-tracks on the stained glass to the other. "Where did your Dark Birds go? Did I kill them all?"

"No. Two of them are dead on the floor over here —I'll have someone come in and deal with the corpses—and five of them ran off to steal a sip of the Dark." The old man had produced various pouches and boxes from under his robe, and was already cleaning and dressing the wound.

"Shouldn't you be—ouch!—stopping them?" Aurelianus had got out a needle and thread and was stitching the cut now; Duffy felt no real pain, just a tugging sensation across his left cheek and temple.

"Oh, no," the wizard said. "Gambrinus has defenses against such as those; as they probably suspected, since they wanted me to fetch the stuff for them. Still, desperate men will face almost anything, and trapped rats throw themselves into the catchers' nets. I'm glad to let Gambrinus finish the job for us."

"The wall is down, by the southeast corner," Duffy muttered sleepily. "Wrecked our barracks. I'm going to sleep here, out in the stables where the Vikings were; I can't remember anything about last night, not one isolated thing, but it certainly doesn't feel like I got any sleep. Those Janissaries just kept *coming,* like it had been a dam that burst. There are corpses everywhere—if tomorrow and the next day are sunny, there'll be plague. I wonder why they pulled back? That was the best chance they could have hoped for, with them in force and us completely taken by surprise."

There was a *snip* sound, and Aurelianus stood up. "There," he said. "You'll have a scar, but at least the hole's closed and it ought not to fester."

Duffy rolled over, got up on his hands and knees, and from there to his feet. "Thanks. Eilif was going to do it. Probably would have got things inside out, so I could grow a beard in my mouth and taste things with my cheek."

"What a disgusting idea."

"Sorry. The charming, sprightly ideas aren't so easy to come by anymore." He picked up his sword, wiped it and sheathed it, and strode wearily out of the dim chapel.

Anna worried for a while about the five wild-eyed men who'd burst past her and clattered down the stairs to the brewing cellar, and when she heard thin, reedy screams faintly from below she got Mother-tongue, for want of anyone hardier, to go down there with her to see what went on.

A charred meat aroma was blended not unpleasantly with the usual malt smell, and they found Gambrinus placidly juggling a number of small irregular spheres of ivory. He assured them that all was well, and Anna didn't begin to feel ill until, back in the dining room, Mothertongue asked her where she supposed the brew-master had got those five little monkey skulls he'd been playing with.

At eleven the rain began to abate, and by noon the clouds were breaking up, letting a strained, pale sun-light play intermittently over the sundered section of wall. The gap was roughly two hundred feet wide, and the wall as it continued on either side—a surprising hundred-and-fifty feet thick in exposed cross-section —leaned dangerously outward. While sharpshooters with fresh loads hammered into their rifled guns watched the distant Turkish lines, hastily assembled gangs of soldiers and laborers built solid barricades in a straight line across the rubble-choked gap, and threw up a fifty-yard-radius semicircle of deep-moored open-frame wooden obstructions on the slope outside. Chalk dust was scattered thickly beyond the semicircle, most of it darkening into gray mud as it soaked up moisture from the wet ground.

Several smoldering fires started by the explosion were finally put out, a task that hadn't been top priority because the rain had prevented them from spreading. All three corpse wagons were working their slow way across the devastated area, collecting their grisly cargo —one had already filled, left, and returned.

During that morning and afternoon the hunchbacked figure of Bluto was to be seen everywhere along the battlements, ordering the re-laying of many cannon and culverins, overseeing their cleaning and loading, shouting ignored advice down to the men outside who were building braces and buttresses to prop the leaning wall in place.

Count von Salm, ostensibly in charge, paced the

street and watched all the activity, content to let experts pursue their crafts. He had ordered most of his troops to go eat and rest in what barracks remained, keeping only a minimal force on watch; there were men along the wall, though, who kept their eyes on the Turkish lines, ready at the first sign of offensive movement to signal von Salm and the bellringer in the St. Stephen's spire.

Through the afternoon there was shifting along the Turkish front, banners moving back and forth above the occasional distant glint of sun on metal, but they seemed to be grouping to the west, toward the southern front of the city and away from the break in the wall.

At four the haggard von Salm climbed the stone stairs of the wall at the Schwarzenbergstrasse and walked a hundred yards west along the catwalk to confer with the hunchbacked bombardier. The freshening western breeze swept the crenellations, drying the sweat on the commander's face and neck; in no hurry to climb back down to the muddy, windless streets, he chatted with Bluto about various aspects of the morning's battle.

"I'm tempted to cluster a large number of guns right along here," Bluto said presently, "from the Carinthian gate to the western corner."

"Because of this shift of theirs? It's got to be a feint," von Salm objected. He ran his fingers through his graying hair. "Obviously they're not going to attack here, along this completely fortified and unweakened side, when there's a damned two-hundred-foot hole in the wall around the corner a hundred yards east."

"Look at them, though," said Bluto, leaning between two merlons and pointing south across the cloud-shadowed plain. "There's *no one* moving around to the eastern side; they're all focusing straight ahead, due south. Hell, man, if it is a feint it would take them a good half hour to re-group on the eastern plain—unless of course they want to run up close to the wall here, and run that hundred yards within range of our guns."

"That could be what they have in mind," von Salm said.

"They'd lose a thousand Janissaries, even if half our lads were asleep."

"Maybe Suleiman doesn't care. He's got more soldiers than time at this point."

Bluto shook his head. "Very well, if Suleiman isn't concerned about massive casualties, why not attack directly at the gap, and push until the defenders give way? Why this westward shift?"

"I don't know," admitted von Salm. "They may shift back under cover of darkness. That's what I would do, if I were Suleiman. But yes, set up . . . five guns along here, and I'll see you get enough men to work them. And if I see them come this way, or hear it during the night, I'll send more." He gnawed a knuckle and stared at the plain. "What's the date today? Oh, the twelfth, of course. I wish there'd be more moon tonight, and a clear sky. I'll have a gang trot outside here and dump chalk in a wide line along this front, just to make you feel better, eh?"

"Both of us," said Bluto dryly as the commander turned and began walking back the way he'd come.

The hunchback strode back and forth along the catwalk, peering through the crenels and thoughtfully laying flagged sticks at each point where he felt a gun should be wheeled up and bolted down, as the red sun sank behind the wooded hills to his right, and lights began to glow in the windows of the city at his back and, distantly in front of him, among the tents on the plain.

Since he'd lit the snake just as the bells overhead had ceased their deafening, bone-jarring announcement of nine o'clock, and it was now nearly burned down to his fingers, Duffy deduced that it must be nearly time for him to brace himself for the one stroke of the half hour. He flipped the coal-tipped stub spinning out over the rail, and watched it draw random red arabesques as it tumbled toward the square far below; then he turned to the wizard who was crouched over the telescope. "Aren't we about due for—" the Irishman began, but he was interrupted by the preludial mechanical grinding from above, so he closed his eyes and shoved his fingers in his ears until the single *bong* had been struck, and the echoes were ringing away through the dark streets below.

"Dut for what?" snapped Aurelianus irritably.

"Never mind." Duffy leaned out on the rail and looked up at the stars that were visible behind the high, rushing clouds. The crescent moon was nothing but a pale blur glowing intermittently in one of the widest patches of cloud.

A gust of particularly cold wind buffeted the cathedral tower, and the Irishman shivered and got back in under the sculptured arch of the small observatory alcove. Their narrow and drafty vantage point was not the highest or most easily accessible, but von Salm and various military advisors had two weeks ago sealed off and taken possession of the platform that commanded the best view. Aurelianus had said it didn't matter, that the little open landing they now occupied was high enough above the rooftops and street-smokes to make star-gazing possible; and for what Duffy considered to be a very long hour now that was what he had been doing.

Finally the old sorcerer leaned back from the eyepiece, rubbing the bridge of his nose with one hand and balancing the telescope on the rail with the other. "It's chaotic," he muttered. "There's no order, nothing to be read. It's . . . unpleasant to see the sky this way, it's like asking a question of an old, wise friend and getting imbecilic grunting and whining for an answer." The image seemed to upset Aurelianus, and he went on quickly. "You're the cause, you know, the random factor, the undefinable cipher that makes gibberish of all the trusty old equations."

The Irishman shrugged. "Maybe you'd have been better off without me from the start. Saved your time. Hell, I haven't really done anything so far that any hired bravo couldn't have done."

"I don't know," Aurelianus said. "I'm limited to what I can actually see and touch—I don't *know!*"

He looked at Duffy. "Did you hear about the newest movement of the Janissaries?"

"Yes. They've shifted west, as if they intended a suicide charge at the unweakened southwestern front. What about it?"

"What do you think would happen if they did attack there?"

Duffy shrugged. "Like I said—suicide. They'd lose a thousand men in five minutes."

"Might one call it a . . . sacrifice?"

"To gain what? There'd be no sense in sending the Janissaries, their finest troops—oh my God." The Irishman carefully sat down and leaned his back against the rail. "I thought you had one of the only two copies of the damned thing in the world."

"So did I." Aurelianus squinted out over the dark rooftops. "And maybe I do. Maybe Ibrahim has got the Vatican copy . . . or hopes somehow to get mine." He shook his white head thoughtfully. "As soon as I heard of the shift it occurred to me—it's the *Janissaries,* the troops conscripted from among the children of conquered Christians . . ."

"At *least* a thousand baptized souls."

"Right."

"Look, he's probably got spies in the city—it may very well be that he doesn't yet have a copy of Didius' Loathesome Whatnot, and is counting on having yours stolen." The sorcerer stared at him blankly, so Duffy went on. "Isn't it obvious? Destroy your copy."

Aurelianus looked away, frowning deeply. "I'm . . . not ready to do that."

The Irishman felt a wave of pity and horror. "Don't even consider it, man! There must be clean strategies— and even if we do lose Vienna, you've said the main thing is having the Fisher King alive. You and he could escape through those tunnels the Dark Birds mentioned, and set up for a better stand somewhere else. The Turks can hardly come any further into Europe *this* season."

"Quite possibly true, Brian, but how can I *know?* With the right kind of sorcerous aid maybe they could come farther, maybe much farther. Maybe the Fisher

King will die if he doesn't get a draught of the Dark—
he'll certainly get no better. Hell, it's not hard to do
the honorable thing when you can see, up ahead, how
it is going to turn out. *Damn* this blindness," he hissed,
pounding a fist against the stone, "and damn Ibrahim,
and damn that old painter."

Duffy blinked. "What old painter?"

"What? Oh, Gustav Vogel, of course. He's clairvoyant, as I've told you, and he isn't allied to the
presently occluded old magic. If I could have got that
sanctimonious old bastard to do a few more visionary
paintings, I might have been able to see what is coming, and be able to forget this . . . terrible move. But
the old wretch was afraid of me—may the Janissaries
use his head for a cannon ball!—and in the last two
years he has done nothing."

"That's true," agreed Duffy with a sympathetic nod.
"Aside from that crazy *Death of the Archangel Michael*
on his wall, I guess he hasn't."

Aurelianus emitted a choked scream, and the telescope spun away over the rail. *"What,* damn you?
Llyr and Mananan! Such a work exists?" He was on
his feet, waving his fists. "Why didn't you tell me this
before, fool? *You* are Michael the Archangel to him—
don't you remember the portrait you sat for, that led
me to you? Michael is the only Christian identity he
can put to what you are. Idiot, don't you see the importance of this? This old artist has clairvoyant, and
likely prophetic, powers. And he's done a picture, I
gather, *of your death.* There may very well be a clue
in it to the outcome of this battle."

From below came the muted crash of the telescope
hitting the pavement. "Oh?" said Duffy, a little stiffly.
"Whether or not it shows my corpse surrounded by
bloody-sworded Turks, you mean?"

"Well, yes, roughly. There would be a lot of other,
more esoteric, indications to look for as well. But
haven't you seen this picture, at least? What is it of?"

The Irishman shrugged apologetically. "I seem to
recall a lot of figures. To tell you the truth, I never
really looked. But if you're right about all this, I hope

it's a picture of an incredibly old man, surrounded by hundreds of friends, dying moderately drunk in bed."

Visibly controlling his impatience, the wizard took a deep breath and exhaled slowly. "Let's go and see," he said.

They clattered down the stairs and set out across the city at a trot that brought them to the old Schottengasse boarding house in ten minutes, and left Aurelianus gasping asthmatically for breath. "No," he croaked when Duffy indicated a bench to sit down on in the entry hall. "Onward!"

They had not brought a light, and so had to grope and stumble up the dark stairs. For a moment Duffy was nervous about having the lake-vision again, but then he sensed that in some way things had gone beyond that. It was not a reassuring thought.

When they reached the third floor landing Duffy himself was panting heavily, and Aurelianus was incapable of speech, though he managed jerkily to wave one arm in furious query. Duffy nodded, found Gustav Vogel's door by touch and pounded on it.

There was no answer or sound of any kind from within. The Irishman knocked again, louder than before, and several people opened other doors in the darkness to complain—Aurelianus summoned enough breath to damn them and order them back into their holes—but Vogel's room was silent.

"Break it," the wizard gasped, *"down."*

Duffy wearily stepped back two paces, which was all that was possible in the corridor, and leaped at the painter's door, curling his shoulder around to take the impact. The door sprang out of the frame as if it had merely been propped there, and it and the Irishman crashed into the room, overturning shabby furniture.

There was a lamp, turned down to a dim glow, on a table in the corner; when he got dizzily to his feet he saw Epiphany sitting beside it, her oddly unstartled face streaked with tears. He took a step closer and saw the body stretched out face-up on the floor—it was Gustav Vogel, and from the look of him he had died, perhaps a week earlier, of starvation.

"Good God," he murmured. "Oh, Epiphany, I—"

"He's dead, Brian," she whispered. She tilted an empty glass up to her lips, and the Irishman wondered how many times she had done it, and when she'd notice that it was empty. "I stopped bringing him food, because I was always drunk and couldn't bear to face him. It wasn't the boys' fault. It was my fault, and your fault, and mainly—" She looked up and turned pale as Aurelianus lurched in through the broken doorway, "it was that monster's fault! Has he come to gloat?"

"What . . . is this?" gasped Aurelianus. "What's happened?"

Epiphany's answering yell started as words but quickly became a shriek. She got up from the table, snatched a long knife from under her apron, and with surprising speed rushed at the exhausted sorcerer.

Duffy stepped forward to stop her—

—and then abruptly found himself standing at the other side of the room, out of breath. Aurelianus was leaning against the wall, and Epiphany, he noticed after glancing around, was huddled in a motionless heap in the corner. He looked back at Aurelianus.

The wizard answered the frantic question that burned in the Irishman's eyes. "It was Arthur," he said in an unsteady voice. "Seeing me in peril, he . . . took over for a moment. Caught her and tossed her aside. I don't know—"

Duffy crossed the room, crouched, and rolled the old woman over. The knife hilt stood out of her side, with no metal visible between the hilt and the cloth of her dress. There was very little blood. He bent down to listen for breath, and couldn't hear any. There was no perceptible pulse under her jaw.

His whole body felt cold and empty and ringing like struck metal, and his mouth was dry. "My God, Piff," he was saying reflexively, not even hearing himself, "did you mean to? You didn't *mean* to, did you?"

Aurelianus pushed himself away from the wall and caught the vacant-eyed Irishman by the shoulder. "The *picture*," he snarled, cutting through Duffy's babbling, "where's the *picture?*"

After a few moments Duffy carefully lowered Epiphany's head to the ground. "Much has been lost, and there is much yet to lose," he said softly, wondering where he'd heard that and what it meant. Dazed, he stood up while Aurelianus seized the lamp and turned up the wick.

The Irishman led him to the wall. "Here," he said, waving at it. He didn't look at it himself—he just stared numbly back at the two bodies.

Several seconds passed, then Aurelianus said in a strangled voice, *"This?"*

Duffy turned, and followed the wizard's gaze. The wall was solid black from end to end, from top to bottom. The artist had painstakingly added so many fine penstrokes of shading and texturing, his concern for detail growing as his sight diminished, that he had left no tiniest strip or dot of plaster uncovered. *The Death of the Archangel Michael,* which had, the last time Duffy had seen it, seemed to be taking place in deep twilight, was now shrouded in the unredeemed darkness of starless, moonless night.

Aurelianus was looking at him now. "He," Duffy said helplessly, "he just kept adding to it."

The wizard gave the wall another minute of silent, useless scrutiny, and then turned away. "You're still a cipher."

He led the way out of the room and the Irishman automatically followed him.

Duffy's mind kept replaying for him the moment when he'd rolled Epiphany's body over. Epiphany is dead, he told himself wonderingly as they made their way down the dark stairs, and soon you'll become aware that that's one whole chamber in your head that you can close up and lock, because there won't ever be anything in it anymore. She's dead. You came all the way back from Venice to kill her.

They walked together, without speaking, until they came to the Tuchlauben; there Aurelianus turned north toward the Zimmermann Inn while Duffy continued on in the direction of the barracks and the gap, though it was still well short of midnight.

Chapter Twenty

AT LONG LAST the waxing glow of dawn divided the irregularly edged paleness of the gap from the high blackness of the leaning walls; what had two hours ago been no more than three stippled lines of bright orange dots in the dark could now be seen to be three ranks of silent, kneeling harquebusiers along the crest of the rubble mound. Behind them, though still outside the new barricade, stood two more companies apiece of landsknechten and Reichshilfe troops, motionless except for the occasional bow of a head to blow on a dimming matchcord.

One of the companies along the mound was Eilif's, and Duffy was crouched in the center of the front line. He unclamped his hand from the gunstock and absently stretched out the fingers. It seemed to him that in the depths of his mind a bomb had been detonated, which, though too far down to be directly perceptible, had blown loose great stagnant bubbles of memory to come wobbling up to the surface; and he thanked God for even this faintest first light, for it restored to him external things to focus his attention on. During the last five hours he had been staring into a cold blackness as absolute as Gustav Vogel's final drawing.

The faint click of metal on stone, as one of the sentries up on the wall grounded his pike, finally snapped Duffy completely out of his terrible night-meditations. He breathed deeply the chilly dawn breeze and tried to sharpen his senses.

The man to his right leaned toward him. "You couldn't *get* me up on those walls," he whispered. "The mines have got them tottering."

The Irishman raised his hand in a be-silent gesture.

Damn this chattering idiot, Duffy thought—did I hear another sound? From the shadowy plain? He peered suspiciously along the barrel of his propped-up harquebus. Every patch of deeper gloom on the plain beyond the white chalk line seemed to his tired eyes to seethe with wormy shapes, but he decided finally that he could see no real motion. He sat back, shivering.

Several long minutes passed, during which the gray light brightened by slow degrees. Through carefully cupped hands Duffy peered at his slowmatch, and was relieved to see that the dawn dampness had not dimmed its red glow. His mail coif was itching his scalp, and from time to time he instinctively tried to scratch his head, forgetting that he had on a riveted steel salade.

"I sure hope that hunchback's kept his cannon-primings dry," muttered the man on Duffy's right again. "I think—"

"Shut up, can't you?" Duffy whispered. Then he stiffened; he'd seen the gray light glint on metal a few hundred yards away, then at several points along a dark line. He opened his mouth to whisper a warning to the other men, but he could already hear the rustle as they flexed chilled joints and looked to their powder and matches. There was a low whistle from atop the warped wall, showing that the sentry too had seen the activity.

The Irishman screwed his match into the firing pin, made sure his pan was filled with powder, and then looked along the barrel at the furtively advancing line. His heart was pounding, his fingertips tingled and he was breathing a little fast. I'll give one shot, he thought —two at the most, if they're slow in getting over the obstruction-fence—and then I'm flinging this machine down and using my sword. I just can't seem to feel really in control with a firearm.

Then there was the muted drum-roll of boots on dirt as the Turks broke into a run—they're akinji, Duffy realized, the lightly armed Turkish infantry; thank God it isn't the Janissaries, whom half the men expected to shift back to this side during the night. The man beside Duffy was panting and scrabbling at the trigger of his gun. "Don't shoot yet, fool," the Irishman rasped.

"Want your ball to drop short? Wait till they reach the chalk line."

In perhaps thirty seconds they reached it, and the gap in the wall lit up briefly as the first line of harquebuses fired, followed a moment later by a flame-gushing blast of gravel and stones from one of the culverins on the battlements. The front of the advancing akinji tide was ripped apart, scimitars flying from nerveless fingers as torn bodies tumbled and rolled across the dirt, but their maniacal fellows pressed on without a pause, over a wide segment of the fence that had been blown down. A rank of standing harquebusiers fired into the Turkish force, and then the akinji were mounting the slight slope below the wall.

There was clearly no time to reload, so Duffy tossed his still-sparking gun aside and, standing up, drew his rapier and dagger. I wish the light were better, he thought. "Two steps back, my company!" he called. "Don't get separated!"

Then the Turks were upon them. Duffy sighted the man who would hit him, parried the flashing scimitar with his rapier guard and stabbed the man in the chest with his dagger. The jolt of impact pushed the Irishman back a step, but didn't knock him over. A sword-edge rang against his helmet, and he gave its owner a quick slash across the face as another blade snapped in half against his hauberk. The defenders' line was slowly giving way when a harsh call sounded from behind them: "We're reloaded back here! *Christians, drop!*"

Duffy parried a hard poke at his face and then fell to his hands and knees even as a mingled roar of gunfire went off at his back and the cold air around him was filled with the whiz-and-thud of lead balls striking flesh. "On your feet!" he yelled a moment later, hopping up to meet the next wave of akinji as their predecessors reeled back and fell.

The man on Duffy's right took a sword through his belly and, clutching himself, somersaulted down the slope, so that the Irishman suddenly found himself facing two—then three—of the akinji. All at once his cautious confidence in his own skill was eroding, and he sensed the nearness of real, incapacitating fear.

"Get over here, somebody!" he yelled, desperately parrying the licking scimitars with sword and dagger. His troop of men had retreated away from him, though, and he hadn't even a wall to get his back to. He took a flying leap at the Turk on his right, trusting his hauberk and salade to absorb the worst of the attacks of the other two; he swept the man's scimitar away in a low line with both his sword and dagger, and riposted with a long thrust of the dagger that he accurately drove into the Turk's throat. The other two akinji struck at Duffy then; one of them swung a hard cut at Duffy's shoulder, and though the blow stung, the mail blocked the sword-edge and the scimitar flew into three pieces; the other lunged in with his sword extended straight, and his point, cutting through the Irishman's leather doublet, found one of the gaps in his mail shirt and sank an inch into his side.

Duffy whirled back when he felt the shock of cold steel in him and sent the Turk's wide-eyed head spinning from his shoulders with a furious scything chop. The field momentarily clear, he scrambled a few steps up the slope and through one of the openings in the barricade that divided the rocky crest, to rejoin his fellow Austrians.

As he lurched up over the top, with the scuff and rattle of the pursuing akinji sounding loud behind him, he caught a glimpse of soldiers standing behind a line of what appeared to be narrow, chest-high tables, and he heard someone's agonized yell: "My God, dive for it, Duffy!"

He caught the urgency in the voice, and without pausing kicked forward in a long dive down the inward slope, ripping his leather gloves and banging his helmet and knees as he tumbled across the raw stones. Even as he moved, a quick series of ten loud explosions concussed the air in front of him like very rapid hammer-strokes; there followed two more stuttering blasts of ten, and then there was a pause.

Duffy had rolled to the gravelly bottom of the slope with his face down and his legs up, and by the time he'd struggled into a sitting position he realized what the tablelike things were—sets of ten small cannons braced together like log rafts, fired by putting a match to the trail of serpentine powder poured across all the touchholes. *Orgelgeschutzen,* the Austrians called them, though from his stay in Venice Duffy thought of them as *ribaldos,* their Italian name.

"Quick, Duff, get back here," came Eilif's voice. The Irishman got to his feet and sprinted ten yards to where the troops were clustered. "Why did you stay out there?" Eilif demanded. "You knew we were to fire two volleys and then fall back to let them run into the teeth of these things." He waved at the *ribaldos.*

"I," Duffy panted, "figured our retreat would look more convincing if a man or two hung on."

The Swiss landsknecht raised a dusty eyebrow and stared hard at Duffy. "Really?"

There was another rush of akinji over the splintered barricade along the top, but it seemed disspirited; when two more bursts of the small-calibre cannon-fire whipped them apart, the survivors backed off fast, and a few seconds later the sentries on the wall called down the news that the akinji were retreating back toward their lines.

"Well of course really," Duffy answered. "What did you think, that I just forgot?"

Eilif grinned. "Sorry." He gestured at the new corpses on the crest and shrugged. "I guess it was a clever move." He trotted away to the slope and began climbing up to see in what direction the Turks retreated.

The Irishman felt hot blood running down his side and gathering at his belt, and suddenly remembered the wound he'd taken. He pressed a hand to it and plodded through the reassembling ranks, looking for a surgeon. His mind, though, wasn't on the sword-cut —in his head he was listening again to his brief dialogue with Eilif, and uneasily admiring his own quick improvisation. Because actually, he thought, your first suspicion was right, Eilif. I *did* forget. And what does *that* say about me?

The sun had risen above the eastern horizon, but the bulk of the ruined wall cast a shadow that was still dark enough to make readily visible the watch-fires up and down the street. Duffy stumbled about randomly until his eyes adjusted to the dimness, and very shortly he was surprised to see Aurelianus warming his hands over one of the fires. Their eyes met, so the Irishman reluctantly crossed the littered space of cobbles to where the wizard stood.

"Keeping the home fires burning, eh?" Duffy said with a pinched and artificial smile. "And what brings you so uncharacteristically close to the front line?"

"This is childish enough," the wizard said bitterly, "without a theatrical rendition of ignorant innocence from you. What were you thinking, a—ach, you're bleeding! Come here."

Newly awakened soldiers were dashing up from the direction of the barracks, shivering in their chilly chain mail and rubbing their eyes, and other men were dragging the wounded back inside. Duffy sat down beside Aurelianus' fire. The sorcerer had taken his medicine box out of his pouch and fished from it a bag that was spilling yellow powder. "Lie down," he said.

Duffy brushed away some scattered stones and complied. Aurelianus opened the Irishman's doublet and lifted his rusty mail shirt. "Why the hell don't you keep your hauberk clean?" he snapped. "This doesn't look too bad, though. He obviously didn't lean into the thrust." He tapped some of the powder into the wound.

"What's that stuff?" asked Duffy, frowning.

"What do you care? It'll keep you from getting poisoned, which is what you deserve, wearing a rusty hauberk." He took a roll of linen from the box and expertly bandaged the wound, running strips around Duffy's back to hold it in place. "There," he said. "That ought to hold body and soul together. Get up."

Duffy did, puzzled by the harshness in the wizard's voice. "What—" he began.

"Shut up. I want to know about your little trick last night. What were you thinking, an eye for an eye, a girl for a girl?"

The Irishman felt something that might become a vast anger begin to build up in himself. "I don't think

I understand," he said carefully. "Are you talking about my . . . the way I . . . the way Epiphany died?"

"I'm talking about your theft of my book, damn it, while I was pottering about in the chapel afterward. You will give it back."

Sudden apprehension scattered the kindling of Duffy's rage. His eyes widened. "Good God, do you mean Didlio's Whirling Gambits or whatever it's called? Listen, *I* didn't—"

"No, not Didius' Gambit." Aurelianus was maintaining his offended frown, but his wrinkle-bordered eyes were beginning to look disconcerted. "I hid that Monday night, after talking to . . . you. No, I mean Becky's book."

"Who the hell—oh, that book your witch girlfriend gave you, three hundred years ago? I didn't take it." Duffy shrugged. "What would I want with the damned thing?"

Aurelianus' expression held for another moment, then without too much change became a frown of worry. "I believe you. Hell! I was hoping it would turn out to have been you."

"Why?"

"Because, for one thing, I'd have been able to get it back without much trouble. You wouldn't have been troublesome about it, would you? I didn't think so. And for another thing, I could have assumed no one had interfered with my guards."

Duffy sighed and sat down again beside the fire. "What guards?"

"Little birdlike creatures that live in that dollhouse structure above my door—pretty things they are, with fine leathery wings of a mother-of-pearl luster, but savage as kill-trained dogs and quick as arrows." Aurelianus crouched near him. "I have a dozen of them, and I've trained them to refrain from attacking me, or any visitors that come into the room with my evident approval. When you were there five or six months ago I conveyed to them by signals that you were to be permitted to enter the room alone. Don't be too flattered—I just figured that in the heat of these last battles I might sometime want to send you back there for something, while staying at the scene of the action myself."

Duffy nodded. "Ah. Don't worry, I wasn't flattered. And there is no one else they've been instructed to let in alone?" The wizard shook his head. "Then you've got inadequate guards," the Irishman said helplessly. "Somebody got by them. Did you check whether they're still in their nest, and alive?"

"Yes. They're in there, in perfect health." He rubbed his eyes tiredly. "That means the intruder was an initiate of certain very secret mysteries, or the lackey of such a one. Those creatures are from another sort of world, and very few people know about them. Ibrahim probably knows, and no doubt whoever broke in was a spy of Ibrahim's which I should have anticipated. Why do I keep failing to—"

"How would this person have knocked them out?" Duffy interrupted. The sun was beginning to clear the mound, and he raised a hand to shield his eyes.

"Oh, there are two notes which, though pitched too high to be audible to the human ear, can counter and blank out the brain waves of these things; the two notes correspond to the pulse of their brains, but are contrary, and have an effect like stopping a garden swing by leaning back and forth at the wrong times. I've seen it done—the man used a tiny one-holed pipe and blew a long steady breath, rapidly covering and uncovering the hole with one finger: the cageful of little fellows just pitched over as if dead. Then when he stopped they all got up again."

"Could he do it inhaling?" Duffy asked sharply.

Aurelianus looked started. "No, as a matter of fact. The tones would be wrong—two low, maybe even audible. No."

"Quick as arrows, you said. By how far is that an exaggeration?"

"Not very damned far." The sorcerer smiled sheepishly. "I see what you mean, of course. For anything more than the quickest look-and-grab it would have had to be two men taking turns, one piping while the other catches his breath and uses two hands on something."

Duffy got to his feet and moved to the side, so that he could see Aurelianus without squinting into the sun. "Are you *certain* someone got in? To judge by the mess that room is in, losing one book would be so easy as to be almost inevitable."

"I'm certain. I know exactly where I left it. Besides, there were other signs of an intruder—things were picked up and replaced in not quite the same position, a number of books were looked at, to judge by the scuffing of the dust on the shelves, and one of my smoking-snakes was bitten. Someone evidently assumed it was a sort of sweetmeat."

Duffy shuddered, imagining the person's surprise and dismay. "It was Werner," he said.

"Werner? Don't be ridic—"

"I saw a one-holed pipe on the table in his little wine-closet, and I remember it wouldn't produce any noise I could hear. This poet friend of his, this Kretchmer, must be a spy for the Turks. Wait a minute, don't interrupt! Through flattery of Werner's doubtless trashy poetry, and the bestowal of sexual favors by some woman pretending to be Kretchmer's wife, the man has got your poor innkeeper into a state where he'd do anything for him."

Aurelianus was silent for a few moments. "Even a woman, eh? The silly old fool. Fancies himself the great poet and lover, I expect. I'll bet you're right. Damn, why wasn't I suspicious of Kretchmer from the start?" He slapped his forehead. "I'm as easily taken in as poor Werner. Kretchmer must have been ordered by Ibrahim to get my copy of Didius' Dire Gambit Overwhelming. Yes, and wasn't Werner asking me months ago if he could borrow some books sometime, with the hint that he'd like free access to my library? Then when I refused, Kretchmer would have had to learn of my little guards—I'd like to have seen *that* brief encounter—and then consult Ibrahim for a way to get around them. It must have taken some time to get in touch with the Turkish adept, for it was only this last Monday I thought I saw footprints in the dust on my floor; the two of them must just have been taking inventory that time, after which Kretchmer would somehow have got outside to show the list of books to the then nearby Ibrahim. Right! And Ibrahim would have known which of those books it would be in, and he sent them back to get it."

"But you hid it Monday night," Duffy remembered.

"Yes. So last night, Tuesday night, they whistled their way in again, failed to find the book where they'd last seen it, and grabbed probably several books at random, of which Becky's is the only one I've missed. I'll have to do an inventory myself. Damn. I should probably check the wine cabinet, too."

Duffy started to speak, but Aurelianus interrupted him with a bark of laughter. "Do you remember when Werner turned up all bloody and limping, and claimed one of your Vikings had got drunk and tried to kill him? No, that's right, you had already moved out by then. In any case, Bugge denied it when I asked him about it."

"So?"

"So Werner was probably the one who first discovered my guards. He couldn't have got more than a step or two into the room, or he'd never have got back out alive."

The cool west wind had blown away the gunpowder smell, and now Duffy could catch the aroma of a pot of oniony stew cooking somewhere. He looked up and down the street, and soon noticed the half-dozen men huddled around one of the fires fifty yards south of him. The Irishman yanked straight his hauberk and tunic with, he hoped, an air of finality and conclusion. "So what will you do now?" he asked.

"Kretchmer and Werner won't know we're aware of their deceits, so I don't think they'll be hard to find. We'll go confront them, make them return whatever they took, and then you can kill them."

Duffy stared at him. "I can't leave this area. I'm on call. I'm defending the West, remember? Hell, why don't you just go sift something deadly into their wine?" He started to leave, then paused. "Oh, and I'd try to get them to admit some of it. It's just possible that Werner had some other reason to own that silent whistle. Here, I've got it—put some disabling venom

in their wine, and then tell them they can have a sip
of the antidote only after they've told you all. Then if
they should somehow happen to be innocent, you can
give them the antidote and apologize."

Aurelianus shook his head. "You're all right with a
sword, Brian, but you'd make a hair-raising diplomat.
No, I think Werner alone I can effectively crack without the stage props, and with his testimony I'll be able
to get a dozen armed men to grab Kretchmer for me
. . . assuming he's still in the city."

"Ah. Well, good luck in capturing the pair." Duffy
yawned. "I guess the main thing is that they didn't get
Didius' Horrors, eh? And now if you'll excuse me there
is a plateful of stew down there waiting for me to ladle
it out of the pot, and beyond that, under an improvised
canvas roof, is a cot waiting to fulfill its purpose in the
scheme of things by letting me fall asleep on it."

"Good enough," said the wizard. "I'll go set my
traps. Oh, and I've got to try to see von Salm, and tell
him that the Turks are likely to re-form in the vulner-
able east again, since Ibrahim no longer has any reason to sacrifice his thousand baptized souls."

"Well, give him my regards," Duffy said, his words
made almost incomprehensible by a huge yawn. "And
thanks for this latest patch-up job."

"You're welcome. Get a new hauberk, hmm?" Aurelianus turned and strode away west. Duffy pointed
himself south, toward the stew. The sun was up now,
shining through a break in the golden clouds, and
Duffy had to squint against the glare.

Throughout the long morning, patches of light and
shadow dappled the plain in shifting patterns, and
once or twice veils of rain whirled across the city or
the Turkish tents like the skirts of the passing clouds.

As Aurelianus had predicted, the Turkish troops
were shifting around to face the eastern wall with its
gap like a missing tooth in a stony jaw. Sentries
crouched to lay their ears against the pavement, and
many claimed to hear the digging of miners at several
points north of the collapsed section of wall. There
was sporadic trading of booming cannon-fire, but,

aside from a particularly heavy burst of Turkish firing by the south wall at about noon, the cannonade was little more than a desultorily observed formality.

Battle was anticipated, and the sellers of horoscopes and luck pieces did a good business among soldiers and citizens alike. Prostitutes and liquor vendors clustered around the makeshift landsknecht barracks, taking their own share of the weirdly inverted economy common to all long-besieged cities. The solace of Faith was free, but nothing else was—and food was much harder to buy than luck, sex, or a drink.

Duffy opened his eyes and crossed without a jolt from unremembered dreams into wakefulness. St. Stephen's was tolling two, and the gray light that slanted in under the awning waxed and waned as the tattered clouds moved across the sun. He stood up and put on his boots, hauberk, doublet and sword, pushed the curtain aside and stepped out into the street. A wine vendor was wheeling his cart past, and the Irishman called for a cup. The man's young son trotted over with it and asked an exorbitant price, which Duffy paid after bestowing his fiercest frown on the unconcerned lad. His company wasn't due to muster until three o'clock, so he took the wine—which proved to be sour—over to a corner where the tumbled wall of a warehouse wall formed a rough bench.

He leaned back and closed his eyes, and ran one open palm over a gritty stone surface. He was mildly surprised to discover that he felt now none of last night's stark, guilty horror—just a tired sadness about the losses of a lot of things, of which Epiphany was admittedly the most poignant. There was a distance to it, though—it was the sort of melancholy that can be taken down from the shelf and bitterly savored during a leisure hour, and not any longer the plain pain that is no more escapable than a toothache. He suspected that this not unpleasant abstraction was the numbing effect of emotional shock, and would, like the quick, natural anesthesia of a serious injury, wear off before long. It did not occur to him that it might be resignation to the idea of his own death.

Opening his eyes and straightening up, he was not surprised to see Aurelianus in the area again, fussily picking his way toward him over and around the scattered chunks of masonry. As he stepped closer Duffy noticed a new bandage tied around his forehead and under his ears that had blotted red over his cheek.

Duffy smiled, a little surprised to discover that he could find no anger in himself toward the ancient sorcerer. "What ho, wizard?" Duffy boomed politely when Aurelianus was in earshot. "Did von Salm take a poke at you with his rapier? You were probably explaining to him how things are not what they seem, am I right?"

"I didn't see von Salm," Aurelianus said, trying to scratch his forehead under the bandage. "They wouldn't let me up in the cathedral spire to speak with him." He shook his head in angry exasperation. "Damn it —if this impasse between Ibrahim and me didn't render the whole magical field so inert, he'd be no more necessary than a child with a sling-shot."

"Well, you can still do low-power magics, right? Couldn't you have got by those guards?"

Aurelianus sighed deeply and sat down. "Oh, certainly. I could—with a mere gesture!—have given them all . . . some damn thing . . . the bowel-quakes, say, and made it impossible for them to stay at their posts. But it's so *undignified*. And I know von Salm wouldn't listen anyway. Yes, the small-time country type spells still work as well as ever, but there's not any battle-handy magic in them—just homey lore on how to harvest your wheat, milk your cows and brew your beer, or how to foil a disliked neighbor's attempts to do those things. Hell. I hope Ibrahim is as discouraged as I am." He looked up cautiously. "You missed Mrs. Hallstadt's wake."

Again the Irishman felt a wash of the almost mellow regret, as if of events that happened centuries ago. "Oh? When?"

"Early this morning they . . . found the bodies. When the news reached the Zimmermann a spontaneous wake developed, and Werner wasn't due back until nightfall—he and Kretchmer are off somewhere,

I don't know where—so the affair proceeded un-hindered for several hours."

"Ah." Duffy sipped his inferior wine thoughtfully. "So what are you going to do about our two poets?"

"I've got a half-dozen armed men waiting for them, led by my man Jock—Giacomo Gritti, remember?— and they'll capture them and bind them to await my interrogation."

Duffy nodded. "I see." He emptied his cup and shuddered. "Incidentally, what *has* made the bandage necessary? Did you cut yourself shaving?"

"Oh—no, I was on the wall watching Mother-tongue's charge."

Duffy raised an eyebrow. "Mothertongue's charge?"

"Didn't you hear about it?"

"I've been asleep," Duffy explained.

"Huh. I would have thought all the cannon-fire would have awakened you." The wizard shrugged sadly. "The poor idiot. He got a full suit of old plate armor from the stores somewhere, made somebody lock him up in it, and then rode his horse through an unguarded ferrier's door in the outer wall, right beside the Wiener-Bach—that little stream that runs along the eastern side of the wall."

"I think I know the door you mean," Duffy said. "I didn't know it had been left unguarded, though. So poor old Mothertongue charged off to save the day, eh?"

"That's right. All by himself, too, since Bugge and the northmen have finally convinced him that they don't want to be knights of the round table. He even carried a makeshift lance and banner, and recited a lot of poetry or something outside the wall before he galloped off. All the men on the battlements were cheering him on and making bets on how far he'd get."

"How far *did* he get?"

"Not far. A hundred yards or so, I guess. He must have startled the Turk gunners—this high-noon charge by one rusty old knight. They soon got over their sur-prise, though, and touched off several guns. It was mostly canister and grapeshot for cutting down troops, but they even let go with a nine-pounder or two. That's how I cut my cheek—a few bits of flying metal or stone came whistling around the parapet."

"And they got him . . . ?"

"Mothertongue? Certainly. Blew him and his horse to bits. It served one purpose, at least—we sealed up that door and included it in the sentry's rounds."

"Damned odd," said Duffy. "I wonder what pushed him over the edge."

The hollow cracking of four cannons interrupted Aurelianus' reply. Duffy looked up at the battlements. "Sounds like the twelve-pounders," he observed. "I guess Bluto figures the Janissaries have no business taking afternoon naps . . ."

Two more cannon detonations shook the pavement, and then he heard the cracking of the sharpshooters' rifled guns. He was on his feet immediately. "It must be a charge," he snapped, and was running toward the square by the gap even as the cacophanous alarum bells began clanging across the city from the St. Stephen's tower.

Abruptly, with a peal of thunder that rattled his teeth, the pavement punched his running legs aside and rushed up to slam his chest and face and bounce him over onto his back. For an instant he lay dazed, choking on his own blood and watching the top of the wall, which was leaning inward toward him, slowly dissolving from an architectural structure into a churning cascade of bricks, stones and dust. Then he was rolling, tumbling and crawling back, his breath blowing in and out in wet wheezes, trying desperately in the seconds remaining to put as much distance as possible between himself and the collapsing wall.

It seemed to take forever to come down. His wounded-spider scuttling had taken him past the midpoint of the square when a vast hammer impacted on the street behind him and he was tossed forward in a multiple somersault that ended in a painful twenty-foot slide. He wound up lying on his side, and managed to sit up. His ears were ringing, and for almost a minute the air was so thickly opaque with smoke and dust that trying to breathe was a solitary nightmare of gagging and coughing.

Then he could hear gunfire, a lot of it, and the steady western breeze was blowing the mushrooming dust cloud back through the new gap, into the eyes of the charging Janissaries. Several companies of soldiers were trotting up in orderly formation as the hastily assembled harquebusiers fell back to reload, and trumpet calls were sounded to summon more troops. Duffy looked over his shoulder and saw Aurelianus fifty yards down the street hurrying away.

He took a long breath, coughed deeply twice, then got to his feet and plodded forward into the gathering press of European soldiers.

The two fallen segments of wall had left an unsteady tower between them, and for twenty furious minutes the fighting seethed around it like waves crashing around an outcropping in the surf, with no ground really being gained by either side. Presently, though, the Viennese forces managed to bring some bigger guns to bear—six ten-barrelled *ribaldos* adding their *rat-tat-tat* snare drum detonations to the din, and a dubiously moored culverin, on the southern edge of the solid wall, that every five minutes rocked back and sent loosened stones clattering down as it whipped charge after charge of gravel into the ullulating mass of white-robed Janissaries.

Through the early afternoon the Turkish troops kept advancing and falling back, and losing hundreds of men in a vain effort to summon up the impetus that would break the desperate ranks of Europeans. Finally at about three-thirty they retreated, and the Viennese forces took turns standing in the gaps, trooping outside to construct advance defense positions, and marching back in for a brief respite in which to sit and drink wine and croak queries and braggadocio declarations at each other.

The sun was well down the western side of the sky, silhouetting in red the rooftops and steeples of Vienna, when several hundred of the akinji came yelling down along the wall from the north, evidently trying to shear off the body of Viennese soldiers that was outside. Eilif's company was out on the plain when they came, and led the way in a counter-charge that drove the Turkish footsoldiers back up to the Weiner-Bach, the narrow sub-canal that flanked the north half of the east wall. The mob of akinji—for they were too undisciplined to be called troops—broke at the banks of the little canal, and only those who retreated to the outer side of it managed to survive and return to the Turkish lines. As night fell the guns of both sides set about making the plain a hazardous no-man's-land of whistling shot and rebounding iron balls.

Chapter Twenty-one

THE DIRTY WATER of the Wiener-Bach, agitated by the occasional spray of ripped-up earth or shattered stone, reflected the blasts of flame from the cannons on the battlements above, so that Duffy, standing by the bank a hundred yards north of the new gap in the wall, saw two flashes for each shot when he looked behind him. The Turkish guns returned fire, distant flares of red light in the gathering darkness.

"Back inside, all of you!" shouted Count von Salm from the battlements. "They won't be coming back to-night—it looks like we're just going to trade shot for an hour or so." As if to emphasize his words, there came the jarring thumps of a couple of Turk cannon balls falling short.

The three companies outside the wall trotted wearily south, and though Duffy tried to hold his position in the lead company, he fell gradually back and was among the last to stumble over the mounded jagged stones of the new gap. He heard a clanking, realized he was absently dragging his sword, and carefully sheathed it. It took some nicks today, he thought; I'll have to get them pounded out sometime.

Inside the wall the soldiers were gathering around a fire. "Hey, Duffy!" barked a tired, dust-streaked Eilif. "It's past six, and Vertot's crew will stand in the hole for a while. Come here and have a cup of mulled ale. You're looking bashed-about."

The Irishman strode on stiff, aching legs to the fire, and sat down in front of it with a deep sigh. He accepted a cup of hot ale from someone and took a long sip, exhaled, and then took another.

"Ah," he breathed, stretching like a cat after a minute of letting his muscles adjust to the luxury of sitting down. "Well, you know, lads," he said expansively, "I wouldn't *like* an *easy* defense. It wouldn't give me the feeling my capabilities were being truly tested."

The men paused from drinking and tying bandages to laugh at that, for Duffy was paraphrasing an inspirational sermon a priest had made to the troops during a respite period that afternoon. There followed a few weak jokes speculating about the battle tactics that priest would probably employ, and how he'd be likely to disport himself afterward, and whether Suleiman's troops had to put up with similar speeches from Godknew-what sort of Mohammedan elders.

"Dead!" came a call from up the dark, rubble-choked street, extinguishing the men's good humor like a bucket of sand flung on a candle. "Night call for the dead!" A creaking, high-sided cart appeared from the shadows, and no one looked at the grisly cargo stacked in it. The driver was gibbering garbled prayers between calls, and his eyes glittered insanely between his tangled hair and beard. Somehow, though, Duffy thought uneasily, I think I know that man.

A crew of anonymous laborers left off their attempts to clear the street of debris, and set about carrying the day's corpses to the wagon and flopping them into its bed. While this was going on the driver buried his face in his hands and wept loudly. Whoever he is, Duffy thought, he's clearly mad. The soldiers around the fire shifted uncomfortably, embarrassed and vaguely upset in the presence of lunacy.

"Why can't they get a sane man to do that?" one of them whispered. "We fight all day and then have to put up with this."

"Listen," said Eilif, wiping dust and ale from his moustache, "he may have been sane when he started."

The cart loaded at last, its tailgate was swung up and latched, and the vehicle squeaked and rattled away down the street, the driver once again voicing his melancholy cry.

Duffy knew he'd seen the man before, but these days he was not one to prod sleeping memories. "More ale here," he said. "Top everybody up, in fact, and heat another pot of the stuff."

Gradually, with the telling of a few jokes and the singing of an old ballad or two, the group around the fire regained their cautious, fragile cheer. Most of the soldiers who'd fought that day had plodded away to the barracks immediately; but, the Irishman reflected, there are always a few who prefer to stay up and talk for a bit, and get some distance between themselves and the day's events before submitting to the night's dreams.

After an hour they began to yawn and drift away, and a light sweep of rain, hissing as it hit the fire, sent the remaining men trudging off to their bunks. Duffy had just stood up when he heard a sharp call: "Who's that? Identify yourself or I'll shoot!"

A moment later he heard a scuffle, and then the bang and ricochet of a gunshot, and a burly, red-bearded man burst out of a doorway under the wall and came pelting up the street, running hard.

"Guards ho!" came a shout from behind the fleeing man. "Stop him! He's a spy!"

Wearily, the Irishman drew his sword and dagger and stood in the man's path. "Very well, Kretchmer, you'd better hold it," he said loudly.

The bearded fugitive whipped out a sword of his own. "Stand aside, Duffy!" he yelled.

Two guards came puffing up from one of the side streets, and a sentry on the wall was taking aim with a smoldering harquebus the rain had not yet damped, so the fleeing spy ran directly at Duffy, whirling his sword fiercely. Just before they collided, the red beard fell away on a string and Duffy was surprised to glimpse the fear-taut face of John Zapolya. Knocked unharmed to the side, the Irishman mustered his faculties and aimed a backhand cut at Zapolya's shoulder. It landed, and the Hungarian gasped in pain as the blade-edge grated against bone, but he kept running. The wall sentry's gun went off but was badly aimed in the uncertain light, and the ball spanged off the street several yards away. Duffy started after the fugitive, but, off balance, he slipped on the rain-wet cobbles and fell, cracking his knee painfully on a stone. When he wincingly got to his feet Zapolya had disappeared up the dim avenue, pursued by two of the guards.

"God damn it," Duffy snarled, hobbling to the shelter of a dry doorway.

Pounding hoofbeats echoed now from the same direction Zapolya had come from, and a moment later a horse and rider appeared and paused in the middle of the street. The firelight was dimming in the rain, so it wasn't until the rider called for the guards that Duffy recognized him.

"Hey, Aurelianus!" the Irishman called. "Zapolya was just here! He ran away up the street."

The wizard wheeled his horse and goaded it over to where Duffy stood. "Zapolya too? Morrigan help us. Did the guards go after him?"

"Yes, two of them."

"Did you see Kretchmer? I was chasing him."

"That was Zapolya! Look, that's his fake beard on the street there."

"Mananan and Llyr! I wonder if Kretchmer has always been Zapolya."

Duffy rubbed his knee and limped a step or two on it. "Well, of course," he snapped irritably. "Think about it—remember, Werner said Kretchmer wasn't home, the night of Easter Sunday? That was the night Zapolya was at the Zimmermann with his siege bombard."

Aurelianus shook his head. "A false *beard,* of all

things." He spat disgustedly. "Follow me. What, have you hurt your leg? Hop up behind me here, then, we've got to get out of the rain and do some talking."

Duffy swung up onto the horse's rump and they clopped down the street to the southern guardhouse, where they dismounted. "Hey, Duff," said the captain who opened the door, "I saw you land one on that spy. Too bad you couldn't get some muscle into the blow, you'd have split him."

"I know," said Duffy with a rueful grin as he and Aurelianus clumped inside and pulled a couple of chairs to a table in the corner. "What was he doing when the sentry challenged him?"

"He was trying to open that old ferrier's door," the captain answered. "The one that crazy man sneaked out through this noon. They bricked it up, but apparently nobody told old Redbeard; he was trying to pull the bricks loose when Rahn saw him."

The Irishman and Aurelianus sat down and the captain returned with a jug of fortified wine he'd been working on. When he had left the room Duffy poured two cups and looked up at the sorceror. "What went wrong with your trap?"

Aurelianus gulped the liquor. "I should have had a whole landsknecht company. Kretchmer and Werner came back to the inn just a few minutes ago, and I let them scuttle halfway across the dining room before I gave the whistle that brought two armed men out of every door. I called to the pair that they were under arrest. Werner just stood and shouted, but Kretchmer —Zapolya!—snatched up a chair and brained one of my men, then drew his sword and disembowelled another. The rest of them cornered him, but he jumped through a window and sprinted east, so I got a horse and came after him." He topped up his cup. "He's fast."

"I know," said Duffy. The rain drumming on the roof had found a hole, and a drop plunked into Duffy's wine. He moved the cup absently.

"Werner ran for the window when his mentor had gone through it," Aurelianus went on, "and one of my eager lads put three inches of sword into his kidney.

I don't know if he'll survive or not." He looked up at the Irishman, a hard speculation glinting in his eyes. "There's something you have to do tonight."

"You mean catch Zapolya? Hell, man, he could simply hide and sneak out through one of the gaps, or lower a rope outside the wall at some secluded—"

"Not Zapolya. He's a played card."

The roof-leak thumped its slow drum beat four times on the table top. "What, then?" Duffy asked quietly.

Aurelianus was picking at the candle on the table now, not looking at Duffy. "This afternoon I got to wondering just exactly what spells were in Becky's book. I have a—"

"What does it matter what spells were in it?" Duffy interrupted. "You and Ibrahim have blocked all the useful types of magic, haven't you? That's what you keep saying."

Aurelianus shifted uncomfortably. "Well, all the major types, yes. But not, I'm afraid, the kind of barnyard conjuring Becky dealt in. Hell, in a tense cease-fire, do warring kings think to forbid pea-shooters? Anyway, I keep a bibliography of all my books, so I looked up Becky's. I'd listed the entire contents page of the book, so I could see what each of her spells is supposed to do." He looked at Duffy unhappily. "One of them is how to fox beer."

Duffy was tired, and staring at the widening puddle on the table, and not concentrating on Aurelianus' words. "So?"

"*So,* you say? Are you even listening? How to fox beer! Have you ever seen—worse, tasted—foxed beer? It's ropy, thick, like honey; spoiled, undrinkable. Ibrahim, if he noticed that spell—and I think we'd better assume he did—can fox the Herzwesten vat, spoil the beer for decades, maybe forever! We might just be able to save the higher levels with hyssop and salt, but the bottom levels—the Dark, do you understand?— would be hopeless."

"Oh. That's right." Duffy raised his eyebrows helplessly. "I don't know what to tell you. Set up some shields against it now. Or draw a keg off and hide it somewhere. I certainly—"

"It would take at least twelve hours to arrange counter-spells—you think Ibrahim will wait? And hiding a keg of it won't do. For one thing it has to mature right there, over old Finn's grave, and for another, the spell will ruin any beer within its range—every drop of beer in the city will go foul, wherever it's hidden."

"Are you sure Becky's spells work?" Duffy asked, trying to be helpful. "I've known a lot of country witches, and they were all out-and-out fakes."

Aurelianus shook his head. "They work. Becky was the real thing. We have only one hook for hope. She was, as you say, a country witch, and her spells have a range of only about a mile. Also, nearly all of them have to be performed at precisely noon or midnight. The natural laws that must be overcome are weakest at those moments."

"So?" said Duffy stonily. By God, he thought, let him say it clearly.

The sorcerer pursed his lips and spoke harshly. "Ibrahim will try it tonight. He knows he can't delay—for one thing, the moon's waxing, and Becky's spells were all dark-of-the-moon ones. And because of the limited range, he'll have to come up quite close to the walls to cast it. What you'll—"

Duffy swept the puddle on the table pattering onto the floor. "You want me to go try to stop him? While you and the old King get ready to escape through the tunnels, I suppose, in case I fail. Well, listen while I tell you something: no. Think again. Get yourself another reincarnated hero."

The captain, who'd apparently been dozing in the next room, leaned his tousled head in through the doorway, wondering at the anger in Duffy's voice. Aurelianus waited until he'd returned to his bench before replying. "That is not what I'm proposing," he said quietly. "I . . . have decided that it would be best to make our final win-or-forfeit stand right here, in Vienna. It would, I'm afraid, be madness to think of falling back and re-grouping somewhere and hope for even half the advantage we've got here and now. After all, the Turks are at least several weeks behind schedule, and Ibrahim has failed to acquire Didius'

Gambit, and we've unmasked—unbearded, I should say—what must have been their chief spy."

Duffy refilled their cups. "And on their side of the ledger: they can ruin the beer from outside the wall."

"Yes, but we know they'll have to be pretty close, for the Zimmermann is nearly half a mile into the city from the wall. And we know he'll do it at midnight. If this beer-fouling trick of theirs works, then I believe they'll have won even if we could physically retreat; and if it fails they'll go home and the Dark will be drawn on schedule. Therefore I attach a lot of importance to the outcome of tonight's venture." His pose of calm rationality fell away for a moment and he banged the wet table top with a fist. "Alone, or even with a body of soldiers, you couldn't go out and fight Ibrahim. For one thing, he's got personal bodyguards, of the species you saw when we fetched the King into the city—oh, that's right, Arthur had the reins in that fight, you wouldn't remember them; but they'd be something like the two things that tried to hypnotize you back in April. Anyway, they'd laugh at your swords and guns—if they were the sort of creature that ever laughed." Though clearly apprehensive, the pale sorcerer managed to smile. "It's a big wager, but I don't think we'll ever have better odds. I have decided to break the deadlock."

"Good God, you mean you'll *use* Didius' Gambit? Why, how can you even—"

"No. Since I choose to view this as the decisive incident in the question of any continuing lifeline of the West, I've decided to . . . do the other thing." He sighed. "The Fisher King and I will accompany you tonight."

Duffy frowned. "The three of us? And you and I holding either end of his stretcher? Not exactly an imposing attack force."

"It won't be quite that bad. Von Salm would never let me have any troops, of course, for an unexplainable midnight sortie, but he did say once that he'd be grateful if I'd take Bugge and the other northmen off his hands."

The Irishman stared at him in disbelief, then gulped some of the wine. He shook his head, laughing in spite of himself. His laughter grew like a rolling snow-ball, until he was leaning forward on the table and gasping, with tears running from the corners of his eyes. He tried to speak, but managed only, ". . . Parade . . . damned clowns . . . funny hats."

Aurelianus hadn't even smiled. "So we won't be entirely alone," he said.

Duffy sniffled and wiped his eyes. "Right. And how many men will Ibrahim have?"

"Aside from his . . . bodyguards? I don't know. Not many, since of course he doesn't want to be seen." He shrugged. "And after the deadlock breaks—who can tell? A lot of sorcerous pressure has built up on both sides; both of the forces will change, out there tonight, when the King of the West joins the battle."

After opening his mouth, Duffy decided not to pursue it. Instead he said, "I'm not sure I'm even ready for these bodyguards."

"No, you're not," Aurelianus agreed. "But you will be, when you're carrying the right sword. That blade you're wearing now is fine for poking holes in Turkish soldiers, but if you're going to face . . . well, those other things, you need a sword they'll fear, one that can cut through their flinty flesh."

The Irishman saw Aurelianus' direction and sighed. "Calad Bolg."

"Exactly. Now listen—you get some sleep, it's only about a quarter of eight. I'll—"

"Sleep?" Duffy's momentary mirth had evaporated completely. He felt scared and vaguely nauseated, and rubbed his face with his hands. "Is that a joke?"

"Rest, at least. I'll fetch Bugge and his men, and the King, and get the sword, and come back here. We'd better head out at roughly eleven."

Duffy stood up, wishing he'd left the fortified wine alone. Am I bound to do this? he wondered. *Well, if Merlin wants me to* . . . But why should I care what Merlin wants? Does he care what *I* want? Has he ever? Well, to hell with the old wizard, then—you're still a soldier, aren't you? All the bright, vague dreams of a slate-roofed cottage in Ireland died last night, fell on a knife in a shabby room. If you aren't a soldier, my lad, dedicated to fighting the Turks, I don't think you're anything at all.

"Very well," he said, very quietly. "I'll try to get some rest."

Aurelianus laid his hand briefly on Duffy's shoulder, then left. A moment later the Irishman heard the horse's hoofbeats recede away up the street.

Under the rain-drummed roof of a lean-to that had been added onto the side of the southern barracks, Rikard Bugge hummed a dreary tune and pounded his dagger again and again into the barrack wall. Soldiers, trying to sleep on the other side, had several times come round to the lean-to's door and tried to get him to stop, but he never looked up or even stopped humming. The other Vikings, sprawled on straw-filled sacks in the slant-roofed structure, stared at their captain sympathetically. They knew well what was bothering him. They had all come on a long and troublesome, if not particularly risky, journey in order to defend the tomb of Balder against Surter and the legions of Muspelheim; and they had found the tomb, and Surter was now camped not three miles south—but the men in charge would not let them fight.

So they'd languished for several months in this hurriedly built shed, oiling and sharpening their weapons more from force of habit than from any hope of using them.

Wham. *Wham. WHAM.* Bugge's dagger-blows had been gradually increasing in force, and he put his shoulder into the final one, punching the blade right through the wall up to the hilt. There were muffled shouts from the other side, but Bugge ignored them and stood up to face his men.

"We have," he said, "been patient. And we are stowed here like chickens in a coop while the dogs go hunting. We have waited for Sigmund to lead us into battle, and all he does is drink and make the old woman at the inn cry. We have obeyed the wishes of the little man who masqueraded as Odin, and he mouths burning serpents and tells us to wait. We have waited long enough." His men growled their agreement, grinning and hefting their swords. "We will not be lulled into forgetting what Gardvord sent us here to do," Bugge said. "We will take action."

"You have anticipated me," Aurelianus said in his fluent Norse as he stepped noiselessly into the lean-to. "The time for action, as you have observed, has arrived."

Bugge scowled skeptically at the sorcerer. "We know what needs to be done," he said. "We don't need your counsel." The other Vikings frowned and nodded.

"Of course not," agreed Aurelianus. "I'm not here as an advisor, but as a messenger."

Bugge waited several seconds. "Well," he barked finally, "what is your message?

The wizard fixed the captain with an intense stare. "My message is from Sigmund, whom you were sent here to obey, as you doubtless recall. He has discovered a plot of the Muspelheimers to poison Balder's barrow by means of filthy southern magic, which Surter's chief wizard, Ibrahim, will perform outside our walls tonight. Sigmund will ride out to stop him, armed with Odin's own dwarf-wrought sword; he sent me to tell you that the period of waiting is at an end, and to arm yourselves and meet him two hours from now at the guard-house down the street."

Bugge let out a howl of joy and embraced Aurelianus, then shoved the wizard toward the door. "Tell your master we'll be there," he said. "It may be that we'll have breakfast with the gods in Asgard, but we'll send Surter's magician to keep Hel company in the underworld!"

Aurelianus bowed and exited, then galloped away toward the Zimmermann Inn as a chorus of Viking war-songs began behind him.

Duffy was lying down on a cot the captain of the guard had told him he could use, but he was far from asleep, in spite of the extra cup of fortified wine the captain had insisted he drink. Odd, he thought as he stared at the low ceiling, how I can't imagine death. I've seen a lot of it, cautiously flirted with it, seen it take more friends than I'll let myself think about, but

I have no idea what it really is. *Death.* All the word conjures up is the old Tarot card image, a skeleton in a black robe, waving something ominous like an hour-glass or a scythe. I wonder what we will be facing out there, besides wholesome Turkish soldiers. Ibrahim's bodyguards . . . I don't remember the fight in the Vienna woods, but I suppose they'll be like the things that flew over me that night on the south shore of the Neusiedler Lake, speaking some eastern tongue, and destroyed Yount's hides-wagons.

Then his stomach went cold at a sudden horrible comprehension. Good Jesus, Duffy thought, *that was him.* I had supposed, mercifully hoped, that he was dead. God only knows how old Yount escaped those demons and made his way, mad but alive, to Vienna, to be given the village-idiot's job of driving the night-shift corpse wagon; to be still, by some ghastly cosmic joke, a dealer in hides. Recoiling from these thoughts, the Irishman cast his mind's eye back again to the skeletal image of death. I guess it's not so bad, he decided hesitantly. Clearly there are worse cards in the deck.

The floor creaked as someone padded into the room, and Duffy sat up quickly, making the candle flame flicker. "Oh, it's you, Merlin," he said. "For a second I thought it might be . . . *another* very old, thin, pale, black-clad person." He chuckled grimly as he stood up. "Is it eleven?"

"Coming up on. Bugge and his men are outside, armed and ready to chop the Fenris Wolf to cat-meat, and the King is lying in the wagon bed. Here." He handed Duffy the heavy sword, and the Irishman took off Eilif's old rapier and slid his belt through the loops on the scabbard of Calad Bolg.

"It'll probably weigh me down on one side, so I walk like a ship wallowing in its beam ends," he said, but actually the sword's weight felt comfortable and familiar.

Although the gutter in the middle of the street flowed deeply and roof spouts still dribbled onto the pavement, the rain itself had stopped. A wagon stood by the wall; Bugge's men waited for Duffy in a group on the street, and torches in the hands of two of them reflected in their slitted eyes and on their helmets and mailshirts. Their coppery blond hair and beards had been braided and thonged back out of the way, and their callused hands fingered the worn leather of their sword grips expectantly. By God, Duffy thought as he grinned and nodded a greeting to them, whatever Turkish hell is churning out there in the dark, I couldn't ask for a much better crew of men to face it with . . . though it would be handier if we had some language in common.

But that's silly, he thought a moment later. Aren't these Vikings? Don't they understand Norse? He barked a greeting in a Norse dialect so archaic that Bugge could barely phrase an equivalent reply.

Duffy stepped up into the wagon's braced rear wheel and smiled at the white-bearded old man sitting up in the bed with a rich-looking tapestried blanket over his legs. "Good evening, Sire," he said. "A peculiar battle it is in which the soldiers stay home and the leaders go fight."

The King chuckled. "I think it makes more sense this way. It's the leaders that have the quarrel." He stared more closely at the Irishman. "Ah," he said softly, "I see that both of you are awake."

Duffy cocked his head. "Yes, that's true, isn't it? You'd think that would be . . . clumsy, like two men in one outsize suit of armor, but it's more like two perfectly matched horses in harness; each one knows without thinking when to take over, when to help, and when to back off. I don't know why I spent so much time being afraid of this and trying to resist it."

He hopped down onto the street and walked over to where the wizard stood. "Do you know for sure that Ibrahim is *out* there?" he asked quietly. "And if so, where? We can't just go calling for him."

Aurelianus seemed both steadier and more tense than usual. "He's there. Perhaps two hundred yards east of the northeast corner of the wall, behind a low, weedy bluff. I've had watchers on the walls since eight, and it was only twenty minutes ago that Jock got a positive sighting."

"Did he see any . . . did he see them very clearly?"

"Of course not. They've got dark-lanterns, apparently, and he only caught a couple of reflected blue flashes. He claims he heard them rustling around, too, but I told him he was too far away for that."

He waved vaguely to the north. "I think we should go over the wall—lowering the King and me in a pallet and sling—at the east end of the Wollzelle, and then find a sheltered spot where the King and I can get busy on the magical offensive, while you and your Vikings make a dash straight east—"

"No, no." Duffy shook his head. "Certainly not. A direct frontal attack? There's not even enough moonlight to keep us from tripping over shattered tree branches; it'd take us ten minutes to reach them, and they'd have heard us coming for nine." Aurelianus started to speak, but the Irishman raised his hand. "No," Duffy said. "We'll go over the wall near the north gate, cross one of the bridges over the Donau Canal and get to the little pier off the Taborstrasse where they've got Bugge's old Viking ship moored. Untying her will be easy and quiet enough, and then we'll all of us simply drift east down the canal. Our sails will be reefed, of course, to avoid being seen, and we'll use a couple of the oars as barge poles, to keep us clear of the banks. It's from the north, you see, that our attack will come, and with, I hope, no warning at all. That'll put you and the King among the canalside willows—a position that's both more secluded and closer to the action than any hillock on the eastern plain."

The sorcerer bowed. "Very well. Your idea is obviously better. You see my . . . ineptitude with matters of warfare."

Duffy squinted at Aurelianus, suddenly suspicious. Had the old wizard intended from the start that they should attack by way of the canal, from the north, and only suggested a direct charge east so that the Irishman could gain some self-confidence by contradicting him?

Then Duffy smiled. Merlin was always devious, and it became a problem only at those rare times when his intentions differed significantly from one's own. He clapped Aurelianus on the shoulder. "Don't feel bad about it."

He waved at the northmen. "Very well, then, lads, climb aboard!" he called. They just grinned and waved back, and the Irishman repeated his order in the Old Norse. Bugge translated it for his men, and they all clambered in, being careful not to kick or step on the King.

Duffy swung up onto the driver's bench and Aurelianus got up beside him. "Everybody in?" Duffy asked. He took for assent the growls that came from the back, and snapped the long reins. The wagon rocked, wheeled about and then rattled away up the street. The two Vikings had extinguished their torches, and the street and buildings were palely illuminated only by a silvery glow that showed where the half moon hid behind the thinning clouds.

They all managed to climb unseen to the north wall catwalk, and with a couple of long lengths of rope and the aid of three of Bugge's men, the job of lowering the Fisher King to the ground outside proved to be much easier than Duffy had imagined. Aurelianus was lowered next, and Duffy and the northmen were about to follow when the Irishman heard, a dozen yards to the right, the rutch of a pebble turning under a boot.

He turned, and the flash, bang and whining ricochet were simultaneous. The lead ball had struck one of the merlons he'd been about to climb between. He froze.

"Nobody move, or the next one takes off a head," came a shout from the same direction as the shot, followed by hurried footsteps.

"Don't move or speak," the Irishman hissed in Old Norse. Bugge nodded.

"Oh, Jesus, it's Duffy!" exclaimed a voice Duffy recognized after a moment as Bluto's. "Just what the *hell* are you doing, you troublesome son of a bitch?" Bluto hobbled up, accompanied by a burly guard who carried a fresh matchlock and blew vigilantly on the glowing end of the cord.

"That's a real quick-trigger man you've got there,

Bluto," Duffy observed mildly. The ball had struck so close to him that it was clear the man hadn't intended to miss.

"He was following orders, damn it," snapped Bluto. "All the sentries have been alerted that a spy was sighted and then lost in the city a few hours ago, and are ordered to stop anyone trying to go over the wall, and bring them, if still alive, to von Salm. I know you're not a spy, Duff, but I don't have any choice—you'll have to come with me."

In the unsteady moonlight Duffy's eyes measured the distance from his right hand to the gun barrel; with a sideways lunge he might be able to knock it out of line. "I'm sorry, Bluto," he said. "I can't."

"It wasn't a suggestion, Brian," the hunchback rasped. "It was an order. To put it bluntly, you're under arrest." The sentry took a step back, putting him out of Duffy's reach.

The Irishman heard the first notes of the bells of St. Stephen's tolling eleven o'clock. "Look, Bluto," he said urgently, "I have to go out there. A sorcerous attack is building up out there on the plain, and if I, and my party, aren't out there when it starts, then things won't go too well for Vienna. You must have seen enough in the last six months to know that magic is playing a part in this struggle. I swear to you, as your oldest friend, who once saved your life and who carries a certain obligation in trust, that I have to go. And I will. You can permit it or you can have him shoot me in the back." He turned to Bugge and gestured toward the rope. The Viking stepped up into the crenel, seized the rope and leaned outward, walking down the outside of the wall.

There was a scuffle and thud, and Duffy looked quickly around. Bluto was holding the long gun by the barrel with one hand, and with the other arm was lowering the unconscious sentry to the surface of the catwalk. He looked up unhappily. "I hope I didn't hit him too hard. I don't know anything about any magic —but go, damn you. I've bought you some time with my neck."

Duffy started to thank him, but the hunchback was

walking away, and not looking back. Soon all the northmen had descended the rope, and Duffy climbed up and stood between the two bulky stone merlons.

As he looped the line behind his thigh and over his shoulder he sniffed the night air and wondered what quality had changed. Had a persistent sound ceased? A prevalent odor disappeared? Then he noticed the stillness of the air. That's what it is, he thought uneasily. It's stopped, the breeze that has blown from the west these past two weeks.

Chapter Twenty-two

THEY CARRIED THE KING over the bridge to the far bank of the canal, lifted him aboard the old ship, got in themselves and then untied all lines. Duffy and three of the northmen used long oars to push the ship away from the bank and into the current, and within a few minutes the high-prowed ship was gliding between the dim, masonry-crowned banks of the Donau, silent under the stark crucifix of its mast. The night air was cold, and smelled of wet streets; Duffy breathed it deeply, savoring the stagnant taint of the lapping water. The northmen stood at the rails, peering ahead into the darkness.

The rains had swelled the Danube, and the offshoot Donau Canal was moving swiftly. Duffy had been afraid they'd have to row to make any speed, with the unavoidable clatter of the oarlocks, but all that proved to be necessary was an oar-butt shoved forcefully against a bank from time to time to keep them from running aground. Soon the high bulk of the city wall had slipped past on their starboard side, and only stunted willows bordered the canal.

Standing to the right of the upswept prow, Duffy

carefully scanned the southern bank, trying to look beyond the dark foreground foliage to the silent group he knew was out there. Do they see us? he wondered. Not likely. We're making no noise, they have no reason to believe we even know they're out here, and it's only from the west they'll be looking for possible attacks.

After about a third of a mile the canal began to curve gently to the north, as if prematurely anticipating its eventual re-merging with the Danube, which didn't occur until several miles further south. If Merlin's wall-watchers know their business, the Irishman thought, Ibrahim's party is now due south of us. He turned, hissed to the northmen and signalled them to put in at the southern bank. This wasn't difficult, since the current had been trying for ten minutes to run them aground on that side; the men at the starboard rail simply stopped bracing the oars against the canal-edge, and within a minute the keel raked the mud and the ship canted over toward the bank, stuck fast.

Duffy stepped across the slanting deck to the starboard rail, leaning backward so as not to pitch right over into the canal. Aurelianus came up beside him. "That jar didn't do the King any good," the wizard whispered accusingly. "But he's ready to be carried to the bank."

"Good. Now listen, I'm going to go over there. When I wave, send Bugge and two others. We'll make sure it's safe. Then when I wave again, the rest of you carry the King across. Have you got that?"

"Yes."

"Very well. See you soon, I trust."

The Irishman carefully lowered himself over the side, clenching his teeth at the bitter chill of the water swirling around his thighs, and waded to the humped, tree-furred bank. Half peering in the darkness and half groping, he found a quiet way up and then waved back at the ship. Soon three of the northmen were crawling up the muddy slope beside him, shivering and rubbing their legs. Beyond the willows the landscape they faced was nothing but a black horizon of uncertain distance.

A flash of blue light pricked the darkness ahead for a moment, then was cut off as if a door had been shut.

Over the splash and slurry of the water through the reeds Duffy now fancied he could faintly hear chanting voices and the rushing of great wings, and he was suddenly afraid to look up for fear the tattered clouds would begin to form malevolent Oriental faces. The canal at our backs, he thought, connects with the Danube, which stretches far south; has some vast white serpent crawled north along the riverbed from Turkish regions to suck us up now from behind?

Fearfully, he turned to look—and saw in the dim moonlight the wide-eyed, terror-stark faces of the three Vikings. They must have seen or heard something I missed, Duffy thought, feeling his own fear spiral higher at this corroboration; or else, he thought suddenly, we're all responding to the same thing, which is not an object or a sound, but simply the atmosphere of outré menace that hangs in the still air here like a vapor.

That's it, he thought with sudden conviction. Ibrahim is doing this to us. He's set up some kind of wizardly fear-wall around himself to drive away anyone who might interrupt him. With the thought, the Irishman was able to unfasten the terror from his mind and push it away, like a man holding a snake by its throat at arm's length. He forced a soft chuckle and turned to Bugge. "It's a trick," he whispered to the trembling northman. "Damn it, it's magic, it's only a fright-mask hung over the door to keep children from barging in!"

Bugge stared at him without comprehension, and the Irishman repeated the statement in Old Norse. Bugge caught the gist of it, gave Duffy a strained grin and then passed the message on to the other two. They loosened up a bit, but none of the four on the bank looked really at ease.

They scouted up and down the watercourse edge fifty yards in both directions without seeing or hearing anything untoward, and Duffy waved again to the ship. By the patchy moonlight he watched the remaining northmen wade across, four of them holding up, clear of the water, the pallet on which lay the old King.

When they had all made their way into the cluster of willows, Aurelianus crossed to where Duffy was standing. "The Fisher King is on the field of battle," he said, quietly but with a savage satisfaction.

All at once the oppressive weight of unspecific fear was gone, and Duffy was able to relax the control-holding muscles of his mind. Suddenly he got the feeling that there were more men on the bank with him than he knew of—he turned, but the moon was behind a cloud and the shadows among the willows were impenetrable. Nevertheless he could sense the presence of many strangers, and from a little further down the bank he caught sounds that seemed to be those of at least one boat pulling in to the bank and disgorging silent men in the darkness. There was flapping and a windy rushing in the air, too, and soft swirl-sounds from the water, as of lithe swimmers just under the surface. The air was as tensely still as if they were in the eye of a vast storm, but the willows all up and down the bank were now twisting and creaking.

Bugge came up beside the Irishman, and by a flitting sprinkle of light Duffy looked for signs of heightened fear in the northman's face, but was surprised to see only an eager reassurance. And he realized that these northmen, like his horse when he was, months ago, so eerily escorted through the Julian Alps, could instinctively recognize allies of this sort, while Duffy tended to be blinded by the fears Christian civilization had instilled in him. The Viking touched him on the shoulder and pointed ahead.

The cloud cover was breaking up and clearing, and Duffy could clearly see three tall men waiting on a low hillock. Without hesitation the Irishman strode up the slope to join them while the large but indistinct body of warriors waited along the bank behind him. When he reached the rounded crest the three turned to him with respectful nods of recognition.

The tallest was as massive and gray and weathered as a Baltic sea cliff, and though an eye-patch covered

an empty socket, his good eye looked from Duffy's
sword to his face, and glittered with an emotion almost
too cold and hard to be called amusement. The second
man, though just as big, was darker of skin, with a
curly black beard and white teeth that flashed in a
fierce smile of greeting. He wore a lion-skin and carried
a short, powerful-looking bow. The third was rangier,
with long hair and a beard that even in the leaching
moonlight Duffy knew must be coppery red. In his
fist he held a long, heavy hammer.

The four of them on the height turned to survey
the fair-sized host gathered by the bank of the canal,
which must somehow have become wider, for at least
half a dozen ships were moored in it—a Spanish carack,
a Phoenician galley, even a dim shape that seemed to
be a Roman bireme. There was a long sigh, and the
limp banners began to twitch and flap on the masts.

Looking southeast, Duffy could see an equal host
gathered around a vast, black tent on the plain, and at
the vanguard stood four tall figures in eastern armor.

The one-eyed man raised a hand, and the wind
came up behind him, tossing his gray locks; then he
brought the hand forward in a spear-casting gesture,
and with the wind the Western force moved forward,
gathering speed and sweeping toward the black tent.
Running effortlessly in the front rank, Duffy heard the
sound of hoofbeats mingled with the thudding of boots,
and he caught too the flapping of wings and a soft
drum-beat of great running paws.

For Duffy the battle that followed was mainly a con-
fusion of quick, unconnected images and encounters.
He clove in half a huge, beating butterfly-thing, between the wings of which was a woman's face, mouth
agape to sink long teeth into him. A grossly fat, bald
man with thick snakes for arms seized Duffy and
moaned in wide-eyed imbecility as he began to con-
strict the Irishman's breath away; he became silent
only when a glowing-eyed cat shape had surged past
and with one swipe of powerful jaws snapped the bald
head off. At one point Duffy faced one of the four
tall Turkish warriors who had stood out in front of
the assembled Eastern host—the man's left hand,

though as mobile and quick as his scimitar-wielding right, was a brassy metallic color and rang like a dagger when he used it to parry Duffy's blade; the Irishman finally managed to sever the arm at the elbow; and when Duffy had delivered the final, beheading stroke, the golden hand was still moving, crawling on the ground like a spider.

Things with the heads of crocodiles contended with dwarfs perched one atop another to form an adversary of conventional height; men enveloped in roaring yellow flames rushed here and there, seeking to embrace their enemies; hollow-eyed corpses lurched past, pulled along by animated swords as pliant as snakes; and, above even the winged warriors that battled with scimitar and longsword high overhead, impossibly tall, luminous figures could be glimpsed rushing across the sky.

Finally Duffy burst through the far side of the seething press. Glancing around he saw that six of the northmen were still with him. Bugge grinned at him as they trotted in to re-group. Less than a hundred yards in front of them stood the circular tent of black cloth, flapping like a big, crippled bat on the moonlit plain. Even as Duffy caught his first clear glimpse of it, part of the drapery flipped back and half a dozen turbanned men, back-lit in eerie blue, stepped out of the tent, drew gleaming scimitars and waited grimly for the attack to arrive.

In ten seconds it did, and two of the Turks fell immediately, chopped nearly in half by the northmen's swords; the other four handled their crescent blades skillfully, but refused to give ground or retreat to the flank, and so were each inevitably engaged by one man and run through by several others. Before Duffy could even get in a lick the Turk guards were dead, while his own crew had suffered nothing worse than a nicked forearm or two.

"Come out of your boudoir, Ibrahim, and share the fate of your boys!" yelled Duffy, leaping forward and with a whirling slash cutting the tent flap across the top.

The cloth fell away—and a shape out of nightmare

stood, turned, and stared incuriously down at him. It seemed to have been crudely chiselled out of coal, and its face was twisted and distorted as if it had spent centuries under powerful, uneven pressure. Muscles like outcroppings of rock ridged its shoulders, and a shrill, grating yell trumpeted from its mouth as its blunt-fingered hands reached for the man.

Duffy fell over backward like an axed tree, and, when the thing rushed forward, raised his sword as a man might instinctively raise his arm while a tidal wave curls over him.

The creature moved in so quickly that it impaled itself on the long blade, which encountered no resistance in penetrating the stony flesh. A moment later it had wrenched itself back with a moan like layers of rock shifting. Dropping to the ground, it curled up in a ball as a cloud of things like blue fireflies swirled upward out of the gaping wound in its belly.

Lifting himself on his elbows and looking over the fallen monster's bulk, the Irishman saw a dozen robed figures inside the tent, standing around a fire that gleamed bright blue. Then the northmen had bounded past him, howling with rage and swinging their swords, and Duffy hopped shakily to his feet to join them.

The tent shook then with a madman's percussion concert as swords clanged and rasped, mail shirts jingled and helmets were ringingly struck from surprised heads. Duffy sprang at a tall, wiry Turk he took to be Ibrahim, aiming a slash that would have cleft the man in two pieces if it had connected; but the Turkish sorcerer leaped back out of the way, and Duffy spun half around with the force of the wasted swing.

Ibrahim snatched up a small book and hopped nimbly toward an open flap at the back of the tent. The Irishman saw him, realized he was too far away to catch, and flung his sword like a Dalcassian axe. It whirled through the air and struck the magician solidly in the shoulder. The suddenly blood-spattered book dropped to the ground, but the wizard regained his balance and, wincing and clutching his gashed shoulder, ducked out of the tent.

"Not so fast, you bastard," growled Duffy, striding after him only to find his way blocked by a desperate-eyed Turk, who drove a quick cut at the Irishman's face. Swordless, he parried it with his left hand while drawing his dagger with his right. He lunged savagely in, snarling with the pain of his mangled palm, and buried his dagger in the man's chest.

A scimitar snapped in half on his steel cap, stunning him as he tried to parry another with his dagger guard; he deflected the blade from his face, but it whipped as he struck it aside and opened a furrow along his forearm. Fearing to riposte with the short dagger, Duffy waited tensely for another thrust—but the Turk gasped, buckled at the knees and collapsed, stabbed from behind. The Irishman whirled to take in the entire tent . . . and then slowly relaxed and lowered his blade, for the only figures still standing were Vikings. A few of the blue fireflies had found their way inside, but were dimming and falling silently to the ground.

The book lay where Ibrahim had dropped it, and Duffy slowly crossed the tent, picked it up with his right hand and flipped it open. In faded brown ink the flyleaf was inscribed: *"For Merlin Aurelianus, these modest magics, from your own little succubus, Becky. Beltane, 1246."* After a moment's hesitation he tore that page out, folded it and tucked it in a pocket, and then dropped the book into the blue fire. He wiped and sheathed his sword, then pulled down a strip of the tent fabric and laid it in the flames.

"Let's go," he panted to the blood-streaked Bugge, who nodded. Three of the other northmen were still standing, and one of them was bleeding badly from a cut in the side. Duffy led them out of the tent.

The wind was high, and raising rushing clouds of dust in the moonlight, but the plain was empty. Duffy stared around thoughtfully, and then pointed toward the city wall that stood in high, ragged silhouette three hundred yards west. With his sorcerous powers restored, Duffy reflected, Merlin can certainly transport the Fisher King back into the city without our help. The five of them set out, one of the northmen hopping on one leg and leaning on a companion. Before they'd taken a dozen steps their long-legged shadows were cast across the dirt in front of them, for the tent behind was now a crackling torch of wholesomely yellow and orange flame.

After a while there were shouts from the top of the wall, and the Irishman waved. "It's me, Duffy!" he bellowed. "We're Christians! Don't shoot!"

Then the Turk guns began thumping, and there was a shattering splash to the north, in the canal. They're trying to find the range, Duffy realized. They haven't had cause to shoot at this corner before now. Ibrahim must have signalled them somehow . . . or could he have reached the Turk lines already?

Two more cannon balls struck, one breaking away several yards of the wall crenellations and one slamming into the water of the Wiener-Bach, directly in front of the wall. The wind carried the high-flung spray to Duffy's face. And they're finding the range, he thought grimly; we'd better find a bridge across this midget canal and get inside. I think there's one just a bit north of us.

He turned to wave the Vikings to the right, and at that moment a muscular black shape beneath two wide-ribbed wings swooped down out of the night sky and swung a scimitar in a terrible chop at Duffy's head. The edge clanked into the Irishman's steel helmet and knocked him violently forward in a rolling tumble. The flier, with a low laugh and a snapping of huge wings, thrashed back up in to the darkness.

He shivered in the cold, damp wind, trying to stand at respectful attention despite his weariness and the pain of wounds. They had handed the mortally wounded Arthur aboard the barge now, and the old monarch lifted his bloody head and smiled weakly at him. "Thank you," the king said quietly, "and farewell."

Duffy nodded and lifted his sword in a salute as the old man let his head sink back upon the cushions. With the handful of others, Duffy stood on the shore of the moonlit lake and watched as the barge was poled away by the woman at the stern and slowly moved out across the glassy water until it was lost in the mists.

Bugge got to Duffy first, and helped him to his feet. The Irishman's helmet had been split, and blood ran down his back from a great gash at the base of his skull.

"I'm all right," he muttered blurrily. "I can . . . still walk." He touched his forehead. "Wow. Did it go? What was it? Wow."

Bugge didn't understand the Austrian words, but took one of his arms while another Viking took the other, and the five battered warriors limped over the northmost Weiner-Bach bridge. A narrow gate was opened for them just short of the Donau canal, and bolted shut again as soon as they got inside.

"What the hell happened out there?" barked a scared and angry sergeant. "What were you doing? You've roused the Turks, that's certain." The northmen couldn't answer him, and Duffy hadn't heard the questions. He was staring absently down the street at a house under the wall whose roof had been shattered by falling masonry and from which flames were beginning to lick. The sergeant looked at the bedraggled crew more closely and then called a young lieutenant over. "These men appear to be in shock," he told him, "and at least two need some medical ateention. That big gray-haired fellow especially—it looks like somebody ran over his head with a plow. They should be taken to the infirmary in the south barracks."

"Right." The young man nodded. "This way," he said. "Follow me." He took Duffy's arm and led him down the street, and the northmen followed.

"Hey, Duff!" came a shout from up on the catwalk. "Are you all right? What was that thing?"

The Irishman stopped and looked up, trying to get his eyes to focus. "Who is it?" he called. "Who is it?"

"Are you drunk? It's me!" He saw a waving arm and squinted; it was Bluto, standing beside one of the cannons, his face lit from beneath by the mounting flames.

"I was—" Duffy started to answer, but he was interrupted by the explosive impact of a Turkish cannon ball against the battlements; bits of shattered stone sprayed everywhere, and a rebounding chunk of the ball caved in a wall across the street. A moment later a hail of rocks clattered down onto the pavement, sending the northmen and the young soldier ducking for cover.

"Bluto?" Duffy shouted. The hunchback was no longer visible on the catwalk. *"Bluto?"*

"Sir," said the lieutenant, stepping warily out of an alcove he'd leaped into, "Come with me. We've got to get you to the infirmary."

"If you'll wait a minute, I'll fetch you someone else to take there," the Irishman said, shoving him away. "I think that fool hunchback is in a bad way." He strode to the stairs and bounded up them.

The wind was whipping the blaze below the wall, and Duffy thought he heard flapping wings. "Keep off, you devils!" he snarled when he reached the top of the stairs; he whirled out his sword, but its unfamiliar weight was too much for his slashed hand—it slipped out of his grasp and fell, glittering in the firelight a moment before it clanged against the cobbles of the street below. "Damn it!" he gritted. "I'll strangle you with my bare hands, then!" He glared up into the night sky, but no winged afrits came diving from the darkness at him. "Hah," he said, relaxing a little. "I'd stay clear too, if I were you."

The catwalk on both sides of the chewed-up section of the crenellations was littered with jagged bits of stone, and Bluto lay crumpled face down against the wall.

"Bluto." The Irishman reeled unsteadily along the walk, ignoring a slight underfoot shift of the whole stony bulk, and knelt by the hunchback. He's clearly dead, Duffy thought. His skull is crushed, and at least one stone seems to have passed right through him. He stood up and turned toward the stairs—then paused, remembering a promise.

"God damn you, Bluto," he said, but he turned back, crouched, and picked up the limp, broken body. Duffy's head was spinning and his ears rang throbbingly. I can't carry you down the stairs, pal, he thought. Sorry. I'll leave a message with someone . . .

Smoky hot hair beating at his face and hands reminded him of the burning house directly below. He cautiously inched one foot toward the catwalk edge and peered down; the crumpled roof of the building was smoking like a charcoal mound between the flames belching from the windows, and collapsed inward even as he watched, in a blazing, white-hot inferno of flames. The heat was unbearable and a cloud of sparks whirled up past him, but he leaned out a little and cast Bluto's body away before stepping back and beating out embers that had landed on his clothes.

I've got to get down, he thought dizzily, rubbing his stinging, smoke-blinded eyes. My neck and back are wet with blood. I'll pass out if I lose much more.

He turned once again toward the stair, and with a grating roar the whole weakened section of the wall-top sheared away outward like a shale slope, and in a rain of tumbling stones Duffy fell through the cold air to the dark water of the Wiener-Bach, fifty feet below.

Chapter Twenty-three

THE DONAU CANAL was empty except for the old Viking ship, which rocked once again at its mooring by the Taborstrasse bridge. Dawn was no more than an hour away; the sky, though still dark, was beginning to fade, the stars were dimming, and before long the bow and stern lanterns would be unnecessary. The wind from the west blew strongly down the canal and swept the deck of the ship, eventually causing the Irishman to shiver all the way back to consciousness. He sat up on the weathered planks and leaned against the rail, gingerly touching the bandage wrapped around his head.

Aurelianus had been crouched in the bow, talking in an undertone to Bugge and the three northmen, but rose when he heard Duffy stir.

He walked back to where he sat. "Don't fool with the bandage," he said softly. "Luckily your skull wasn't cracked, but you could start it up bleeding again." He shook his head wonderingly. "You're fortunate, too, that I've regained my sorcerous strengths. You were a mess when they fished you out of that canal. I had to rebuild your left knee completely—you'll always limp some, but I figure it will lend you color—and a couple of things inside you had to be encouraged to return to their proper places and recommence functioning. I looked into your skull, and there's no bleeding in there, though you may be nauseous and see double for a day or two. I've told Bugge what to watch for and what not to let you do."

Duffy glanced over at the northman and opened his mouth for a feeble joke—then closed it. "I . . . I no longer know his language," he whispered to Aurelianus.

"Yes. Arthur has gone back to Avalon, and you're completely Brian Duffy now. That ought to be a relief —for one thing, I imagine you'll dream less often, and less vividly." He snapped his fingers. "Oh, and I went through your pockets, and I want to thank you," he said, holding up a wad of pulpy paper, "for the thought that made you save the signed flyleaf from Becky's book. The ink washed out while you were in the water, of course, but it *was* a . . . kind thought." He stepped to the gangplank. "You and these men will be rowed away northwest, along the canal and up the Danube. There's nothing you can do here now. Now it's just a clean-up job for young soldiers."

"Who's going to row?" the Irishman inquired. "There's not one of us with even enough strength left to chop an onion."

"Good Lord, man, after that production tonight, do you think it'll be any trouble for me to conjure a few mindless spirits to row your ship for a while?"

The old wizard looks exhausted, Duffy thought—

probably more than I do. Yet at the same time he looks stronger than I've ever seen him.

"Here," added Aurelianus, tossing a bag that clanked when it hit the deck. "A token of the gratitude of the West."

Rikard Bugge stood up and stretched, then spoke to Duffy. The Irishman turned inquiringly to Aurelianus. The wizard smiled. "He says, 'Surter is turned back, and must now retreat to Muspelheim. Balder's grave-barrow is safe, and we won't see Ragnarok *this* winter.'"

Duffy grinned. "Amen."

Aurelianus stepped across the gangplank to the shore, stooped to pull the plank away, and the oars shifted aimlessly for a moment and then clacked rhythmically in the locks. The wizard untied the line and let it trail out through his fingers and slap into the water.

The Irishman got cautiously to his feet, leaning heavily on the rail. "Do you have one of your snakes?" he called to the dim figure on the bank that was Aurelianus.

"Here." The wizard fished one from a pocket and tossed it spinning through the air. Duffy caught it, and lit it at the stern lantern.

The ship was moving now, and Duffy sat down in the deep shadow of the high stern, so that all the wizard could see of him, until the ship rounded the nearest bend and passed out of sight beyond a stone arch, was the tiny ember at the head of the snake.

epiLoGue

October Fourteenth

IT WAS CLEAR that Suleiman was preparing an attack. Through the dawn mists von Salm, from his perch in St. Stephen's spire, could see across the plain the gathering ranks of mounted Janissaries and the milling mob that was the akinji. Inside Vienna's walls the soldiers, their breath steaming as they trotted from the barracks, gathered about the points where the wall had been crumbled by mines. Frightened women peered tearfully from windows, priests hurried from regiment to regiment dispensing general blessings since there was no time for individual confessions, and dogs, puzzled and upset by the air of tension, huddled under carts and barked furiously at everyone they saw.

Merlin stood on the wall at the northeast corner and smiled a little sadly. The west wind had resumed and gained strength all through the night, and it blew his white hair into his face now as he lifted the massive sword and laid it in one of the battered crenels.

Merlin leaned in the wide notch and stared moodily down at the surface of the muddy Wiener-Bach. So long, Arthur, the magician thought. I wish we'd had a little leisure in which to talk, this time around. And so long, Brian Duffy, you disagreeable old Irishman. You were a lot of trouble, more than I expected, but I liked you. Werner never did . . . poor Werner, who succumbed to his wound this morning at about the same time you were casting off in Bugge's ship. Oh, and you were right about Zapolya, by the way. They found a bloodstained rope hanging outside the wall somewhere near the southern gate. I suppose he's on his way back to Hungary now.

"Good morning, sir," said a portly sentry in a stern tone, edging past the thin wizard as he walked his rounds.

"Hm? Oh, good morning."

He sighed and looked up at the patch of dark clouds in the east that was giving way before the fresh wind. Yes, he thought, in spite of all the setbacks and reluctances, you two did what you were called on to do. You saved the beer, and therefore the King and the West. This Turkish attack this morning can accomplish nothing; it's the last desperate blow of a defeated opponent who is determined at least to leave as much ruin behind as he can.

Merlin picked up the old longsword with both hands, stared at it as if to fix it in his memory for a while, and then tossed it spinning end over end toward the water below.

He turned and ambled thoughtfully toward the stairs. I guess I'll be leaving for England in about a week, he calculated. I will leave the brewery once again in Gambrinus' capable hands . . . and there are things at home that could bear a bit of meddling with. Perhaps—

The sentry came puffing up. "What did that mean?" he gasped.

Merlin was puzzled. "What did what mean?"

"That sword you just dropped into the Wiener-Bach—didn't you watch it fall?"

"No." the magician smiled. "What did I miss?"

"Well, I couldn't see it too clear through the ground mist, you know, but I'll swear that a hand rose out of the water and . . ." The sentry paused, scratching his nose and frowning.

"Go on," prompted Merlin politely. "A hand . . . ?" The wind was twitching his hair again and he shook it back out of his face.

"Never mind, sir," said the sentry stolidly. "It was a fancy, I'm sure. I haven't been getting near enough sleep these days."

The wizard smiled sympathetically. "Few of us have." He walked past to the stairs and stepped down them to the ash-dusty street. From the southeast the Turkish cannons began firing, but the wind blew most of the sound away, and to Merlin it sounded like nothing but plodding footsteps receding away in the distance.

About the Author

Tim Powers is twenty-five years old, a native New Yorker now living in Santa Ana, California. A graduate (in English) of California State University at Fullerton, he works in a Tinder Box tobacco shop—a considerable improvement on his previous jobs, which have ranged from janitor to bartender to pizza cook to caricaturist.

He became interested in fantasy at an early age, when his mother read him such stories as Chesterton's *Lepanto*, Grahame's *Wind in the Willows*, and Lewis' Narnia stories; more recently he has enjoyed the works of Leiber, Cabell, Marquez, and the best of the old *Weird Tales* writers.